Forbidden Things: Book Two

Exile

By Nikki McCormack

Published by
Elysium Books

Written by Nikki McCormack
www.elysiumpalace.com

Cover Art by Robert Crescenzio

First Edition 2015
978-0996319645

*For my sister, Holly, one of the most
courageous and caring women I know.*

CHAPTER ONE

Yiloch sat upon his newly won throne, patient and wary, watching the black-skinned man approach up the length of the magnificent room. Guards, adepts, and creators stood alert along both sides. Even the eyes of the men and women in the subtle etchings along the blue marble walls seemed more attentive than usual. Two lines of three warriors flanked the man, each carrying an ornate spear top-ped with a slender, curved blade. Elaborate markings down the length of the shafts made them appear more ceremonial than functional, but he knew better than to doubt the effectiveness of those weapons or that of the men bearing them. Kudaness warriors were skilled fighters. In their hands, those delicate-looking blades could practically decapitate a horse with a single strike. Allowing armed visitors into the room at all was a declaration of his confidence in the many ascard users present.

The thin, sand-colored straps of a few satchels he carried were all that covered the leader's chest, exposing a broad, muscular build. A warrior at first glance, but prior experience with the Kudaness, coupled with years of political education, gave Yiloch the knowledge to translate a few of the messages written on the man's skin. An elaborate tattoo on his right cheek marked him as part of the Ithik Ani, the Kudaness priesthood. The black swirling tattoos over his arms, shoulders, and legs announced his role as a suac, a high priest. Another tattoo with three black lines running parallel to the line of his jaw on his left cheek and two black dots beside his left eye informed others he belonged to the Murak tribe. Long black hair, braided back into countless strands, several woven through with patterns of beads, swung heavily down to his lower back. He wore intimidation in place of armor, and his copper eyes, discolored by the potion the Ithik Ani used to initiate a connection with their gods, gleamed with feral intensity.

Only a month into his reign and Yiloch was hosting a most unusual visitor. The presence of a suac in his halls could be a gesture of respect or a warning. Perhaps both.

"Emperor Yiloch." The Lyran usher, his light skin stark white beside the dark Kudaness, offered a deep bow to Yiloch, then inclined his head toward the visitors. "I am honored to present Suac Chozai Galal un Murak un Ani."

The usher's introduction confirmed everything he had read from the tattoos. This man was very important among his people. Kudaness high priests held more power than their tribal chieftains did. Even among other tribes, this man's rank made him second only to their suac.

Before the throne, the high priest lowered his chin in the slightest intimation of a bow, his odd metallic-eyed gaze never leaving Yiloch's.

This is a man whose power is never challenged.

Yiloch needed to proceed with caution, especially

given the unexpected nature of the visit. Whatever the reason for his unannounced arrival, the suac had the political advantage for the moment.

Yiloch nodded to him, offering reserved respect. "Suac Chozai, your visit honors us."

The suac's answering expression curled his lips into a predatory snarl, and his eyes sparkled as if he found something amusing.

The irrepressible twitch of a muscle in Yiloch's jaw was the only thing that might expose his annoyance, but only a careful observer was likely to notice. A heightened sense of vigilance rose in him in reaction to the thinly veiled animosity lurking behind those eerie eyes, but he kept his expression neutral. Kudaness priests had a notorious lack of respect for rank outside of their own culture and, at least in his limited dealings, they treated most everyone with some amount of disdain. It made them challenging to work with, but the Kudaness were a powerful people and the border they shared with Lyra boasted a long trade history beneficial to both countries. His father's madness nearly destroyed that trade, and Yiloch wouldn't risk its revitalization over such a small measure of insult.

"The Murak have seen that Lyra's new Emperor respects the trade relationship with Kudan," the priest began, his accent thick enough that Yiloch had to listen closely to understand him. It might have been easier if the man spoke in his native tongue, but using the Lyran trade dialect was appropriate here, showing some deference to Yiloch's rank in this setting. "The Murak, the greatest tribe in Kudan, wishes to express our gratitude for your efforts."

He resisted a smirk. How many of the tribes would lay claim to that status? "It has long been a beneficial arrangement. Emperor Rylan insulted all our people by disrespecting that relationship. That will not happen under my rule. However, while I appreciate your gratitude, I do not believe you traveled all this way to express a simple thank you. Why have you come here?"

Tension rippled out from the high priest. His copper eyes glinted in the sunlight shining down through the faceted crystal ceiling as he returned Yiloch's measuring regard, perhaps trying to determine whether he intended some insult with his abrupt manner.

Yiloch could have been more tactful, wasting time on niceties, but the mere rarity of a visit from a Kudaness suac was enough to inspire interest and unease. He itched to know the reason.

"I am suac to the Murak tribe, chosen by the gods to bear the burden of their gifts for the benefit of my people." Suac Chozai's somber expression and weighted tone communicated the significance of his status. "One of those gifts is the ability to foresee possible futures. The gods have shown me that our lands and people will soon face a terrible threat. Not only the people of Kudan, but all our people"—he swept a hand out to suggest a wider area—"are under threat from a tribe not of Kudan. This tribe is mighty. They come in great numbers and use ascard in ways none here have seen before. They ride on the backs of sturdy horses and will decimate all in their path if not dealt with through quick and decisive action. We require the aid of the Blood Prince to defeat this threat."

Yiloch narrowed his eyes, making little effort to hide his disapproval of the old, hated title. His hand itched to move closer to his sword. Whether Chozai's use of the title was a mere slip from long habit or an intentional insult, the suac tried his patience. A careless approach, considering he was requesting military aid.

He waited a moment to see if the suac would apologize. When he didn't, Yiloch spoke, biting off his words with the effort of keeping them civil. "I would be a fool to extend my resources so soon after taking the throne. My empire is recovering from significant upheaval. I have many soldiers and adepts out hunting for the adept Myac, who remains a threat. What benefit is there to Lyra in sending aid to the Murak against an enemy who is, as yet, mostly unknown even to you?"

The suac's smile broadened, giving a glimpse of incisors filed to a subtle point. It enhanced the predatory appearance, but he couldn't intimidate Yiloch with tribal gimmicks. The confidence in his smile, however, was a trifle unsettling.

"You need us, Blood Prince," Chozai stated, making it apparent that the use of the title hadn't been a slip.

Yiloch scowled, losing the struggle to contain his irritation. Kudan and Lyra held an uneasy peace balanced on the benefits they could offer one another and a shaky mutual respect for the extreme differences in their cultures. That balance felt even more precarious at the moment.

This one man is not worth the destruction of that peace.

"You insult me in my palace, then expect me to accept on your word that I should extend you aid at a time when I have need of my soldiers here. You had best be able to offer more concrete proof of how this will benefit Lyra." He infused his tone with an edge of warning. He would not continue to suffer disrespect in his own palace.

Like a man struck dead, the suac's face lost all expression. His eyes clouded over, a translucent white masking the brilliant copper, and his voice assumed a deep, rhythmic cadence. "The emperor of Lyra will be thrice betrayed; by ally, by family, and by love. To escape the dark consequences of those betrayals, he must send forth his army to the aid of those favored by the gods. In return, salvation will come from beyond his borders to mend the rifts created by those betrayals. If such aid is not given, salvation will not come and his empire will fall in a storm of fire and blood to a savage power from beyond the Rhuakine."

Yiloch glanced at Ian, the youngest and strongest creator in his army. The young man shook his head. If the suac was using ascard to change his eyes and voice, Ian couldn't detect it.

A chill passed through Yiloch, and he noticed his cousin, Lord Terral, shifting his feet near the foot of the dais. Was that from the same unease they all felt at the suac's dark fore-telling, or something more insidious?

Betrayed by ally, by family, and by love.

The Rhuakine was a canyon-scarred desert to the east of Kudan, implying that the savage force the suac spoke of was the same one that threatened the Murak. If so, his people would fall before this new power first if Lyra didn't send soldiers to their aid. Under those circumstances, he would have expected a more respectful approach from the man. Was the disdain for foreigners so ingrained that he couldn't overcome it even for the sake of diplomacy?

Yiloch stood. With his sword riding comfortably at his hip, he descended the steps and walked up to stop a few feet from the high priest. Suac Chozai was a big man, several inches taller, but his eyes, which had regained their usual abnormal color, took on a hint of wariness. The Murak warriors tightened their grips on their weapons, and some of Yiloch's guards took hold of their swords. His bold approach had extracted some reluctant respect from the arrogant high priest and his guards.

He met those deep copper eyes with a steady gaze. "You have intrigued me, Suac Chozai. I give little credit to fortune-telling as a rule, but if I discounted all such things completely out of hand, I would not be where I am now. Perhaps we could discuss this in a more casual setting."

Chozai nodded, and two of his warriors moved up closer behind him. Adran, one of Yiloch's captains and a lifelong friend, and Ian came forward from either side of the dais to flank him. It was given that they would attend him, just as the two lead warriors of Chozai's retinue accompanied him. The suac stepped aside to let Yiloch walk ahead of him, more out of a lack of trust, he suspected, than any show of deference to his rank within the realm. Among the Kudaness, the suacs were exempt from the laws of men. Knowing that, Chozai's manner wasn't surprising, but it still chafed him.

Yiloch led them to a set of doors on one side of the main room. The usher hurried ahead, opening the doors into the map chamber. Maps hung on the walls and covered the surfaces of every table. Old maps, new maps, maps of places he knew as well as he knew his own bedroom, and maps of places he wasn't certain even existed. A few chairs sat along the walls to provide the option of comfort if desired, but the room served primarily as a place to peruse maps and plan strategies.

Adran and Ian flanked him as he walked around the back of a table with a map of Kudan stretched across it, then they moved off to the sides where they could keep watch over him and his visitors and still be close enough to react to an attack.

The map they stood over was a rare, beautifully detailed piece. Yiloch's father, the late Emperor Rylan, purchased it from a Kudaness sea captain before Yiloch was born. The tribal borders within Kudan had changed since its creation, as they often did, but it still gave a reasonable approximation of reality, and he appreciated the artistry of it.

Suac Chozai approached the opposite side of the table while the usher shut them into the room. His dispassionate gaze fell upon the map.

Yiloch considered the situation for a moment. He had noticed Lord Terral's unease when the suac mentioned betrayal. It might have merely been discomfort caused by the suac's strange display, but Terral was one of very few left in his empire who could claim to be family. If there were any truth to the suac's prophecy, Terral would be a prime suspect, a possibility that prompted the relocation to a more private setting. If guilt brought about Terral's unease, then perhaps the desire to find out what occurred behind these doors would drive him to carelessness.

"From your words, Suac Chozai, I gather you believe the Murak will fall to this savage foe if I refuse to send aid." Yiloch kept his eyes upon the map to avoid showing too much interest in the answer. The suac expected no more courtesy than he gave when dealing with unbelievers from outside his lands. It was tempting to meet his expectations.

"You understand correctly. If our fates were not inter-twined, I would not be here."

Yiloch pinned the Murak priest with his gaze. "Then tell me, who will betray me?"

Chozai reached a tattooed arm across the table. One finger, tipped with a thick, cracked nail, came to rest upon the ring that lay hidden under Yiloch's shirt, pressing it against his skin. "Your greatest undoing shall come from here," he stated with conviction.

Defensive rage, wild and unreasoning, blazed to life in Yiloch. He wanted to tear the man's hand off. To leap across the table and strike him down. Chozai drew back from him in response to the change in his bearing. The ring, Indigo's ring, burned against his skin for a few seconds, blazing with the intensity of the emotions tied to that delicate band. Every second he had spent with her, all the sacrifices she had made and risks she had taken for him, rushed to the forefront of his mind. His ascard ability flared, rising with his emotions so he had to wrestle back control.

Ian, highly sensitive to ascard use in others, tensed, his eyes growing wide.

"All this talk of foresight," Yiloch snarled, fury driving the words past his lips. "I saw that display out there. I thought the Kudaness considered it sacrilege to use ascard."

He attacked their religion, seeking to repay some of the turmoil the suac's accusation caused him, and it worked. Chozai's copper eyes flashed, and his warriors shifted into wider stances, moving their weapons out of ceremonial position to something far more threatening. Adran's hand dropped to his sword hilt, and he also moved into a combat-ready posture.

Calm washed over and through Yiloch then. He glanced at Ian, whose pale eyes had taken on a familiar inward-facing intensity. The manipulation was unsolicited and unwanted, but not unwise.

Chozai followed his gaze, reading something different into the glance. He motioned to his warriors, who assumed their previous stance. The suac wasn't fool enough to pit his men against the power of a creator, and Ian had become renowned for his exceptional ascard strength since helping Yiloch take the city from his father. Ironically, several of the acts that earned the youth the respect he now held were Indigo's accomplishments, but allowing Ian to take credit for them increased his influence and allowed her to keep her power hidden. It also made the creator an effective political asset.

"I do not manipulate the power of the gods for my visions. The gods grant them to me." He turned a sneer on Ian, not so wary of his power that he wasn't willing to express his disdain. "Not stolen."

The tension in his tone told Yiloch he had gotten under the man's skin, but if the suac, as representative of the Murak un Ani, had no more respect to offer him, the tenuous relationship between their people was not apt to change anytime soon, certainly not for the better.

"Suac Chozai, I require more to build a military alliance on than prophecy and brash accusations. I have an empire to fortify, one the former emperor made a fair attempt at destroying the foundations of, and a dangerous criminal to bring to justice. I need my army at hand until I have brought all my lords to heel, preferably with as little bloodshed as possible. There is much to be done to secure my rule. If you can offer me no greater proof of your need, or of my own, if you cannot even respect my rank, then we have nothing more to discuss. You are welcome to return and present your case again if these things change. For now, all I can offer is refreshment and rest before you depart."

Suac Chozai's expression darkened, growing more hostile with every word. Disregarding the man's foretellings and his confidence in their accuracy made Yiloch uneasy, but as Emperor, he couldn't allow the man to disrespect him. Gambling resources on mere prophecy might also make his subjects wonder if he shared the madness his father suffered from in the end.

Chozai's lip lifted in an animalistic snarl, exposing one sharpened canine. "You will destroy yourself and your empire with your arrogance."

"Just as your arrogance will destroy your people if your visions come true," Yiloch countered. "You have not offered me enough sound information to work with.

As I said, come to me with more, and I will reconsider my position."

The suac narrowed his eyes and gave a curt nod. "So it shall be."

Chozai turned from Yiloch, and his warriors fell in behind him. Yiloch watched them stride from the room, making no move to follow. The suac hadn't stood upon ceremony, nor had he behaved in a manner respectful of Lyran customs. As such, it seemed appropriate to let him show himself out of the map chamber. The usher would see to him from there.

Yiloch turned to Ian when the door shut behind them. "The foretelling he did, where did he draw his power from?"

Ian stared at the door, his lips pressed in a troubled line. After a few seconds, he looked at Yiloch and shrugged. "I don't know. I didn't sense him connecting to his inner aspect or drawing on ascard around him, and he wasn't masking anything that I could tell."

Yiloch stared at the closed door. Silence filled the room. Several minutes passed before Adran coughed and Yiloch met his worried amber eyes. His slightly darker skin and dusty blond hair betrayed impure blood, but he was a lifelong friend and advisor. Lineage carried little weight before the trust that existed between them.

"The suac didn't look pleased." Adran's tone carried a trace of displeasure with the way the situation had gone.

Yiloch nodded once, dismissing the underlying message. "I have been thinking, Adran." He walked to another map. This one depicted the allied kingdom of

Caithin across the Gilded Strait. "We need healers in our army. Not borrowed healers, but our own formally trained healers."

Adran walked to the other side of the table and rested his hands on it. His fingers tapped the surface a few times, the only expression of his annoyance at the change of subject. "We could ask King Jerrin for an instructor, though it might be more beneficial to send some of our adepts to train at their academy."

Yiloch touched the city of Demin with one finger, trying to ignore the ache in his chest at the thought of Indigo there. "Discuss it with Ferin and see what he thinks of sending adepts to Caithin for training. Ask him how many he would send and who, then prepare a missive to King Jerrin and bring it to me."

"My lord." Adran inclined his head, the concern in his eyes taking on a more personal nature.

Yiloch looked away. They had been friends far too long for him to expect Adran to miss the distress that hid behind his carefully controlled regard, but he had no wish to discuss it until his head was clearer. Besides, there were more urgent matters to worry about. "Any news of Myac?'

"Still nothing."

He nodded, suppressing the chill of dread that always came with thoughts of the dangerous adept who had nearly killed Indigo. "You may both go."

The two men left him, Adran lingering in the doorway a few seconds before moving on. When the door clicked shut, Yiloch reached down the collar of his shirt and brought out the ring that hung there. Two clear stones nestled in a delicate band to either side of a larger gem the color of her eyes—the color of her name.

"Indigo." He let her name roll off his lips like a caress.

Holding the ring, he closed his eyes and played back every touch they had shared, every kiss and intimate moment, in his mind. Extraordinary power filled her, hidden beneath a gentle beauty and charming vulnerability. She had helped him take the throne from his father, using her uncommonly strong ascard connection to assist him to the point that she had almost lost her life more than once. She gave everything for him because she loved him, and though his motives for using her power had been selfish at the start, he couldn't help reciprocating that love by the end. Still, she was Caithin, and the exalted pure blood of Lyran royalty was part of its power. He could not ask her to be his bride, not without losing the approval of his people, and she had her own battles to fight in Caithin. Now he had only her ring and a deep ache in his chest.

No, betrayal couldn't come from Indigo. She would never turn against him after all they had gone through together. His trust in her made him suspicious of everything the suac said after implicating her. And yet, as he twisted the ring about in his fingers, a deep disquiet took root in his heart that hadn't been there before.

CHAPTER TWO

Indigo rubbed the thumb of her left hand over the barren spot on her ring finger while she gazed out the window of her new residence at people passing in the street below. There was comfort in knowing that they couldn't see her. Comfort but also sorrow that she felt it necessary to work ascard into the glass so her windows would always appear empty from the outside. Jayce would never see her standing there, though she had spotted him a few times. Even Andrea didn't know where she was living now, and Indigo intended to keep it that way. As much as she missed her friend, Andrea's relationship with Jayce made her nervous about spending time together outside of their classes. For all that she appreciated her new sanctuary, watching people going about their lives through those windows left her feeling more isolated than ever.

The light of dawn spilled over Demin. Across the Gilded Strait, the sun would already be shining over Yiroth, its light dancing through the magnificent created crystal ceiling of the palace throne room. Was Yiloch there, sitting upon his throne? Did he think about her, or did his new role as emperor demand so much of him that she no longer crossed his mind?

Her gaze lifted to the brightening sky. Who else

watched that sunrise? Was Myac somewhere, his wounds healed, observing the arrival of a new day while plotting his revenge?

No, she refused to think of him right now.

She released a long exhale and closed her eyes, remembering the feel of Yiloch's fingers on her skin and the taste of his lips, letting those memories chase Myac away. If only...

"Are you sure you cannot sort out your differences?"

Drawn from her reverie, she glanced around at her uncle, Lord Theron, where he relaxed in a plush chair, sipping from a goblet of wine. This was his first visit to the city since her return from Lyra. Recently trimmed dark hair hung neatly arranged around his stately features. His dark eyes peered at her with a casual impatience that somehow conveyed displeasure with the situation without disrupting his tranquil composure. Propriety was everything to him, she knew, but he wouldn't force her hand, even though he had the right to as her guardian. The deaths of her disgraced parents left her in his care, but he claimed to enjoy the responsibility, despite her sometimes-unconventional choices and conduct. This decision, the dissolution of her engagement, had to concern him, but he never let inner turmoil show on his cultivated features. Such admirable self-control.

"I am sorry, Uncle, but this was the only way. Lord Jayce was becoming dangerously violent. Lord Caplin told you what he was like the day I left with the healers bound for Lyra. I tremble to imagine what he might have done if Caplin and his men hadn't been there to help me move out of the residence upon my return."

She faced him fully now, catching the briefest flicker of disappointment in his expression as she went to sit across from him.

The chairs were a soft ivory in color, the embroidery done in silver and blue. Colors better suited to Lyran décor. Much of the room shared a similar palette. She had spent several lonely evenings using ascard to transform the traditional Caithin rich golds and reds into colors reminiscent of the Imperial palace in Yiroth. It was during her brief stay there, in fact, that she had studied the created crystal ceilings and windows to learn how to bind off a working so she could make the changes permanent.

Once, such frivolous use of ascard for purposes other than healing would have gotten her arrested by the Ascard Watchmen, specially trained adepts who patrolled Caithin, alert for illegal use of ascard. She could mask her workings well enough now that they never knew. Theoretically, she was exempt from those regulations as a member of the King's Order, a secret organization of adepts and creators trained to do more than heal with ascard. Until she spoke with Serivar, however, she wasn't willing to assume her immunity still stood. She had, after all, blackmailed and threatened the headmaster to make him let her go to Lyra.

"If Lord Caplin felt the situation was dangerous, I imagine it was. I appreciate the effort he made in finding this place and helping you get out of that engagement. You know I support you in this. I would, however, like to discuss that little adventure of yours," he remarked, latching on to her passing mention of her trip to Lyra, a subject she had put some effort into drawing him away from earlier. "I must insist that you at least consult with me before running off again. Until I find a suitable husband for you, you remain my ward. I cannot ensure your safety if you don't allow me to be involved in such significant decisions."

Until he finds me a suitable husband? Can I wed now that my heart belongs to a man I will never have?

She took several long sips of wine before responding. "I should have let you know, but nothing you said would have changed my mind about going."

Theron rolled his gaze to the ceiling as though some great wisdom waited there that might help him manage his headstrong niece. "I am painfully aware of that, Indigo. I have never been under the illusion that I could expect obedience from you. For a woman, you have proven to be rather"—he picked at an imaginary bit of dust on one sleeve—"independent. You are your father's child. No one could stop him from doing anything he felt strongly about either."

That dark gaze considered her, reminding her of her father's eyes. On rare occasions, the family resemblance showed. Those flickers of physical similarity were the only likenesses between Theron and his late brother. Where her father had possessed a passionate temper, she had never heard Theron so much as raise his voice. Theron dedicated his life to the service of the king, most often acting as a royal emissary to handle delicate political situations. Her father had been executed for trying to destroy the king's slave trade with Lyra. They were so very different it was hard to believe they had grown up together.

Theron heaved a sigh and gazed into his wine, ending the mutual silence. "Sometimes I wish you were my son."

A feeling of warmth infused her at his words, and she smiled to show her appreciation for the sentiment. From him, there probably was no greater compliment. He had three sons, all of whom had followed whatever path in life proved easiest, seeking recognition through their father's name rather than their own accomplishments. His remark exposed a reluctant admiration for her determination, despite his frequent attempts to convince her to act in a manner more befitting a lady.

"Thank you, Uncle."

He shrugged off her gratitude. "You will return to your schooling soon."

It was a statement, not a question, and she understood he would press her on that. It was one thing to endanger her already precarious social standing with the dissolution of her engagement. He wouldn't fight that, knowing Jayce had hurt her before and might do worse given a chance. Theron would never tolerate her falling behind in her training as a healer, however, especially given how skilled she had proven to be. Becoming an accomplished healer could earn her a stable place in society even without marrying a man of rank, though she didn't doubt he was already searching out new prospects for her.

Apprehension sparked in her chest when she glanced at the scroll sitting on the table beside her. It was a request from Headmaster Serivar for her to attend him at her earliest convenience in his offices at the Caithin Healers Academy. The missive had arrived nearly three weeks ago. So far, it had not suited her to attend him. She convinced Master Healer Siddael, who led the healers in the campaign to help Yiloch overthrow his father, to approve a temporary leave of absence from her schooling after their return from Lyra. It was easy to do. He was so impressed with her healing skills during their time in Lyra that he allowed her the same recovery period more senior healers from the campaign received.

"You know more than many of your peers already," Siddael had said. *"If we hold you back a little, they may feel less threatened by you."*

There would be much catching up to do, but she couldn't help smiling at the thought of Headmaster Serivar waiting on her convenience. "Yes. I'm going to speak with the headmaster this afternoon."

"I am glad to hear it." He set his empty goblet on the table and rose from the chair. "You have had your adventure. It is time now for you to turn your attention back to your future. If I can be of assistance..."

She detected a hint of discouragement behind the offer. He would provide her with anything she needed, but he respected her more because she asked for almost nothing. He made the offer so that he could appreciate her refusal.

She rose to walk him out. "Thank you, Uncle, but I am fine."

The satisfaction in his smile reinforced the correctness of her answer. "So you always are, dearest Indigo.

You know how to reach me should that change."

"I do."

He kissed her on the cheek before striding regally from the room, satisfied that he had done his duty as her guardian.

He should have been royalty.

She gave a small shake of her head as she watched him descend the stairs with a swift elegance that reminded her of Yiloch, though even her uncle would pale in his commanding presence.

Leaning her head against the door, she gazed down the now empty stairwell for several quiet minutes. Memories haunted her of people she had killed and helped kill with her power. Of spattered blood and staring eyes devoid of life. She pushed those away, drawing upon pleasurable memories of the times she and Yiloch had made love, of sneaking moments to be together without the knowledge of her countrymen, of sitting on the steps beneath the throne in the imperial palace with his arms around her, gazing up through the created crystal ceiling at a starlit sky.

Shaking herself from her reverie, she went to retrieve a brightly colored shawl that matched her colorful summer dress. The outfit contrasted her mood, but donning a pretense of good cheer might set the headmaster off his guard.

Members of the King's Order were supposed to be a clandestine group acting on behalf of the king in defense of the kingdom. Not long before her departure to Lyra, she discovered that no one else knew of her training. The time had come to find out why Serivar was keeping her training secret from everyone, even the king she supposedly served. She had used the information to blackmail the headmaster, offering to keep his secret and continue working with him only if he let her join the force of soldiers and healers going to Lyra. When he resisted, she used ascard to intimidate him into going along with her. Whatever plans he had for her, she needed him to understand that she wouldn't be his docile pawn. The training was important to her, though, so she hoped her fear of some sinister intent behind his actions proved unfounded.

She connected to her inner aspect and drew on ascard as she descended the stairs with a forced lightness of step. If she acted cheerful, perhaps she could persuade herself to feel that way. Extending her ability, she swept the area for anyone she might want to avoid, searching for the unique signature of the inner aspect within those individuals. She primarily wanted to avoid Jayce, but also Andrea and some other shared acquaintances. Discovering Serivar's intentions had to be her sole focus today. She needed no distractions.

With ongoing practice, she had increased the range of her reach and could now pinpoint Serivar's location within the academy administration building well ahead of her arrival. Interestingly, he was in the hidden training room behind his office where she had done most of her Order training, and he wasn't alone. She didn't recognize the inner aspect signature of the individual with him. Perhaps he was training another adept for the Order, like herself.

The prospect kindled curiosity. When she agreed to

become an adept of the King's Order, Serivar told her she would probably never meet the others. It was tempting to dig deeper into the stranger's skills and learn more about them.

After a moment of vacillating on the edge of morality, she withdrew her ability, respecting the stranger's privacy, and waited until she was almost at the headmaster's office. Then she reached out once more and touched Serivar, using ascard to notify him of her arrival, earning a pleasing startle from him. She had never done such a thing with him before. The skill was one she had worked out on her own in Lyra. Tracking his movement with ascard, she waited outside the office door until she sensed him within. Whoever was with him had also come out to the office.

After giving him a moment to compose himself, she knocked.

"Come in."

She entered the familiar room, shutting the door behind her before he could ask her to, and seated herself across from him without awaiting the offer. Her gaze skimmed over the narrow, youthful features of the headmaster before coming to rest upon the room's other occupant.

The individual, standing off to one side feigning interest in a book, was a young, bronze-skinned Caithin man with a well-defined jaw and balanced features. His unkempt, mid-length hair was a dark, dingy brown that detracted a little from an otherwise pleasant visage. His dark eyes, when he glanced her way, held a keen alertness that belied his casual posture.

She drew on ascard, masking her ability as she probed deeper into the stranger. His ascard connection was strong, but not extraordinary. Still, something seemed familiar about him when his gaze flickered over to her again. For now, she gave up her uninvited exploration and faced the headmaster.

"You wished to see me, Lord Serivar," she stated, expressing with her sharp tone that she remained upset with him. Time hadn't diluted the distress caused by his lies, and she refused to let its passage soften this encounter.

A flash of irritation lit Serivar's eyes as he considered her, lips pressed together in a tight line. His obvious frustration pleased her. "Your time away seems to have dulled your sense of propriety. I suppose it must be the Lyran influence."

She said nothing, beating down the burning desire to rise to the defense of Lyra to avoid rousing his curiosity on that subject. She breathed in the familiar aromas of the office: books, ink, and the ever-present decanter of wine. Strange how much she had missed that distinctive blend.

When she offered him no response, he continued, "Indigo, this is Edan Lindis. He is another adept in the King's Order."

She gave a respectful nod but didn't rise to curtsy as he might expect in other settings. She was not in the mood to play the role of a proper noble lady today. If this man was one of Caithin's secretive force of adepts and creators, then he was an equal of sorts, and she would treat him thus.

Edan faced her, amusement sparkling in his eyes when they met hers, and she again had that unsettling sense that she knew him from somewhere.

"It is a pleasure to meet you, Lord Edan." Though Serivar had given the man no title, she added it based on his rich attire and the hint of refinement in his bearing.

He inclined his head, reserved yet respectful. "Likewise, my lady."

She considered him a moment longer, trying once more to place him before giving up and turning back to Serivar. "I didn't think we were allowed to meet others of the Order."

"Edan is part of something more exclusive than our normal membership. Like you," he added pointedly.

She raised her eyebrows, but held her silence, curious to see where this was leading and unwilling to offer him anything until she had some answers. This was the first she had heard of any more exclusive group.

"Before we move on to business, why don't you have some wine and tell me of your experiences in Lyra?" Serivar gestured to the three goblets waiting on his desk.

Edan walked over to sit in the chair next to her, angling it so he could face her and the headmaster. He took one goblet and reclined in the seat, swirling the wine before taking a sip. Serivar took another goblet, and she claimed the third, inspecting it with ascard on a whim.

Should she mistrust Serivar enough to be wary of poison? Had he earned that level of suspicion, or was she being paranoid?

To be fair to herself, the headmaster had not yet

explained his actions, and she was still on edge after her time in Lyra. Myac haunted her thoughts often enough to perpetuate a sense of dreadful anticipation in her. She saw him in her nightmares, always standing in the street below her residence and staring up at the window, somehow seeing through her workings to where she waited within.

When she was confident that the wine was only wine, she took a sip and swallowed it along with the sense of dread that accompanied thoughts of Myac.

"There are many things about that experience that I am not ready to discuss yet," she answered. "As I recall, you had some things to explain to me, and I would have those explanations now if possible. I want to continue my training with the Order, but I will not work with you behind a veil of lies and deception."

Serivar smiled and raised his cup to her, the sudden fondness in his expression disconcerting. "It is refreshing to have you back, Indigo. I missed your fiery temper and lack of respect more than I would have thought possible."

The comment was disarming, forcing her to cling to her anger. "I find that rather surprising." She offered a tepid smile, noting with interest that Edan's expression had soured in response to Serivar's words. Was that the mere jealousy of a rival adept or something more?

"The king's life is always under threat of some kind, but Edan has been investigating information we got our hands on that someone is preparing to make an attempt on King Jerrin's life. What we need in the face of such a threat is people working outside of the king's knowledge, Indigo. People within the order who he could not betray if someone were to take him hostage. People who could protect his heir. That is why I kept your training secret, but I could not risk telling you until I was confident of your dedication to our cause."

A chill swept through her. His explanation made more sense than her fear that he was hatching some plot against the king himself. He was working to protect the kingdom in the event they could not protect the king, and she had been too new yet for him to trust with that information. She almost felt bad about her harsh treatment of him.

"Why me?"

"Because I have no one stronger than you." Serivar leaned in, the fire in his eyes backing his earnest tone, and she noted again a souring in Edan's expression. "I know you do not want to be a weapon, but I need you to be one. We need the strength of your ability and your aptitude for picking up new skills. You could be our ultimate weapon against such a threat. Simply put, I need you, Indigo."

The sincerity in his expression and the way he leaned close, his eyes seeing only her, finally disarmed her, breaking her shield of anger, leaving her uncomfortable and a little afraid. She didn't want him to need her in this way, not him or her kingdom. Yiloch had needed her this way, and she had given him everything, nearly losing her life. Could she give so much again? It was exhausting and scarring. Without the precious reward of Yiloch's affection, she wasn't sure she could have given him as much as she had. Loving him as she did, she couldn't have turned him away. Could she turn away from this? If what Serivar said was true, could she deny her own kingdom the same effort she had given to Lyra out of love for its emperor?

"That's all there is to it?" She arched a brow, holding on to a mask of cynicism to hide her inner turmoil. "No greater plan than that?"

Serivar gave her a mystified look. "Is that not enough?"

"All this secrecy. You should have told me before I left. You could have spared so much worry, so much stress, simply by telling me the truth." She felt knots of that stress releasing in her mind and gut that she hadn't even known were there, and it infuriated her to realize what his evasiveness had been doing to her.

Serivar's features softened, a hint of sympathy in his gentle regard. "You were so set against being made a weapon, and I wasn't sure at the time how legitimate the threat was. I had no way of knowing if some of those you would be fighting and traveling with might be part of that threat. In retrospect, I realize I should have handled things differently. I am sorry, Indigo. I should have been upfront with you and saved you the entire ordeal of going to Lyra. That was my mistake."

"Knowing the truth wouldn't have altered my decision to go to Lyra," she countered, a touch of guilt warming her cheeks at having toyed with his emotions. "But I might have done so without a mountain of worry weighing on my shoulders."

"I cannot say that surprises me. You are a willful creature. Now that you are back, however, there is much to do. If you are ready and willing to defend your own people..." he trailed off, letting the challenge hang in the air, and leaned back in his chair behind the large wooden desk, taking a sip of wine.

Indigo returned his scrutiny. She wanted to continue learning. Knowledge was power. Power was freedom. Her thoughts wandered back to encounter with Myac again. As far as she could tell, his ascard ability could be as strong or stronger than hers. The battle with him almost killed her. Myac was still out there somewhere, and knowing that turned her blood to ice. Even if she didn't want to be more prepared in case she ever met up with him again, she didn't think her conscience would let her turn away from her king, the leader of her country and a man who had always treated her kindly, if he truly was in danger.

"If you believe I must become a weapon for the good of our kingdom, then I will learn what you have to teach me."

Serivar sat up, looking pleased and moderately surprised by her response. Not as surprised as she was to discover how important her training was to her. She had gained enormous confidence from what he had taught her so far. Learning more could only be to her benefit.

She took a sip of her wine, holding the headmaster's gaze as she did so.

"When will you be ready to resume training?"

"Tomorrow?"

A slow smile curved his lips, and he raised his cup to her. "Tomorrow, then."

CHAPTER THREE

She yearns for more power. More control.

Myac observed the exchange between Serivar and Indigo with considerable interest from behind the safety of his feigned identity. He had known a mere surface illusion of the Caithin man called Edan wouldn't be enough to fool the woman he fought in Lyra, and seeing her now made him appreciate the effort he had put into his disguise. Two of Serivar's most powerful creators helped him build up complex layers of masking and illusion to bury the ascard signature that would betray his identity. That masking also concealed the strength of his ascard connection.

Even so, his first moments in the room with Indigo were nerve-wracking. He knew from prior experience that her ascard connection was extraordinary and almost expected her to find a flaw in the illusion, but after a brief investigation, she accepted him for who Serivar said he was, and her initial suspicion eased into curiosity.

Now that he could observe her in a casual environment, he marveled at disarmingly delicate the fierce woman he had faced in Lyra could appear. She wasn't as tall as his memory had made her. Average of height and elegant in bearing, her slender build made her appear almost fragile. The determined gleam in her brilliant blue eyes brought life to fine features, warmed by soft bronze skin tone and thick locks of dark brown hair that cascaded around her face with a hint of wildness. A playful, brightly colored dress clung to her figure, defiant of her distrustful manner.

She was as remarkable in appearance as she was strong in ascard connection. Had Yiloch perhaps chosen her for something other than her ascard ability? What an interesting possibility. If Yiloch had discovered her power first, that alone would have motivated him to draw her into his circle. But how could he have uncovered the one thing she worked so hard to hide? It made more sense that the arrogant prince might have sought the pleasure of her flesh and stumbled upon the magnificent adept within purely by accident. A fortuitous accident for him, if so.

He probed further with ascard, taking extreme care not to alert her to his actions. She kept her ability almost completely masked. In her own home city, he would have expected her to be less vigilant. When he encountered her in Lyra, she masked her ability with such incredible skill that he hadn't learned of her presence until he faced her in person. That element of surprise almost cost him his life. When he fled to Caithin after Emperor Rylan's fall, he had done so hoping she hadn't survived. Now her survival filled him with a morbid pleasure. As Edan, a fellow member of this very exclusive subset of the King's Order, he had an opportunity to influence her, so long as he could ignore the irritating fondness his old healing mentor, Serivar, had for her.

That affection flowed off the headmaster even now, subdued only by a thick layer of frustration.

They were both an open book to the ascard skill he had developed for sensing emotions, though she kept hers restrained, a hint of anger edged with the sour tang of distrust. Such emotions seemed out-of-place coming from a student facing her teacher. Digging for more, he ran up against a thick core of sorrow, the foundation beneath all her emotions. Even without knowing the source of that sorrow, it inspired an unaccustomed twist of sympathy in him. It tasted to his ascard sense much like the sorrow he felt after his mother was murdered and his father turned him away.

He pushed those thoughts aside, leaving darker things to dwell in the shadowed places where they belonged.

What he most wanted to understand was why she risked so much for Prince Yiloch. Was it merely a sense of duty to help her kingdom fulfill the alliance they had forged with the Lyran prince? Could she have been guilty of the same error he had made? Believing there was little risk because she had never come upon another adept as strong as herself? With her strength, as with his, it would have been a reasonable assumption to make.

Strange as it was, there was something glorious about being wrong. Having someone else around who rivaled him in power made everything more interesting. Until he knew more, however, he couldn't risk her finding out who he really was, which also meant he couldn't let her know of the power they shared.

He drew on more ascard, preparing to search deeper still. There was so much to learn about her, and he wanted to know it all.

"I would like you to work with Edan," Serivar said. "He has an advanced skill in sensing emotion that I think would be useful for you going forward."

As Serivar spoke the words, the emotions Myac was digging through vanished, and his ability ran up against an icy wall of apparent indifference. She met his eyes, offering a tight, challenging smile. If he'd had any warning, he might have countered the block, but he would never have expected her to put up such a barrier so fast. The speed with which she adapted an existing skill to this new use was remarkable.

"Impressive." He acknowledged the sudden shutdown with grudging admiration.

"Thank you, Lord Edan." She offered a curt nod. "No offense, but I like my privacy."

"None taken." He made his voice light despite the surge of irritation with Serivar for alerting her and with how easily she slapped away his power, like someone swatting a fly. He had minimal strength invested in the exploration, but being so effortlessly cast off still stung. How novel.

Masking was never one of his greatest strengths. He would have to learn to mask his own emotions better before he taught her too much about detecting them. He also needed to make Serivar understand that any further revelation of his skills in her presence could undermine their efforts. They might have learned more about what motivated her before making her aware so she could shut him out. Every skill she developed gave her additional advantages, and she already had a plethora of defenses that were going to force him to find ways outside of ascard to understand her.

Serivar glanced at each of them, and Myac dared to narrow his eyes in a brief warning. The headmaster's slight shoulders rose in a shrug, and Myac bit back on the petty punishments he yearned to deal out. The headmaster refused to acknowledge how dangerous his precious little prodigy could be if they didn't keep her under control. Then again, Serivar had never shown enough sense to withhold anything from him either. Expecting him to have the foresight to filter what he taught this woman, whose very presence demanded an influx of knowledge, was perhaps asking too much. The best Myac could hope for was to win her trust as Edan, which promised to be an entertaining endeavor if he went about it correctly.

"About Lyra…" Serivar began.

Myac returned his full attention to Indigo, still hoping to learn something, though it would have been easier before she blocked him out. Now he had to rely on body language and tone to read between her words.

She straightened in her chair, shoulders pulling back, defiance hardening her features. "Many things happened in Lyra, and I used skills I should perhaps not have used. I have no regrets, however, and no one in Caithin can prove I did anything more than heal with my abilities."

So many careful words used to convey absolutely no useful information. Well done.

Serivar's eyes narrowed, as unsatisfied with her answer as Myac was, though for different reasons. "No one in Caithin?"

Myac smiled to himself. No one in Caithin that she knew of could prove she had done more than heal, but he had been on the receiving end of her power. Since he arrived here, he and Serivar had many lengthy and often heated discussions about the skills she used against him, so there were at least two people in Caithin who knew some of what she had done. To her credit, she had no reason to believe she wasn't telling the truth.

"I used abilities other than healing to aid Emperor Yiloch directly on at least one occasion, so obviously he was aware, as were a few of his closest companions."

Serivar shook his head. His icy tone, when he spoke, could have frozen a river in flood. A fine show, since none of this was actually news to him. "Why would you risk exposing everything? We had an agreement. You were to go as a healer, like the others. Nothing more. Certainly not as a personal adept to the prince."

Her regard matched the ice in his tone, and she lifted her chin, refusing to accept his chastisement. "My reasons are my own."

"Not when they put everything we have done here at risk," Serivar shouted, a sudden flare of rage striking Myac's extended ability with enough power to make him jerk back. Even Indigo flinched. "Not when you vowed yourself to secrecy. I would be within my rights to have you stripped of these memories and turned back into a simple healer."

Her eyes widened a fraction, hands tightening on

her skirt below Serivar's line of sight. Myac didn't need his ability to see how much she feared what the headmaster threatened.

Serivar was quiet for a few seconds, folding his hands on his desk and reclaiming his composure. When he continued, his calmer voice held a lingering edge of warning. "While that may be what I should do, you are far too valuable, and you at least made some effort to hold to our bargain in a challenging situation. Be warned, however, I cannot afford to let such behavior go unpunished a second time."

Her shoulders rose and fell with a deep breath to refresh her courage. The movement of her collarbones drew Myac's eyes to the soft hollow at the base of her throat. Delicate, vulnerable flesh.

"I understand your position, Headmaster Serivar. I have no intention of putting you in this situation a second time."

He marveled at her exemplary composure as she sipped from her wine, the draping fabric of her sleeve sliding back to reveal one slender wrist. Her hands were steady, but a light touch of ascard told him how her pulse raced. She set the goblet back on the desk, and he watched the dancing of delicate bones and muscles required for that simple action with a rush of unexpected yearning. She rose from her chair, her bright dress clinging to her hips and falling in loose layers over her legs.

"Until tomorrow, Headmaster," she nodded to Serivar, then turned to Myac, who composed himself to hide the startling hunger she had sparked in him. "Lord Edan." She offered him a nod as well.

Before he could question his own inclinations, he was on his feet, offering her a slight bow. "Lady Indigo."

The glimmer of appreciation in her eyes rewarded his effort, and he watched her stride from the room with a walk that conveyed both pride and femininity. When she pulled the door shut behind her, he sank into his seat again, a smile tugging at the corners of his mouth. It was no longer hard to understand why Serivar coveted her the way he did and let her get away with so much.

"Charming and exasperating, isn't she," Serivar remarked, gazing into her empty chair with more of that annoying fondness softening his features.

"When not trying to kill me, yes, she can be rather enchanting," Myac mused.

Serivar's attention snapped to him, a sharp warning in his narrowed eyes.

Don't want me playing with your toy?

Myac took a sip of wine to hide his amusement. The temptation to try seducing her appealed to him in so many ways. He wasn't about to let the Caithin headmaster set the rules in this game. "She is willful. That makes her dangerous, more so than I think you realize, but I believe we can bring her to hand. We just have to do it delicately."

Serivar nodded, the warning fading. "Can you manipulate her?"

Myac shook his head. "Not with ascard. She has protections and maskings wrapped around her like an iron cocoon. She wisely distrusts you." The comment earned him a scowl. "I will have to win her trust the slow way if we want her to believe it's her decision to do what we need her to do."

Serivar stared at the door, his scowl deepening. "That's unfortunate, but I can't say I'm surprised. Which brings me to the next order of business..." Myac felt the headmaster engage his ability and spend a few minutes reinforcing barriers that already surrounded the room to prevent eavesdropping of the traditional kind and from someone using ascard. "King Jerrin received a missive from Emperor Yiloch's adept advisor yesterday. The emperor has requested to send three of his Lyran adepts here to the academy to train in the healing arts. He wants to build up his own organized force of healers. I approved the request, of course."

Myac smiled. It was almost too good to be true. "Three Lyran adepts in the city, gives us three perfect victims. We can frame the trio for the king's assassination, and there will be little doubt of the new emperor's involvement since he sent them here. We won't even need to use Indigo for that part, but Yiloch trusted her in that throne room, which will make her extremely useful when the time comes to make him pay for his crimes. When will the adepts arrive?"

"It could be anytime. You must begin working on Indigo right away, but I expect you to keep things professional," he emphasized the last word, pinning Myac with a stern gaze.

Myac regarded his old instructor. After watching his mother fall beneath Yiloch's blade and barely escaping their burning home with his life, he fled to his noble father, Lord Terral, only to be turned away. He found sanctuary in an unlikely place. Serivar, not yet headmaster, had been traveling in Lyra a few years before the growing slave trade made such travel inadvisable. He took pity on a burn-scarred youth and brought him back to Caithin, where he taught him healing while picking his mind about other uses of ascard. With Serivar's help, Myac learned how to heal his burn scars and expanded his knowledge enough that he gained Emperor Rylan's notice when he returned to Lyra.

How much courtesy was all of that worth now?

Myac smirked. "And if I don't keep it professional, Serivar, what will you do then?"

The headmaster's eyes darkened with the anger that poured off him in thick waves; laughably impotent anger. Myac took another sip of his wine and rolled it over his tongue, delighting in his advantage. He swallowed, then set the empty goblet down and stood. Without a word, he strode from the room, leaving Serivar to fume in silence.

In the end, the man with the most power made the rules, and Serivar was smart enough to recognize that he was not that man.

CHAPTER FOUR

Myac stood by the table in the hidden training room the next morning, his gaze continuously drifting to the door in anticipation of Indigo's arrival. This was his first chance to work with her. To discover what she was capable of and, more importantly, what made her vulnerable.

What would it take to win her favor?

One finger traced the edge of the leather-bound book he held as though it were the cheek of a lover.

Why stop there? Perhaps with the right approach, he could also entice her. Make her not only trust him but fall for him as well. She seemed, for all her intelligence, to be the type who would place stock in foolish notions like love. So much power and beauty in one splendid creature. She captured his imagination. That she had almost sent him to his death before only added to her allure now that the element of surprise was on his side. What a pleasure it would be to see Yiloch's face if the same woman who helped put him on the throne returned to take it away from him.

Long hours spent working with some of Serivar's most skilled creators were paying off. They were creating prisons that existed beyond the confines of space and time, like the Serroc prison Emperor Rylan had placed Yiloch in once before. Only these new prisons wouldn't share the flaws of the original. Yiloch would not escape this time. They would frame his adepts for the assassination of King Jerrin and his family, tracing the ultimate responsibility back to Emperor Yiloch himself. Then they would imprison and execute him for his crimes and, if all went as planned, the woman who stood at his side before would now stand at the side of his executioners.

The king's brother, Gavin, who Serivar had already built up considerable influence with, would assume the Caithin throne, and Myac's father, Lord Terral, would ascend to the Lyran throne and acknowledge Myac as his son. When all the pieces were in place, Myac would return home to Lyra as a prince, one with significant influence in Caithin thanks to Serivar's relationship with the current king's brother. They had to move within the year if they were to take Emperor Yiloch down before Lyra recovered from his father's destructive rule and the unrest caused by the war between the two. Still, some tasks were far too pleasant to rush overmuch.

So much power.

Myac closed his eyes, remembering the feel of Indigo's ability clamped around his inner aspect, blocking him from interfering while Yiloch and his father faced off in the throne room. The surprise, the panic, and the swelling of molten resentment like a fire on the verge of exploding out of control. He could still see her vivid blue eyes focused on him, the way they widened in desperation when she felt her hold on him weakening. Those same blue eyes were exquisite with pain and terror seconds later when she lay on the floor, injured and unable to do so much as breathe before his retaliation. Eyes so entrancing, filled with the realization she was about to die an excruciating death at his hands, he almost loved her in that moment.

She should have died.

Myac startled, snapping from his reverie when Indigo entered the training room. Her masking was so perfect, betraying no hint of her remarkable ascard ability to his extended awareness, that he wasn't aware of her arrival until she stepped through the door. A spirit could have entered the room as far as his ability was concerned, but the alluring fragrance of her and the way the supple fabric of her saffron dress clung to every curve stirred senses he was far less accustomed to acknowledging.

Who's going to be seducing whom?

He smiled to himself, annoyance fading with the irony of the situation. Was she oblivious to the potency of her physical presence, or would he be a fool to think anything she did was accidental?

He returned his attention to the book he held as though her arrival was of minimal interest by comparison. With a bump of her heel, she shut the door, lighting the rest of the candles around the perimeter of the room, half of which he hadn't bothered to light, with a quick touch of ascard. He felt her power as it swept through the room, the working unmasked for once, and shivered at the strength of it. Coupled with her very feminine presence, it brought about an awkward arousal that he countered with some creative ascard use before she could notice anything.

How long had it been since someone elicited such a response from him? Had any woman ever enticed him so? As attractive as she was, physical beauty alone had never been enough to sway him, but combined with her power, it was almost irresistible.

"Lord Edan," she greeted after a brief glance around the room, during which she extended another bit of ascard to check the many wards that guarded that space.

He hesitated, caught up in a swell of loathing for the contrived personality he wore. Every moment he spent with her, she would spend with someone else. Every smile he earned from her would be for a man who didn't exist. The thought of her shock, the delicious spark of fear he knew would light her eyes if she saw who he really was, ignited his hunger far more than the clinging fabric of her dress and the light summery scent of her. His groin tightened in response, and he immediately appreciated that she had turned to move around to the other side of the table. It took more effort this time to tame his physical response this time. There had to be a better way to manage the situation.

"Lady Indigo." He looked up from the book with a show of deliberation, acting as if the contents of those brittle pages caused his delayed greeting, then he inclined his head to her. "I expected Lord Serivar to join us." He glanced at the closed door. He had pushed Serivar to allow him to work with her alone, but the headmaster vehemently rejected the idea.

"I told him I didn't see a reason for him to waste his time supervising us. I can get him, if you like, but we are both adults. Are we not?" She met his gaze, those striking blue eyes steady and unreadable.

He yearned for the ability to sense her emotions, still awed and disturbed by the effectiveness of her masking and the speed with which she had adapted it to hiding her feelings in addition to her ascard connection. How much might he learn from her if he could only convince her to open up to him? He wasn't used to having to work for something like this. It was new and exciting somehow.

"We are adults," he agreed with a rare, genuine smile. It felt strange, as if someone else had taken charge of his face. "I am quite impressed by your masking, my lady. Perhaps at some point you would consider working with me to improve my skills in that area."

She considered him for a few seconds. Resistance showed in her eyes and the slightest backward lean in her stance, a sudden distance that made little sense in response to such a simple request, but she eventually nodded.

"I would be happy to," she said, though her tone didn't quite reflect the sentiment.

So much reservation. He caught himself extending his ability toward her and pulled it back before he could suffer the humiliating crash against her barriers that would alert her to his efforts.

What made her so reluctant to engage with him? His illusion and the barriers that kept her from knowing him for who he was were far too complex for that to be the problem. If her distance had nothing to do with who he was, then it must be something more personal. Serivar mentioned an engagement gone sour. Could that be at the root of her wary manner? It might be worth investigating as a potential point of vulnerability.

"Lord Serivar was rather harsh with you yesterday." He noted the page number as if he had actually been reading the book and closed it.

She shrugged and sank into one chair by the solitary table. Even that movement somehow exuded a certain distance and separation, as if she were alone even in his company.

"He was probably right to be. I shouldn't have done the things I did in Lyra, given our agreement and the risk of exposing the Order."

"Why did you do them then?"

She gave him a sharp look, prickling with warning.

So much for building any rapport today. If she didn't trust Serivar enough to talk about it, she certainly wasn't about to spill her secrets to a man she had met the previous day. "I apologize. It's not my business."

Those deep blue eyes considered him, the flash of irritation sinking away in their vibrant depths. Her gaze fell to her fingers, where they rested on the table. "I did what I felt I needed to at the time. I will not belittle those decisions with pointless regret. Serivar can choose to accept that or not."

When she looked up at him again, her eyes narrowed, and he became aware of the pleased smile creeping across his lips.

"I'm sorry. I was just...," he paused, trying to pick his

words with more care. "You possess so much spirit, my lady. I cannot help wondering if the headmaster would have invited you into the King's Order at all had he known that beforehand." Her eyes sparked with anger again, and he held up a placating hand. It was like fishing with an actual line and bait, as he had seen people in Caithin doing when he lived with Serivar in his youth. He had always thought fishing that way a silly process when ascard could accomplish the desired results so much faster. The comparison was all too fitting here. Without ascard, he had to manipulate her in other ways. Hook her anger, draw her in, soothe her, provoke her closer, and soothe her again. "I don't mean that as an insult. You express considerable strength and conviction. I find it rather admirable."

"Oh." Her cheeks flushed a pretty shade of rose, and she averted her gaze, shifting as though her chair had become uncomfortable.

Myac sat, relishing the small triumph, and leaned across the table toward her. "Shall we begin?"

She nodded, her expression relaxing with the change of subject.

"Very well." He settled back to put her more at ease. "Recognizing emotion with ascard can be difficult, but given the strength of your connection, you have probably already done it accidentally at least once. A person's inner aspect reacts to every emotion they experience, even when their connection is too weak for them to control ascard intentionally." Interest flared to life in her eyes now that they were working, and he allowed an approving smile to touch his lips. Her hunger for knowledge was exquisite in itself. "That reaction is slightly different for every individual emotion. Sorting through and understanding the thousands of tiny variations is one of the harder skills to master. The easiest way to start doing so is to study emotional responses in yourself. Once you can reliably recognize how your inner aspect reacts to emotions, you can start applying that knowledge to other people. Does that make sense?"

"It sounds similar to distinguishing the different ascard signatures in people," she remarked, hands clenched before her on the table now, eager.

"Yes." It was a heady feeling, being the focus of her attention. But the time had come to see if he could manipulate her hunger for knowledge to learn more about her. "There are several ways we can approach the process. The most effective teaching method I have found is for the student to talk about things that stir a variety of different emotions in them. Being focused on their inner aspect during this process allows them to study their ascard reaction while they are experiencing the emotion."

She started picking at the fingernails of one hand with those on the other. "Couldn't I just think about things instead of talking about them?"

That was exactly the response he expected. Perhaps this wouldn't be so hard after all. "Your emotions will be more poignant if you have the added vulnerability of sharing the provoking thoughts with someone else."

"Precisely." She smiled as though he had agreed with her.

"Out loud." He gave her a stern look.

"With a stranger?"

"Unless you know someone else who can teach you this." She pressed her lips together in an irritated line, and he forged ahead. "When you feel you have grasped the effect different emotions have on your inner aspect, we can trade roles. I will be the subject, and you can try to determine my emotional response to different topics based on what you learned from observing your own. When we are through today, we will no longer be strangers."

Role-swapping was risky given the secrets he was keeping, but it was the only effective way to teach this skill, and knowing he would have to expose himself in front of her eased a little of the resistance in her eyes. Besides, while he wasn't particularly good at masking, he was proficient at controlling his emotions, at least outside of the unexpected passion she inspired in him, but that wasn't something he had practiced much in the past.

Her gaze turned inward while she considered his proposal, and she began picking at her fingernails again. The soft clicking of her nails was the only sound for several seconds. Then her hands stilled, and he felt her ease back the masking safeguarding her emotions. Meeting his eyes, she nodded to signal that she was ready. The uncertainty bombarding his senses now belied the gesture, but he wasn't about to squander the opportunity.

To begin the session, he asked her simple questions. Did she like horses? What was her favorite color? How did she feel about the rain? The sunshine? At first, she answered even those basic questions with reluctance, pondering each one for much longer than should be necessary. Then she began relaxing into the lesson, enthusiasm with the results overcoming some of her resistance.

When he found a suitable place to slip it into the string of questions, he asked, "Do you have any romantic interests?"

Her expression closed. "I was engaged for a time."

So much sharp, burning anger edged with an intense spark of fear. Why? The intensity of her reaction suggested some kind of lingering trauma. Regardless, it pleased him more than it probably should that she wasn't bound to anyone now.

Throughout the entire process, there remained that undertone of sorrow and solitude he had detected the day before. When she spoke of her deceased parents, however, she did so with a curious aloofness and brevity, speaking more fondly of her time spent growing up in her uncle's home with his sons. When he dared to ask about her time in Lyra, she closed off again, refusing to say any more than she had to Serivar. An almost painful itch of curiosity urged him to press the subject, but he resisted, wary of distancing her again.

Her head tilted to one side, her gaze drilling into him with that captivating burn of boundless inquisitiveness. "You're frustrated now. Why?"

Apparently, she was ready to move on to the next step in their training, and Myac had allowed frustration with her avoidance of a subject he was exceedingly interested in become foremost in his mind. Several responses leapt forth. He settled for something near the truth, if only part of it.

"I apologize." He forced calm upon himself as he spoke. "The truth is, I am rather fascinated by you. I was hoping to learn more about what motivates you from this session, but you seem reluctant to speak of those things."

A fresh flare of irritation ignited in response to his partial confession. Resignation, and perhaps a sense of grudging tolerance, quenched it a moment later, and she leaned back in her chair. So discerning was her scrutiny that he fancied he could feel his disguise crumbling before it. Not the most comfortable sensation.

"You don't come across as the timid sort, Lord Edan. Why not simply ask me outright what you want to know?"

She had him unsettled. His mind scrambled for a reason to excuse himself from the session before something went terribly wrong, but he refused to run from her. That would only make it harder to work with her again. "Would you answer me honestly if I did?"

She met his eyes, a tremor of temptation charging the air. So many unspoken words hung around them. Things she wanted to share but wouldn't for reasons that he couldn't pretend to know. She wanted a confidant. There was no doubt in his mind about that now. If only he could convince her to let him fill that role.

The tremor vanished when she shrugged, stubbornly casting off temptation. "Probably not."

"Then I must be clever enough to earn my way past your defenses."

"You will have to be exceedingly clever, my lord." Her smile was almost playful, but the masking returned, blocking her emotions from him once more.

He wrestled down the urge to incinerate something with his power. He couldn't lose patience, especially not with her tuned to him. Learning to mask his emotions better couldn't happen soon enough.

"I am sorry if I have upset you, Lady Indigo. Perhaps we should move on to something else since you are picking up on this with such ease."

A tiny, satisfied smirk touched her lips, and Myac fought another war with his temper as he tried to puzzle out the thoughts behind that look without the advantage of ascard senses. He relied on his ability to read people with ascard far too much. It put him at a significant disadvantage in this situation.

"Lord Edan, I do appreciate your time, but I would prefer to cut our session short today, if you don't mind. I know we talked yesterday about working together on your masking. If you speak with Headmaster Serivar, he can explain the basics of this kind of masking. I can help you build upon that tomorrow afternoon if you like."

Why was she in such a hurry to get away now? Had he upset her? "If you wish it, we can call an end to today's session. I do hope I haven't offended..."

The smile she gave him then was sincere and sweet enough to make his breath catch in his throat. "No, Lord Edan, you have done nothing wrong. I'm flattered that you find me so interesting, but I have my own anxieties to deal with, and I feel unequal to the task of managing them right now. You shouldn't have to suffer for that. I think it best that I go."

She rose, and he followed suit, hurrying to the door so he could open it for her. On a whim, he held it shut instead, forcing her attention to him. "The headmaster was kind enough to grant me a room in his home. I don't think he or his wife would object if you were to join us for supper some evening."

Outrage flashed across her features, so fierce that he almost backed away.

Everything I say and do is wrong.

A fresh burst of frustration left him fumbling for a way to salvage the encounter. Then her protections slipped, only for a heartbeat, but long enough for a deep, aching sorrow to wash over him, drowning his frustration. The emotion vanished again as suddenly as it appeared, tucked back safe behind her walls. Her anger faltered, crumbling before uncertainty. A touch of sadness darkened her eyes. She lowered her gaze.

"I have had misfortune in my relationships over the last few years," she murmured. "I need time to figure those things out."

On a whim, he reached out, placing a gentle finger under her chin and lifting until her eyes met his. The gesture might ignite her rage again, but she was vulnerable at that moment, lapsed into a victim state she undoubtedly struggled to be rid of. He had seen it in enough people to recognize it and know how easy those fragile moments were to exploit. He needed to capture this one. Use it to his advantage.

"I am truly sorry." He offered her a smile as gentle and cautious as his touch. "I won't mention it again. But should you change your mind, the invitation will remain open."

She met his eyes, searching them for several long seconds, and he wondered what she thought she saw there. A web of lies and deception? A deep and earnest longing? Neither would be wrong.

"Thank you, Lord Edan. I value your offer and your understanding."

He nodded, pleased that the gamble had paid off, and opened the door for her, offering a slight bow as she left the room. She had slipped the hook as fish often did, but the bait was out and she would try it again. She was much too curious not to.

CHAPTER FIVE

Indigo strode from the room as fast as she could without breaking into a run. Part of her wanted to turn back and tell Edan that yes, she would join him for supper. What would be the harm? All he was asking for was her company at a meal. Besides, what good could come of spending all her free time hiding away in her residence, pining over the man she could never have?

Serivar's office was empty, so at least she didn't need to fake her composure with him. She hurried away from Edan, from the temptation to confide in someone, reaching out with tendrils of ascard to make sure no one she wanted to avoid was in the area. Even knowing the Watchmen wouldn't come after her for it, using ascard to sneak through the streets avoiding people made her feel like a criminal in her own city. It was still better than running into Jayce.

Forcing her discomfort with her current situation aside, she turned her thoughts to the session with Edan. It wasn't hard. She found him intriguing for some reason she couldn't quite put her finger on. The man didn't hide that he found her attractive, which made her uncomfortable, though he had given adequate respect to the distance she maintained, except perhaps the moment by the door. There was nothing unseemly about his showing interest. She wasn't married or even engaged anymore after all, but he would undoubtedly continue to express that interest if she didn't discourage him.

And yet, setting aside the fact that something about him felt unnervingly familiar at times, she had no reason to push him away beyond a pointless romantic entanglement that had no future. Part of her resented him because he wasn't Yiloch, which wasn't at all fair. She would never be with the Lyran emperor again. Edan was attractive enough, seemed nice, and had asked for nothing from her outside of their professional relationship beyond the sharing of a meal. Why not take a chance and get to know him better?

Jayce had also seemed nice in the beginning.

Also not fair, she chided herself.

Being honest with herself about it, she had to admit to a reckless urge to let him in for the sole reason of finally having someone to talk to who knew about at least one of the biggest secrets in her life, and that worried her. It was the wrong reason to encourage his interest.

Joining the King's Order made it so she couldn't be completely honest with anyone about who she was and how she spent her time. Now her dissolved engagement with Jayce also made her the subject of cruel gossip and estranged her from Andrea. Lord Caplin, the king's nephew, had been her best friend in the city for many years, only now that she knew his feelings for her extended beyond friendship, despite his engagement to Andrea, she felt it best not to spend too much time around either of them. That left her with no one in the city.

She wrapped her arms around her middle where someone had hollowed her out and filled the empty space with remorse. How had things gotten this way? Helping Yiloch take his father's throne should have been a step toward asserting control over her future, but every step she had taken since left her feeling only a little more in control and a lot more alone.

It doesn't matter. This is my fight.

She lifted her head and set back her shoulders, unwrapping her arms from around herself. All she needed to do was finish her training and move on. As a healer, she could find a position in most any town. It might be better to relocate to a place well away from Demin. After all, if no one knew her, it would be easier to keep the Order's secrets, and she wouldn't have to make excuses to anyone any time the Order called upon her.

She passed through the gates marking the entrance to the academy grounds with ascard still extended around her. An Ascard Watchman standing outside a nearby residence tensed and glanced in her direction. She felt the light touch of his ability and saw him relax with an almost imperceptible nod to her before he looked away. She bit her lip. The Watchmen had their inner aspects tuned to recognize the signature of those who had permission to use ascard for non-healing applications, but she would prefer it if they never noticed her at all now that she had mastered her masking.

She stopped and pretended to look for something in her bag while turning her attention to the masking around her ascard connections, testing different weaves to reinforce potential weaknesses. Once satisfied, she resumed her walk. She hadn't gone far when her extended ability touched on a familiar ascard signature and her heart stuttered in her chest.

Jayce was a block up the street and heading her way. With so many people in the area that he didn't appear to have noticed her yet, but she had mere seconds to come up with some way to avoid him. She glanced around, trying to maintain calm. Stepping into the shadows of the building next to her, she drew on more ascard and molded it, adding the illusion of more weight on her body, darkening her hair to black, and altering her features enough to throw him off.

She waited a moment, letting a few people pass by before stepping back into the street and continuing along her route. Jayce came into view, dusty brunette hair tidy as always, his handsome features lit by a boisterous smile as he talked with a man she recognized from his archery group. Her chest tightened with remembered pain, the force behind his kicks the night he had knocked her to the floor, strong enough to crack her ribs. If she hadn't had her ascard ability to stop him with, would she even be alive now?

She shuddered.

What right did he have to be happy after all the pain he had inflicted upon her? The temptation to do something, to cause him pain or at the very least trip him up with a bit of ascard manipulation, was almost overwhelming. Her heart pounded with a toxic blend of fear and hatred.

I shouldn't fear him. I could destroy him with a thought.

The knowledge did nothing to ease the frantic flutter in her chest, urging her to run or hide.

Jayce glanced past her. His gaze snapped back for a second look as the two men continued past, his smile faltering. Then he shook his head and resumed his conversation, his smile not as easy as it had been before. He feared her too, but not enough to outweigh the resentment she knew he harbored toward her now. She'd struck a devastating blow to his pride when Caplin helped her dissolve their engagement.

She maintained the illusion for the rest of her walk, discarding it with a shudder at the bottom of the staircase leading up to her rooms. Her gaze drifted up those steps to her door, and she deflated. The unfortunate truth was she hated to be alone, and that craving for company undermined her purpose. How could she continue taking control of her life when doing so had brought her nothing but sorrow so far?

Perhaps she would take Edan up on the offer of supper after all. It might be amusing to see how Serivar responded to the situation, and perhaps she would find a friend in the young lord if she gave him a chance. Knowing she wouldn't have to hide the King's Order from him was enough by itself to make befriending him worth some effort.

Tomorrow.

Several minutes later, she stood staring into her wardrobe, uncertain of what had compelled her to open it in the first place. After a few more seconds of staring at her assortment of clothing, she drew out the soft gray cloak Yiloch had given her the day she left Lyra. It belonged to his deceased mother, whom he had loved very much. A precious gift from a man she couldn't stop loving, no matter how many miles stretched between them. Wrapping the cloak around her shoulders, she walked out to the couch and curled up against a pillow, closing her eyes to savor the welcome memory of his touch.

* * *

Indigo squeezed her mother's hand as tightly as she could. Her seven-year-old heart fluttered like that of a tiny bird as twelve well-armed soldiers marched into the foyer of their home, moving around either side of the scowling guardsman at their head. All but two began spreading out through the house, searching for something. Those two remained, awaiting orders.

She glanced up, seeking comfort, but her mother was busy glaring at the guardsman, her lower lip trembling while her red-rimmed eyes filled with moisture.

"Serana Milan, you will wait here until the search is complete," the guardsman ordered. His dark eyes were cold and wary.

What could her mother, fragile as she was, have possibly done to earn the distrust in those eyes?

"I demand to know what's going on. This is my home." Her hand trembled in Indigo's grasp as she shouted at the guardsman.

That cold gaze sank to Indigo, and she stepped closer to her mother's side. "Your husband, Desgard Milan, was arrested this morning for leading an attack against a slave caravan. We have evidence connecting him to numerous other such attacks. He has been summarily stripped of all lands and titles. He will stand trial for treason and face the appropriate punishment for his crimes."

A shudder passed through her mother, shaking her like an autumn leaf in the wind, clinging to its branch. Icy fear spread through the pit of Indigo's stomach. She squeezed her mother's hand even tighter. There was no reassurance to be found there. The hand wasn't any stronger than her own.

"And what is to become of me?"

Indigo winced at the lack of inclusion in her mother's question. It stung, though it didn't surprise her somehow.

The guard's gaze was still on Indigo. She wanted to run from those judging eyes, but then something stirred in their depths, a glimmer of sympathy that vanished when he looked at her mother again. "You will stay here under watch until such time as your husband's trial and sentencing are complete. If there is no evidence found suggesting your knowledge of or involvement in his crimes, you will be free to leave this place."

"To go where?" Her voice cracked. She yanked her hand away from Indigo and fled down the hall, her sobs echoing back to them.

Indigo watched her go, one of the remaining soldiers giving chase at a nod from his captain. She tried to feel abandoned but couldn't even generate a sense of loss. How many days of her life had her mother wasted crying and fretting while Indigo's Lyran tutor educated and cared for her daughter? Her mother cried for her father not to go whenever he left them, sometimes for months at a time, and wept harder *still when he returned and took his frustrations out on her. Indigo resented them both at that moment, but her mother most of all. Perhaps if her mother weren't so weak, her father wouldn't stay away so long or be so angry when he was home.*

Never, she promised herself then, she would never be like her mother.

A hand opened next to her in offering. Indigo took it, the rough, calloused surface so different from her mother's, and the soldier led her to an adjacent sitting room to wait.

* * *

Indigo woke to the sound of a horse nickering as it passed in the street below. She sat up, keeping the cloak wrapped snugly around her shoulders. Judging by the light, not much time had passed since she lay down. She brushed her cheek with one hand and felt tears there. The dream came back to her then, not so much a dream as a memory banished to the vulnerable realm of sleep.

Her father came home eventually, about a week after a court inquisitor arrived to question her mother. He arrived in a wooden box that she remembered thinking was a bit too short for him, along with an escort of ten soldiers. One soldier had come to the door a few hours after dawn that day. Her mother took her along when she answered it, perhaps seeking whatever comfort Indigo's presence provided.

"It is my duty to inform you that Desgard Milan was tried and found guilty of multiple counts of treason and sentenced to immediate execution," the soldier had informed them, his professional tone offering no sympathy.

Her mother had said nothing. She took Indigo's hand and led her out into the courtyard of the estate. Something about the wagon waiting there struck Indigo as alarming and ominous, so much so that she folded her arms about herself even now, remembering it. Such a common thing made cold and foreboding amidst an escort of soldiers who sat their mounts in disapproving silence. This traitor had paid the price for his crimes, and they were ready to be done with him. Even at seven, Indigo had recognized that sense of annoyance in the air and lifted her chin in defiance of it, taking pride in knowing her father had defied them for so long. For all that he'd been an infrequent father and a terrible husband, he had been brave enough to stand against the slave trade and free many of its victims, giving them the time and effort he couldn't seem to give to his own family.

When they approached the wooden box, two men removed the lid. The man beside it, garbed in healer's robes, had regarded her with pity, an expression that undermined her courage and slowed her steps so that her mother had to tug her the last few feet to the back of the wagon. The healer was there to preserve the body until it could be properly placed into the ground.

Her mother had taken a deep breath, a sound like a wailing wind in Indigo's ears at the time, and peered into the box. Indigo looked as well. Within the box a man lay, his head tucked under one arm like a grotesque satchel. She remembered staring at his face, so familiar and beloved in life, made foreign by this unnatural stillness. When she tried to move away, her mother's hand tightened on hers again, forcing her to stay. Her gaze drifted away from his face, moving up to the bloody stump where his head should have been. Perhaps she remembered it worse than it was, but the stump had seemed so ragged. Not as clean a cut as they had made when they executed her Lyran tutor, Hadris, for illegal ascard use several months earlier. Almost as if the headsman had used a dull sword to do the deed, hacking away at his neck as one might at a tree.

Her mother spoke with the soldiers then, though Indigo remembered almost nothing of what they said. Her father had left them for the last time. That reality had been stark. Agonizingly real. The silence of his flesh and the blood that soaked his clothing burned into her mind.

Quiet tears ran down her cheeks now, as they had then.

Then something a guard said had caught her attention. "You have two days to gather your personal items. This property now belongs to King Jerrin."

This is the beginning of the end, she remembered thinking, and so it had been in a way. The end of that life and the opening of a door that would start a new life for her.

She would remember the soldier's words forever for the sad irony in them. Two days was more than they would need, as it turned out. Her mother told her not to pack that evening. They would do it tomorrow. The next morning, Indigo wandered out to the garden where her mother often sat to watch the sunrise in the summer months, waiting for her husband's next return. The sun rose, and the gentle light of dawn greeted her, falling with a surreal glow upon the broken figure twisted upon the stone bench in the garden. Her mother lay there, her back spine in the wrong direction over the back of the bench, her neck turned at an awkward angle, so her cheek pressed against the flagstone walk. Deep blue eyes, so like Indigo's own, stared blankly at a red begonia, the first to bloom that year.

Serana Milan had thrown herself from the highest peak of the manor, apparently unwilling to live without her abusive husband. What did it matter that she left behind a seven-year-old daughter? Indigo still felt icy resentment at the memory. She had wept, sobbing inconsolably for days over the death of Hadris. She shed a slow stream of silent tears even now, years later, for her father. Not once had she cried for her mother. The passionate adoration Yiloch had for his mother, which had driven him to do such hideous things in his search for her killer, was unfathomable to Indigo.

And what of the Lyran slave trade her father had died trying to bring to an end? When she first met Yiloch, though she hadn't known at the time who he really was, she'd agreed to help him partly because she hoped that doing so would further her father's dream. She had assumed, given his pride in his country, that Yiloch would want to end the trade, to end the enslavement of his people, but she had never asked. Now that he was Emperor of Lyra, would he try to end that practice? Could she still love him if he didn't?

What does it matter if I love him or not when we can't be together?

A clicking sound drew her attention. It took a second to realize she was picking at her fingernails again. She stopped herself, but not before remembering the way Yiloch had placed his hands over hers to quiet that nervous habit the first time they spoke. They had barely known each other then, and yet that touch had moved her so deeply. An instant of gentle contact was all it took to show her just how far wrong her relationship with Jayce had gone.

Curling back down on the couch, she lay alone with her memories and brushed another tear from her cheek.

CHAPTER SIX

Yiloch gazed through the created crystal windows from where he lounged in the sitting room of his private chambers. He had often found his father sitting in this very spot, gazing in contemplation out toward the sea as he was now. They were not so different in some ways, but the ways in which they were had been irreconcilable. If his father hadn't been so callous about his mother's death or so willing to use Yiloch's sorrow to manipulate him, perhaps things would not have gone the way they did. Rylan might still rule Lyra with Yiloch at his side. Yiloch's brother and others close to him might still be alive. Myac might never have entered the picture.

Indigo wouldn't have either.

He frowned at the waves in the distance.

It had gone this way, though. Rylan's manipulations fueled a heated falling out that led to him exiling Yiloch from the capital. After that, his father turned more to the kinds of behaviors that led to their parting of ways, using the slave trade to control nobles and criminals alike, and eventually putting Yiloch's younger brother to death for being too gentle. Revolution became inevitable. Leading it himself allowed

Yiloch to mitigate some of the damage, though there was still much rebuilding to do and an abundance of loose ends to tie up.

Thinking back on the day he had taken the throne, it wasn't the climactic moment when his blade cut clean through his father's neck that he remembered. It was the moment of horror when he feared Indigo might die in service to his thirst for revenge and need to savor that experience. How like the woman to overpower even that long-awaited satisfaction with her unassumingly captivating presence.

He smiled at the thought, unable to maintain any semblance of irritation toward her. The only other memory that stuck with him so strongly was that of his mother's death. Love was truly a waste of effort, was it not? It left you vulnerable to so much pain and there was no way to get rid of it once it had infected your very being.

Indigo.

He exhaled, clenching his fist around the ring that usually hung at his neck. The ring he had taken from her as a keepsake of their first encounter, which she later told him to keep so it might be with him when she could not be.

Myac was dangerous. The adept would pay for what he did to Indigo once they found him, but he wouldn't suffer. Yiloch would indulge no drawn-out moment of vengeance. Yiloch had almost lost Indigo to such hubris when he defeated his father. He had learned his lesson.

The door to his chamber opened. He reached out with ascard, touching on Adran's presence as expected, and made no move to acknowledge him. Adran entered, cloaked in respectful silence, and sat in another chair, the very chair Yiloch himself used to sit in to wait for his father's acknowledgement. His longtime friend didn't stare at him with the expectancy of a child trying to please his father. Instead, he set his booted feet on a table and turned his gaze to the windows, watching moonlit waves dancing in the distance. Perhaps he sought answers in those shimmering waters just as Yiloch did.

"You keep telling me to let Eris go," Adran chided, his gentle tone taking some of the sting from his words, "can't you do the same for Indigo? She has her own life to lead. Isn't it about time you left her to it?"

Remorse twisted in his chest at the mention of Adran's sister, who had died for him in their fight to take the empire. She had been an integral part of Yiloch's life as much as Adran always had. The three of them grew up together in the capital, and the siblings had gone into exile with him to help him raise and lead an army against his father. It was hard to accept Eris's vigorous spirit being snuffed out so easily, and the absence of her unfailing enthusiasm left a deep chasm in both their lives. Still, while he sympathized with Adran, Eris and Indigo were not comparable in this case.

"Indigo is still alive," he answered, keeping his tone equally gentle but unyielding. "She is merely beyond my reach for now."

"Unless you intend to make her come back here, she might as well be as lost as Eris is." Adran's voice caught this time when he spoke his sister's name.

Yiloch clasped the chain back around his neck and slipped the ring under his shirt, suppressing a quick surge of resentment. It was unfair to get angry with his friend when he only spoke the truth. Indigo had made her choice. Lyran custom wouldn't allow him to take her as his bride, and could he really blame her for not accepting less?

"You may be right," he acknowledged once the ring settled against his skin again.

"But you will continue ignoring me, regardless." Adran's wry grin showed he expected no less.

Yiloch said nothing.

"King Jerrin has extended his welcome to our chosen adepts, with the stipulation that they not use ascard outside of the Healer's Academy. They must also avoid speaking of Lyra's less restrictive ascard uses with anyone other than Lord Serivar or those approved by the headmaster while they are training in Caithin. The headmaster also requested that, in trade for their training as healers, they share knowledge of some of their non-healing skills with a few select students in confidence while they are there."

Yiloch nodded. "The arrangement is fair given Caithin's laws protecting their fragile citizenry from the dangers of ascard use. Have Ferin select his adepts and get them on their way. Make sure he makes his choices based on their existing skills as well as their willingness and aptitude to learn healing. We should be somewhat selective about what we teach Caithin's adepts."

"Already done." Adran smiled in response to his appreciative look. "They head out for Demin in two days.

Ferin will go with them for a short time to ensure the initial process goes smoothly. He has assigned Ian to oversee your ascard users here while he is away."

"I take it he is sending Adept Galyn?"

A hint of envy for the other man's successful relationship strained Adran's smile. "Yes. The two of them are practically inseparable."

Yiloch had to push aside his own jealousy of Ferin, who would be spending time at the Caithin Healers Academy where he might run across Indigo. Would he get to see her? Speak with her even?

"I hope you warned Ferin to be cautious. Caithin isn't known for its tolerance of foreign adepts or alternative relationships. They will need to be discreet, even with those specifically assigned to work with them." Adran nodded, and he took quick note of the melancholy in his friend's eyes before continuing. "Ian has come along well, but that timid streak still creeps to the surface now and then. I think a taste of leadership will do him good."

Adran smiled and shook his head. "I never imagined simply giving him the opportunity to use his abilities in your service would do such amazing things for his confidence. He's doing remarkably well."

Yiloch chuckled. "There was a time not so long ago that you were ready to tear me apart for getting him involved in my war."

"Our war, my lord," Adran corrected. "Even I can be wrong on rare occasions. There is a reason you're the one in charge."

"Royal blood," Yiloch replied, dismissive.

Adran gave him a long, affectionate look. "There is far more to it than that."

Yiloch held his silence, and Adran joined him in gazing out the crystal windows again. The waves rolled in with a steady, soothing rhythm. The motion was peaceful tonight. It helped to wash away the stress of the day. He spent most of his days of late dealing with complicated political maneuvering to settle the recent upheaval in the empire, along with the tedious daily tasks that were an inevitable part of ruling. The ocean was the only thing that soothed him. Did the knowledge that Indigo was out there on the other side of the Gilded Strait play a part in that?

Earlier today, he received word that Kudaness raiding parties were attacking farms and settlements near the southern Lyran border. A part of him suspected it was retaliation from Suac Chozai for his refusal to offer aid. He dispatched a small force to protect the settlements with orders to avoid instigating further conflict and sent the part Kudaness warrior, Cadmar, with them to conduct a discreet investigation of the situation. Cadmar had the knowledge of Kudaness culture and territory necessary for discovering the root of the problem without provoking the people. He was even welcome among many of the tribes.

The first order of business would be to determine what tribe or tribes were responsible for the attacks. If the Murak were behind them, then Yiloch could be confident of his suspicions, and his retribution would be more severe. Otherwise, he would seek a more peaceful resolution with the offending tribe before resorting to aggressive action. For now, he trusted Cadmar to assess the situation and would wait upon his assessment.

As the silence drew on, he glanced at Adran, noting the slightest tension in his posture that only a lifetime of friendship made apparent.

"You have something else you wish to talk about? Myac perhaps," he ventured, hopeful.

"No. I'm afraid that search has borne no fruit yet." Adran met his eyes. "You need an heir. Soon," he added with extra emphasis.

"I doubt the royal penis is going to shrivel up and fall off on the morrow." Flippancy wouldn't get him anywhere, but he detested the subject.

"All your reasons for not doing so are naught but excuses for clinging to Indigo in your heart."

Yiloch scowled.

"She can keep your heart, my friend, but you need to give your seed to someone else."

Only Adran would be so bold, and Yiloch couldn't bring himself to argue about it again, despite the ridiculous resentment that arose at the thought of marrying someone other than the splendid Caithin adept. He could never marry her. Lyran tradition held that only the purest Lyran blood could sit upon the throne. His empress couldn't be some Caithin woman, regardless of her rank or his feelings for her. Adran was correct in his assessment. An empress and a child would give the people promise for the future. That would help bring calm and a sense of stability to the empire.

"Lord Vyram has a lovely daughter of proper age, if I recall," Yiloch commented. If he remembered correctly, she also thrived in social settings. A woman who would require little attention so long as she had fine clothes and plenty of courtiers to hold her attention. "Selecting her would also offer him recognition appropriate to his efforts in helping me take the throne."

"Yes, Lady Auryl. Lord Vyram commands considerable respect among the nobility, and his lineage is flawless. She would be a good choice," Adran agreed, though Yiloch caught a touch of uncertainty in his voice and raised an eyebrow in question. "To be honest, I'm not sure she has the spirit you seem to prefer in a mate."

Yiloch gave him a sour look. "I don't see how that matters."

"I assumed you would want more than a pretty face?"

"I have had more than a pretty face, my friend," Yiloch returned. "Now all I need is a visible empress who is pure of blood and fertile."

Adran nodded, though he looked as if he had bitten into something sour. "I will see what arrangements can be made then. Will you use one of your mother's rings, or shall I have a new one commissioned?"

"A new one." There was no reason to bestow one of his mother's treasures on Lady Auryl now. Perhaps one day she would prove worthy of such a gift. "I would appreciate it if you would present the proposal yourself, Adran. Lord Vyram will take insult if I send someone of lesser import when his beloved daughter is the subject of negotiation. No sense offending him from the outset."

"Certainly, I will head out tomorrow for Vyram's estate after I've arranged the rings."

Yiloch nodded and touched the small lump of Indigo's ring through his shirt while he gazed out at the moon. The soft, glowing orb reminded him of a pearl in one of his mother's favorite rings. When he was young, she told him how his father had commissioned a dozen adepts to take a piece of the moon to fashion the stone in the ring. It was a ridiculous story, but he loved to hear her tell it, smiling while her hand rested on his arm as he lay in bed at night, the ring turned so that the pearl would catch the glow of moonlight through his windows. The memory gave him an idea, one that had nothing at all to do with Lady Auryl.

"Adran, could you send for Ferin and Ian?"

"At this hour?" Yiloch gave him a stern look, and he shrugged, his slender frame lifting with the gesture. "As you wish." He let his boots fall to the floor and stood.

While Adran leaned out the door to send a servant for Ian and Ferin, Yiloch walked over to the vanity where most of his mother had stored her jewelry. A quick search found what he was looking for. The ring had a delicate gold band with a perfect pearl set at the top. Fine strands of gold wound around the perimeter and tapered up to hold it in place. To either side were two brilliant diamonds, one set just below and the other set just above the main band, also wound with delicate tendrils of gold.

Adran came to stand next to him and eyed the ring.

"That doesn't look like a wedding ring," he commented.

"I don't intend it to be." Yiloch eyed the delicate piece, a satisfied smile curving his lips.

Adran sighed. "What purpose will it serve?" His weary tone expressed a world of sympathy, edged with a warning.

"It shall bear my gratitude for her efforts in our war and act as a token." He did not say as a token of what. An explanation was unnecessary. "Humor me, Adran. It is all I can give her."

Adran inclined his head in solemn acceptance. "I always do."

* * *

The speed with which the messenger found and returned with Ian and Ferin told him they had already settled in for the evening. Ferin wore silken trousers and a long night robe, his mussed hair attesting to the fact that he had gotten so far as to climb into bed. Ian, dressed in rough brown pants and a shirt that would be more appropriate for working the stables than attending his emperor, was bright-eyed and eager. What he lacked in proper attire, he made up for with boundless enthusiasm, and Yiloch, hungry to share his idea, appreciated that fervor.

He held the ring out in his palm. "I would like to have this ring enhanced with protections. What chance is there that you could have something prepared by morning for Ferin to take with him to Caithin?"

Ian and Ferin stared at him, looking perplexed for several seconds, then Ian's eyes lit up.

"For Indigo!"

Showing unusual disregard for their disparity in

rank, Ian plucked the ring from Yiloch's fingers and eyed it closely. He whistled his appreciation, a huge smile cracking his narrow features in two, and a smile pulled at Yiloch's lips in response to the young creator's exuberance. Ian adored Indigo and had a strong admiration for her power and skill with ascard. The thought of applying his abilities to create a gift for her appeared to have him burning with palpable enthusiasm.

"I think I can come up with something. Perhaps work some defenses into it and strengthen the ring itself to keep it from harm. Though I imagine we won't want anyone knowing it's enhanced." He glanced at Ferin. "Do you have someone who could work a masking into it to hide my improvements?"

"Of course," Ferin answered, his eyes brightening as his sleepy brain began working on the idea. "If only we had her here, we could also tune it to her ascard signature..."

"We can," Ian declared, his delighted grin making him look more like a lanky schoolboy than an accomplished creator in service to the emperor.

Ferin stared at him, his blank gaze calling for clarification, and Yiloch raised an eyebrow in question.

Ian looked between them expectantly, as if the answer were so obvious he was certain they would come up with it themselves. When neither spoke, he chuckled and explained. "The ascard links she created to you and me while she was here." He gestured to Yiloch and himself. "Those links are still within each of us, even if she can't reach us through them from this distance, they bear her signature. We can use that to tune the ring to her. That way, no one else will benefit from the ascard we work into it and, with a little help from a few other adepts, we can mask its nature from others. I can also add an extra bit of beauty to the stones. Make it the envy of all her friends," Ian added with a pleased little laugh, tossing the ring and catching it, his long fingers closing over the fine piece.

Yiloch nodded in satisfaction. This task was in the best possible hands. "Ferin, see that he has the help of any adepts or creators he needs, then get some rest. You are in charge, Ian. Make what you can of it. Make it worthy of her."

Ian clapped Yiloch on the shoulder before turning to leave, enthusiasm overcoming his usual timidity. "It will be worthy of her, Emperor Yiloch," he said, the tightness in his voice betraying the strength of his feelings for her. "Don't worry about that."

Staring after Ian with a mystified look, Ferin followed the young creator from the room.

Adran shook his head, holding his silence until the door closed. "You gave that project to the right person."

Yiloch nodded. "It appears so." Adran shifted, his gaze sinking to the floor, and Yiloch suppressed a sigh. "What is it now?"

"Do you think there is anything to Suac Chozai's warnings?"

Yiloch's jaw tightened. He couldn't believe that Indigo would ever betray him, but the prophet's words lingered in his mind like a festering wound. None of the things he wanted to say in defense of her would come forth. Instead, he simply said, "Does it matter now?"

"I suppose not," Adran replied with a small shrug. "Though we could take some precautions."

"Meaning."

"You could make the ring a public gift, officially recognizing Indigo for her efforts in the fight against your father. You would betray her other ascard abilities to her people under the guise of honoring her, and they would have no choice but to take action against her."

Yiloch gave him a long, probing look. "You would do that to her?"

Adran set his jaw. "To protect you, I would."

"I suppose that should not surprise me."

Adran turned to the door. "Good night, my lord."

"Good night, Adran."

As Adran left the room, Yiloch walked to the created crystal windows to gaze out over the water. He could feel the link she had left within him. He had been furious when he first learned she had done it, but only for a moment. The link was dormant now, with her so far away, and made him feel all the more lonely for its silence. He touched the crystal, pressing his palm flat against the cool surface, feeling the ascard woven into it. Perfectly blended into the window, inseparable from its substance. She was similarly woven into him in more ways than merely that link of ascard. He hoped their blending was not so inescapable, almost as much as he hoped it was.

CHAPTER SEVEN

For the next several days, Indigo made no objection to Serivar joining their training sessions. His presence allowed her to avoid her confusion about Edan. Sensing emotions came easily to her once she understood the fundamentals, so now they focused on new things. Serivar had worked with Edan on developing a solid foundation in the basics of protection and masking before Indigo took over, helping him build upon that foundation. The man was a quick study, picking things up with a speed that matched her own, and the growing admiration she had for his skill made it more tempting to give him a chance. And yet, she couldn't fully relax around him, so she used Serivar's presence to force distance between them.

Today was the last day of training before her next rest day. Serivar sat with a book at the lone table in the hidden training room while she fired arrows of flame at a target on the far wall. Her attack skills were growing fast now that she had given in to Serivar's urging in that direction.

Edan practiced masking his ability while attempting to disarm her protections. At that moment, he was working on managing multiple protections at once, trying to mask his emotions while simultaneously masking his ascard activities. She could still feel the slight edge of frustration in him when he failed to break through her barriers, particularly while she was distracted. She often sensed such exasperation in him when he worked with her, but he remained polite and patient, and she wondered again if she shouldn't give him a chance. Would it hurt anything to see where it led?

She glanced at Serivar, holding back the wry smirk that tugged at her lips. The headmaster wouldn't approve of their associating outside of the training room, which made it even more tempting.

Serivar's head snapped up, his gaze cutting into her. "The target! Not the wall!"

She winced and stopped what she was doing.

Serivar used his ability to smother the fire she had started on the far wall.

"Sorry. I got distracted."

"I couldn't tell from my end," Edan commented, a mix of grudging admiration and irritation coming through in his tone.

Serivar turned the strict gaze on him. "There is no room for petty jealousies here. Have you forgotten that we are all on the same side?"

Indigo started at the sudden flare of fury from Edan, then flinched when a barrier slammed down over his emotions, knocking her ability aside. She met his eyes, her cheeks burning.

"My apologies. I should be more respectful of your privacy. I just get so caught up in practicing new skills."

There was an immense leveraging of self-control

evident as he closed his eyes and took a deep, calming breath. Was he that angry? With her or with Serivar? Perhaps both.

She did a quick inspection of the barriers around the room before changing the subject. "What about the rumors of a threat against King Jerrin? Have you learned anything new, Headmaster?"

Worry ground the edge off Serivar's gaze. "There were some arrests made, but it turned out to be a false trail."

"How do we even know there is a genuine threat?"

"He's a king. There will always be threats," Edan responded, the snap in his tone making it clear he remained annoyed with someone.

Indigo gave him a chastising look and stuck out her tongue, attempting to ease the tension with silliness. He shrugged it off, but she caught a hint of a smile tugging at his lips, and a giddy sensation bubbled in her gut. She turned back to Serivar, who was now scowling at them both.

"This is no joke."

She did her best to look contrite, avoiding Edan's gaze lest it bring the tickle of amusement back.

"There were traces of ascard found within the palace, signs that someone has been watching the king's movements. The exceptional masking not only made it impossible to detect the source but also made it clear the watcher wasn't supposed to be there. With our only lead turning up false, our investigation is at a bit of a standstill right now."

"I would like to be of more help." Hopefully, he

would take to heart the sincerity in her tone.

Serivar regarded her for a moment and shook his head. "You are not quite ready. Soon, I think, but I see no point in putting your life at risk with inadequate preparation."

Edan opened his mouth to respond when something disturbed the barriers around the room from outside. His mouth fell shut, and he glanced toward the door leading back to Serivar's office. It appeared he kept his ascard senses on alert as much as she did.

Serivar smiled. "Ah, there are some people here I would like you two to meet." He rose. "If you will both join me in my office."

With that, he left the room, and Edan moved to follow. Acting on a whim before the moment of courage could pass, Indigo intercepted him, touching his arm to stop him, then stepping back to a polite distance. Edan eyed her, a certain wariness and cautious hope in the way he drew in his breath and held it, his lips ever so slightly parted as if about to whisper something.

She forced herself to speak past the sudden tightness in her throat. "Does the offer of supper still stand?"

He smiled, releasing the breath. "Of course it does."

"I think I would like to take you up on it," she blurted, her pulse quickening and nerves dancing so wildly she wondered if this might be a bad idea after all.

"Wonderful. How about this evening? Around seven?"

Taken aback, she stared at him in silence for a few seconds, then said, "Isn't that too soon? There would only be a few hours for Serivar's wife to prepare."

His eyes brightened with enthusiasm. "It will be fine. I can help Lady Vera. I would love to have you join us."

His smile was infectious, and she returned it. "Very well. Tonight. We should join Serivar."

Edan nodded and gestured for her to precede him down the hallway, his improved mood apparent to her ability even with his careful masking. When they arrived in his office, Serivar shut the hidden door behind them and went to his chair, gesturing for them to sit across from him. He started to say something then but halted and looked up at the door. Now that she was paying attention again, she could feel someone outside the room reaching out with ascard. Mere seconds after the search swept through, there was a knock on the office door.

"Come in."

Serivar rose as the door opened to admit five individuals: a healer in student's robes, two Lyran men, and two Lyran women. One man, a slender individual with pale, neatly cropped blond hair and pale gold eyes, caught Indigo's attention. She stood, and Edan followed suit.

"Lord Serivar." The healer bowed between the headmaster and his guests. "May I present Adept Captain Ferin of Lyra, and Adepts Kade, Sine, and Galyn."

"Thank you." Serivar responded with a dismissive nod. The young healer left the room, shutting the door as the headmaster greeted the fair-skinned Lyran adepts. When he turned to introduce Indigo and Edan,

Ferin smiled and stepped forward, taking her hands in his.

"My Lady Indigo, it is a pleasure to see you again. I trust you have fully recovered from your efforts in Lyra?"

She returned his smile, pointedly ignoring the scrutiny she was receiving from the rest of the room's occupants. A quick and discreet ascard sweep of their audience told her Ferin's warm greeting surprised most of the others, though Edan's emotions were more carefully locked away than ever. The rather beautiful woman, introduced as Galyn, responded to the greeting with a small twist of jealousy, and Indigo flushed at the implications.

"Lord Ferin, it's a pleasure indeed. I am well. And you?" She yearned to ask him of Yiloch, but it would be unwise to express too much interest in the Lyran emperor before her Caithin colleagues. Only Caplin knew the depth of that relationship, and she meant to keep it that way.

"Very well." He held her hands a moment longer, his eyes alight with some unspoken message that stirred hope in her, then he released her hands and faced Serivar. "Apologies, Lord Serivar, but as you can see, I am already acquainted with Lady Indigo."

"Yes." Serivar bit off the word, tension in his voice accompanied by a flare of anxiety that puzzled her. "Lady Indigo and Lord Edan will be working with your adepts part of the time. Indigo is one of our most skilled healing students. She and Edan are also developing other skills that your adepts may have experience with."

Ferin nodded. "Of course."

"Lady Indigo, Lord Edan, if you would please excuse us. I need to go over some things with our guests. There's no need for you to linger."

The headmaster's words didn't exactly deny them the right to stay, and Indigo considered pushing the matter, but Edan touched her elbow and made for the door. Not wanting to cause a scene, she nodded to Serivar and started following him out.

"Lady Indigo." She turned back to Ferin, trying not to appear as hopeful as she was for some word—any word at all—from Yiloch to prove that he still cared for her. "Perhaps we can find a chance to catch up before I head back to Lyra. I will be staying here for a while to see that things get off to a smooth start."

Again, she sensed a puzzling surge of anxiety from Serivar and struggled not to look at him since she didn't have his permission to be poking about his emotions. "I would like that, Lord Ferin."

"I will search you out later in the week, perhaps," he said, his words somehow both a question and a suggestion.

How about now? She nodded, forcing herself to be patient. "Until then."

Ferin returned the nod, and she received a sense of satisfaction and anticipation from him. Whatever he wanted to share, it must not be bad, or he wouldn't be so pleased. Turning away to hide an eager smile, she left the room with Edan. When the door closed behind them, he fell into step alongside her.

"Lord Ferin. He is one of Prince Yiloch's closest captains, isn't he? Part of his inner circle?"

She glanced at him, her step faltering. "You mean Emperor Yiloch."

Edan's expression slipped, an instant of confusion flickering across his features, then it vanished behind a smile, and he dismissed the moment with a casual shrug. "Of course. That is a fairly recent development still."

She continued walking, though she felt more ill at ease again now. "You are familiar with the emperor's captains?"

"Not really, I have heard their names, mostly. Working with Serivar and staying in his home, I hear a lot about current politics." Edan avoided her gaze now, looking as if her unease had spread to him. "From what I saw in there, you are the one who is familiar with the captain. As only one of fifty healers, I would not have expected such a strong camaraderie to develop with the Lyran soldiers, let alone their leaders."

She stopped and stared at him. Edan continued a few more strides, then he also stopped and rotated around on the ball of one foot. Drawing on ascard in the surrounding air, she felt for anyone nearby and created a barrier to block sound. Edan's eyes narrowed, then she felt him investigating her construct with his ability, and his expression relaxed a fraction.

"As you already know from my argument with Serivar, I did more than heal in Lyra. I assisted the emperor directly and, as a result, was often in contact with his captains." She stepped closer to him, biting her words off in partially feigned anger. It was cruel, perhaps, but the fastest way to get him to drop the subject would be to act as if he had insulted her. "Does it surprise you so much that they might have found my company agreeable?"

Edan looked alarmed and disconcerted for a moment, then a slow smile curved his lips, and he lifted his hands in a quick gesture of surrender. "Your eyes are amazing when you're angry." He held up a hand again to stop the heated retort she was about to throw at him. "And you make a fair point. I, for one, find your company immensely agreeable, so it should not surprise me to find that others feel the same."

Her anger began melting, though a vague unease remained, tugging at the back of her mind. She let the sound barrier dissolve. "Perhaps we should arrange supper for another night."

Edan reached out to her side and took her hand.

She resisted the urge to pull away from him. She had been somewhat dishonest in manipulating his interest in her. The least she could do was let him try to make amends.

"I hope I haven't pushed you away."

She forced herself to meet his eyes, struggling against the distance this new unease reestablished between them. "No. I am sorry for losing my temper." It was her turn to gesture him to silence when he started to speak. "I just have a feeling Serivar will be here late tonight, and it wouldn't seem proper to come to supper at his house without him there."

Edan nodded, though he searched her face for several seconds, looking for additional explanation she refused to give, before yielding. "You are right. Perhaps tomorrow?"

"I am busy tomorrow. I'm sorry. Can we talk about it next week?"

"Certainly." There was disappointment in the way he averted his eyes and in his tone as he gave her hand a gentle squeeze before releasing it.

She forced a smile. "Good night, Lord Edan." After offering him a polite nod, she continued down the hallway.

Outside, the soft, pale gray of dusk was settling over the city, bringing a chill to the air. She drew her amber shawl tight around her shoulders and walked faster, both to keep herself warm and to outrun the discomfort that still clung to her. Why had it disturbed her so when Edan called Yiloch prince instead of emperor? It was an easy enough mistake to make, but there was something about it that nagged at her. The error in title didn't actually bother her by itself. It was the way he said it. Prince Yiloch had rolled off his tongue easily, as if he were used to saying it, and there had been an edge of resentment in his tone. It was subtle, but she was sure she had heard it.

She walked up to the fountain courtyard in the education district and sank into memories. It was the first place she had ever seen Yiloch. His aristocratic beauty and mystery captivated her from the first moment, and he had proceeded to steal her heart completely in the ensuing months. She held her hand under the water. It was icy cold in the chilly evening, and she sucked in a breath with the shock of it. That instant of shock also awoke her to the fact that she risked encountering Jayce or Andrea if she lingered here.

She made herself resume her walk. The unease faded by the time she entered her building and climbed the stairs to her door. Out of habit, she did an ascard sweep as she opened the door and discovered that she was no longer alone. She spun, stepping backward through the doorway while drawing on more ascard. A split second before she launched an attack, she recognized Ferin and released the gathered power.

"Lord Ferin." She breathed, placing a hand to her chest, feeling the pounding of her heart as she staggered back a few more steps. How could she have let her guard down enough to allow someone to get that close unnoticed? The potential consequences of such carelessness left her trembling. "I could have killed you."

Ferin gave her a shaky smile, and she felt him releasing the defensive barriers he had thrown up in response to her near assault. They wouldn't have been enough. His connection wasn't that strong. "Believe me, my lady, I do not doubt that."

"How did you find me?" She gestured him in.

His gaze lingered on her trembling fingers as he shut the door behind him. Then he met her eyes, a pleased smile chasing the last vestiges of alarm from his features. "I have a gift for you," he said, "from Emperor Yiloch."

Her heart skipped a beat, but it wasn't from fear this time. Her cheeks flushed with the bombardment of emotions that answered his words. The joy bursting through her must have been apparent in her face, because Ferin chuckled and drew an object from his pocket. He held his hand out to her, a small blue silk bag resting on his palm. She took it, hands trembling even more now than they had been a moment ago, and used ascard to force her hands steady so she wouldn't drop the bag. Opening the drawstring, she shook the contents into her hand.

A delicate gold ring landed in her palm, a perfect pearl set in it. The ring itself was lovely, and she immediately sensed ascard bound into it, some of it bearing her own signature. Tears stung her eyes.

"It's created?"

"Partly," Ferin replied. "The original foundation was his mother's favorite ring. Ian and I worked with a team of creators to enhance it and tuned it to your signature using the links you placed upon him and Yiloch, which is also how I found you. Then we added masking so no one else will sense the power bound in it. It has protections woven into it so that if someone attacks you with ascard, the ring will absorb some of the attack. It will also amplify the links you have created to others. Not enough to bridge the Gilded Strait from here," he added in response to her hopeful glance, "but enough to extend them considerably should you ever need to. It will also enhance all the barriers and the masking you place upon yourself."

She gazed at the ring, in awe of the magnificent gift. It was so delicate, meant for a woman with fine hands. Were her hands slender enough? What if it didn't fit?

"Don't fret, the size will adjust to fit whatever finger you choose to place it upon," he said, anticipating her concern.

Feeling as though she might burst with happiness,

she slid the ring onto the ring finger of her right hand, and the band adjusted down a small fraction to fit perfectly, as he had said it would. The power woven into it reinforced her already substantial ascard connection. The sensation was comforting. Stepping forward, she threw her arms around Ferin's neck in an embrace full of gratitude. After a second's hesitation, he tentatively returned it.

"Thank you, Lord Ferin."

"I am merely the messenger." He chuckled, apparently satisfied despite his words of protest. "Without Ian's creation skill, I doubt we could have done more than offer you a pretty ring."

"That would have been enough, but this is extraordinary." She stepped back. "Can I offer you some wine? I hope you can stay for a bit. I would love to hear all the news from Lyra."

"I will happily stay until your questions run dry, my lady, and I would love some wine."

Gesturing for him to take a seat, she retrieved two goblets and selected a wine Caplin had given her, leftover from some gathering of the King's High Council. A far more expensive selection than she could have afforded on her own.

Ferin looked around the room, a knowing smile turning his lips. "I detect a Lyran influence in your décor," he remarked. He chose one of the plush ivory chairs to sink into, tracing a line of blue embroidery with one finger.

"Do you like it?"

"Very much so. I may have to visit you often while I am here just to get a taste of home."

A warm flush rose in her cheeks. "I would welcome the company," she replied in earnest as she handed him his wine, then settled into the chair across from him. "Tell me about Galyn."

Ferin flushed, and she sipped her wine to hide a smile. "I hope it isn't so obvious to everyone. I did not intend it to be a distraction." A trace of sincere worry tightened his voice.

"I sensed jealousy from her when you greeted me. Not many here use ascard for more than healing, though, so I doubt it will come up," she reassured. "Edan is skilled at sensing emotions, but I can't imagine him taking exception to the two of you being intimate, especially given that you won't be here the entire time."

Ferin nodded. "To answer your inquiry, Galyn and I have been together about a year and eight months. She is... quite remarkable." His candid smile drew a soft laugh from her, then his expression turned serious. "What about you? I thought you were engaged."

Sorrow and frustration muted some of the happiness Ferin brought to her lonely residence. She gazed into her wine. "Lord Caplin leveraged his status to help dissolve the engagement. So far, there have been no serious repercussions, other than a few raised eyebrows, but I have avoided Jayce with a little ascard assistance. Who knows what will happen when our paths finally cross."

"Yiloch will be glad to hear that you are free of that situation."

"Why do you follow him?"

Ferin rotated his wineglass in his hands. "I am truly

powerful at no skill. I developed my ascard ability a little in as many varied skills as I could so that I could put my efforts to guiding others in developing those skills. I sacrificed expertise for the ability to teach a broad range of skill sets. Because of that, all my students surpass me."

It wasn't an answer, but she went along with his train of thought, determined to be patient. "You always wanted to teach?"

He nodded.

"But I didn't think Lyra had any organized schools for using ascard."

"We do not, not yet, but Yiloch wants to establish schools. That is not the only reason I follow him, but it is a significant one. We share the same dream in that respect."

She sipped her wine, then swirled the cup, staring into the red depths of the liquid. "How is he?"

"He is..." Ferin paused until she met his eyes. After a few seconds, he nodded in response to whatever he saw there. "He is as difficult as ever and, when he is not pining away over you, he makes a fine emperor."

"I doubt he pines over me all that much." She tried to sound flippant, but the flicker of sympathy in his eyes told her he disagreed.

"He does, but he does not let it interfere with his goals and responsibilities any more than he has ever let anything stand in his way. Yiloch is nothing if not focused when it comes to his empire. He is a good leader. Cruel when it is called for and generous when needed. Unfortunately, there is still much unrest after his take-over, and Myac remains a threat."

She nodded and sipped her wine again to settle the twisting of dread in her gut. She didn't want to think about Myac. There was little she could do for Yiloch on that front. "He should marry. An heir would settle the people."

Ferin's brow rose a fraction. "You are right, but I would not have expected you to say as much. You are an intelligent and capable woman, Lady Indigo. It is a shame you were born Caithin. You would have made a good empress."

A bitter edge crept into her laugh then. "I don't know that I'm all that, Lord Ferin, but I thank you for the compliments and I share your regret."

His smile was rich with understanding when he leaned forward, raising his cup to her. "To love, ill-fated or otherwise."

She lifted her cup, meeting his with a soft click, and they both downed what remained a touch too eagerly. Heartache and worry, it seemed, went well with wine.

"More?"

He nodded, holding out his cup. "If you wouldn't mind."

"Not at all." She rose to bring the decanter closer. "The night is young."

CHAPTER EIGHT

Embracing deepening shadows, Myac blended himself with the night and waited. Across the street, he could still sense Ferin's presence within the building. Indigo was there as well, at least, he suspected as much. If so, her presence remained thoroughly masked, as always. The window of the upper residence where he sensed Ferin was dark, but someone had altered the glass with illusions that, upon deeper investigation, bore the signature of her work. What he saw in that window most likely did not reflect reality.

Whatever the Lyran adept was doing there, it became apparent after almost an hour of waiting that he was in no hurry to leave. Myac might have suspected some romantic intent, but the casual nature of what little emotion he could leach through the barriers around the place made it clear neither of them harbored such intentions. Perhaps they merely intended to chat away the evening. An evening she should have spent with him.

Bitter self-disgust swelled within him.

How could he be so careless? Indigo was attentive and as wary as a wildcat. Too much so for him to get away with thoughtless slips in conversation. He ground his teeth and sent a cautious tendril to probe at her barriers again. What would he give to listen in on their conversation? He could determine very little from reading Ferin's faint emotions. The only thing he was certain of was that the man felt comfortable in her presence. It might simply be because she had helped them win the campaign against Emperor Rylan, but Myac sensed there was more to it. What had she done to gain not only the trust but also the companionship of Yiloch's inner circle?

When prolonged investigation failed to expose any weaknesses he could exploit, Myac turned away from the pointless vigil, determined not to let the evening go to waste. With fresh purpose, he started toward another part of the education district in search of other diversions. It had taken little effort to find out where her discarded fiancé, one Jayce Sendir, lived. With what he had gleaned from Serivar and from his sessions with her, he thought he had enough background information to confront the young lord. Now was as good a time as any to see what more he could learn about her history and maybe stir up a little trouble in the process. Some pain from her past might be the perfect catalyst needed to get her to turn to him. If he could only nudge the young lord in the right direction without implicating himself, the rewards for his efforts might be considerable.

Myac ascended the stairs of the residence and knocked at the door, a soft, tentative knock. When it opened, the man standing there glanced over his shoulder at the darkness falling outside and scowled. At first glance, he was attractive enough, but the sour expression found a natural home on sharp features framed by precisely trimmed hair. Irritation radiated from him, with a bottomless well of anger beneath it, boiling anger, eager to lash out at anyone who dared to press him. Myac got the impression, from the strength and depth of the emotion, that it always lurked there, right below the surface. In the first few seconds, he knew everything he needed to about why Indigo left this man and why she was going to so much trouble to hide in her own city.

"Lord Jayce Sendir?"

A puzzled frown curved his lips, and he narrowed his eyes. "Do I know you?"

"No. Pardon my intrusion. I was actually searching for your fiancée, Lady Indigo Milan."

Rage. A surge of pure, white-hot rage blazed forth as Jayce's hand tightened on the edge of the door, and he recoiled a bit as though accosted by a sudden foul odor. Myac pulled ascard in around himself, carefully maintaining the outward appearance of concern and some uncertainty while he prepared a few precautionary defenses.

Jayce clenched his jaw, taking control of himself. The young lord balanced on the knife-edge of a quick, dangerous temper. It was more than likely that he had taken his temper out on Indigo in some physical way, Myac realized, his jaw clenching with an unexpected surge of antipathy toward the man before him.

And why does that thought bother you so much?

He shoved the question aside, focusing on the task at hand and taking care to control his expression.

"Indigo left," Jayce stated, his tone frigid as a wind

coming off the glaciers on Mount Serst in the heart of winter.

Myac manufactured an expression of surprise. "Oh. I'm terribly sorry. I haven't spoken to her in about a year, so I didn't realize..."

Jayce regarded him for several seconds, resentment at war with the jealous curiosity in his eyes. Eventually, curiosity won. "How do you know her?"

"I knew her before she joined the academy. We were close friends for a long time." The jealousy flared again, and Myac had to fight back a smile. It was so easy to bait him. "I'm Lord Edan Lindis." He offered his hand when the silence lengthened.

Jayce's eyes narrowed more. "She never mentioned you."

Myac let his hand sink back to his side and picked at one sleeve, making a show of looking disappointed.

Jayce nodded as though he had expected the response, and then he nodded a second time, more firmly this time. "Care for a drink, Lord Edan?" He stepped back to offer entry.

Myac lingered on the doorstep, considering the interior in apparent thoughtful silence so as not to look too eager, and then he shrugged. "I don't see why not."

Myac followed him into one of the more upscale residences in the district, more than adequate for an active student of any status who wanted to be near their place of study. It was also painfully unkempt, something he suspected was a recent development. He had spent enough time around Indigo that he couldn't imagine her living in such disarray. Jayce had to move a jacket, a longbow, and a quiver of arrows to make a place for Myac to sit. Hiding his disgust, he settled on the chair, a nice, comfortable piece made ugly through lack of cleaning. Jayce vanished and returned a moment later carrying two clay mugs of some rank-smelling alcohol. As he lifted the mug to his lips, Myac used a touch of creation skill to turn it into a complex wine more suited to his tastes, careful to mask the altered aroma.

Jayce sat in another chair, leaning forward with his elbows resting on his knees, his posture aggressive and demanding. Hazel eyes stabbed into Myac, hungering for something, perhaps a justification for the vile jealousy that coursed through him. It was a poison, that jealousy, and it was apt to kill him someday, hopefully sooner rather than later.

"What exactly is your relationship with Indigo?"

Myac finished his visual inventory of the room before speaking, though he continued his search with ascard when he turned his attention toward his host, seeking anything that felt strongly of Indigo. The other man's impatience infused the air with tension, but Myac pretended not to notice. Nothing in the residence held the signature of her power, but her neutral signature was present, if faint, in many places. He sensed nothing here he could learn much from, which narrowed his purpose down to the one thing that might be of use to him: Jayce.

Taking another drink, he finally met that intense gaze. "Are you studying at the academy?"

Anger flared, promptly smothered. How exhausting must it be to live with such constant rage? Was it always this bad, or had Indigo's departure exacerbated the issue? Dissolution of an engagement, at least among the noble classes, was frowned upon in Caithin society. He could only imagine what a public disgrace like that would do to such a man's ego... and his temper.

"No. I do practice archery near here if you're wondering why I still live in this sty."

A sty you created.

"I was merely curious. It seems a nice place for this area."

Jayce shrugged and waited, still expecting an answer to his previous question.

Myac cleared his throat and shifted in his seat, encouraging the other man to read discomfort in the actions. "Indigo and I were... close... before she moved here. We spent a lot of time together when she wanted to get away from her uncle's sons. I was passing through Demin, heading south to Leisburg and thought it might be nice to see her again and catch up a little, maybe reminisce about old times."

The jealousy coiled in Jayce like a serpent ready to strike. To his credit, he sat back in his chair, taking a long draw from his mug, and managed to appear almost calm despite the storm of emotion raging inside him. Yet, even if his emotions hadn't been an open book to Myac, the flame of cruelty burning in his eyes would have betrayed him. With a lot of practice, the young lord might learn the politics of deception well, but he was playing the game against a connoisseur of the art. He stood little chance.

"I hate to disappoint you, but I'm afraid all she cares

about now is her training as a healer. So much so that she has excluded friends and family from her life."

The bitterness that oozed off him belied his casual tone. The words themselves rang false as well. Indigo was passionate about her studies, he had discovered that much without effort. There was no reason that pursuit should have driven her into hiding, as she obviously was. This man provoked that and many of Indigo's other frustrating behaviors Myac now struggled to work past. He was a base and worthless creature, barely worth the power it would take to kill him under normal circumstances. Myac yearned to be away from him. This man had no true ambitions, no admirable goals, just a selfish need to control those around him and blame them for his failings. He was repulsive.

Myac drank more wine and sighed, giving no hint of his disgust. "That is unfortunate. She always was a motivated woman, though. I appreciated that about her." Jayce scowled at the praise, but Myac continued as though he hadn't noticed. "I will be here a few weeks before I continue on. Maybe I'll get a chance to catch up with her before I leave. It sounds as though asking around the academy might bear more fruit."

Jayce arched an eyebrow, took another long draw on his drink, then said, "Slim chance of that. They don't allow non-students into the training buildings. You can try if it amuses you, though."

"There must be some way to get in touch with her," Myac persisted. "I have so much I want to tell her about and so little time."

"I wouldn't mind having a chat with her myself,"

Jayce said, managing a lighter tone. "I hated leaving our relationship on the sour note it ended on. Unfortunately, I'm not sure where she's staying. I haven't had time to do much investigating."

Liar. He had learned from his own investigations that Jayce spent several weeks hunting for her after the force of healers and soldiers returned from Lyra. Indigo covered her tracks well, and Serivar refused to meet with Jayce, brushing the young lord's frequent visits off on subordinates who didn't have the authority to disclose information about Academy students.

How infuriating it all must be for him. The thought was curiously satisfying.

"I have another old friend in the academy who might be able to find out where she's staying," Myac muttered, adopting a distant look to give the impression that he was only thinking aloud.

Jayce leaned forward, the intensity in his manner rekindled. "Perhaps you could let me know if you learn anything. I'd really like to apologize for a few things and clear the air between us."

Hunger and anticipation flowed from the man. Myac smiled inwardly. Jayce would be an easy tool to manipulate. That was all he needed to know. If things turned around soon, he wouldn't need to make use of this tool. If she remained closed off, the young lord was dry grass waiting for a match, and Myac was more than willing to be that match if it became necessary.

Not yet.

"Of course. I'll reach out if I learn anything." He finished the wine and stood. "I should be going."

Jayce stood so fast that Myac's defensive reflexes kicked in again, and he drew upon more ascard. The young lord's unrelenting tension and anger put him on edge. He turned toward the door and stiffened, bristling with contempt when Jayce dared to stop him with a hand on his shoulder.

I could destroy you with a thought, whelp. Biting back his temper, Myac turned and met that feverish gaze.

"Promise me you'll let me know where she is. I really need to speak with her."

"I will," he said. *When and if it serves my purposes to do so.*

Jayce gestured to the door.

As soon as he was outside again, Myac allowed himself a shudder of revulsion. Maybe he had been something more once, maybe not, but Jayce was nothing more now than a beast whose existence served no purpose. If the repulsive waste of flesh didn't die when he finally confronted Indigo, Myac vowed to kill the man himself.

Rather than head straight back to Serivar's home outside the education district, he let curiosity lead him back to Indigo's place. It was only about ten minutes off course, a perfectly reasonable diversion. The window remained dark like the sky, but it had yet to show anything different. A black, lifeless mirror to the night. It gave him the feeling that he could somehow peer through it back into himself. Somewhere beyond that window, life existed, vibrant life, existing well beyond his reach. Would he even recognize it if he connected with it, or was he too far removed from that which he sought beyond the taunting darkness of the window?

He shook himself, casting away the melancholy that had swept over him. Beyond the barriers around the place, he could feel Ferin. The man was still there, in that enhanced state of relaxation that only alcohol could bring, a deep, amused satisfaction running below the surface. Did Indigo's emotions reflect his? Was she finding the same pleasant comfort in the adept's company that he found in hers? Myac probed the barrier more aggressively and finally broke a tendril of power through. Through that breach, he had a vibrant link to Ferin's, and he left part of himself behind, riding in on his power to listen to their words.

Laughter greeted him, gentle, like the soft trill of a flute, unforced and beautiful. Jealousy, much like that he'd sensed in Jayce, seared through him, breaking his focus as her laughter ended and she spoke.

"You know, I rather envy you. You..."

Her voice trailed off, and Myac felt a whisper of her power touch his own. Drawing back into himself, he laid a quick, false signature upon his working to divert her from his presence. Let her think one of their oppressive Ascard Watchmen was poking around her barriers. Not wanting to gamble on the effectiveness of his ruse, he moved away from the building, hurrying out of the education district.

A short time later, he stepped into the front entry-way of Serivar's luxurious home. Being headmaster of the Academy, a member of the King's High Council, and head of the King's Order came with considerable benefits. Discarding his jacket in a heap on the ornate bench inside the door, he walked into the front sitting room, seeking more wine to soothe his nerves. He caught the taste of Serivar's presence the instant after he was already stepping into the room. The other man waited silent in the near darkness, a single candle flickering on the table as he sipped wine from a delicate, created glass.

Not willing to be put off by the headmaster's unexpected presence there or his long, accusing stare, Myac walked to where the decanter waited, also made of created glass, and poured wine for himself.

"Give it up, Myac. She will never come to you."

Rage flared, and his hand clenched around the glass, unmaking and shattering the delicate piece with a thought. He dropped the remains and shook wine from his hand, already working ascard to heal the minor cuts his fit of temper had earned him.

Donning a calm facade, he began pouring another glass and said, "I imagine you thought these glasses unbreakable."

"You have nothing she wants or needs," Serivar persisted.

Myac spun.

Serivar's eyes shone with defiance in the light of that single candle, the headmaster emboldened by too much wine.

"You are mistaken," Myac said, his voice a venomous whisper. "She needs someone as fire needs air. Fear, longing, and sorrow hound her every moment. She will wear down, and her need for someone will become a need for anyone. I intend to be the one who is there for her when that happens."

Not interested in Serivar's response, he strode from the room, smothering the single candle with his power. An immature and harmless gesture, but that didn't make it any less satisfying. Not nearly as satisfying, however, as it would be when he proved Serivar wrong. He stalked to the room the man had lent him and slammed the door, maliciously hoping to wake Lady Vera. Then he sat by the one window and took a long drink of the wine. Resting his head against the back of the chair, he closed his eyes to the darkness and played her laughter back in his mind.

CHAPTER NINE

Rain poured over them, drumming mercilessly down upon the fields beyond the outer wall of the capital city of Yiroth, where the ground still bore scars from Yiloch's brief siege. Dark clouds showed no promise of letting up anytime soon. It suited Yiloch's mood. If only it could rain hard enough to wash away the fast-approaching entourage.

Mud sprayed up in sheets from the wheels of five carriages speeding toward the outer gates, forcing the mounted escort to grant them a wide berth. Five carriages. The first would carry Lord and Lady Vyram and their daughter, Lady Auryl. The remaining four would contain her belongings, which doubtless included an extensive wardrobe, and those things her parents brought along for their extended visit. They would take up residence in the palace until after the wedding. The entire process was a considerable amount of bother, though he recognized most of his resistance came from a refusal to move on. He would attempt to be a gracious host and husband, though he wanted to be neither on this occasion.

Standing on the outer wall under an invisible barrier Ian had created to block the rain, Yiloch eyed the extra carriages, a bitter smirk creeping across his lips. Would the closets in the palace be large enough? All he could remember of Auryl from visits to Lord Vyram's estate were her distinct, pure-blooded beauty and her father's frequent, exasperated comments about her penchant for fine clothing sucking his coffers dry. Now she would have the coffers of the empire to dip into. This empire was being reborn, however, and mending the wounds his father's careless rule had inflicted upon it would be expensive, so he would have to tell the steward to keep close account of her spending.

A cool breeze came up, blowing his long silver hair into his face and bringing a cold misting of rain in under the barrier. He raised an eyebrow at Ian. The young creator answered with an awkward grin and brushed a lock of pale blond hair out of his face. Exerting no obvious effort, he extended the barrier down around them to block the breeze in addition to the rain.

"What's she like?" Ian's tone carried the weight of many tactfully unvoiced questions. Was she anything like Indigo? Did she have any special traits that might set her apart from any other eligible lady in the kingdom? Was there anything that would make her something more than a reminder of the woman they wanted her to be?

Adran, who had returned the evening prior with Lord Vyram's acceptance of the offer of engagement, shifted next to him. Yiloch knew where Adran stood on the subject. Though the other man was fond enough of Indigo, he was very pragmatic and believed the time had come to move on. He was right, but Ian, like Yiloch himself, found it much harder to let go.

"She will never be Indigo," Adran replied with sharpness in his tone and a warning glance that encompassed them both.

He expected them to treat Lady Auryl well regardless of the love for Indigo that remained within them both, rooted there quite effectively by the bit of ascard she had used to link to them during the campaign against his father. Even without the memories, that link was an intimate reminder of her presence. The knowledge that Ian also shared that enduring connection to her made him jealous in a way, but he also took some comfort in knowing someone else struggled with the constant reminder as he did.

A hint of red colored Ian's cheeks in response to Adran's chastisement, and he stared at the approaching group with an air of avoidance. Yiloch sympathized, but an heir was necessary, and he would not compromise his rule for anything, not even Indigo.

Without her, I might not have a throne. She almost lost her life getting me here. How many people would do that, even for someone they love?

The thoughts came unbidden, in defiance of his determination to set her aside. The leadership of Lyra was what he had wanted all his life. This was his birthright, an undeniable part of the blood that ran through his veins. Nothing would come between him and his empire, not even a greater love than he had ever dreamed possible.

Once, he had thought that what his father and mother shared before her murder was love, now he realized how pale a thing that had been. Theirs had been an arranged marriage, a poor political match that they had worked to hide the truth of from their children. Rylan chose her for her lineage alone, as Yiloch now chose Lady Auryl. That realization did help him understand some of why his father might not have suffered such a devastating sorrow upon her death. Perhaps he and his father were more alike than he once thought. Both of them would do whatever was necessary to achieve their goals, including discarding the ones they loved. His father's greatest mistake was in thinking Yiloch would sit quietly in exile and watch him destroy the empire.

"It would be a thoughtful gesture to meet them at the gates," Adran suggested.

Yiloch pushed away his gloom, inhaled the clean smell of the rain, and set his shoulders back. He focused on the lead carriage and shook his head. "No. She will want to freshen up after the journey, and Lord Vyram will want to present her formally. Besides, I am the emperor, not some minor lord. You will meet them at the inner gate, Adran, and show her to her rooms so she can prepare herself. I will see them in the throne room in an hour."

Adran nodded, his expression revealing approval of the decision as he left to act on his orders. Was the man trying to drive him mad? If he thought one thing, why did he suggest the other?

Yiloch shook his head after his friend and stayed to watch until the lead riders reached the outer gate. Then he turned and started walking along the wall. Ian kept pace, staying a few steps behind him and maintaining the barrier against the elements. For a moment, he considered dismissing the youth. The thought of being drenched in a cleansing rain was appealing somehow. Another part of him, a needful part he still hadn't quite come to terms with, wanted the company of the one person who understood his melancholy better than anyone else could.

When he came to the place on the wall above the door where he and Indigo had entered the night he took the throne, Yiloch stopped and gazed out over the landscape. He could retrace every step of that night in his mind.

His newest young captain, Leryc, had let them in, allowing them to infiltrate the palace undetected with the help of Indigo's masking. Her reluctance to kill the guards in the palace helped him understand what it cost her to save him the night she had killed the group of creators who had almost succeeded in assassinating him and ending the war before it had truly begun. She had saved his life at substantial personal cost, risking everything so he could become emperor of a country she wasn't even a citizen of.

He couldn't say exactly when he had fallen in love with her. It might have been the night he realized she was willing to risk her life for him. Or maybe it was the first moment he looked into those brilliant blue eyes and saw the strength deep within her, trampled upon and ragged, needing only a nudge in the right direction to blossom. Regardless, he did love her, and he wanted her near for that reason, even if he could never marry her. Perhaps he should have offered her a position as a personal adept working with Ferin and Ian, but she wouldn't have accepted. Not at the time. Maybe never. She had her own goals to accomplish and her own battles to fight. Though he resented her choice in a way, he couldn't help admiring her determination. Maybe she would return someday, but how would she feel about trying to fit into this new equation?

He continued to the next tower and descended the spiraling stone steps within. Ian's barrier fell away when the tower door closed. The youth continued with him in solemn silence, sharing his mood and immersed in his own thoughts. They meandered back to the throne room, and Yiloch sat upon the throne, looking up to watch rain running over the faceted crystal high above. The effect was both beautiful and disheartening: the lamentation of a dark gray sky.

Without a word, Ian took up his place behind and to the left of the throne. To the right of the main throne, another now stood, resurrected from storage where it had sat untouched since his mother's death. Both finely wrought in silver and ivory, elegantly detailed, but the second throne had a feminine delicacy to it that Yiloch's heavier throne lacked. Now, freshly cleaned, it reclaimed its rightful place alongside the emperor's throne.

What would Indigo look like sitting there? He could almost imagine her, that beautiful bronze skin defiant of the pale seat, arresting blue eyes calming the heart of every man and woman who came before them.

He shook his head.

Before the time came for Auryl and her parents to arrive, Captain Paulin and Lord Terral joined them, each leading three guardsmen, and took up places along the sides of the long room. His second, Commander Hax, also entered, giving him a suggestive wink and a nod to express her approval of his chosen bride before taking up her place below and to the left of the dais. Yiloch made himself grin in response to her. Hax was the last person he wanted interrogating him over his dour mood. He had last seen Lady Auryl several years ago. If Hax approved, then she had blossomed since then and would at least be a complementary political and social accessory. Time would tell what more she could offer.

Adran entered ahead of Lord and Lady Vyram and Lady Auryl, who walked a few strides behind them. He strode to the front and took up a position opposite Hax as the usher introduced the other three. They continued to the front with formal, measured strides and knelt before the dais.

"Rise and be welcome," Yiloch greeted.

Lady Vyram rose and stepped aside. Lord Vyram also rose, sweeping an arm back to present his daughter.

"It is our honor, Emperor Yiloch, to present to you our daughter, Lady Auryl Desile." He stepped aside then, taking a place next to his wife as Lady Auryl stepped forward and executed a graceful curtsy at the foot of the dais.

"My family and I are honored to accept your proposal, Your Majesty."

Her voice was soft and melodic, trained to a perfect tone. Long, silvery hair with a hint of the same violet that accented her pale eyes framed slender, snow-pale features. Several fine braids wove through her hair, wound back into an elaborate knot held in place using pins studded with diamonds and purple sapphires to match the brilliant necklace she wore. Her long, off-the-shoulder dress was pale silver, accented with deep purple embroidery and lace. Altogether a beautiful display, designed to suit an emperor. Much like a bouquet one might find centered on the dining table. She was every bit the proper choice as far as presentation went.

"It is my pleasure, Lady Auryl," he replied, infusing his voice with a sincerity only partially forced. "I hope your chambers suitable."

"More than suitable, my lord." She answered with a calculated pause, careful not to make him wait while demonstrating proper refinement in tone and manner.

The formal greetings aside, Yiloch considered her for a few seconds, noting that she was steady under his gaze. Confidence born of vanity, or was there something more behind that well-trained facade?

"If it would please you, Lady Auryl, you may take time to rest before supper, or if you would rather, you are welcome to join me for a walk on the ocean terrace."

"It would please me greatly to walk with you, my lord."

There was a spark of something in her eyes that coaxed a smile to his lips. She brightened in response, a hint of color flushing her pale cheeks.

Rising, he offered a slight bow to her parents. "By your leave..."

Both nodded vigorously before he could say more. "Please, my lord," Lord Vyram said, extending one hand in a symbolic gesture to pass along his daughter.

Yiloch nodded and offered his arm, which Auryl accepted, laying her hand ever so delicately at the crook of his elbow. "If you have need of anything, please ask any of the servants," he added to her parents. "Captain Adran will show you around the palace."

He turned to Auryl, resting a hand over the one she had placed on his arm. "Would you like to see the shore gardens?"

"Certainly, my lord, but the rain is fierce without."

"Indeed it is." Yiloch glanced over one shoulder. "Creator Ian, please join us."

Ian walked down from the dais, stopping to bow before them. "It would be a pleasure to offer my services." He gave Auryl a charming smile that earned a light laugh from her.

"This is my lead creator, Ian."

"Oh, yes. The young prodigy my father mentioned." She addressed Ian directly, then. "When he came back from Emperor Yiloch's campaign, he spoke quite highly of your skill."

Ian flushed brightly, still an awkward boy around ladies. "I'm flattered to hear it, my lady," he muttered.

Her conduct was pleasing. If this were her normal manner, then she would not only make a fine empress, but might also prove to be reasonable company as well.

With Ian following behind, Yiloch led the way out to the multi-level terraces between the palace and the shore gardens. The moment they stepped outside, Ian created a barrier to block the wind and rain. Auryl laughed and held one hand out into the rain beyond the invisible barrier. Playing along with her, Ian extended the barrier out over her hand, and she laughed again, beaming over her shoulder at him. They walked down the stairs that wound between the levels, gradually descending to the lower gardens that opened onto a rocky coastline. Waves crashed against the rocks, sending a magnificent spray into the air against the backdrop of the stormy sky. It was the type of breathtaking display that only nature could create.

Auryl stopped, tugging gently on Yiloch's arm. When he paused and looked down at her, she turned to gaze out over the strait for a few seconds, then looked back at the palace that would soon be her home.

"It is truly a magnificent palace."

Yiloch glanced up at the massive structure now looming above them. It was stunning, towering over the landscape in shades of blue, white, and silver like a castle of ice, but it had lost some of its glamor for him. He humored her, though. "It is. Every emperor adds something to it. I believe my great-grandfather added the most extraordinary feature with the crystal ceiling he had created over the throne room."

She looked up at him, pale violet eyes dusky in the dim gray light. "And what will you add, my lord?"

"Melancholy," Ian murmured.

A laugh escaped Auryl, and she quickly put her fingers to her lips, looking embarrassed.

Yiloch gave Ian a warning scowl.

The young creator bowed his head a touch, fighting to hold on to a more serious expression, though Yiloch could see the smile tugging at the corners of his mouth.

"Apologies, my lord. That was most inappropriate."

"Indeed," Yiloch snapped.

"Perhaps I can help with your melancholy, my lord," Auryl offered, her smile more hopeful now.

Yiloch caught Ian's grin before the creator looked tactfully away. Facing her, Yiloch took her hands in his and met her eyes. Indigo's striking blue eyes and brilliant smile filled his mind. Would he ever look at another woman without seeing her?

"Do you think you can be happy here, my lady?"

She met his eyes searchingly. "Of course, my lord. Why wouldn't I be?"

Yiloch made no effort to explain as he took her hand and placed it back on his arm, turning to continue their garden walk.

CHAPTER TEN

For the next few weeks, Indigo kept herself occupied working with the Lyran adepts when she wasn't in her regular morning classes. Serivar had her training them in healing arts while they reciprocated by sharing with her the skills in which they were adept. Kade had considerable expertise in manipulating fire, Galyn's focus was illusion, and Sine was developing a mastery of physical enhancements such as creating sudden bursts of speed or transferring herself over short distances in mere seconds. Physical enhancement was something Yiloch was skilled at, and Indigo, having seen it in use, was eager to learn more. Sine also confessed to a side interest in mental manipulation, which Indigo also found intriguing.

Edan wasn't included in her training sessions with the Lyran adepts. The headmaster decided to split the adepts up between them most of the time, setting them to training in separate rooms. Indigo appreciated the arrangement. Her encounter with Edan the night Ferin gave her the ring still lingered in her mind, carrying with it an inexplicable weight of foreboding.

"Lady Indigo?"

She glanced at Galyn. The slender young woman

was watching in her quiet way, pale green eyes full of patient curiosity. She had silken, almost white hair that cascaded elegantly over her shoulders, worn long as was popular with both genders in Lyra. Combined with the pale, refined features that were a trademark of pure Lyran blood, the long hair only added to her enticing beauty and power of presence, much as it did with Yiloch. She was lovely and fortunate in the love Ferin had for her.

Indigo touched the ring, twisting it on her finger, comforted by the power it held and the concern it represented.

"What is it, Lady Galyn?" She used the Lyran Trade dialect, as the other woman had. The dialect was widely used in Caithin because of the active trade with Lyra and the large population of Lyran slaves, so most anyone with an education could hold up their end of a conversation in it. Indigo's Lyran tutor had seen to it that it was almost as natural to her as her native language. For the three adepts, it was easier than Caithin, and it reminded Indigo of her time with Yiloch.

"I was wondering if we might review the healing of broken bones again."

"Certainly, Galyn," Sine piped up, tossing her long hair, almost white with an odd hint of red at the roots, over her shoulder. She pinned Indigo with her gaze, her eyes as white as her hair with a thin line of red around the iris. "After I'm finished with her."

Galyn crinkled her nose and made a rude face at Sine after she looked away, and Indigo bit back a laugh. The two adepts snipped at each other like siblings, which made sessions with the two of them together amusing and challenging. When either of them teamed up with Kade, whose patience appeared to have no limits, the sessions were more peaceful, but far less entertaining. Today, Kade was working with Edan in another room.

"Mental manipulation is easier when the subject can't use ascard," Sine said, resuming the conversation they had been having. "They can't sense that you're doing anything. With anyone who has a decent connection to their inner aspect and is even a little sensitive to ascard use, it's much harder to put suggestions in their head without them catching you doing it and resisting or retaliating. It is also predictably hard to find people willing to let you practice on them, so the skill is challenging to develop."

Indigo nodded. "What if you had an exceptional masking ability?"

"Are you and Edan planning something?"

Unease sparked in Indigo. "Edan?"

"He was asking similar questions. I thought maybe you two were planning to convince the headmaster there isn't any attraction between you so he might stop forcing you apart." Sine winked knowingly at Galyn, who nodded conspiratorially, as though they had uncovered a secret.

"No. Of course not. There isn't a... I just..." Indigo sputtered before Sine's teasing grin.

Galyn laughed.

"Masking would help," Sine answered with a gentle smile, taking mercy on her. "But I can't do that. My connection isn't strong enough to split beyond my existing skill set and the healing you're teaching us. Besides, healing is complementary to the physical enhancements."

There was a knock on the door then, and Indigo caught Galyn's frown of frustration at the prospect of further delay on the subject she wanted to dig into. Reaching out with ascard, Indigo touched on Kade's signature and an unreadable barrier she suspected was Edan. He was getting much better at masking.

Giving Galyn a quick smile she hoped was encouraging, she used a flick of ascard to unbolt the door and smiled a welcome to the two men. "Kade. Edan. Are you joining us for more training?"

Edan shook his head. He looked tired, as though even the effort of responding was a drain. She had barely seen him of late, so the apparent exhaustion surprised her.

"Lord Serivar has a task for me. I'm dropping Kade off with you for the remainder of the afternoon." A sigh whispered across his lips, and his gaze focused past her, his weary look fixating on something not in the room.

"That's unfortunate," she offered, putting forth a modest effort to cheer him up. "I have seen very little of you lately."

Her words held more power than expected. His focus shifted, settling on her, and a warm smile curved his lips, a fresh spark of interest replacing the weariness in his eyes. "Indeed. Which reminds me, I had hoped to entice you to supper tomorrow evening."

Misgivings or no, she had evaded him for as long as

she could without it becoming insulting. She felt the eyes of the other three adepts on her, curious as they awaited her answer. She twisted the new ring on her finger and forced a nod. "It would be my pleasure," she lied.

His expression brightened more, animation returning to his features, and she felt some gratification that she had at least improved his day, even if she had added stress to her own. "Would seven be acceptable?"

"Of course."

"Wonderful. I look forward to seeing you then, Lady Indigo." He turned to leave the room, his steps quicker and lighter now, then stopped, glancing back at her hands. He tilted his head, looking puzzled, then met her eyes. "That ring is new, isn't it?"

She started to cover the ring with her other hand and caught herself. He had already noticed it and asked. Attempting to hide it now would only make it look suspicious. Forcing her hands to stillness, she said, "This? Not really. It belonged to my mother. Uncle Theron had it cleaned up and gave it to me a few days ago."

Edan considered the ring for a long moment. Did he have a reason not to believe her? Although she might not, given the uncertainty in her response that made it almost sound as if she had been asking him if that was where she got it, rather than telling him.

After several tense seconds, he nodded to himself. "It is quite beautiful." He met her eyes again. "Tomorrow then," he reconfirmed and strode from the room.

She bolted the door behind him. Did any of the three Lyran adepts know the truth about the ring? It was likely

Galyn did, given her relationship with Ferin. When she turned, she met the lovely young woman's eyes. Galyn gave her a small, clandestine wink, and she bit back a smile. Yes, she knew, but she wouldn't expose Indigo's secret.

"You're too good for that one," Galyn commented.

"Leave off, Galyn," Sine snapped. "Her relationships are none of your affair."

Indigo ignored Sine's attempted intervention and held Galyn's gaze, bothered by her judgment. "What makes you say so?"

Galyn stepped closer, her expression solemn, which somehow made her more alluring. "He's hiding things."

Indigo frowned, reaching out with a tendril of ascard to touch Edan's careful barrier as it moved away from them through the building. "Aren't we all?"

"Perhaps. Though some of us carry darker secrets than others." Then Galyn smiled, the expression offsetting some of the warning carried in her words. "Regardless, you are a woman who has won the affections of an emperor and his men, you should never settle for less."

Indigo searched the other adept's eyes, longing to believe that what she said mattered. "You are very dear, Lady Galyn," she said, trying to keep the intense longing from her voice. "But one must be practical. My station makes me an unsuitable match for anyone of such lofty status."

"Perhaps you are right." Her gaze flickered to the ring and back to Indigo's face, sending a message contradictory to that passing between her lips.

Indigo huffed and rolled her eyes. "Romantics."

Galyn only grinned and shrugged, happy to accept the accusation. "About healing bones…" she prompted.

Sine started protesting, but Kade got his words out first. "I would love to learn more about mending breaks and fractures."

Sine's shoulders sank in defeat, and she gestured for Indigo to proceed.

* * *

Indigo pondered what to wear for a long time the next evening. She had considerable reservations about Edan, especially after Galyn's dubious assessment of him. As a result, she didn't want to dress in a manner that he might consider encouraging. However, her usual attire, when she wasn't wearing her student's robes, tended toward flattering and playful to distract from the sorrow that clung to her. Any attempt to downgrade her appearance below her usual standards was going to draw more attention than if she overdressed for the occasion.

Perhaps I am being unfair to him again.

Galyn's association with Ferin, and thereby Yiloch in her mind, certainly influenced her easy acceptance of her and willingness to trust her opinion. In contrast, her lingering misgivings about Serivar colored her attitude toward Edan. If she were to be honest with herself, placing her absolute trust in Yiloch was probably a mistake, given how ruthless he could be in pursuit of his goals. He would always set her aside in favor of his ambitions, or so she preferred to tell herself. It made his absence from her life less painful.

"You will die an old maid in love with a memory," she warned her reflection in the mirror.

Is that so bad?

She cast the thought aside and considered the three dress options she had left after an extended process of elimination. Torn, she settled on a pale blue gown that opened at the chest and below the waist to expose an ivory layer beneath. Some sparing silver embroidery and lace showed at the bosom, waist, and the hems of the sleeves and skirt. It was shapely and fashionable enough to suit her usual style, though the colors were admittedly more suited to Lyra, but not revealing enough to suggest intimate intentions. Over that, she donned the pale gray cloak Yiloch had given her on her last morning in Lyra, drawing it around her as though the fabric were his arms enfolding her.

For a moment, she struggled with the desire to sit down in one of her Lyran-inspired chairs and wallow in the recent past for the rest of the evening. She gazed at the comfortable chairs for a minute, perhaps more, lost in the memory of a gentle touch she would never feel again, of his lips, his arms, his strong naked body moving against hers...

Her heart started racing, and she gave herself a firm shake.

Not only Edan but also Serivar and his somewhat caustic wife, Vera, were expecting her. She would pay them all a considerable insult by not showing up. Abandoning that commitment would only make her life more difficult when she encountered them again. Drawing a deep, bracing breath, she cleared her mind of distracting things and left the residence. A carriage waited outside. Edan had sent it to pick her up, as appropriate. She nodded polite acknowledgement to the footman when he gave her a hand up.

It took less than five minutes to reach Lord Serivar's home in the palace district, not far outside the education district. Much too quick a trip for her to puzzle through any of the reservations she had about going. Could it be her devotion to Yiloch alone that stood between her and Edan, driving her to come up with excuses why she couldn't be interested in him, or might he truly be harboring some sinister secret?

The carriage pulled up into a small courtyard before the handsome multi-story home. The front door, framed by broad pillars wrapped in a flowering vine, opened as she stepped down from the carriage, accepting the footman's aid though she hardly needed it. Etiquette required many unnecessary actions.

Edan came out and strode over to take her hand as the footman released it. "I see your time in Lyra had considerable influence."

She parted her lips, ready to defend her color selections, but he disarmed her with a quick, teasing smile.

"You look stunning." He transferred her arm to his elbow to escort her in.

She hesitated, resisting the light tug on her arm, and he stopped, glancing at her inquisitively. "I apologize. I'm a little nervous. Lady Vera has never been that fond of me. She all but accused me outright of seducing her husband at one point. How is her temper this evening?"

Edan chuckled. "I would never have expected you to hesitate in the face of Serivar's snippy housewife."

She gasped and put her hand to her chest, giving him a look of mock offense. "This is quite serious. That snippy housewife is cooking the food I'm expected to eat," she infused her tone with exaggerated alarm, though she couldn't help a touch of genuine concern that the woman might really do something wicked to her meal.

Edan assumed a repentant look. "My sincerest apologies, my lady. If it will put you at ease, I would be happy to inspect your food and drink with ascard before we dine." A grin tugged at the corners of his lips.

She shook her head and smiled, the banter easing her misgivings, then gave his arm a light pull. "I think I can manage. Let's go face the terrifying lady of the house."

Lady Vera's greeting was civil. She seemed to have put behind her the bitter jealousy she had displayed upon their first meeting, when she had suggestively accused Indigo of taking up all Serivar's time. In fact, in a sense, the accusation had some validity behind it before Indigo left for Lyra. Serivar had stayed late nearly every night at the academy training her, but Vera's tone implied a far more intimate use of their time. With Indigo's long absence and the other activities keeping her busy since her return, however, the woman's ill temper toward her appeared to have faded.

Dinner itself was a pleasing affair, the table laid out with an array of savory dishes and fine wines. A far nicer meal than she usually settled for on her own. It reminded her of the luxurious meals she had enjoyed when living with her uncle, Theron. Those meals were often noisier, given the never-ending teasing between Theron's sons, but they were always delicious.

As servants carried away the plates from a last course of glazed pheasant, Vera held a hand across the table to Indigo.

"That's a beautiful ring, my dear. May I have a closer look?"

"Thank you," Indigo held her hand out to the other woman, fighting the urge to guard the ring from prying eyes. With the expert masking woven into it, no one was going to suspect that it was anything other than an ordinary, if rather lovely, ring.

Vera took her hand and turned it one way, then the other, letting the light play upon the center pearl and the diamonds to either side. "Gorgeous," she commented. "Where did *you* get such a piece?"

"It belonged to my mother." Indigo swallowed back bitterness inspired by the insulting way Vera had emphasized *you* as if Indigo were unworthy of such fine jewelry. "My father brought it back from one of his trips to Lyra."

She released Indigo's hand. "Probably stole it from some poor noblewoman." Vera glanced meaningfully at Serivar while Indigo choked back her own fury. Edan looked at Indigo, his eyes wide and mouth slightly agape with surprise. Vera went on as though she had said nothing out of line. "I don't suppose you have any trips to Lyra planned soon. My hand would appreciate such a burden."

Serivar cleared his throat and chuckled. He eyed Indigo with mock accusation. "See what you started."

"See how he avoids answering," Vera countered. There was a hint of tension beneath her teasing tone. Perhaps she had noticed the fury burning in Indigo's expression, or maybe it was simply her husband's lack of interest in acquiring expensive gifts for her that vexed her. Either way, she moved on to a new subject. "It's good to see you considering new prospects after your unfortunate experience, Lady Indigo. Lord Edan is a fine young man."

Indigo flushed, her rage unbalanced by a surge of irrational panic in response to the pleasure in Edan's sudden smile. It was Serivar who reacted most strongly, however, his expression darkening with a sudden scowl. Where he had done nothing to soften his wife's insulting insinuation about Indigo's father, he was more than willing to step in on behalf of her virtue.

"I think you are overstating their relationship, my dear." The sour look he gave each of them made it apparent that he expected those words to be true.

Edan glanced at Indigo, giving her a fond, sympathetic smile, in plain defiance of the warning in Serivar's look. "While training alongside her every day, I find it hard not to be enraptured by her beauty and wit."

"You are too generous," Indigo replied, making her tone light in an effort to undermine the sincerity in his.

"Yes, isn't he just," Serivar grumbled under his breath.

A fleeting smile escaped Indigo, which she wiped away when Serivar turned his fiery gaze on her. She lifted the fine silk linen from her lap and set it on the table. "It has been a pleasure," she avoided looking at

Vera when she spoke the words, "but I have early plans tomorrow and should not be out too late."

Serivar stood when she did, almost bouncing up with relief.

Edan and Vera rose as well.

"Of course, Lady Indigo, you must get your rest. I'll show you to the door," Serivar offered, but Vera caught his arm.

"I imagine Edan can handle that," she insisted.

Serivar watched Edan escort her from the room with a look that bordered on alarm. It almost surprised her when he didn't come running after them. His desire to control her irritated her to no end, and the opportunity to defy him was invigorating, especially after the insult his wife had paid her father. His look of distress was gratifying enough to lift her spirits a touch on the way back out to the courtyard where the carriage waited.

The footman stepped down, opening the door and standing by to assist her.

"Thank you for coming. I wish you didn't have to leave so soon." Edan's eyes dulled with genuine disappointment, though he still kept his emotions carefully masked, making it hard to determine the depth of his sincerity or his intent. "I apologize for Vera's cruel comment."

"She's not your responsibility. Besides, she is not the first, nor will she be the last, to think ill of my father." She kicked back the threatening melancholy. "I am also sorry to leave so soon. Though it's probably for the best. I think Serivar was getting uneasy."

"Yes." He chuckled. "I found it rather delightful."

She managed a light laugh, and he laughed with her, taking a step closer. The small distance between them crackled with anticipation and hope. It would be so easy to take one more step closer and surrender to his intentions. His lips would be warm, his arms welcoming.

She touched the ring, a painful twisting in her chest. "Thank you, Lord Edan, for an interesting evening. Goodnight."

She turned before he could say or do anything more and accepted the footman's aid into the carriage, unable to relax again until she was back in her residence, well away from the temptation and confusion he inspired. The need to flee from his interest made it more obvious than ever that she wasn't ready for a new relationship. Discarding the dress, she pulled the gray cloak around her bare skin and lay on her bed. She let her thoughts turn to Yiloch, wondering as the wine helped her drift to sleep if he might be thinking about her too.

CHAPTER ELEVEN

Myac watched the carriage disappear around a corner. Frustration rushed through him like potent alcohol, clouding his mind. He simply didn't have any time left. Preoccupation with training the Lyran adepts and evening visits from Ferin had diminished Indigo's loneliness, making her less susceptible to his advances. Still, a chance existed that the events of this night would push her closer to the breaking point, and a little nudge, perhaps with the help of her estranged fiancé, might be enough to drive her into his embrace.

He sensed Serivar walking up behind him.

"She will never be yours," he stated with galling confidence.

Myac bristled. "She's already come quite close to giving in. Whatever is holding her back won't keep her there forever." He stayed silent for a moment, basking in the heat of Serivar's protective anger, then he turned away from those thoughts. It was time to focus on other things. Ever cautious, he constructed a barrier around them to prevent anyone from eavesdropping. "Your assassins are moving in an hour after midnight, yes?"

"Yes." There was the slightest hint of regret in the whispered word.

Turning, Myac met the headmaster's eyes with a calculating stare. Was the man determined enough to see this through? "They will make a mess of it?"

A flash of annoyance, then Serivar nodded. "I trust in them far more than I do in you."

Myac responded with a cynical smile. "Perhaps you're getting smarter." He turned back to the street where evening traffic still meandered through, the leisurely milling of people whose evenings were nearing their end or, in some cases, just starting. His was about to start. "The Lyran adepts?"

"I encouraged them to rest early tonight as I have a rigorous day of working with injuries planned for tomorrow. I have someone monitoring their quarters to make sure they don't go anywhere."

Myac nodded his approval. "Good, we can't afford for them to be seen by anyone tonight."

He slid a hand into the pocket of his dress jacket and touched the leaf Galyn had mended in training the prior day. Plants were easy subjects for the practice of healing minor cuts and similar wounds. This one now bore Galyn's ascard signature. One of Serivar's adepts had considerable skill in a variation of masking which she could use to mask her workings with the ascard signature of another. That adept would accompany two others, one who specialized in working with fire whose task was to kill the queen and her son, and the third to make them all invisible. She would disguise their workings, weaving a faint trace of Kade's ascard signature into them.

Myac's job was to kill the king. It was a prestigious

task, the appointing of which contradicted Serivar's claimed lack of trust in him. He would weave enough of Galyn's ascard signature into the king's body to make it appear as if the Lyran adept had tried to mask the working. It would take a powerful adept to detect it, and there were few adepts with the required skills in the King's Order, none of whom had the capacity to dig deep enough to find the actual truth behind the deception. Indigo might, but Serivar wouldn't be using her in the investigation. The headmaster had another role for her to play in all of this.

To make the illusion complete, they had another adept ready to implant false memories of the murder in the minds of Kade and Galyn while they slept tonight. Memories the inquisitors could root out, along with recollections of orders from Yiloch to carry out the assassinations. Ferin, because of his years of working with ascard, and Sine, because of her dabbling in mental manipulations, would be too risky to implant with false memories. Once they found Kade and Galyn guilty, however, they would assume the other two adepts were involved.

Serivar stepped forward, eyeing him expectantly. Myac smirked. Fear was a savory emotion, exquisitely wild and unrefined. The release of ascard within a person at the moment of their death was as sweet and satisfying as sexual climax. Better, perhaps. How fine would the fear and death of a king taste? A shiver of anticipation swept through him. Opening to his inner aspect, he allowed himself to feel the full strength of his connection for a few intoxicating moments. His mind blazed with power, fierce and glorious, feeding his greatest desires.

Serivar, watching the change in his expression, took a step back, a sweet chill of fear breaking away from him like ice splitting from the bank of a thawing river. Myac closed his eyes, struggling for control as the taste of the other man's distress tempted him.

You need him. He pulled back from the tempest of power.

Narrowing his eyes at the headmaster, he stepped back into the shadows, taking ascard from the air and weaving it around himself. The headmaster's eyes narrowed, straining to see into the darkness as Myac's illusion hid him from sight. With a malicious smile, he crept up next to the other man, entirely invisible now, and leaned close to his ear.

"Goodnight..." he whispered, and Serivar startled away from him, his eyes darting about for anything that might betray Myac's presence. In a soft, sinister voice, Myac quoted the last few lines of a favorite poem.

> "'Goodnight,' he whispered as her last
> breath misted in the air.
> 'Goodnight, my love,' he whispered as
> her gaze became a stare.
> 'Goodnight, and know I do this because
> to me you have lied.
> Goodnight, I shall not mourn you, for by
> my hand you died.'"

"This isn't the time for games," Serivar snapped, his

growing fear thickening the surrounding air.

"As you command," Myac replied, but he didn't leave right away. Instead, he stood and watched, pondering, while Serivar hurried into the house and shut the door, the bolt clicking into place.

Would the headmaster turn on him if something went wrong tonight? Did he have the guts to even consider it?

Probably not.

Chuckling to himself, Myac wandered deeper into the palace district. Through one of their sources within the castle, they learned that King Jerrin played dice in the barracks twice a week with several of his captains and a few lords. Tonight was one of those nights, but this night, he would never make it back to his chambers.

Stars shimmered, stark and beautiful in the dark sky as Myac made his way unseen into the palace courtyard. Already he could feel the slight tug of weariness from the extensive use of ascard that kept him hidden from sight. Blending with ascard in the air was a complicated working, requiring considerable strength and focus. He might have waited to hide himself until he was closer to the palace, but it was safer to ensure that no one saw him anywhere away from Serivar's house tonight. This night would be monumental in Caithin and Lyran history. Two men, one from each country, would be the unseen masterminds behind a magnificent future.

Myac practically vibrated with thrilling anticipation. Discipline and the understanding that nothing was certain until the end kept him focused and silent. He could use ascard to silence his movement, but he relied on patience and awareness to prevent audible detection instead. Too much power was already being expended to maintain his invisibility. He needed to have enough strength not only to kill the king, but also to mask the working, plant the evidence, and get out undetected. It was a lot to ask of a single adept.

Sending out a tendril of ascard, he searched for King Jerrin, and a bolt of panic shot through him. The king was already heading back toward the palace, probably on route to his chambers, much earlier than usual. He considered trying to warn the others, and then his touch on the king brought back to him a strong sense of arousal. King Jerrin was returning early because he was hungry for a different manner of play this night.

This could be fun.

Myac grinned. He would follow and allow the king to walk in on the other adepts as they were killing his wife. The timing should be almost perfect.

To be certain, he sent a tendril out and touched first on the queen resting in their chambers, then on to the prince. His power brushed the youth's ascard signature as it flared and went silent in agonizing death. Spreading it through the boy's chambers, he found the three adepts, all well masked, though not well enough to hide from him. They were leaving the room. They might finish the deed before the king arrived, but Myac would still get the satisfaction of letting Jerrin see his wife lying dead before he completed his job.

He came around the side of the palace near the main barracks and spotted the king with two guards opening a side door into the building. Using a technique he learned from Sine, Myac swapped himself with ascard in the air inside the open doorway, careful to maintain all his illusions when he arrived in front of them. Stepping out of the way, he let the king and his guards pass by, then crept after them. The transfer drained him more than he expected, and a moment of dizziness slowed him. When it passed, he quickened his steps to keep up, forced to use a touch of ascard to keep from making too much noise.

The trio paused outside one doorway that led into a lush private sitting room furnished in dark wood with rich red and gold accents. It looked warm and inviting. The king stopped to consider the room, his desire losing some of its potency. Myac tapped into his sense of arousal and magnified it incrementally. After a few seconds, the heavyset man shifted his stance, a hint of flush coming to his bearded face. Clearing his throat, he turned and headed onward.

Outside the king's private chambers, the two guards stopped and took positions on either side of the door. Myac slipped through the door before it closed. Reaching ahead into the bedchamber, his ability met up against a wall of purest terror, then silence. Seconds later, the king opened the door to the room, his eager grin mostly hidden by his beard. Surprise from the three hidden adepts enveloped Myac only to be overpowered a second later by the mix of horror and anguish from the king when he spotted his wife lying crumpled on the floor.

She might have been asleep if not for the smell of burned flesh and the scorch marks around her lips and empty eye sockets that left little to the imagination. The adept had burned her to death from the inside. A nice touch. Myac nodded his appreciation, though no one would see the gesture. He dropped his invisibility as the king turned. Jerrin's mouth opened to cry out, but all that emerged when his wide moisture-filled eyes focused on Myac was a strangled croak.

Myac grinned, wishing he could afford to discard the illusion of Edan. Those maskings and illusions weren't all his own though, and there was little chance that they could rebuild the disguise precisely the same. The tiniest flaw might be enough to catch Indigo's attention.

The king stepped back from him, unaware of the other adepts waiting in silence throughout the room.

"Why?" Jerrin's voice was a pained whisper.

"Nothing personal," Myac replied. "You're simply in the way."

The king's brow furrowed, and defiance flickered in his eyes when he realized the answer gave him nothing to bargain with. Jerrin reached for the dagger at his belt, his mouth opening again, perhaps to shout for aid. Myac lanced his throat with a slice of power. Blood sprayed forth. The king's mouth worked, making only wet choking sounds. The shock and pain in his eyes faded fast, his life draining away down the front of his fine clothes. For a few seconds, he wavered there, then he sank forward, coming down on his knees where he teetered a moment more before falling forward. Myac stepped out of the way, his Lyran reflexes giving the movement a distinct precision and grace.

Blood pooled around the silent figure, darkening the large, decorative carpet that covered much of the decorative parquet floor around the bed. He watched it spread for a few heartbeats, appreciating his work, then looked up, his eyes settling on the closest of the hidden adepts.

"Finish your work with the queen," he said, noting that her body still bore the wrong ascard signature. When the ascard signature in her began transforming with the complex weaving of deception, Myac nodded, recreated the illusion that hid him from sight, and did the same with the king's body.

"Now go," he muttered once the false signatures were in place.

He could feel them leave. With the masking, their presence was faint, but he was strong enough to probe past it. He was also exhausted. Before leaving, he checked that the other adepts had left no trace of their presence, cleaning up a bit of sloppy work in the young prince's room where one of them had used ascard to unbolt the door. By the time he slipped away, dawn was threatening. Someone would discover the bodies soon, and he was weary to the core. Far too tired at this point to risk being caught in the palace after the alarm sounded.

He entered Serivar's home shrouded in silence less than an hour later and went straight to his room. He had to rest if he wanted any chance of holding up the subterfuge effectively. Fortunately, Serivar had all the adepts he needed to complete the arrests and start the interrogations that would find the Lyran adepts guilty of this horrific crime.

Myac smiled, a weary satisfaction curving his lips. He had barely enough energy left to undress before falling into bed and the deep, rewarding slumber that soon followed.

CHAPTER TWELVE

Indigo woke with a start. Blinking sleep away.

What had woken her so suddenly?

She was cold, wrapped only in the gray cloak. Perhaps the chill had awakened her. Then a loud knock made her start again. Reaching out with ascard, she identified Caplin's signature outside her door. The emotions pouring from him were so intense and jumbled that she couldn't quite read any of them.

"One moment."

She hadn't bothered to light a night candle, so she was unsure of the hour, but a faint glow coming in the window suggested the approach of dawn. She scurried to find suitable dressing robes, lighting candles with ascard as she went to fight the mournful pallor early light cast over the room.

The knock came again, much more insistent, before she finally made it to the door. It wasn't like Caplin to be so impatient. Worry wormed its way through her, making her gut ache. She opened the door, stepping back in surprise when he charged in without waiting for her leave to do so. His face was pale and drawn, eyes bloodshot and rimmed in red as if he had been weeping. She shut the door and met those eyes, the worm of worry growing into a vast, dreadful beast inside.

"What's wrong?"

"Jerrin, Livia, and Marich were assassinated last night." His tone wavered on a hysterical edge between rage and misery.

For a moment, she could only stare, feeling as if an icy wind had frozen her to the spot. Gooseflesh rose on her arms. She couldn't have heard him right. "The king's dead?"

"Yes," he snarled, rage winning out for an instant, twisting his face into a mask of hatred.

How could that be? What had she been training for as part of the King's Order if not the protection of King Jerrin? The organization she had made a choice to give her life to, this thing that consumed most of her waking hours, had failed. What point was there to it? Was it nothing but an illusion? A false sense of purpose for a few self-important adepts and creators?

"I don't understand. How can the king be dead?" She met his eyes, disconcerted, wishing she could wake from the nightmare. "All three of them are dead?"

"All of them murdered in their rooms," Caplin confirmed, his voice cracked and tears sprang to his eyes.

She felt a painful twisting in her chest as she watched the battle for control waging behind those eyes. He wanted to scream and rage. He wanted to hurt someone, and she wanted to help him, but there was no one to go after yet. No one to hurt. If there were, he wouldn't be there. One tear escaped, running down his cheek unchecked. When he stomped down the remaining tears with raw will, she took his hand and gave it a squeeze.

"What are you doing here, Caplin? Aren't you needed elsewhere?"

He hung his head. "I... I am."

There were no more words. He stepped closer and wrapped his arms around her, clinging like a terrified child as he buried his head in her hair. Startled, she stood still for a few seconds before slowly embracing him. Closing her eyes and stifling her own shock and sense of personal failure, she smoothed his messy hair with one hand and held him. Perhaps it should bother her that he had come to her for comfort rather than to his fiancée, but there would be time later to sort out such things. His tears dampened the shoulder of her dressing gown, giving her something physical to distract her from the storm of anger and grief raging within.

Then another thought struck her, and she stiffened. Jerrin's brother, Lord Gavin, would assume the throne now that the king, his wife, and his only heir were dead. That meant Caplin would soon be the crown prince of Caithin. He was a very important person, far too important to be hiding out in the home of a mere healer whose social status was, to put it mildly, in a substantial state of flux. Still, she needed to know a few things before she sent him back to the palace.

She used the minimum force necessary to get him to release her. Ignoring his forlorn look, she took his hand and led him to one couch. Gentle pressure was enough to make him sit, and she knelt before him, taking both of his hands in hers.

"Dearest Caplin. *Prince* Caplin." She spoke the title with force, and his lips twisted in a pained grimace. He looked down at their joined hands. "Tell me what happened and what's going on now?" Talking about it would make it more real for him, she knew, and for herself. The acknowledgment of reality was necessary for action.

He swallowed hard a few times before beginning, his voice strained. "Someone burned Livia and Marich from the inside in their bedchambers. Jerrin's throat had been cut, but not with a blade. There were traces of ascard in the wound."

Ascard users had done this. The thought sent a chill through her. "Have they identified the ascard signature of the work?"

"Not yet. The signatures were..." he paused, his eyes meeting hers in silent questioning.

"Masked?" she suggested.

His eyes narrowed with a flash of bitterness that, while not directed specifically at her, made her feel at odds with him. Ascard users were high on his list of least favorite people right now. If he knew all the things she could do with ascard, would he be seeking her for comfort like this?

"Yes, masked was the word the Watchmen used. They took the visiting Lyran adepts and Lord Ferin into custody already."

No.

Her chest tightened, making it hard to breathe. She jerked her hands away. Rising, she walked to a bookshelf and leaned on it, facing away from him while she tried to focus past the frantic pounding of her heart. The room swayed.

Be calm. She used ascard to force a mild sedation into herself.

"Indigo?"

She gave the sedation a few seconds to take hold, numbing her emotions, then turned to face him. He was standing now, his brow furrowed with concern, a hint of something else in his eyes. Wariness. Could that be? Was that a spark of mistrust she saw come to light in his eyes? Had her reaction marked as an ascard user above friend?

It didn't matter. She had to defend the people she believed in.

"I can't believe they're guilty," she stated. "I have spent days working with all of them. They wouldn't do this."

He looked confused. "Why were you working with them?"

"Believe it or not, I am a very accomplished healer." She gave him a hard look, hoping he would accept her words and move on.

After a few seconds, he gave a curt nod, letting it go. "Look at the evidence, Indigo. Kade is skilled with fire... Wait." He held up a hand to halt her building protest, and she bit her lip, letting him go on. "Sine does physical and some mental manipulation. Galyn..."

Beautiful, sweet Galyn.

The Lyran woman's gentle manner and kind words rushed to the fore. Pain twisted in her chest, and Caplin, perhaps seeing some reflection of that pain in her face, paused. She wrestled her emotions under control again and met his eyes. He waited a moment longer, his gaze searching, but finally continued.

"Galyn is adept with illusions. Sine and Galyn could quite easily have gotten the three of them in and out of the palace unseen, and Kade..." his voice cracked. He moved on. "We don't train those skills here in Caithin. We smother them. It only makes sense that the assassins would be foreign."

She started to object and caught herself. They did train such skills in Caithin. He had to know about the King's Order, didn't he? Or maybe he didn't know yet. Even considering the adepts of the King's Order, however, the Lyran adepts were still the more likely culprits, given that the entire purpose of the King's Order was to protect the king. Yet, if the Lyran adepts were guilty, did that not also implicate their emperor?

She stepped to the closest chair and dropped into it, suddenly nauseous and dizzy. It made no sense. Even if Yiloch wanted King Jerrin dead, which was certainly plausible, he would never do it so inelegantly. And yet, all evidence appeared to be pointing in that direction. The Watchmen had missed something. They must have.

"They are investigating other possibilities, aren't they? Someone could be intentionally misleading them."

"Of course they are. The investigation has barely started. There are senior healers trying to tease out the masked ascard signatures in the bodies and people searching for additional clues. There are guardsmen and Ascard Watchmen scouring the entire city for clues. Given the seriousness of the situation, they took the four Lyran adepts into custody to be questioned and held until proven innocent, though I don't expect that to happen."

She gave him a scalding look.

Caplin knelt before her now, sorrow flowing off him in suffocating waves, growing more potent in response to her anger. "I am sorry, Indigo. It must be hard after working with them and thinking you knew them, but they haven't been here that long. No one is immune to skilled deception. Even you."

I am more so than most. She pushed the thought away. Too much faith in her ascard ability could lead to reckless mistakes. She was still plenty fallible and perhaps gullible, though she wasn't ready to accept that yet. "They will treat them fairly and give them a chance to defend themselves?"

"Naturally," he replied, though his eyes hardened as he said it, telling her the truth as he saw it. Their guilt was certain in his mind, and if that was true for Caplin, who was always so willing to see the good in people, it would be so already for many others.

"You need to get back, Caplin. Your prolonged absence might cause alarm." *And I need time to think.*

His shoulders sank, and he averted his gaze, understanding the dismissal for what it was and unable to argue against her reasoning. Standing, he turned toward the door but made no move in that direction.

She took his hand and squeezed it once more. "I'm so deeply sorry for all that you have lost this day. For what we have all lost," she murmured.

"As am I." He returned the grip for a moment before releasing her hand and seeing himself out.

When he was gone, she curled into a ball on the chair, wrapping herself around the empty ache that always lurked at her core. Could Yiloch be behind this? Could he really rain this misery down on her so callously?

She longed for the release of tears or anger, but neither came. Hugging her knees to her chest, she rocked in the chair, staring at the wall. After a time, bright mocking sunlight sprayed across the room, and she made herself rise.

After dressing in a sedate dark blue dress, the deep color of mourning, she braided three braids in her hair in acknowledgement of the deceased and left the apartment. With no actual destination in mind, her feet took her to the Academy administration building. Serivar's office door was closed when she arrived, and a quick sweep of power told her the office was empty. Walking in, she closed the door behind her, sat in the headmaster's chair behind the big desk, and waited.

She didn't extend her ability to alert her to anyone's approach. Sorrow made the effort seem too much. As such, when the door opened, it surprised her to see Edan enter. He stopped in the doorway, startled by her presence as well, perhaps more so because she was sitting in the headmaster's chair. She lowered her gaze. He wasn't the one she was waiting for, so she didn't exert the energy required to acknowledge him.

After a moment, the door clicked shut. Though she couldn't read his emotions, his step was soft and tentative when he walked around the desk. He stood alongside the chair, the awkwardness of uncertainty apparent in his hesitation and the shifting of his feet.

"Indigo," he murmured her name, his tone gentle, trying to comfort her.

She closed her eyes, biting the inside of her lip against the sudden swell of anguish and despair that soft voice unleashed. Fingers brushed her cheek, the touch feather-light, moving a strand of hair from her face.

Yiloch.

She whispered his name in her mind, remembering, yearning for a different touch and a different time. Encouraged perhaps by the fact that she hadn't chased him away yet, Edan crouched next to the chair and took her hand. Opening her eyes, she met his searching gaze, hating him because he wasn't the man she wanted to see, appreciating him for the concern that lent maturity and sincerity to his features.

"You've already heard. Lord... Prince Caplin spoke to you?" He ventured, cautious with his words.

She nodded, not trusting herself to speak.

"It's horrible," he murmured.

"I don't understand. I thought we knew there was a threat. How did..." Frustrated and confused, she fell silent, pleading with her eyes for him to make sense of things for her.

"Deceptive trails led us astray, like hounds on a false scent. We failed." Some emotion flashed in his eyes for an instant.

Was it anger, perhaps, or disappointment? Either way, it was comforting to have someone there who understood her feelings of defeat. He looked tired, too. Living with Serivar, who had undoubtedly been one of the first people called to the palace, meant that the dismal news had probably interrupted his sleep at an early hour.

"I can't believe Lord Ferin and the others would be part of such a thing. It makes no sense."

Edan lowered his gaze. "I know. I can hardly fathom the thought, but the evidence is persuasive."

She pulled back her hand and stood fast enough to knock the chair back into a bookcase. Some of the heavier volumes rocked a bit, then stood firm.

It was the same thing she had heard from Caplin. Edan, at least, had worked with the three adepts. Did he not see how out of character this was? Then again, deception was an essential part of being an assassin. Conflicting thoughts and emotions waged war inside her, destroying her composure, pounding away at her self-control. Turning away from Edan before she gave in to the urge to lash out, she stalked to the back of the office and stood staring at the wall where the hidden doorway to the training room was. Not sure what she meant to do next, she began picking at her fingernails.

"Why would Emperor Yiloch do such a thing?" She struggled to keep her voice steady and remember the secrets she was keeping. She heard Edan approach and felt the warmth of his body when he moved up close behind her.

"He has many reasons to hate King Jerrin. His father and Jerrin are the reasons the Lyran slave trade has endured. Besides, when he doesn't like a thing, he hasn't shown himself to be the type to stand by idly and let it go on. I believe you saw firsthand what he did to his own father."

She winced at the memory of cold satisfaction on Yiloch's blood-spattered face after he had cut his father's head off. She shook her head, trying to clear away the image. "No. It just doesn't feel right. He would never be so..." Careless was the word that came to mind, but she held it in, realizing she was dangerously close to revealing more of her relationship with Yiloch than was wise, especially in these precarious circumstances. Hanging her head to hide the tear that had slipped free, she took a deep, shuddering breath and tried to rein in her emotions.

His hand rested on her shoulder. "I'm sorry, Indigo. I wish I could make this less painful."

She turned to him and stepped closer, the way Caplin had with her only a short time earlier, letting Edan take her into his embrace. For once, there was no inclination to pull away. Right now, she wanted someone to hold her, anyone who was willing to do so, and he fit that requirement better than most. Tears fell, but she couldn't let go and weep uncontrollably as she wanted to. Somehow, it didn't seem right to show that much weakness in his arms, despite the gentleness of his embrace.

When she felt more in control, she extricated herself and accepted the linen he offered to dry her tears.

"I apologize." She handed it back to him, rumpled and damp.

"I am not repelled by your tears," he replied with a charming smile.

She managed to return a smile that she discarded quickly, the expression feeling somehow insulting to the dead.

"If you are waiting for Serivar, he said he wasn't likely to make it in today."

Indigo nodded. "I suppose I should have expected as much."

"You don't seem up for practicing anything."

"No. I'm afraid you're right." She wrung her hands, struggling against the fresh surge of misery that his embrace had eased for a brief time.

"Do you want company?"

She met his eyes, contemplating the momentary respite his comfort had given her. Something about him still gave her pause, perhaps those secrets Galyn said he was keeping. Even now, she was so willing to trust Galyn, a Lyran woman being held on suspicion of regicide, and not Edan. Given the monster her late fiancé turned out to be, perhaps it was her own ability to judge character that should be in question. Someday she should give him a genuine chance, but not today. Today, she didn't have the emotional fortitude to work past her reservations.

"Thank you, Edan, but I..." Her words trailed off before a surge of guilt.

"But you need some time alone." Disappointment forced his gaze away, though after a moment's visible struggle, he mustered a soft smile for her. "I understand. Please call upon me if I can do anything for you."

"I will."

CHAPTER THIRTEEN

As the day wore on, Indigo holed up in her residence, alternating between pacing and sitting to stare out the window. A sunny day beckoned, urging her to take a walk in the fresh air to clear her mind, but the risk of having to speak to someone kept her inside. For every bit of evidence and every plausible reason she could come up with why Yiloch would not have ordered the assassinations, she could come up with at least as many reasons he might have. The most compelling argument against his guilt wasn't one of morals or humanity, but an issue of planning. If he were behind the assassinations, the execution was much too reckless. He could come across as impulsive and arrogant, but he was no fool. If someone else were behind it, however, the setup was almost brilliant.

Another party would have known how to prey upon racial prejudices between the two countries and take advantage of the unrest caused by the rebellion in Lyra. They also had the rumors of the former Lyran emperor's madness. How easy it would be to suggest that his son suffered a similar affliction, especially if they brought up the slaughter that had won Yiloch his hated title of the Blood Prince.

The problem was that the true perpetrators of the crime would also have needed to know about the Lyran adepts in temporary residence at the academy. Not only know about their presence there but also have comprehensive information regarding their individual skills. Knowledge of their presence was intentionally restricted, and the training agreement prohibited discussion of their ascard skills outside of a select group. Those things only added support to the argument that the Lyran adepts were at least involved.

She glowered at the fading light outside the window. What she wanted was an update. So much had to be happening outside of her walls, and she yearned to know what new information may have come to light since that morning. If only they would let her speak to Ferin. He would explain their side. Then again, she would be inclined to believe him because doing so would benefit the man she loved, so perhaps she lacked the impartiality necessary.

Were they holding the adepts in the royal prison? She stretched her ability, searching for Ferin, but found nothing. Either he was out of her reach or being kept in a location guarded against ascard. The latter seemed most likely.

As the light faded toward evening, she paused in a round of pacing and stood biting her lip. With an absent thought, she lit a candle. The light vanished seconds later, and she glanced over to see a pile of melted wax on the table. She had exerted a little too much power in her frustration. She lit a few candles in the wall sconces, paying more attention this time so as not to burn them out.

Other possibilities existed, not that they were a great deal more appealing than that of the Lyran adepts being behind it all. Someone very close to the Caithin's king, likely a member of the council who had inside information about the Lyran adepts, could have played a part in the assassinations, helping stage them to frame the visitors. At best, that meant a significant information leak. At worst, there was a key architect in the murders hidden among them. That possibility cast suspicion in uncomfortable places, but it merited consideration.

A knock made her jump, sending her heart racing. Her renewed pacing had taken her almost to the door, the handle within reach, as though she had been expecting someone to arrive just then. A brief brush of ascard identified Caplin. His dark, tumultuous mood had worn him down to a state of weary resignation. The feel of it sent a chill through her, even as she wondered why he had come back here. Reluctantly, she cracked the door, met the darkness in his eyes, and opened it to admit him. He took a few steps into the room, and she noticed a deepening of his frown as his gaze swept over her stylized Lyran décor, something he had commented on in the past with some amusement. He didn't look so amused now.

When she shut the door and turned to face him, she came up against an iron wall of determination. A wall constructed to put distance between them. "Your services are required, Indigo. They successfully extracted memories from Adept Kade regarding his part in the assassinations."

She stared at him, some distant part of her aware of

a crushing sensation in her chest. A vast gulf had opened between them over the course of a single day, and she couldn't seem to hear him properly across it. His words echoed faintly in her head, as though he shouted them from the other side of a vast canyon.

"I am sure you understand that this means Emperor Yiloch and the others are now confirmed suspects in the assassination of King Jerrin and his family."

She shook her head, feeling a surge in Caplin's anger as she did so. Yiloch was too cunning and far too self-interested to risk everything over such a reckless move so soon after securing his throne. She couldn't believe he was behind this.

"What am I needed for?" She asked, wary of a certain volatility in Caplin's current state of mind. He directed his anger at her now, a stabbing, aggressive presence searching for somewhere to lay blame.

"Lord Serivar will set sail for Lyra within the hour. He carries a royal missive requiring Emperor Yiloch to come to Caithin to stand trial in defense of himself and his adepts. Lord Serivar—"

"That's absurd. Yiloch will never agree to that."

Caplin's eyes narrowed. He continued as though she hadn't spoken. "Lord Serivar is waiting below in my carriage. He asked that you accompany him, and that request is being granted."

"Me? Why me?"

"Emperor Yiloch knows you," Caplin stated.

"He knows you as well," she countered. It wasn't that she didn't want to see Yiloch again. She wanted it more than almost anything, but not like this.

"He trusts you," Caplin stated. "He will be more inclined to be reasonable if you are the one to present the missive. Regardless, the High Council has decided they cannot allow the new heir to the throne to be put at risk."

She hesitated. Something darker lurked behind his surface emotions, a trace of guilt that fed the distance between them. He was lying to her or at least holding back important information. "What aren't you telling me, Caplin? I have a right to know if I am to be involved in this. We've been friends for years. You know you can trust me."

He shook his head, a small, abrupt movement, but the anguish that surged through him was enormous. "Not this time, Indigo. Not right now. Please. If you will not do this for me as your prince, do it for me as a friend." He was pleading now, begging with his voice and eyes, the anger drowning under a wave of guilt and sorrow.

"I don't understand, Caplin. This is a futile gesture. He won't leave Lyra when it is still in need of so much healing and Myac remains unaccounted for. At best, he might send someone in his stead." She twisted the ring on her finger, yearning to deny him, but finding it hard to turn him away when his need was so strong. "Please don't involve me in this. You know my heart."

He grimaced, less than pleased at the reminder. He was the only one who knew of her love for Yiloch outside of a few of those closest to the Lyran Emperor. The wall of unyielding determination went up again. "You need to go… now." He pointed to the door.

She lifted her chin, her throat tightening. "And if I choose not to?"

"What is he to you?" Caplin snarled, the deep well of anger resurfacing with stunning force. "He used you. He risked your life repeatedly, and all you have to show for it is some adolescent infatuation and a cloak. Do you honestly believe he would hesitate to let you die if your death was all that stood between him and his objectives?"

Caplin's eyes looked wrong so filled with loathing. They had become the eyes of a stranger, and the underlying jealousy she felt radiating off him made her feel more alone than ever. Even those things were better than the malignant twist of doubt in her mind that feared his words were true.

"I must gather some things first, *Prince* Caplin." She hissed the title and stalked to her bedroom, slamming the door behind her.

When she returned a few minutes later with a bag full of things she felt she might need on the brief journey across the Gilded Strait and back, he stood waiting in icy silence. She set the bag down and donned the gray cloak Yiloch had given her. Caplin's eyes narrowed, but he said nothing. After a few awkward seconds in which neither of them moved or spoke, he took her satchel and led the way down to where his carriage waited, tossing the bag to the footman to be stowed. When he opened the carriage door for her, she saw Serivar waiting inside. One of Caplin's horses waited saddled and ready to depart alongside the carriage, held by one of several royal guardsmen.

"My carriage will take you to the Kilty docks. I have other duties to attend to."

She gave a curt nod. "Your Highness."

Caplin hesitated, the anger that engulfed him faltering, giving her a stark glimpse of his sorrow, a sorrow as potent as that tearing her apart inside. He swallowed, unable to meet her eyes. "Thank you, Lady Indigo. You have my gratitude."

He strode to his horse and mounted, heading off at a swift trot in the direction of the palace amidst his substantial retinue of guards. She climbed into the carriage, ignoring the footman's offered aid and sat in the opposite corner from Serivar. As the carriage began moving, he met her bitter gaze.

"Indigo, I understand that this is all very upsetting, but with your help, we will ensure justice is served quickly and mercilessly."

She pressed back in the seat, increasing the physical distance between them incrementally. "I hope you have irrefutable proof?"

Serivar looked taken aback by her temper, but he was quick to recover. "Yes. In fact, Kade has already signed a confession. He burned the queen and the crown prince to death from the inside," he shook his head, grimacing in disgust. "We're confident that Sine and Galyn helped him get in and out without being detected, given their particular skill sets, though they haven't admitted to anything yet. It makes sense that Ferin may have been involved, since he came here in a supervisory capacity and has a diverse set of skills."

"None of them strong," she defended.

"Perhaps, on our trip over, you might take a little time to consider whose service you are actually in. Your time assisting Lyra is over. You owe your loyalty to Caithin."

Resentment swelled. "I owe nothing to anyone," she said, biting off each word.

Serivar said nothing, his emotions turning cold toward her, which was just as well. She no longer wanted to talk to him or anyone else.

The deep, empty ache of loneliness was growing inside her like an unchallenged weed. She rubbed her temples to fight the accompanying ache in her head and turned to stare out the window into the street. In such a short time, she had developed an attachment to the three Lyran adepts, not to mention a strong affection for Ferin. The depths of her feelings for Yiloch went far beyond that. Could she face this miserable turn of events with her heart torn asunder as it now was? The king and his family were dead, and if they found the three adepts guilty beyond doubt, Ferin may as well be, unless Yiloch could convince them of his innocence.

Yiloch, how could you do this? She drew a deep breath, fighting back tears.

How could he betray an alliance he had only just secured? How could he betray her love and trust? She ran ascard in a caress over the ring he had sent her, feeling the power woven into it. Had he given it to her because he knew this was coming? Was he arrogant enough to expect she might side with him and need extra protection? If so, perhaps the time had come to rid herself of the burden.

She took hold of the ring, pausing as her fingers tightened on it. No, she wouldn't take it off yet. She had to give him a chance to explain. Somehow, he would make this right.

She felt the tears she had been fighting begin spilling warm down her cheeks.

"It has been a hard day," Serivar offered, his tone gentler now.

She continued to ignore him.

"The trip will be over quickly," he said, as though such a thing should reassure her. "We have a swift ship awaiting us at the port, and two of the King's Order will accompany us who can use ascard to speed our passage across the Gilded Strait. We should arrive before news of the success of the assassinations reaches Yiroth."

She tried to show interest in his words, but her heart felt stifled and cold. She managed a soft, noncommittal sound in response, and he said nothing more. Perhaps he believed her broken up over the deaths of the king and his family, which she genuinely was, but the sense of betrayal she felt toward Yiloch was no less powerful and somehow more devastating. Her tears continued to fall as they made their way to Kilty.

CHAPTER FOURTEEN

Yiloch blocked Adran's attack and shoved him back, using ascard to add more force. Adran staggered away, sprawling on his back when he failed to catch himself. Yiloch was already spinning the other way to face Leryc, using ascard again, this time to hasten his movement. He parried Leryc's blade and drove forward, forcing the other man to retreat under a hail of swift blows. Adran was on his feet again, and Yiloch caught him moving in for another attack out of the corner of his eye. Timing his moment, he waited until Adran and Leryc had both committed to their next attacks, then he swapped himself with ascard in the air behind Leryc. Their opponent abruptly gone, the other two men's blades collided, and Yiloch chuckled at them from where he stood, now out of harm's way.

From the balcony overlooking the sparring circle, Auryl and her entourage of ladies, a couple she had brought with her and the rest from wealthy houses in Yiroth, applauded him. Their praise, something he might appreciate under different circumstances, grated at his nerves. In three weeks, he and Auryl would be married. He didn't feel ready to wed, but it was a necessary step. Lyra needed stability and promise for the future in order to grow strong again.

Adran and Leryc both frowned at him with mock severity, and Yiloch grinned. "Don't tell me you weren't expecting that?"

Leryc was rubbing his arm and grimacing, though the sparkle in his eyes was still jovial enough. "Good thing you escaped that blow, my lord," he commented. "I only got part of it, and I think it nearly broke my arm. I suspect Adran was trying to knock you into the next country with that one."

Adran shrugged and grinned, his cheeks picking up a hint of extra color.

Yiloch chuckled, forgetting the rest of his audience for a pleasant moment. "Shall we go another round?" He still had a lot of frustration to burn off.

"Of course, Your Highness," Leryc replied. "What better way to spend an afternoon than to be pummeled into unconsciousness by my emperor."

Yiloch and Adran both laughed, as did the ladies watching from the balcony above. One of them laughed a little too loudly, her cheeks flushing bright when Leryc glanced up at them. Yiloch winked at his new captain. "I think someone has taken an interest in you," he suggested in a low voice.

Leryc flushed, his gaze jumping to Adran for a few telling seconds, a hint of color rising in his cheeks now. "I certainly hope not."

They stepped apart and moved into fighting positions, each eyeing the others for that instant of inattention that would leave them vulnerable. Yiloch rarely used ascard when practicing one on one. With multiple opponents, however, he used it liberally, despite the fatigue it caused. There was little point in having developed combat skills with ascard if he never practiced using them. Such skills needed to be automatic and flawless in an actual fight. The growing fatigue also helped to drive other thoughts from his mind, though Indigo's ring, still a cool circlet of memory pressing against his skin, undermined those efforts.

Leryc and Adran attacked in unison, and Yiloch had to enhance his speed significantly to meet both attacks. As he spun to face another attack from Adran, he felt a familiar gentle touch within him and stopped, lowering his sword. Adran barely managed to pull his attack, but Leryc didn't react as fast. At the last second, Yiloch hardened an ascard barrier over the skin of his arm, and the practice blade shattered when it struck.

Movement from the balcony caught his attention, and he looked up to see Auryl standing, her lips rounded in an O of surprise, fingers clenching the rail. Yiloch met her gaze for a moment, conflicted by the equal parts resentment and sympathy he felt whenever he looked in her eyes. The door under the balcony flew open, and Ian strode into the yard, the animation and bewilderment on his face confirming what Yiloch already knew but couldn't quite believe.

Ian glanced up at the balcony and stepped close to Yiloch, keeping his voice low. "She's here."

Yiloch nodded, tossing his practice sword to Adran, who caught it despite the lack of warning.

"If she has the ring, she should have been able to give us far more warning than this," Yiloch said, striding toward the door. He wanted to be angry with her for the lack of notice, it would be easier to find his composure now if she had given him time to prepare, but the charge of excitement and worry burned away any glimmer of anger. Was something wrong? Why else would she return so suddenly?

Ian fell into step beside him, his long legs matching stride easily. Adran and Leryc hastily stowed the practice swords, leaving the remains of Leryc's sword in the ring for a servant to clean up.

"Perhaps she didn't want to give any warning," Ian suggested, his tone tight with the same excitement and unease. "A surprise visit."

"Indigo?" Adran queried when he and Leryc caught up with them.

"Yes."

"Your betrothed didn't seem pleased with your sudden departure," Adran remarked pointedly.

Yiloch gave him a stern look. "This business isn't her concern," he snapped.

"It will be soon enough."

Yiloch clenched his jaw, biting back several bitter retorts. Adran was right, and as usual with this subject, he hated it.

"She's very close," Ian commented.

Yiloch nodded. He could feel her through the link she had placed in him, which meant she wanted him to know she was coming. Given how close she felt, she had deliberately chosen not to give him much time at all to prepare. If she intended her visit as a pleasant surprise, he wouldn't have expected any warning at all, but this last-minute alert had an air of foreboding about it. It was possible she came to take him up on his offer of a position as one of his personal adepts, though in that case he would have expected some prior contact. Indigo was careful. She would have sent ahead to ensure the offer remained open.

The anxiety he felt could be the Suac Chozai's fault, considering the ominous warning the man had given him that still nagged at his thoughts. Most likely, there was no need for concern.

He glanced at Ian, not comforted by the troubled look on the young creator's face. "Can you tell if anyone is with her?"

"I hadn't checked yet," he replied, his strides slowing as his eyes focused inward.

Yiloch stopped, allowing Ian to do the same and put his full attention to his ascard inquiry. They waited for several minutes before Ian nodded to himself.

"There is someone with her. I recognize the ascard signature from our visit to Caithin. It's the headmaster of the Caithin Healers Academy, Lord Serivar. They have arrived at the inner wall."

"I remember him being a pleasant fellow during the negotiations. So supportive of the alliance," Yiloch commented with a sharp edge of sarcasm. "Ian, greet them and escort them to the east sitting room. Adran, appease Lady Auryl before she runs to her father. Please," he added in response to the other man's scowl. "Leryc, you can return to your other duties. Perhaps some training would do you good." He managed a teasing wink for the young captain.

Leryc grinned good-naturedly. "Yes, my lord."

Adran still looked irritated, but after a moment's hesitation, he bowed his head and strode brusquely down the hall. Ian had already trotted off in the other direction. Yiloch went to his chambers and discarded his sweaty clothes, using the washbasin to sponge away the worst of the sweat before allowing an attendant to dress him in clean clothes suitable for a formal meeting of uncertain nature. The attendant ran a brush through his long hair while he finished fastening the cuffs of his jacket. When the reflection in the created mirror was satisfactory, he went to the east sitting room to await his surprise visitors.

For several minutes, he sat in one of the elegant chairs, considering how it would feel to see her again. Eager anticipation pulsed through him, heady enough that he had to work at focusing his thoughts on anything else. The headmaster's presence suggested official business. That also suggested that her visit might be under orders rather than something she had chosen. If only he could be sure of her intentions. Her touch within him had revealed nothing, though he knew from experience that it could be quite expressive if she wished it to be. Leave it to Indigo to stand behind mystery. Of course, she might be as anxious and uncertain as he was, which would explain the reserved contact.

Anticipation and apprehension warred within him until Ian arrived in the doorway and bowed.

"Emperor Yiloch." He stepped aside and bowed less deeply before the two figures behind him. "I present to you Lord Serivar Lithanus, headmaster of the Caithin Healer's Academy and honored member of the Caithin High Council, and Lady Indigo Milan."

Indigo stood a few steps behind the headmaster. She looked beautiful, even in the sedate attire she wore, though her eyes were tired and troubled, rimmed in red. The three small, simple braids in her hair were one of the Caithin mourning customs, and he recognized the deep shade of her blue dress as a color of mourning. Over that, she wore the gray cloak he had given her, and the ring he had sent circled on one delicate finger.

Serivar bowed and Indigo curtsied as Yiloch rose and inclined his head in an appropriate show of respect for their comparative ranks. He nodded to Ian, and the creator closed the doors before coming to stand on one side of the room as a precaution. Indigo's expression, more sorrowful than anything, added to his sense of apprehension, making him glad he had the talented creator with him.

"Lord Serivar. Lady Indigo. To what do I owe the pleasure of your visit?"

Indigo's jaw tightened, and she took several steps, stopping within arm's length of him. Ian shifted his feet but stayed where he was. He could react to a threat regardless of distance, though if Indigo posed a threat, they were both in trouble. And yet, how could she? The scent of her, like warm spring and roses, was the same as when they first met, when they had first made love. How he yearned to touch her.

She lifted her chin with an endearing hint of that stubborn determination he admired. "I have a missive for you from the king." She drew a sealed scroll from within the cloak and held it out to him. "We may speak after you have read it."

Yiloch hesitated, remembering another scroll in the hands of a man he had thought he could trust. A scroll that left him imprisoned for seven months.

The emperor of Lyra will be thrice betrayed.

But this was Indigo. She had helped free him from that prison and fought at his side to win him his throne.

Bewildered by her conduct, Yiloch reached for the scroll, searching her eyes for some hint of their purpose. Those eyes were as beautiful as he remembered, but he caught a flicker of anguish in them when she met his inquiring gaze. He yearned to reach out to her, to know what loss she had suffered and console her. Unfortunately, political affairs had to come first.

He hesitated at the last moment, glancing at Ian. The creator nodded, signaling that the scroll was safe. The moment his fingers touched it, Serivar's hand came to rest on Indigo's shoulder. A gesture of support, or something else?

Her deep blue eyes narrowed, a chill rising in them.

He realized his error a heartbeat too late.

Trust. He had learned not to fully trust any man, because every man had his price. Why hadn't he learned to apply that lesson to women as well? The agony of her betrayal turned to burning rage when familiar pressure closed in around him, making it hard to breathe.

I will not be imprisoned again.

Yiloch reached for his sword as the three of them reappeared on a long stretch of sandy beach, and the pressure went away. Then he realized he hadn't donned the weapon before coming to meet them. An uncharacteristic oversight, but he would not have expected to need it, not with her. The created prison already suppressed his ability to use ascard as the previous one had, leaving him relatively defenseless. An unpleasantly familiar set of circumstances.

Another man appeared next to Indigo and took hold of her arm. Then the two vanished, leaving him alone with Lord Serivar.

"What's the meaning of this?" Yiloch snarled.

"You have been accused of ordering the assassination of King Jerrin and his family," Serivar stated as though reading from a script. "You will be held and tried under Caithin law."

This was news. He didn't recollect ordering the assassination of the Caithin royal family, though he had certainly contemplated eliminating the king more than once. "King Jerrin is dead?"

Serivar was silent, a certain smugness in his stance.

"This is absurd," Yiloch countered. "I had nothing to do with it."

Serivar smiled a slow, ominous smile. A smile that landed like a stone in Yiloch's gut.

"But you already know I didn't do it."

"You will never be able to prove your innocence," Serivar replied. Then he also vanished.

How could he have let love make such a fool of him?

Yiloch stared at the place Indigo had been mere seconds ago. The emotions he experienced, cutting him apart like wheat before a scythe, were entirely new. This was what betrayal felt like when it came from someone he had trusted implicitly, enough to let her into the one place he tried so hard to guard: his heart. The suac had been right. That suggested many things that Yiloch was not at all happy to consider. Had he truly doomed his kingdom by turning away the arrogant Kudaness priest? Not a comforting notion, especially while trapped in another Serroc prison where he was helpless to do anything to correct his mistake.

He began pacing the long beach, examining the perimeters with what little ascard he could draw upon. When he ended up in the first prison, he had raged against it for days, running himself into the ground so that he nearly died when he first encountered one of the mutated hounds Myac left for him. This setting was beautiful, complete with a brilliant false sunset over the created illusion of the ocean and a shelter in the middle of a small stretch of fruit trees standing opposite the water. Better, in many respects, than the volcanic landscape riddled his father had left him in for those seven months. There was little else to this prison, however. It was much smaller than the former one, if considerably more hospitable, not that the setting made him any happier to be here. The construction was also better than the last one. It suppressed his ability so thoroughly that he doubted he could draw upon enough ascard to find faults in its makeup, like the one that had allowed him to escape the former one. There was no obvious gateway to exploit either.

Captain Renkle had done the same thing, handing him a missive that transported him into his father's prison. This time it was the woman he had dared to give his love to who betrayed him, and the betrayal was far more painful because of that. How could she look him in the eyes, while wearing his mother's ring, and condemn him to this? His first act upon escaping the last prison was to kill Renkle. There was only one way to handle a traitor.

Could he kill Indigo?

Yiloch stopped pacing, reached into his shirt, and pulled out the chain with her ring hanging on it. Carefully removing it, he stared at the beautiful little circlet resting heavily in his palm. He had taken it from her, without her knowing, the night before she helped him escape the former prison. When she later told him to keep it, he had been more than happy to do so, savoring the feeling of it resting against his skin every day since. The anguish that filled him upon looking at it now only fueled his rage. He turned his hand over, letting the ring fall to the sand.

Yes, for this, he could kill her.

With the ache in his chest defying his thoughts, he resumed pacing, stepping on the ring with each pass to drive it deeper into the sand as he started counting strides.

At least it's a long beach.

Someone would come to speak to him eventually, and he would find a way out. Serivar would pay—all of Caithin would pay—and Indigo...

He clenched his hands into fists and stopped. The furious pacing only fueled his rage and wasted energy. He sat near where they had appeared in the prison and faced out over the water, watching the play of light on the false horizon. Heartache filled his eyes with moisture, but no tears fell. She didn't deserve his tears.

CHAPTER FIFTEEN

The surge of hurt and fury she had last felt from Yiloch tore through Indigo repeatedly, like a scream for help that brought no aid.

"You can't steal an emperor," she shouted.

With all the conflicting thoughts running through her mind, she wasn't sure why she settled on that particular one to scream at Serivar when he appeared in the training room at the Healers Academy seconds behind them. Knowing they had used her to entrap Yiloch, telling her to give him the scroll without revealing to her what it was really for, left her feeling betrayed and furious. What she had done to Yiloch and how he must feel toward her because of it made her heartsick. She wanted to lash out at anyone she could reach and make them feel her pain. Serivar and Edan were within range, and they deserved her fury.

"We just did," Serivar replied, calmly setting a small turquoise stone next to several others sitting in a neat line on a shelf between some books.

Indigo touched the stones with her power. They were keystones, she realized, recognizing something in the working reminiscent of the Serroc prison she had spent time in briefly with Yiloch before. The one she had helped him escape so long ago. The prisons existed outside of understood reality, and the keystones were their anchor to the normal world, in this case, allowing them to return to Caithin through the prison. Two of the stones glowed, including the one Serivar had touched. The other three were dark, lifeless rocks. Why were they dark? There were five prisoners now, weren't there?

"Lyra will retaliate."

"We left a message behind to explain why we took him into custody." Serivar's tone remained aggravatingly calm and patient, as though he were explaining something to a child. "They will not act against us rashly without their emperor, especially given the gravity of the accusations against him."

"We don't even know that he's guilty."

"Actually..." Edan started, trailing off when she turned a frosty glare on him.

She resented him for taking her away from Yiloch before she could say anything. They hadn't even allowed her a chance to speak to him and explain herself.

Edan shifted, uncomfortable before her bitter gaze, but continued. "Galyn and Kade both confessed their involvement. Sine tried to deny the charges, but she finally relented when the other two implicated her. Ferin's involvement is still unclear, but Kade admitted his orders came from Emperor Yiloch himself."

Indigo shuddered, a wave of nausea leaving her shaken and unsteady on her feet. Her anger with Yiloch for his probable guilt still wasn't as potent as what she felt toward them for using her. Even now, some part of her refused to believe that he and his adepts had anything to do with the assassinations, despite this new testimony to the contrary.

"What will happen to them?" She made a largely futile effort to keep the concern out of her voice.

He turned a dispassionate gaze to the keystones. "Galyn, Kade, and Sine have already undergone sentencing and execution for their crimes."

Despair expanded within her, bringing a chill to her bare arms as if a winter wind blew through the room. Now she understood why three of the stones were dark. No one was in those prisons anymore.

"Lord Ferin and Emperor Yiloch will face questioning and be dealt with appropriately as well."

His words, and the hint of satisfaction in his tone, made her nauseous. Did Ferin know Galyn was dead? She could see the three adepts clearly in her mind, all no older than she was and so hungry to learn. When she wavered on her feet, Edan stepped forward to offer a steadying hand. She stepped back from him so fast she almost fell, catching herself on the edge of a table.

"I'm..." This couldn't be happening. She shook her head. "I'm sorry. I suddenly don't feel so well."

"Perhaps you should get some rest," Serivar offered, and she yearned to claw the tranquility from his eyes. "It has been a stressful few days, and there is no need for you to worry yourself further with this matter."

In other words, they had gotten what they wanted from her.

She nodded. Let them think it was stress afflicting her rather than horror at the death of the three adepts and the betrayal she had committed against the man she loved. Whether or not he was guilty, what she had done was wrong. Knowing they had tricked her into it was little consolation. After his seven-month imprisonment by his father, he wouldn't take kindly to repeating the experience. Nor would he easily forgive what must seem a vile deception from her. She touched the stones with ascard again, yearning to return to the prison and speak to him. The effort would be pointless. It might assuage her guilt, but it wouldn't help him any.

"I can summon a carriage," the headmaster offered.

"No, thank you. The fresh air may help."

Edan took another step closer. "Shall I walk you home?"

She gave him a warning glare, and he took a quick step back. Before she could reject his offer, Serivar shook his head. "I need you here, Edan." He turned to Indigo. "We can find someone else to walk with you if you like."

She shook her head. Why did he need Edan and not her? How had the other adept, who had only been there for a short time, become so integral to his efforts? Whatever the reason, it wasn't important right now. What was important was fixing this, and she knew just who to talk to about it. "No, I'll be fine."

It took an act of will to keep from running from the room. Stepping out into the academy grounds to see students going about their usual business, appreciating the afternoon sun, their lives unchanged beyond the mourning attire most wore, she had trouble believing she had been in the imperial palace in Lyra only a short time ago. Her mind reeled. This couldn't be happening.

Quickening her strides as if to outrun the horror, she considered where Caplin might be at this hour. His family would have moved into the palace by now, so she headed in that direction, reaching as far as she could with her ability to find him. As she neared the inner wall, she could sense him within the palace. She tried to call him to her, something she had never tried with someone who had no real ascard ability, and felt him react with surprise.

The gate guard stopped her outside the palace courtyard, his expression dark and wary after the recent tragedy.

"What business do you have in the palace?" he barked.

"Prince Caplin is expecting me," she stated, hoping her longtime friend would still welcome her despite all that had come between them. "Lady Indigo Milan."

He turned to one of the other guards. There were five more than usual, she noted. Not a surprise.

"Check to see if Prince Caplin is expecting a Lady Indigo Milan."

She felt Caplin approaching and turned her attention to the main doors. He looked mildly surprised to see her when he stepped out, perhaps expecting to find her ascard summons was just a figment of an overstressed mind. If so, he didn't doubt it now. Gratitude filled her at his willingness to investigate, a precious instant of happiness nudging through her misery.

"She may enter," he called, and the guards turned, dropping into quick bows when they saw him.

The guard who had stopped her now gestured for her to pass. She approached Caplin and stopped a few feet back, held at a distance by his scrutinizing regard. He looked weary, easily as weary as she felt. He searched her face for several seconds, then offered her his arm. When she placed her hand at the crook of his elbow, she noticed the way his muscles tensed and his posture stiffened. He escorted her back into the palace to a quiet sitting room off the main hall, unaware of the barriers she was erecting against eavesdropping of any kind. Neither of them sat.

"I didn't expect you back so soon. Your method of getting my attention was... unique. I can't help wondering what other skills you have managed to hide from the Watchmen." The aloofness in his tone erased the lingering pleasure from him trusting her summons, filling the hollow inside her with more sorrow. "Is Emperor Yiloch in the prison?"

She had to swallow a fresh burst of rage. He had known. He was as guilty of using her as Serivar had been. It didn't matter now. He had to hear her out. He was the only one who might listen. "I don't believe he's guilty, Caplin. In fact, I know he isn't."

Caplin turned away from her. "I know how you feel, Indigo, but you cannot let your emotions cloud your judgment. We have signed confessions proving he gave the orders."

"I know what you have, but couldn't..."

He faced her then, and she saw rigid denial in his eyes, felt his emotions turning cold to her. He had no desire to believe her. Hurt and anger at the death of the king and his family overflowed in him. It was a relief to have someone to blame, someone to punish. Inappropriate as doing so might be, she dug deeper into his emotions and found something more. Hidden beneath the other tumultuous emotions she found a persistent hope, directed at her. Did Yiloch's guilt make him think she might change her mind about him? Now that he was heir to the throne and her beloved Yiloch stood accused of a most terrible crime, did he think she might turn to him for comfort?

Did he think Yiloch's rank was what attracted her to him? Would he set Adriana aside so easily? As she picked apart his emotions with ascard and saw his thoughts written in the faint glimmer of hope in his eyes, she realized she would find no ally there. Her chest felt as if it might collapse into the chasm of loneliness and hurt that realization expanded inside her.

I truly am alone.

"You are right, my lord. I just can't reconcile it in my mind." She lowered her gaze to hide the distress lying brought her. Anger and pain were all she had to keep herself going now. Let him think her resigned to this end.

Caplin stepped closer and rested his hand on her shoulder. "Stay for supper. Rest. We have all faced too much hardship of late."

Rest and dine in the palace with you while Yiloch sits in his prison awaiting judgement? Never.

She shook her head, finding it all too easy to bring tears to her eyes. "No. Thank you. I need a little time alone."

"Indigo." Caplin placed a hand on her cheek, and she strangled the urge to slap it away, quickly blocking out the surge of disappointment that flowed from him.

"Thank you for seeing me. I must go."

"You are always welcome," Caplin said when she turned to leave.

Despair threatened, rising like a wave intent on drowning her. Caplin would be of no help to her. The swell of loneliness made her want to lie down on the cobbles and weep, but that wouldn't save Yiloch or Ferin.

Were they guilty? It was impossible to imagine Yiloch doing something like this. He was far too clever and efficient. It wasn't so hard to believe he might want King Jerrin dead, especially given what the slave trade did to the Caithin attitude towards Lyra's people. Still, if he had ordered an assassination, he would have gone to more trouble, with the many adepts and creators at his disposal, to hide his involvement. It was up to her now to intervene in their fates or let them die. She needed to make her decision and devise a plan before it was too late.

* * *

Myac had watched Indigo leave. The fire in her eyes spoke clearly of the force of her anger without any need to read her emotions. Just looking into those vibrant eyes told him her fury was mighty, and that they had only scratched the surface. Like a poisonous snake that missed its first strike, barely grazing the skin with its fangs, she would withdraw, consider her approach, and strike again. The next time, she would not miss.

That her rage extended to them both now only infuriated him. His own anger was a cold thing, an icy storm within him, no less volatile than hers for all that it manifested differently. From the moment she returned to the academy, Myac warned Serivar not to use her like this. Nurture her, convince her this was the right path, he had advised, but do not use her like a pawn in this game. All the ground he had made toward gaining her trust was lost the instant he appeared in the prison, making himself complicit in the lies she had been told. He should have refused to play that part. Then he could have been her ally against Serivar in this. She would have been that much closer to giving in to him.

"I warned you not to use her. She's a powerful ally and an extremely dangerous enemy."

Serivar shrugged the words off. He shuffled through some items on the training room table and said, "She'll come around. She always does."

"Are you blind?" Myac hissed, and Serivar looked around at him this time. "Every fiber of her being was trembling with hatred for you. For both of us. I didn't even need my ability to see it."

Serivar smirked. "You are only upset because I've ruined your little game. She will not turn to you now. Not ever."

Myac yearned to strike him down on the spot, but the new king trusted Serivar, which meant he needed the wretched fool, at least for now. The situation was far too delicate to strike down a critical player yet. He had made such arrogant mistakes with Yiloch's father, and years of effort went to waste because of it. He would not do so again.

"Perhaps you missed the part about how she is also furious with you. Maybe you don't understand. Indigo is a unique creature. She's much like me. She could strike you down with a passing thought as easily as I could. The only meaningful difference is that, for the time being, I need you. Indigo doesn't." Serivar stared at him, holding onto his composure convincingly enough, if not for the tremor of uncertainty running through his emotions. "Think about that. I have some business to take care of." Myac started for the door.

"Wait."

Myac stopped, not offering the headmaster enough respect to face him.

"I thought you were going to come with me to speak to King Gavin about our new prisoner."

"You sound like a spoiled child no one wants to play with," Myac snapped. "Go talk to your puppet king without me. I have more important things to do." Leaving the room, he used a tendril of ascard to slam the door behind him, appreciating the satisfying crack as wood in the doorframe splintered with the force.

Out in the streets, the mood was subdued. Women wore dresses or shawls in the mourning color, some with the traditional braids in their hair as Indigo had done. Men wore coats or vests in the same shade, but they wore their hair too short in Caithin to braid it as the women did. No pureblooded Lyran man would be seen with such a pathetic head of hair. His lip curled in a silent snarl, despising the need to pass as one of them. It was an insult to a lineage that could be traced back hundreds of years.

He strode through the streets with such a dark, determined glare that people made way for him, the human instinct for self-preservation taking over. It took very little time to reach his destination. He didn't know if the young lord would be in, but given the general state of mourning and upheaval, many people had taken to their homes to make a show of their somber state over the loss of their king.

A grumbled acknowledgment and a few minutes of waiting met his knock. When the door opened, Jayce stood there, a woman in the room behind him, craning her neck to see who was at the door.

The young lord's hazel eyes lit with eager anticipation. "Edan. You found her?"

Myac smiled and nodded.

Jayce stepped to one side to offer entry and turned to the woman. "Andrea, I'd like you to meet my exceptionally good friend, Lord Edan."

CHAPTER SIXTEEN

Adran sat on a couch across from Lady Auryl. He sipped his wine and tried to focus on what she was saying, but his thoughts refused to move away from the circumstances surrounding the unexpected visit from Indigo and Lord Serivar. More specifically, they lingered on the warning from Suac Chozai that Yiloch would be betrayed by love. If Yiloch loved anyone more than he did the charming Caithin adept, Adran didn't know who it would be. What if the suac was right? What if Indigo's unexpected arrival was the start of this betrayal he foretold?

Given the focus of his thoughts, the look on Ian's face when he burst into the room made Adran's heart jump into his throat. The young creator's ashen pallor and the desperation in his eyes said something was very wrong. Something Ian felt incapable of handling on his own.

Forcing a calm demeanor, he gestured with a tiny tilt of his head toward Auryl.

Ian's answering nod was almost imperceptible, and he schooled the distress from his expression, clearing his throat softly. "Please excuse the interruption." There was the slightest tremor in his voice that might go unnoticed by someone like Auryl, who didn't know him as well, but made Adran's heart race. "I need to speak with you for a moment, Captain Adran."

Adran stood, and Auryl placed her hands on the arms of the chair as if to rise, looking up at him and Ian with concern. She wasn't a fool. She sensed something was amiss. Under her querying gaze, Ian, his forced composure already cracking, started to look like a cornered animal.

"Please excuse us, my lady," Adran intervened, feeling a wash of relief when she reluctantly relaxed back in her chair. The spark in her eyes told him she wasn't happy about acquiescing, but she also recognized that she didn't yet have the authority to make demands of him. "I'm certain this will only take a moment."

Fighting the dread that constricted his throat and twisted his stomach in the most unpleasant of ways, Adran led Ian away from the sitting room, leading him to a study down the hall. Once inside, he turned to Ian as the creator shut the door behind them.

"What's happened?"

Ian's fragile calm collapsed, and his hands began shaking. "They've taken him. I was standing right there, but I couldn't act fast enough. When I checked the scroll, I didn't sense any threat. I failed him."

"What do you mean, they've taken him?" Panic exploded within Adran like a potent alcohol set aflame, but he had to be clearheaded and steady. He had the awful feeling Yiloch needed him to be so, now more than ever.

"Lady Indigo and Lord Serivar. I took them to meet with Emperor Yiloch." As he spoke, Adran noticed his eyes losing focus, perhaps searching for some trace of Yiloch with ascard. "Indigo told him she had a missive from the king. As soon as he touched it, Lord Serivar put a hand on her shoulder, and all three of them vanished."

Adran let loose a string of the vilest curses he knew, releasing a tiny fraction of the rage and anguish Ian's news caused him. A sense of desolation at losing his dearest friend once again filled the space left by the outburst, but now he could at least think somewhat coherently. He gestured for Ian to sit in a chair. Too distraught to argue, Ian didn't hesitate to obey the silent command. Adran pulled the string that would ring the servant's bell, then, driven to impatience by the urgency of the situation, he leaned out the door and hollered for a servant. A young man in servant's livery came rushing down the hall. Before he could finish his bow, Adran was barking out orders.

"I need Lord Terral and Commander Hax here immediately."

"Yes, my lord," the man bowed and started jogging back down the hallway.

"And send someone to start a fire to warm up this room," Adran called after him, noticing the chill in the air. "We may be here a while."

"It will be done, my lord," the man called back over his shoulder.

A whoosh behind him preceded sudden warmth. He glanced from the now blazing fire to Ian and shut the door. "Thank you."

Ian held a scroll out to him, and Adran practically leapt back from it. Ian cringed. "Sorry. It has no workings on it. It was lying on the floor where they had been standing after they disappeared. I inspected it before touching it. I'm certain the one Indigo handed Yiloch had no workings on it either. All I can figure out is that Serivar must have been holding some kind of key. That would explain him putting his hand on Indigo's shoulder as Yiloch was taking the scroll." Adran took the offered item and unrolled it while Ian spoke. "It says that they have taken Emperor Yiloch into custody to stand trial for ordering the assassination of King Jerrin Duvox and his wife and son. According to that, Kade and Sine have already confessed to their part in the deaths and claimed that their orders came from Emperor Yiloch."

Adran read the scroll, confirming Ian's words. Then he read it again... and again.

Ian was gripping the arms of his chair as if he meant to tear them off. "What do we do now? We have to go after him, right?"

Adran's pulse pounded in his ears. He reread the scroll one more time. "No. This is a delicate situation that could easily lead to war, and we're in no position to go up against Caithin right now. We must proceed with caution. We'll send someone with a missive demanding the release of Emperor Yiloch and an opportunity to investigate these allegations ourselves."

"He's not guilty, is he?"

Defensive anger flared, and Adran met Ian's eyes, catching his temper before words he might regret slipped past his lips. No matter how dramatically Ian had grown and changed in the last year, no matter how great his creation ability was, he was still very young and inexperienced. "No. I would have known if he were planning something like this."

Ian leaned forward and buried his face in his hands, his elbows on his knees. "I didn't sense the threat. He trusted me, and I failed him."

A strong desire to throw himself down in another chair and languish in his own despair swept over Adran. Instead, he began pacing the room before the large window. He could think better that way.

"They must have used a Serroc prison," he growled, more to himself than Ian. Yiloch would be insane with rage at falling for that trick twice. A shame he trusted the Caithin woman so much. Otherwise, he might have been more careful, but love did strange things to the mind. It was clear now more than ever that he truly loved Indigo, or at least had loved her up to now. "Curse that vile woman," he snarled.

Ian looked up, fierce defensiveness blazing to life in his eyes. "Indigo would never hurt him."

Apparently Ian loved her as well. Adran scowled at him. "She already has." He would have thought it impossible for the young creator to look any more dejected, but Ian's face crumbled at his biting words, and he buried his face in his hands again. "Did either of them say anything to you or to each other when you were taking them to see Yiloch?"

Ian raised his head, his face smoothing with concentration as he thought back over the events in his mind. "Nothing really, though Indigo seemed lost in some deep melancholy. I tried to speak with her, but she said very little."

"We need to—" Adran cut off when the door opened.

Hax stormed in wearing her full commander's uniform, hair braided back out of the way. She was stripping off leather gauntlets as she entered, her helmet tucked under one arm. Sweeping the room with her pale eyes, she considered Ian for a second, then settled her irritable gaze on Adran.

"What's the meaning of this? I was busy training recruits."

"Please sit," Adran replied, gesturing to an empty chair.

Hax sat, but in her usual defiant manner chose a different chair from the one he had specified. When she opened her mouth to speak again, Adran gestured for her to wait and, for a wonder, she glanced at Ian again and fell silent. Just when he thought her patience might wear thin, the door opened once more, and Lord Terral entered. He glanced around the room and perched on the edge of a seat, watching Adran expectantly, almost warily.

"I have you together because Emperor Yiloch has been taken prisoner."

"What?" Hax stood, her face darkening with murderous rage.

Adran gestured for her to wait again, and she held her silence, but didn't sit back down.

"Lady Indigo and Lord Serivar arrived here not an hour ago to see Emperor Yiloch. They handed him a missive, and our current hypothesis is that one of them was carrying the secondary key for a Serroc prison.

Obviously, we need to get him back, but we must approach carefully. According to this missive, he stands accused of ordering the assassinations of King Jerrin and his family." Indignation flashed in Hax's eyes, but she refrained from expressing her thoughts at his look of warning. "We also need someone to be a figurehead in his absence to keep things under control until we can resolve this mess." He gave Terral a significant look. "As Yiloch's cousin, you would be next in line to the throne. It makes sense to place you in the position of emperor regent. I assume there are no objections."

When no one said anything, Terral inclined his head and said, "I will do whatever is necessary to keep things running smoothly until we get this mess straightened out."

"Perhaps one of us should go to Demin," Ian suggested.

"Absolutely not," Terral stated as Adran shook his head.

Terral nodded to Adran, deferring to him. Adran considered Ian. Despite the immense power the creator possessed, he looked disconcertingly young and vulnerable at that moment.

"We can send a missive, but they already have Yiloch, and we don't yet know the status of Ferin and the three adepts who went to Caithin with him. We can't afford to provide them with any more valuable captives. For now, we will have to settle for a simple messenger until we have more information."

Terral sank back in his seat, gazing into the fire. "We will need to speak with Lord and Lady Vyram and Lady

Auryl. The wedding is almost upon us. If we can't recover him soon, we have hundreds of guests to notify."

Adran sighed. What he really wanted was to find a quiet spot to indulge his rage and anguish. Hax, given her more aggressive nature, would find someone to spar with when they finished here and would probably send that someone to bed with a limp. Perhaps he should volunteer to be her victim. A little physical pain would be a welcome distraction. She met his eyes, and he saw his torment mirrored there. Hax hadn't been with Yiloch as long as he had, but she loved him as a leader and friend.

Adran looked at Ian and promptly turned away from the despair in his eyes. Like the rest of the inner circle, Ian had come to love Yiloch, but the pain was twofold for him. Where they had all developed some fondness for Indigo, Ian had learned to love her almost as much as Yiloch did.

Then he met Terral's eyes. There was tension in the man's posture and expression, but even though he was Yiloch's cousin, the two were never terribly close and the upset was less profound. Perhaps it would work in their favor having someone less emotionally entangled with the situation sitting on the throne. Adran had misgivings about the man, though he had no concrete reason for them. Regardless of those groundless uncertainties, Terral was Yiloch's closest living relative. That made him the leading option for a figurehead.

Adran refused to consider what would happen if Yiloch didn't return. He had to return. The last time, when Emperor Rylan had imprisoned Yiloch, Adran survived day to day with a fading hope and a growing sense of emptiness. Then, at least, he had Eris to keep him going and bolster his failing optimism. Now she was gone. Without her, how could he hope to face the loss of the man he had built his life around? He had given up every other ambition so he could stay by his side and serve him as a friend and subject? There were no other options. They had to get Yiloch back.

"First, we need to prepare a created missive to send to Caithin's new leadership. When that's done, I will tell Lady Auryl that Yiloch was called away on urgent business, and we must postpone the wedding. That will be what we tell everyone for now. He has left you in charge until his return," he gestured to Terral, who nodded sagely. "We have a great deal of work to do. Let's get to it."

They all stood, and Adran turned to Hax, who was already pulling her gauntlets back on.

"Would you care to spar later, perhaps in the practice ring near the ocean terraces?"

Hax met his eyes for a long moment. They both knew she was better with a sword than he was, and she rarely took pity on her opponents. Because of that, he usually avoided sparring with her, preferring not to lose the use of a limb in a practice match. Whatever she saw in his eyes now met her approval, and she nodded.

"I would care to," she replied. "Do you want me to speak with Lady Auryl?"

It surprised Adran to find he could still choke out a laugh. "No, please. This matter needs to be dealt with delicately."

Hax's eyes started narrowing, then they relaxed, and she grinned. "I suppose you're right. Diplomacy isn't my strength. I'll head out to the practice ring in five hours."

Adran nodded.

He spent the next several hours working out the contents of the missive demanding Yiloch's return and the right to investigate the accusations with Ian and Terral. Ian created it so that only the new King Gavin or his son, Lord Caplin, would be able to read its contents. When that was done, Adran went in search of Lady Auryl. A meeting he dreaded. He found her on a covered terrace accessible only from the throne room.

"My lady," he said, his careful tone, a tone reserved for the sharing of bad news, drawing a worried look from her.

"What has happened, Lord Adran?"

"There was an incident in Demin involving Lord Ferin and his adepts. Yiloch departed in haste with a personal entourage to address the issue himself, hoping to preserve the peace with our Caithin allies." Adran's heart went out to her when her face fell with the understanding of what this news meant. Her gaze drifted out to sea for a few minutes, moisture rising in her eyes. Then she rallied, setting her head high and her shoulders back with determination worthy of an empress. If only Yiloch could see how suited she was to the role.

"Then the wedding is to be postponed?" His slight nod was sufficient confirmation. "So it must be. He cannot set aside the affairs of an empire for the sake of a mere wedding."

Adran deemed it wise not to point out that this particular wedding was an affair of the empire. "My lady, you are truly deserving of the station you will soon hold. This will all be resolved quickly and your wedding will proceed without further delay." He took her hands in his and gave them a gentle squeeze.

"Thank you, Lord Adran. Emperor Yiloch is fortunate to have you at his side."

Adran could barely muster a smile, fighting hard not to let his worry break through. "I should speak with your parents."

Auryl shook her head. "No. I will speak to them. I know how to deal with my father better than anyone."

Relief crashed over him so hard at the thought of not having to deal with anyone else for now that it left him stumbling for words for a few seconds. Gratitude brought his smile back. "As you wish, Lady Auryl."

As soon as he had taken leave of her, Adran went to his rooms to change and headed out to the practice ring near the ocean terraces. It was raining, which seemed appropriate for the occasion. Though it was earlier than their proposed meeting time, Hax was already there, sitting under a shelter constructed to provide observers shelter from the rain or sun. She had a flask in one hand and two more on the bench beside her. As he walked up, she took a long swig from the one she held and offered it to him. He accepted it, taking a long drink of the fiery liquid, a crude alcohol imported from Kudan. When he met her eyes, he could tell this wasn't her first drink since they had last parted ways. He spotted an empty flask discarded in one corner.

"Trying to even the odds, are you?"

Hax grinned, a wicked gleam in her eyes. "Actually, I'm even less forgiving when I've had a few drinks."

"Perfect, shall we start?"

Her expression softened, a rare glimmer of concern showed through in her hesitation. "Are you sure? We could have sex instead. It's just as satisfying and typically less painful. Have you ever slept with a woman, Adran?"

He grinned ruefully. "No, and I do not intend to start today."

"I could send for Leryc."

"Leryc? Why Leryc?"

Hax only stared at him as though he had spoken a foreign language, and hundreds of brief moments raced through his mind. Leryc always offering to help him with the most menial of tasks. Leryc constantly asking to watch him work so he could learn something about the political side of things. The way the new young captain smiled at him and watched his hands with that hint of wistfulness that Adran always assumed meant he wasn't really paying attention. The way he colored when Yiloch had harassed Adran about his romantic preferences.

What a fool I am.

A spark of joy struck through the anger and sorrow that filled him then, a speck of light in the darkness. Perhaps he would ask Leryc if he wished to help him in his rooms later, since he would almost certainly be suffering from some injury or other.

"Shall we?" He reached for a practice sword.

Hax shrugged, grabbed a sword, and walked out into the rain. After taking another long drink from the flask, Adran joined her.

CHAPTER SEVENTEEN

Indigo breathed a sigh of relief once she was safely back in her residence. Here, in the silence of her rooms, she could take a little time to come up with a plan. There had to be something she could do, someone she could reason with. Caplin would be of no help, which destroyed her best chance of fixing this by following proper procedures. He was far too willing to accept Yiloch's guilt under the circumstances. Without Caplin's backing, would his father even listen to her arguments?

There would also be no help coming from the academy, not with Serivar advocating for Yiloch's guilt. That left her few options other than trying to reach out to someone in Lyra. Ignoring the very real danger that they would have her put to death on sight after her involvement in their emperor's abduction, the time it would take to get to Lyra and back might be more time than Yiloch had, given how swift Caithin justice was moving.

Caithin justice indeed.

Despite the nearly overwhelming fury that burned through her, she forced herself to step back and look at the situation.

How could she be right when the rest of the King's

Order and the Ascard Watchmen had all reached the conclusion that he was the one behind this hideous crime? She was more powerful in base ascard strength than any of them according to Serivar, but there must be adepts among them with the ability focused on digging through false trails to find the truth. Then again, none of them would have enough personal knowledge of Yiloch to doubt that this was his doing. What motivation would they have to dig any deeper than necessary to confirm what they already believed to be true? If what she had heard so far was any indication, whoever was behind this subterfuge had known just how to exploit the tenuous relationship between the two countries.

But what if he is guilty? She scowled at the created window, twisting his mother's ring around her finger. *I must prove that for myself before I condemn him.*

She sat in one of the plush chairs and searched her mind for viable alternatives. The only wild notion she could come up with that had a halfway decent chance of success was that of freeing Yiloch and Ferin herself. That option, however, wouldn't convince anyone of their innocence. It would only make her look guilty as well. If she did such a thing, would she actually be helping anyone? She certainly wouldn't be helping herself. It might buy her time to investigate the assassinations, but it would be harder to do so as a wanted criminal, and would anyone take the evidence she found into consideration after that. She had the advantage of her significant ascard connection, but she needed to decide how to best use that power in this situation.

As evening fell outside, she leaned back in the chair,

staring through the fireplace and deep into the churning tangle of thoughts that made her head pound. She lit a candle to ward off darkness and drew her knees to her chest, chewing at her lip while she considered every conceivable scenario, finding compelling reasons to discard each new idea as fast as she could come up with them.

How much time did she have before they executed Ferin?

The sound of footsteps on the stairs tickled at the edge of her consciousness. It was important that she acknowledge the sound, but she still hadn't solved her dilemma, and the distraction was unwelcome. When the sound finally drove into her awareness like an arrowhead piercing the skin, she glanced at the door in alarm. She didn't recall bolting it on her way in, and that quick glance confirmed she hadn't done so. Jumping up from the chair, she reached out with a tendril of ascard, jerking it back when the door flew open before she could correct her mistake.

Jayce stormed in, slamming the door behind him, his face flushed with wrath or drink, or both. He glanced around the room. "You think I'm going to let you have a little haven all to yourself after you publicly disgraced me?" The slight slur in his speech confirmed the involvement of an excess of drink.

Her heart pounded, and she stepped back, realizing too late that it would be her second mistake of the evening.

Encouraged by her show of fear, Jayce sneered and came forward.

"Jayce." She managed a soothing tone despite the

tremor of remembered fear that vibrated through her. "Let this go. It's over and done with. *We* are over and done with." She opened to more ascard, feeling that power fill her. As she did so, she also checked her masking to be sure she wouldn't draw attention if she had to use it against him.

Please, just let it go.

She wasn't supposed to know how to do most of the things she could do with ascard and it could bring trouble if she let him in on those things. If only she could talk him down this time—get him to give up.

Jayce's lip lifted in a silent snarl. "You won't get the last word, Indigo." He spat her name as if it was some foul thing that people only whispered of in dark corners. "That isn't the way this is going to work."

He moved forward again, and she backed up a few more steps, trying to maintain the distance between them. This time she came up against a table and had to move to one side to clear her way. "Why don't we sit down and talk about it? Maybe we can find a sensible way to settle things that works for both of us."

He shook his head. "No one else gets to have you."

She narrowed her eyes, the ring growing heavier on her finger, reminding her that someone else had already had her, someone handsome and powerful who needed her now. Stopping her retreat, she straightened and sneered at him. "It's much too late for that."

Lightning flashed in his eyes, and she cursed herself for letting her emotions get the upper hand. A moment of reciprocated anger, a mere flash of defiance, was all he needed to keep his rage burning hot.

"Whore," he yelled, his voice cracking. A tear ran down his cheek, and her stomach twisted into knots. Did he honestly believe he had ever loved her or that she somehow belonged to him? "I'll drag you down to the docks and sell you to the slave traders. Maybe they can find a use for you."

Anger and frustration pounded their way to the surface. She was wasting precious time arguing with him. People she cared for were in danger. "Get out."

Jayce lunged at her then, the movement so sudden that she didn't have time to evade him. He grabbed a fistful of hair, using it to pull her head back and down. She staggered, a second of panic overriding rational thought. One knee struck the floor, sending a bolt of pain up through her hip. His eyes were wide and a lunatic grin warped his handsome features. He drew back his free hand to strike her. The gesture took her back to the last time he had attacked her, before she had gone to Lyra. Everything stopped. A razor's edge of hatred erased her fear. She wasn't about to let him strike her again. Not ever.

She slammed a wall of ascard power into him. His hand jerked open in surprise, freeing her, and he reeled back into a table. The decorative candelabra on the table crashed to the floor. He caught himself, looking con-fused for a moment, and then he glared hatred at her, hatred edged with a bitter note of fear that felt like a scream crashing into her wide-open ascard abilities. She climbed to her feet, using another side table to steady herself. Her heart pounded so hard in her chest that it sounded like war drums beating in her ears.

This is war. It won't end until one of us is dead.

She could scare him with her power or put him to sleep as she had once before, but there would always be another day that drink would make him bold and bring him back to her door.

"I've had a miserable day, Jayce. Now isn't the best time to test me." She returned his glare while she struggled to take control of the loathing boiling up inside her. Such an abhorrent emotion, one that planted cruel thoughts in her head.

Jayce's lip curled up in a feral snarl. "I'm done doing things on your schedule." He drew the hunting knife from his belt.

She shook her head, keeping a hand on the table. Her mind spun with possible outcomes for this confrontation, none of them good, and part of her wondered what the harm would be in ridding the world of such a man. Today, that part of her was more persuasive than usual.

"Don't do this," she warned. "It isn't worth dying over."

He hesitated for an instant, brow furrowing with uncertainty, and she hoped he would remember that she had put him to sleep and burned his hands on prior encounters with nothing more than a thought. Then that brief sanity vanished from his eyes, and he lunged. Her hatred stepped in to meet him, a release after long hours of uncertainty and sorrow. It filled her mind with pure, scalding fury. She grabbed the knife by the blade, protecting her hand with a shield of ascard, and twisted it from his grasp. At the same instant, noting the rise of horror in his eyes with an odd sense of detachment, as though she watched from a distance, she dove into him with ascard, closed it around his heart and squeezed. Somewhere someone screamed a denial in her voice. When his heart fell silent in his chest, she released the crushing hold. He collapsed at her feet like an oversized marionette with cut strings.

For an uncertain length of time, she stared at the body, uncomprehending. Then the reality of what she had done crept in.

Murderer.

Still holding the blade of his knife in one hand, she sank to her knees next to him. She pressed her fingertips to his neck and searched for a pulse even as she confirmed with ascard that the force of her power had crushed his heart into pulp.

Murderer.

How was she going to explain this? She had murdered someone. She had so many other ways she could have stopped him. So many ways she could have used her power to disable him long enough to call the authorities. Instead, she had killed him in cold blood.

He would have come back. He would have always come back.

Her stomach turned. There was no excuse for what she had done, and no way to call it an accident. Any decent healer could detect that. Her hands started to tremble as she knelt there beside him, still holding the cold steel blade of his knife. This wasn't who she was. Or was it? Serivar skewed her training toward making her into a weapon. Yiloch had let her be his weapon. Was this what she was now, a tool suited more for killing than for love? An adept groomed to hurt rather than heal?

"What have I done," she whispered, fighting back nausea and fear that threatened to overwhelm rational thought.

I must not panic. The trembling spread through her body, every muscle shaking.

"You appear to have killed him."

She flinched and glanced over her shoulder. Edan stood in the doorway of her bedroom, gazing down at her. Too calm. Too composed. When had he come in? How long had he been there?

She looked back at Jayce, lying dead before her, the panic she warned herself against blossoming in her chest.

Focus. She struggled to keep her breathing steady. *Look where your carelessness has gotten you and learn from it.*

"You're masking has improved." Somehow only a hint of a tremor came through in her voice despite her heart threatening to pound its way through her chest. Still leaning over Jayce's body, she slipped his dagger into the sleeve of her cloak and checked all her masks and barriers, ensuring Edan wouldn't sense her fear or the deception that lurked beneath it.

"Your former fiancé?" His tone was far too casual, too devoid of alarm or surprise, for the situation.

"How did you find me here?" Her voice shook more this time despite her efforts. She hoped he would assume that was a predictable rising panic over what she had done. If so, he would be at least partly correct.

If I get out of this, I will never let my guard slip again. For an instant, she considered praying to the Divine, but having just killed someone, she didn't think the Divine was likely to listen to her.

"I apologize for my intrusion, but I was concerned about you. You were so upset earlier. I decided someone should check on you. The other evening, I glimpsed you entering the building, so I assumed this was where you were staying. I thought I heard something when I was coming up the stairs, so when you didn't answer my knock, I let myself in."

His tone sounded too flat, making his words sound like lines in a play memorized by someone who had never acted before, lacking in emotion and sincerity. She managed not to jump when his hand appeared next to her face, offering to help her up. Jayce's eyes stared in accusation at her. She closed her eyes, trying to clear her mind, searching for clarity and control. If only it would all be gone when she opened her eyes, like a vivid nightmare.

"It was obviously self-defense," Edan reassured, his voice destroying her moment of glorious self-delusion.

Opening her eyes, she took the offered hand and allowed him to help her stand. When she was on her feet, he pulled her around to face him, placing her back to the wall with a bookcase on one side and a hand on the opposite shoulder to keep her from moving away. He ran the fingers of the other hand along her jawline in a gentle caress. She sensed that the secrets he kept were very close to surfacing. Those secrets might be of use to her now. Forcing herself not to recoil from the passion burning in his eyes, she straightened and met his gaze.

Concealing her workings, she extended several tendrils of ascard, skimming over all the layers of his protections in search of a way through. His masking, though much improved, was still not perfect. As his desire flared and he moved close enough that their lips were almost touching, she felt his barriers shifting with his distraction.

Drawing on the additional power woven into the ring, she found she could dig past his outer barriers, masking the tendril of ascard she used to bore her way in. Beneath the outer barriers, she encountered deeper layers of masking and illusion bearing the ascard signatures of several other individuals. The work was magnificent. Drilling down through those layers, she finally found his true inner aspect, and the ascard signature there was all too familiar. She peeled back her masking, allowing him to feel the tendril of ascard as she retracted it.

A cold calm filled her. The vast supply of ascard she drew into herself now drove fear and revulsion into a deep, secluded corner of her mind where they couldn't interfere. Now that she knew who she was dealing with, every fiber of her being understood that she couldn't afford to show any weakness or make any mistakes.

"You almost fooled me," she murmured, a soft, sensual whisper.

The illusions melted away, and Myac stood before her, his black eyes shining with dark humor, long obsidian hair adding a ghostly pallor to already pale features.

"What gave me away?"

"It was something in your eyes when we met." Though she couldn't place it at the time, she recalled sensing something familiar about Edan the first time she met him.

Myac leaned in and kissed her, his lips warm and soft against hers. She returned the kiss. The calm moved aside to make room for the defensive indifference she had perfected with Jayce rising on a comforting wave of ascard power as she slid the dagger from her sleeve.

Myac moved back from her the tiniest bit, his predatory smile filled with a deep satisfaction and a hunger that declared his intentions without a need for words.

"I told Serivar we were the same, you and I." He traced the line of her jaw again, his gaze following the motion of his fingertips, admiring.

"You were right." A pang of remorse pierced her chest at the truth that lived in those words. *We are both murderers.*

Then she shoved the dagger into his chest and pushed him away, pulling the weapon free when he staggered back. Pain and surprise burst from him as his eyes widened. Falling to one knee, he looked down at the blood spreading over his shirt, then up at her, silenced by shock. A swell of fury darkened his expression, and she erected a protective barrier when she felt him opening himself to more ascard. Jumping over Jayce's body, she threw open the door and fled the room.

She had no time now for pondering options. Very few options remained.

CHAPTER EIGHTEEN

It was dark now. Indigo slid the bloodied dagger up into her sleeve again on her way out the door and hurried back to the academy. Myac would have to focus his power on healing for a time if he were to have any chance of surviving the dire injury she had inflicted on him. Given his power and association with Serivar, it was all too likely that he had the skill and knowledge to do so. The process of saving his own life would at least buy her some time. She could only hope it would be enough.

Outside the administration building, she hid in the shadows, waiting while she searched the building for any sign of Serivar. With a growing sense of hope, she finished her search and found no trace of him. Doing her best to look focused, as though she had some purpose for being there, she entered the building. Those few healers present at that hour were there primarily as emergency support for the neighboring medical buildings. They greeted her politely, so used to seeing her there now that they didn't question her. She kept her pace casual and returned their greetings, keeping her hands folded in front of her and covered by the fabric of her sleeves to hide their shaking and the blood that still stained them.

Knowing who she was up against now, she didn't dare squander precious ascard resources to clean or steady her hands.

She slipped into Serivar's office and went back to the hidden training room where the keystones waited, lined up on the shelf. Grabbing the two active stones, she placed one in a pocket and held the other, the one Serivar had touched that she was sure would take her to Yiloch's prison, in her palm. The stone pulsed warmly in her grasp, its response to her touch drawing forth a small gasp of surprise. She didn't know if what she was planning would work, but there was no time to come up with a better idea. No time to waste on indecision. She focused her power on the stone and entered the prison.

The long beach stretched out before her. Several yards away, she spotted Yiloch sitting cross-legged, gazing out over the water. He turned to look at her, handsome as ever under the false night sky, a false moon giving shine to his silvery hair. Anger flared to life in his pale eyes. Rising in one smooth motion, he started walking toward her, rage adding a deadly threat to his powerful strides. She longed to speak with him alone, to explain what had happened, but she couldn't risk doing so just now. Ignoring him with effort, she pulled the other keystone from her pocket and focused her power on it. It grew hot enough to scald her palm, disintegrating seconds before she could react to the pain, and Ferin staggered out of nothing beside her, gasping for air.

Yiloch stopped and stared at Ferin with a puzzled expression. Then the rage surged up in his eyes again as they refocused on something behind her, giving her a few precious seconds of warning. She spun to find Myac standing behind her, disguised as Edan once more, though the illusion was far more superficial this time, a hasty working meant to hide him from the vast majority of people who didn't have the skill to dig past it. He was holding a stone like the one she held. A secondary key to the prison. He must have had it on him already to have healed and followed her so fast.

She refused to let him get to Yiloch. Grabbing his hand, she trapped the secondary stone between their palms and focused a flood of power on the keystone she held for Yiloch's prison. The stone scalded her already burned palm and disintegrated like the first had. The resulting surge of light as the prison imploded blinded her for an instant.

When her vision returned, she was back in her room, Jayce's body still lying on the floor, and Myac was with her. The secondary key took them both back to where he had been when he entered. Because Yiloch and Ferin had no key and the prison existed outside of normal space, she had no way of knowing where they would end up, but she had made certain that Myac didn't end up with them. For now, she could only hope they were safe.

Myac was gasping, climbing to his feet with the halting movements of a man many times his age. A quick inspection told her he had healed the wound too fast in his rush to come after her. She stood and moved away from him. The strain of all the power she had been casting about was taking its toll. Her thoughts were becoming sluggish, her muscles beginning to shake with fatigue. How much more could she do before it became too much?

It doesn't really matter now. Yiloch and Ferin were free, and no one, herself included, knew where they were.

Finally standing, Myac smirked, though she could see a world of pain and exhaustion in his eyes.

"We are more alike than I realized, you and I," he commented, taking a few staggering steps toward her. "You don't think this is going to stop me or save them in the end, do you?"

"It certainly evens the odds a bit, don't you think?" She took another careful step back.

"Why are you willing to risk so much for Yiloch?" he asked, sneering as he spoke the name.

She measured the space between her current position and the door with a glance. They were both about the same distance from it now, but his injury should slow him down. Could she count on that to be enough of an advantage with fatigue setting in?

"Why are you so determined to destroy him?" she asked, refusing to indulge him with an honest answer to his question. "I can't imagine it's out of some sense of vengeance for the death of his father."

"No. Let's just say that he and his father owe me. I wanted to destroy them both, but was easier to let one of them kill the other. Less explaining to do that way. However, in retrospect, I now realize that it would have been easier had Rylan come out the victor. I didn't expect Yiloch to be so bloodthirsty that he would rather kill me than employ my skills." He tilted his head to one side, in an almost dog-like, or rather, wolf-like fashion. "Perhaps I should ask what it is you have against me?"

"You tried to kill me." She forced herself to stand her ground. If she retreated any further, he would be closer to the door than she was.

"Only after you tried to help the Blood Prince kill me," he countered, measuring her distance to the door with a glance as she had done.

"I..." She trailed off, her argument dying on her lips when she realized that what he said was true.

"Now you see, my lady. Our conflict started with you. It didn't have to be this way." His superior smile grated on her, but it boded well that he was letting his arrogance show. Maybe he would be careless if he believed he was gaining the upper hand. Then he glanced down at the blood over the front of his shirt and scowled. "In fact, it looks like you are ahead. I have some catching up to do."

She felt him drawing on ascard energy, sucking it from the surrounding air like oxygen. His attack ran harmlessly up against her barriers, reinforced by the power bound to the ring. Injury and ascard exertion had left him too drained to overpower her that easily.

She smiled and unleashed her rage into the ascard all around them. The room burst into flames with a roar. Myac's eyes narrowed, flames reflecting in them as he turned his own failing strength to shielding himself from the fire that now surrounded him.

For the second time that night, she fled from her residence, feeling a brief pang of regret for all the things she would lose in the fire. They were only things.

She ran as far as she could, but long hours of stress and wielding ascard were wearing her down. Leaning against a building, she focused on catching her breath and trying to control her trembling. Already she could feel Myac searching for her. Now that she knew who he was, he no longer bothered to conceal his efforts from her. Deflecting his search away took far more effort than it should have. She couldn't hide from him for long. Which one of them would break first?

Knowing that Myac was in Caithin made her more confident than ever that Yiloch and the others had nothing to do with the death of the king and his family. She might reach out to Serivar, but Edan had been living with him. She couldn't trust him now, not that she ever really had. Caplin allowed himself to be blinded by grief, anger, and his jealousy of Yiloch. She couldn't seek his help. All else aside, now that she had set free the remaining suspects in the assassination, she had technically made herself a criminal. It would only be a matter of time before they rescinded her immunity to the Ascard Watchmen and came hunting for her.

The sound of hooves clacking on the cobblestones reached her. Ducking back further into the shadows, she waited until the horse was almost past. A young nobleman sat astride the big chestnut, the exaggerated sway in his seat hinting that he may have had a bit too much to drink. He was probably heading home now to sleep off the excess.

Drawing on ascard around her, she put him gently to sleep and stepped out to take hold of the chestnut's reins, using more power to lower him to the ground before he could fall off, then led the horse into the alley. Leaving the animal for a moment, she rolled the young man into the shadows and searched his pockets.

You are not a thief, a voice in her mind protested when she drew out his coin purse and tucked it into her cloak.

I am now.

Leaving him lying in the alley, she mounted his horse and urged the chestnut into a long, fast trot. Once she had exited the city proper, she reached back with her rapidly fading ascard ability to wake the young man so he wouldn't fall victim to any other unsavory persons who might be out wandering the nighttime streets. That done, she urged the horse to a canter and pointed him toward the port town of Kilty, a few miles east of Demin.

Tears trailed down her cheeks, and she trembled with more than just the chill of the night as they raced down the dark road. In Lyra, she had killed people, but only to save Yiloch's life. Tonight she had killed her former fiancé when she could have subdued him without bringing him harm and called the authorities to deal with him. Then again, they would have done nothing more than give him a warning and set him free again. He would never stop trying to get back at her. His vanity demanded it.

That knowledge brought no comfort.

"No," she scolded herself aloud, "you will not justify this murder."

If she justified his death to herself, then it would become easier to rationalize killing again. She had many less violent ways of dealing with such a threat. Ways that would only work if he never caught her unaware.

She ground her teeth and focused on the night ahead, trying not to think anymore.

Sometime after midnight, she rode into the Kilty Docks. Trade was a business of expediency. As such, several crews were busy unloading or loading cargo despite the hour. She tied the horse outside an inn. Someone would take care of him when it became clear his rider had abandoned him. His owner might even get him back eventually. Leaving the horse to whatever fate awaited it, she started toward the ships, using ascard to hide her ring to avoid it becoming a factor in bargaining.

For a few minutes, she stood in the shadows and watched. Selecting a ship whose crew was loading cargo with considerable haste, their urgency suggesting that they were running behind schedule. She approached a crewman as he reached the bottom of the plank on his way to get another crate. He sidestepped as if intending to ignore her and continue past, so she moved into his path again, forcing him to stop.

"Excuse me, sir, but I would like to speak with your captain."

His dark eyes overflowed with weary resignation. "We carry cargo, not passengers. Try another ship." He gave a curt nod and sidestepped to move around her once more.

"I'm sure your captain can tell me that just as well as you can." She placed a hand on his shoulder with enough force to turn him back toward her.

The man scowled at her hand and turned to the ship, gesturing with his head to an older man standing to the side of the gangplank on the deck. The man looked like all the others working the ship, but since he had at least enough rank to be supervising rather than carrying, she decided it was worth a try.

"Thank you."

"Won't do you any good." The man shook his head and moved on toward the stack of crates they were loading while Indigo wove her way up the gangplank amidst the curses of the laboring crewmen. The man at the top watched her with a deepening scowl.

"We carry cargo, not passengers," he stated gruffly when she reached him.

She forced a sweet smile. "So I've been told. I'll pay well and be no trouble."

"Never met a woman who wasn't trouble."

She continued to smile, swallowing the string of insults that wanted to come out. "Really, Captain..." she trailed off, pressing for a name. The way his gaze flickered away when she used the title confirmed her suspicions. "You aren't the captain, are you?"

He narrowed his eyes at her. "Look, lady, we're running two days behind already. The captain doesn't have time for you."

"What if I told you I could get you to Yiroth in a day?" she asked, reasonably confident she could emulate what the two adepts had done for the ship she and Serivar had taken to Yiroth. Had that really been such a short time ago? It felt like weeks. Several long, exhausting weeks.

The man, probably the quartermaster, guffawed. "I'd say you were running light on cargo up top."

"Is it because I'm a woman?" Time closed in around

her, and she struggled not to let her impatience show. Eventually, someone would look for her here. It was too obvious an escape route. Then she noticed the smugness coming from him and realized she had guessed wrong. A quick ascard search of the captain's quarters gave her all the information she needed. "No. It isn't my gender, is it? It's my race. Your captain is pure-blooded Lyran, isn't he?"

The quartermaster's eyes darkened, and he took a menacing step toward her. "You'd best go find another ship before I toss you overboard."

She held up her hands in a show of surrender. "Very well. I'll go."

He gave a gruff nod, glancing back at the men loading cargo now that he considered the problem solved. She turned as if to walk away, but rather than head down the gangplank, she stopped the turn early and strode swiftly toward the captain's quarters. After a few seconds, she heard the quartermaster stomping after her, but she was well ahead and moving at a brisk walk. The annoyance rolling off him told her he didn't consider her much of a threat, which explained why he wasn't running to catch up.

"It's locked anyway, you fool of a woman," he called after her.

Of course, they would keep it locked here. She found the inner latch with a tendril of ascard and searched out the bolt. She was almost at the door when she slipped the bolt free. Pulling it open, she stepped inside to be greeted by the sound of steel sliding free of a leather sheath. She continued inside, stopping a few inches shy of the point of the blade. The pale Lyran captain glared a warning down the length of sharpened steel.

"Who are you?" he snarled.

She sensed the quartermaster stopping in the doorway behind her. Reaching up, she laid a finger against the flat of the blade and pushed it aside. As irritation and amusement battled across the captain's features, she walked past him into the cabin. She sensed the amusement winning out and heard the sword sliding back into its sheath while she pretended interest in the layout of his cabin.

"Go see to the cargo, Renth, I think I can handle this one." His Lyran accent added an exotic charm to his light tone, but the underlying hint of a more intimate interest warned her to be wary.

She glanced over her shoulder to see the quartermaster nod once and shut the door, leaving her and the captain alone. The captain turned and made a show of appraising her that bordered on outright rudeness, but she herself hadn't been overly polite thus far. Not willing to let him upset her composure, she returned the scrutiny, taking in the light blond hair, braided back out of the way, and pale blue eyes in a face that remained light of skin and barely lined despite many long hours at sea.

He cocked his head slightly, curiosity growing as they regarded one another. "By all appearances, I'd say you are a noblewoman, but if so, you look as though you've had a rough night. What do you want with me?"

"Captain...?"

"Murchadh," he replied, drawing a chair up and gesturing for her to sit.

She accepted the seat gratefully, her weariness cascading over her the moment she was off her feet. The desire to give in to misery and exhaustion was powerful, but she forced it aside and met his eyes. The night wasn't over yet.

"Captain Murchadh, I need to get to Yiroth."

"And why would I take you?" he asked, claiming another chair and placing his feet up on the one table in the room. The approval in his eyes suggested what form of payment he might accept.

Indigo ignored it. "I can get you across the Gilded Strait in a day," she stated, though she wasn't entirely certain her strength would hold out for such an effort.

"Using ascard?"

She nodded, relieved that his Lyran heritage made him more willing to accept such a possibility, and his need for haste sparked interest in his pale eyes.

"Can I ask you one question?"

"Certainly," she replied, wary of the sudden tension she felt in him.

"Do you keep slaves, my lady?"

The tension immediately made sense. "I am of noble blood, Captain Murchadh, but my family does not now, nor have they ever, kept Lyran slaves."

The captain looked skeptical, but she met his eyes with unfaltering poise, and he finally nodded. "I believe you. Who are you running from?"

She answered with a sly smile. "That is two questions, Captain. It seems to me it would make more sense to ask who I am not running from at this point, but regardless of how you phrase the question, I will not answer it."

The captain shrugged. "What's your name?"

"Indigo."

He searched her face, looking for more information. When she offered none, he nodded. "Welcome aboard my ship, Lady Indigo."

He sat up and offered his hand to shake on their bargain. Though it was not a gesture she was used to, it pleased her to be treated like a business associate rather than a lady under the circumstances, and she shook the offered hand firmly.

Murchadh chuckled. "It's almost a shame this will be such a quick trip. I suspect you have some interesting stories to tell."

"I may at that." She hoped desperately that she had the strength left to hold up her end of the bargain. If not, this could prove to be a grievous mistake.

He glanced at his bunk. "I don't suppose..."

She gave him a chiding look. "It will take considerable energy to speed the ship for our journey, Captain. I appreciate the offer, but I think it best to keep this relationship professional."

He shrugged, his sheepish grin stripping any threat from him. "Not every night a pretty noblewoman walks into my cabin. I had to try."

CHAPTER NINETEEN

Myac stared at the surrounding fire, paralyzed by memories.

It was late at night. He was thirteen—startled awake from a deep slumber. Sweating. Panicked. What woke him was the sound of screaming. Now that he was aware, he heard it all around him, along with the sound of fire, crackling and roaring like some enormous festival bonfire. He could feel the heat of the flames and, considering he was inside the two-room house he shared with his mother, it made his panic soar. He barely had time to look around when someone grabbed his arm with bruising force.

"Myac. Come with me."

It was his mother, dragging him from the bed, her eyes wide with fear. Flames licking up the wall of the house behind her created an eerie red glow around her face. Myac jumped up, grabbing the trousers he had discarded on the floor next to the bed. He hopped along after his mother as he pulled on one leg and then the other. To his dismay, she stopped at the door and motioned him to wait. Her hands trembled, sweat beading on them, the droplets gleaming like gems in the flickering firelight. She cracked the door less than an inch and peered out without exiting, despite the flames closing fast around them, hungry for every speck of fuel, be it wood or flesh. Her hesitation spiked his fear. He wanted to run from the ravenous blaze consuming their home, but he held his ground. He would be brave for her because she had kept him and loved him even though his father rejected him. When she opened the door further, he saw every building in the village suffering the same fate. The whole place was on fire.

His mother nodded and moved cautiously out into the open. No sooner had she cleared the doorway than a figure appeared beside her. Long silver hair and pale eyes reflected the firelight, giving him the look of a mythical night demon. He was dreadfully beautiful, a manifestation of the purest Lyran bloodlines. The blade he swung at Myac's mother dripped with blood.

"Mother!"

Her body crumpled to the ground, a lifeless doll, her head coming to rest at his feet. Myac looked from the head to the man standing before him. Those pale eyes overflowed with blind hatred, an insatiable bloodlust and madness that he couldn't hope to reason with. Myac stepped back, terrified. The man took a step toward him, then a deafening crack split the air and part of the building collapsed around Myac. He screamed and thrashed as his hair and clothing caught fire, struggling to free himself from the burning wreckage that had fallen on him.

Myac's own cry of remembered pain forced him back to the present. Flames were consuming everything around him, but the barrier he had put up against them still protected him. Terror-filled memories faded, an ache of loss lingering in their place, and confidence in his power resurfaced. Calm now, he stepped over the burning body of Indigo's dead fiancé. He walked to the door and hesitated before exiting, glancing around the room with a touch of remorse. He would have liked to search the place to see what he could learn about her, but it was too late now. Regardless, he would find her somehow and make her explain herself. Then he would probably kill her, but that decision could wait. He reached out with ascard as he exited the building and found nothing. If she were anywhere near, her masking was still too strong for him to find her.

You must be wearing down, my lady.

He refused to accept the possibility that her ascard strength might outlast his.

A sharp pain speared through the wound in his chest, almost dropping him to his knees. The healing he had done was insufficient. Like it or not, he needed to return to the academy and have a healer do a more thorough job. Indigo would have to wait, but he would find her. No matter what it took, he would find her, and she would answer for the pain she had caused him.

When he exited the building, a crowd was already gathering, mostly to gawk, though a few were moving buckets. Unless he missed his guess, there would be adepts on the scene before long to put the fire out, Ascard Watchmen perhaps with a few extra community protection skills. If they were too slow, Jayce would be unrecognizable. Sparing a little of the scant energy he had left, Myac reached back into the building and dampened down the fire near the body. Let them discover that Indigo had killed the young lord. Then they would hunt her with more fervor and increase the odds of locating her if she was still in the city. Unfortunately, he didn't think she was foolish enough to remain in Demin now.

With the gawkers' attention too absorbed by the fire to spare him a glance, he hurried from the area. It was tempting to go to Serivar's house and crawl into bed to rest. That need felt greater than any other. Exhaustion pulled at his consciousness, threatening to drag him down in the middle of the street. If he didn't receive attention for his injury, however, an injury that would have been fatal for almost anyone left to tend it alone, then the poor healing job he had done could lead to a permanent handicap. It might be too late already. If Indigo had left the blade in, he might not have been able to get it out and start the healing fast enough to survive the wound, though he suspected she had pulled it free hoping he might lose too much blood to save himself.

As furious as he was with her for attacking him, the encounter sparked a sense of satisfaction too. They weren't so different at all. She was beginning to see that. In her desperation, she might discover that she understood him more. Her situation would give her no easy outs, and he had no intention of helping her if the opportunity arose. The harder things were for her, the better chance he had of running her into a corner and bending her to his will.

As he staggered toward the Academy, the kiss lingered in his mind. It had been nothing more than deception on her part, but that somehow made it sweeter. Just more proof that they were creatures of a similar nature.

He made it to Serivar's office only to find it empty. Drawing on a little more ascard, he reached beyond the office into the hidden training room, not wanting to walk that far if he didn't have to. Serivar was there, so he closed the office door and went through the hidden hallway to the training room. When he entered, Serivar scowled at him.

"Where are the keystones?" he snapped, a slight tremor in his voice.

Myac took a few more steps before weakness made his head spin. Stumbling toward the table, he tried to catch himself on the chair next to it but knocked it away instead and landed painfully on one knee. Serivar's face twisted with alarm, and his focus changed. A querying sweep of ascard brushed up against Myac's weakening barriers. Dropping those barriers, he let Serivar inspect him, the headmaster easily tracking down the injury.

"By the Divine, what happened to you?" He came forward now and helped Myac stand. "You can heal better than that."

"I didn't have time to do it right. Can you fix it?"

Serivar's frown wasn't encouraging. "One of the master healers can improve on it, but I'm not sure how much. What happened?" he asked again.

"Indigo took the keystones. I tried to stop her without killing her." He wondered for an instant if he could have killed her but quickly dismissed the thought. "I got this for my trouble. She destroyed the keystones and fled."

"Where are Ferin and Emperor Yiloch?" An edge of panic raised Serivar's voice now.

Myac gave him a bitter glare as the headmaster helped him to a chair. "How should I know? She wasn't in physical contact with them when she destroyed the last stone. They could have ended up anywhere."

Once Myac was off his feet, Serivar sat on the table, the tremble in his hands betraying his panic. "Why would she do this? Doesn't she realize that she's making herself an accomplice in the king's murder? I don't know that I'll be able to get her out of this mess."

Myac shook his head and instantly regretted it when his vision blurred. He waited for a surge of nausea to pass before trying to speak. "I don't understand why she did it. She's *your* pet project. Perhaps you should have made sure you had her loyalty before you turned her into a weapon."

"You are not laying the onus on me for this," Serivar snapped.

"Of course not. I'd never dream of blaming the idiot responsible," Myac snarled.

Serivar's eyes pinched, his expression turning cold. Myac wondered briefly if the other man might retaliate against him while he was weak or simply abandon him to his injuries, leaving him permanently handicapped. Then the moment passed, and Serivar looked away.

Weak bastard.

"About that master healer," Myac prompted.

Serivar's lip curled with distaste as he helped Myac to his feet again. They walked from the room, Myac gladly taking advantage of Serivar's offered assistance. He hated feeling this frail, but he wasn't too proud to accept the aid when he needed it. Letting his condition get any worse would only give Indigo more advantages.

"What next?" he asked, hoping Serivar would have insight into where Indigo might have gone.

"We talk to Caplin. He was with her in Lyra. He might have information that could help us understand her reckless behavior."

"He didn't tell you anything the last time you spoke with him."

Serivar opened the office door and let Myac continue leaning on him going down the hall. "Under the circumstances, I think he will be more forthcoming. Especially when he realizes the danger she has put herself in."

Myac nodded. If Caplin and Indigo were truly close friends, the new prince wouldn't want her getting hurt. He would be more apt to share any secrets he was keeping if he understood how much danger she was in. "You might be right. After some healing and rest, we should speak with him."

"Is everything okay?"

Myac glanced up to see a young woman in healer's robes stop in the hall ahead of them. Her eyes widened at the blood on his shirt.

"Go to the east building and tell one of the master healers that we are coming. Edan will need some very complex healing." When she hesitated, her ascard brushing up against Myac's poorly rebuilt barriers to assess his condition, Serivar scowled at her. "Now," he snapped.

Her ascard pulled away, and she ran down the hall toward the exit.

When they reached the east building, another low-level healer met them and led them to a private room where the master healer was waiting. She was a middle-aged woman, with deep lines developing at the corners of her dark eyes. A hasty ascard investigation reassured Myac that, while her healing skill was considerable, she didn't have the ability necessary to root out his disguise. The illusion needed rebuilding. It wasn't as flawless as it had been before he let Indigo see through it, but it was adequate to fool most people.

He let her ascard pass through and felt it focus in on the poorly healed wound. Her only reaction to the nearly lethal injury was the pressing of her lips into a tight line. Rising from the chair she had been sitting in, she ushered him to the bed. Once he was lying down, she sat beside him and placed a hand on his chest, her eyes losing their focus as she thoroughly inspected the injury.

"You are lucky to be alive," she said finally. "Who did the initial healing?"

"I did." He could hear the weakness in his own voice as he struggled to stay conscious. Lying down made that even more challenging.

"Remarkably well done. It could not have been easy to heal yourself while in that much pain." Her smile was full of sympathy and admiration. "You saved your own life, but under unfavorable circumstances. If I undo too much of what you have done, it could kill you. I will clean up what I can without putting you at risk. You are going to have some pain there for a long time. Possibly for the rest of your life, which won't be long if you have any more incidents like this one."

Myac grimaced. The wound would be a constant reminder then. Perhaps that was best. He would be less apt to underestimate her the next time they met. "Do it," he snapped, annoyed at how feeble his voice sounded.

He met Serivar's emotionless gaze, wishing he had the strength to read the other man's emotions right then. The healer's hand rested on his forehead. Before he could protest, he felt her ability knock down the last bit of resolve that was keeping him awake, and he succumbed to a deep sedation.

CHAPTER TWENTY

Yiloch's knees struck sand again, only this was hot, dry sand, not the wet, cool sand of the prison beach. Looking around while he tried to catch his breath from the transition, he saw nothing but open desert, baking in the bright sun as far as the eye could see. A few feet away, he spotted Ferin on his hands and knees, gasping for air. The other man had been through two abrupt transitions back-to-back and appeared to be having a more difficult time recovering.

Yiloch got to his feet, the blazing sun becoming a significant concern as breathing got easier. They needed to get moving now if they were going to figure out where they were and hopefully find civilization. Walking over to his adept Captain, Yiloch offered a hand, holding it by the man's face so he would see it. Ferin waved him away and sat back on his heels. Staring at his hands, he brushed them together to clear away the sand, then looked up at Yiloch, squinting in the bright sunlight. There was a gray cast to his skin, and his eyelids were puffy and red from the recent passage of many tears.

"I guess it's good to see you, my lord."

Since he seemed in no hurry to stand, Yiloch knelt before him and placed a hand on his shoulder. "What's happened, Ferin?"

Ferin met his eyes, and then he looked back down at his hands and sighed, brushing at more sand. "Someone assassinated King Jerrin, and his wife and son. They arrested Galyn, Kade, Sine, and me as suspects before the bodies had time to get cold. Somehow they forced all three of the others to sign confessions admitting their parts in the assassinations and stating that the orders came from you. After that, they put them to death."

Ferin looked at Yiloch then, his eyes brimming with liquid misery. Yiloch cringed inwardly. Galyn had meant everything to Ferin. Her execution explained the depth of his sorrow.

"I'm sorry, Ferin." And he was, but he couldn't allow time for grief when their situation was so precarious and so many questions still needed answers. "Why would they have confessed?"

"Caithin has many adepts in their employ. I can only assume they have someone who specializes in mental manipulation who convinced them of their guilt. Sine was the last to give in. Since she dabbled in that skill herself, she would have been harder to manipulate."

Yiloch regarded him with some surprise. Ferin had never mentioned working with mental manipulation himself, but if one of his students had, that implied that he had as well. An unusual secret to keep from one's emperor. "And you?"

Ferin shrugged. "It is one of many skills I developed further before I decided to expand my focus on a greater variety to train others. That, in combination with the protections I put up as a precaution while in Demin, was apparently enough to thwart them. I believe they were about ready to settle for sentencing me on grounds of association."

Yiloch sat in the sand beside his captain and put considerable effort into keeping his rage at a distance so he could study the situation rationally. Molten fury boiled in the background, but their current predicament called for a clear head.

Ferin stood, finally recovered from the two transitions, and walked a few feet away, bending over to pick something up from the sand. "This is the ring you always wear, isn't it, the one you got from Indigo?" He held up the chain so the ring with its large blue center stone dangled before Yiloch, glinting brightly in the extreme sunlight.

Yiloch's composure snapped, and he sneered at the item. "Yes. Indigo, the shameless liar who put me in that prison. I have no need of it."

Ferin's hand sank to his side, the chain dangling from loose fingers. "Indigo? But why would she have done that? She was so ecstatic when I gave her your ring. Bursting with joy, I would say. I can't imagine her ever doing anything to hurt you."

"She is an exceptional performer, it would seem."

Ferin slid the ring and chain into a pocket despite Yiloch's warning glare. "There must be another explanation. She would not have done this to you."

"Suac Chozai said I would be betrayed three times: by ally, by family, and by love. It appears I have been betrayed by ally and by love in one grand strike. She knew what she was doing."

As he spoke, the anguish of her betrayal struck him

like a hammer blow, and he struggled to hide that pain from Ferin. He needed to be a leader now. Ferin's sympathetic gaze showed him how successful that effort wasn't. Jumping to his feet, he stared out into the desert, pretending to contemplate the way forward while he composed himself.

"There must be more to it. She set us free, didn't she? That is how it appeared to me."

"Set us free?" Yiloch let out a bitter laugh. "We don't even know where we are. This could be another prison."

"I don't think so, my lord." Ferin's tone turned wary as he focused past Yiloch.

Yiloch followed his gaze, spotting figures in the distance. There were three people on foot, leading some lean, long-legged pack animals. Dark faces peered out at them from under pale hoods designed to shield from the sun and still be cool. He recognized the animals as well. They were tall, leggy beasts with long necks, small, flat heads, and broad feet suited to the sandy terrain. The Kudaness called them skek.

He shook his head in disbelief. "We're in southern Kudan," he murmured.

"So it would seem," Ferin replied.

If they were in Kudan, then they were somewhere in the long, narrow stretch of inhospitable sand flats that cut through the region in the lower, southern half. The appearance of the trio of Kudaness was comforting, in that it suggested that they were probably close to an edge of the sand flats. If they had any luck at all, it would be the northern edge. He could almost make out the details of the patterns on their clothes that would tell him their tribe and how friendly, or not, they were going to be toward Lyran people. Rather than wait, he took hold of ascard as a precaution and started toward them. Ferin fell into step, flanking him on the right out of habit, and Yiloch could feel him working ascard as well.

The two walking ahead were an older man and a youth, both tattooed with the mark of the warrior under their right eye and the mark of their tribe on their left cheek. Behind them was an older woman with the tribal mark tattooed on her forehead, the tattoo pattern of the Denilik tribe. They were one of the less aggressive tribes, which might be beneficial in one way, but Denilik was on the far southeastern edge of Kudan, almost as far as they could get from Yiroth on the known continent.

The trio stopped several yards away and let Yiloch and Ferin close the remaining distance, watching them with more curiosity than concern.

"Ilikah smile on you," Yiloch said, offering a traditional greeting in Kudaness, and hoping the dialect he had chosen would be close enough to what they spoke.

The woman cocked her head, regarding him with open curiosity, while the young man looked at first surprised by his greeting, then suspicious, his grip on his spear tightening. The elder man, his narrow face heavily lined with age and sun exposure, offered a reserved smile, though his hand lingered near the wide knife at his waist. He considered them for a minute or more, then handed the lead for his skek to the youth and walked closer. Despite being of a small stature that required him to look up at Yiloch, the man exuded confidence and amusement.

"Did Ilikah drop you?" he asked with a broad grin.

Yiloch couldn't stop an answering smile. Given his choice of greeting, it made a kind of sense that the man would think the sky-traveling god of the Kudaness had deposited them here. How else did two well-dressed, poorly equipped Lyran men end up in the middle of the desert on the southeastern edge of Kudan?

"It is certainly possible," he replied. "Regardless of how we got here, we would like to make our way back to Lyra. Can you point us in the right direction?"

The man laughed then, a long, hearty laugh that doubled him over, holding his gut. The youth watched with a disapproving frown. The woman looked away, an amused smile tugging at her lips. Yiloch waited, forcing himself to be patient, though recent events had shortened his temper. When the man regained control of himself, he looked over his shoulder at the woman and quickly rattled off something in a dialect distinct enough from those Yiloch knew that he had trouble following. The woman began digging in the packs on her skek and he turned back to them.

"There must be a mighty need in your spirits for you to be presented with such a journey," he said to them. "The gods will provide for the needs of your spirit, but you will need sustenance for your bodies. We will give you what we can spare and point you to where you go."

The man walked back to help the woman. Uncertain how to respond, Yiloch waited in curious silence, noting Ferin's deliberately neutral expression. This wasn't an expected response, even from a traditionally impartial tribe, but then, he knew little of the southern Kudaness beyond the fact that they were smaller in stature than their northern brethren and not as quick to violence. The younger man continued to scowl at them until the elder scolded him for his rudeness. Then he turned to studying his hands, the sand, the skek, anything to avoid looking at Yiloch and Ferin. The woman folded all the items they had gathered into a light robe, and the man carried it back to where they waited.

"You will head that way for many days," He man pointed behind them as he offered the bundle to Yiloch. "Be watchful. A violent storm comes from the east, beyond Kudan and the Rhuakine."

Yiloch accepted the bundle, a chill touching him as he remembered Suac Chozai's warning. "A storm?"

The man nodded, solemn and certain. "A storm of death, bristling with bladed spears and profane power."

A fresh sense of urgency pressed him to get moving. The prophecy Suac Chozai brought him was no longer something he could bring himself to scoff at. "How can we repay you?"

"I am Korik of Denilik. It is my honor to assist a wandering soul upon their spirit journey. If you must repay me, I ask only this: when the Gods are near, speak of me favorably to them."

Yiloch hoped no Kudaness Gods would come that close, but he nodded his agreement, offering a respectful bow to the small man. "I will do so."

"It is dangerous to delay a spirit journey." Korik shooed them on with his hands. "May Ilikah watch over you both."

"And you," Yiloch replied, as eager to be moving on as the man was to see them moving.

Korik was already rejoining his family, so Yiloch turned, giving a slight nod to Ferin to show that they should get going. Slinging the bundle over his shoulder, he started walking in the indicated direction.

"I should carry that." Ferin reached toward the bundle.

Yiloch sidestepped away from his hand. "Why?"

"You are the emperor."

He managed a dry chuckle, though there was only cynical humor left in him. "Out here, I don't think that matters much."

"It is a long walk."

He laughed again at the understatement. He had to laugh because the other tempting options, such as screaming his frustration, would serve little purpose. "I'll let you carry it later if you insist."

"We have no weapons," Ferin commented.

Yiloch nodded. He wanted for his sword as most men would want for water in this inhospitable place. He had focused most of his ascard ability on skills that enhanced his fighting techniques. Without a sword, many of those skills served little purpose. Ferin had a stronger ascard connection, though he spread it thinly across a wide variety of skills. He would have some defenses at least because of that and would no doubt need them in time. Not all tribes were as easygoing as the Denilik. They also had the added concern of whatever threat was coming across the Rhuakine. Given recent events, he couldn't help beginning to believe in the suac's prophecy.

As they walked, he lamented the absence of both his

sword and Indigo's ring. For a short time, he considered asking Ferin for the ring back so he could ease one of those aches, but he couldn't forgive what she had done. Whatever her reasons, she knew how deeply he resented his first captivity. She had spent the last few days of a miserable seven-month stay in that first prison with him. Knowing what he had gone through before and professing to love him as she did, how could she have played any part in imprisoning him again? Did she really believe he had something to do with the death of her king? After everything they had gone through together, how could she doubt him?

He struggled to push aside those thoughts. Dwelling on heartache and anger wouldn't help him get back to Lyra any faster. Turning his attention to the barren miles ahead of them, he noticed then that he no longer felt the heat of the sun on his face and glanced over at Ferin in question.

"We won't burn or overheat this way," the adept answered.

"How long can you maintain it?"

Ferin shrugged. "It isn't a significant drain on my ability, though I could maintain it far longer if I didn't have to waste so much energy walking in this wretched sand."

Yiloch nodded his sympathy. They needed to find mounts, both for the ability to travel faster and for the conservation of their own energy. There were few horses in Kudan. Many of the tribes didn't keep the animals because they used up precious resources needed to maintain other livestock. The hardy skek could survive with little food and water but were ill-suited to carrying a man's weight. If they found a village with horses, bartering for them would require more than they had to offer in trade.

He scanned the barren horizon. Sand stretched on for miles, nothing but sand. This was a miserable place to end up.

CHAPTER TWENTY-ONE

Indigo leaned on the doorjamb, closing her eyes to the late afternoon sunshine. Captain Murchadh had offered her the use of his cabin for the duration of the trip, leaving her undisturbed to do her work. As promised, she brought them to the port in the Lyran capital of Yiroth in a day. It took less than a day, in truth. Adding that effort to everything else she had done in the last twenty-four hours, she had no reserves left. If Myac appeared now, she would be helpless to fight him.

A hand rested on her shoulder, and she forced her eyes open again, surprised to see Murchadh eyeing her with concern. She smiled, wearily amused that the ship's captain should care so much about the well-being of a woman he had only just met.

"Are you all right, Lady Indigo? You could take a rest on the cot in my cabin while we unload."

She shook her head, and the resulting dizziness made her wary of doing so again. "I'll be fine."

"I have seen ships moved across the Strait this way before, but never by a single adept and with such speed. My crew and I are very much in your debt. You saved me considerable cost by getting my cargo here on time. If there is anything at all I can do..." he trailed off, making it an open offer.

It took far more effort than she was willing to let him see to stand up straight. "Thank you, but I must be moving on now. If anyone asks..."

His sly, conspiratorial grin and wink were even more reassuring than his words. "I never saw you."

She gave him a sincere smile. "Thank you, Captain."

It was a struggle to walk down the gangplank with the constant movement of the water below threatening to unbalance her. She still maintained her masking and other barriers, though without the supplemental power in the ring, those would have failed by now as well. Too much energy expended through ascard use, stress, and long hours of wakefulness was taking its toll.

With a deep breath, she started down the street, determined to make it far enough to at least barter for a carriage to the palace. She wanted to reach out and see if Yiloch he might be there, but she could no longer spare that kind of energy. She made it to the buildings facing the docks before having to stop and lean against one to rest. After all she had been through, it wouldn't do to pass out in the street to be robbed or worse, but that was starting to feel like a strong possibility.

"Lady Indigo?"

The deep voice was uplifting in its familiarity. There was hope after all.

"Cadmar." She breathed his name in disbelief and turned in the direction the call had come from. When her body stopped turning, her head continued to spin, and she spotted the dark-skinned warrior approaching only seconds before falling into blackness.

***

** * **

"Lady Indigo?"

The deep voice made her head throb. An involuntary moan escaped her lips, and someone close by chuckled, the sound provoking an agonizing spike in her headache.

"I told you she would wake soon. She's a strong woman."

"Cadmar?"

She kept her voice low so as not to aggravate her own head. There was little question regarding why she suffered that pain. She had overused her ascard ability by a fair sum. The distressing part was that she didn't yet have the energy to heal the headache. Opening her eyes a fraction, she found herself in a dimly lit room and dared to open them the rest of the way. The elegant furnishings were enough to tell her she was in the palace, so she had gotten that far at least.

Cadmar sat on the edge of the bed, pale green eyes lit with gentle affection and a spark of amusement. Beyond him, Adran stood scowling at her, arms crossed and eyes narrowed with stabbing resentment.

She drew a light breath and pushed herself up into a sitting position.

"Where is he?" Adran demanded.

She winced, both from his volume and from the underlying anguish that rolled out from him. He loved Yiloch as much as she did, perhaps more, given their long history. She closed off her ability, unable to bear that pain on top of her own.

"Easy, Adran, it's clear she's been through a lot." That voice was also familiar.

"Ian." His name came out as a pleased sigh.

The pleasure was fleeting, crushed by guilt and misery. Even after seeing her take Yiloch away from them, the young creator still spoke up in defense of her condition. Did she deserve such consideration from him?

She let her face fall into her hands, trying to fight back the threatening tears. Despite her efforts, exhaustion left her too weak to resist, and they spilled forth. Her shoulders shook with sobs she couldn't control.

"Look what you have done now," Cadmar chastised. He moved closer and put an arm around her, pulling her against him.

"She deserves it," Adran snapped.

She agreed with him, but she couldn't control herself well enough to say as much. The night had nearly cost her life, and she'd taken someone else's life in the process. A despicable life, yes, but she had loved Jayce once, before she found out what he was like behind that charming facade. Now Yiloch and Ferin were missing. Myac was still out there somewhere, seeking revenge against Yiloch and against her for trying to kill him twice, which was a sensible enough reason to want her dead now that she thought about it. And here she was, a sniffling, hopeless mess.

She sank against the iron wall of Cadmar's muscle-bound chest and gave in to anguish and exhaustion. The crying worsened her headache, but at least that made letting the dark warrior hold and comfort her feel like a little less of an undeserved indulgence.

"Honestly, Adran," Ian murmured, his voice now coming from over near the other man. "We should hear her side of this before we judge. Why would she come here if she were seeking to harm Yiloch?"

"Has harmed," Adran amended.

She regained control of herself and pushed away from Cadmar. With a sour look, Adran tossed her a handkerchief to wipe away her tears. She thanked him and murmured thanks to Cadmar as well, but before she could say anything else, the door swung open and Hax stormed in. Her gaze locked on Indigo, her face twisting in a feral mask of fury that made Indigo's blood go cold.

"You," she hissed.

Her hand dropped to her sword hilt, and she started forward. Cadmar snapped to his feet and stepped into her path. If his intervention surprised Indigo, it shocked Hax even more. She stepped back from him, hurt and confusion rising in her eyes. Indigo felt a pang of sympathy for the other woman. She didn't know the full extent of the relationship between the two, but she had noticed a strong bond of some kind there the first time she saw them together.

Indigo stood, keeping one leg pressed against the bed for stability. All eyes turned to her, as she had intended, not quite diffusing the situation, but at least distracting Hax. "Yiloch hasn't returned here then?"

The deepening scowl from Adran provided a sufficient answer.

"Someone assassinated King Jerrin, his son, and his wife ..." she trailed off at Adran's look of impatience.

"That news spread up from the docks this morning," Ian offered. "Besides, we already knew that much from the missive you left behind."

Missive? Another piece of the plan they hadn't bothered to let her in on.

"But Emperor Yiloch had no part in their deaths," Adran stated, his voice as tense as his posture.

She nodded, though the movement made her headache flare again. If Yiloch had been planning to assassinate the Caithin king, Adran would have known about it. His conviction was comforting. "I know that now. When I agreed to come here with Serivar, it was with the understanding that we would present Yiloch with a demand to stand trial in defense of his adepts. If I had known that Serivar was carrying a keystone to a Serroc prison with the intent of transporting him there, I would never have gone along with it."

Adran and Hax looked skeptical, but Ian nodded as though he had expected as much. Cadmar watched, now standing next to Hax, though he kept giving the other woman wary looks as if still expecting some backlash for his defense of Indigo.

"What about Ferin and the three adepts he took with him?" Ian asked.

"Ferin should be wherever Yiloch is—"

"And where is that?" Hax interrupted.

"I'll explain in a moment. Somehow, they got the other three adepts to confess to the crime and implicate Yiloch. They have already put them to death."

Indigo winced and pressed a hand to her head at Hax's cry of outrage. The others held their anger in silence, but the drawn faces and stiff postures were enough to tell her they were no less upset, and she was suddenly quite glad that she had closed off her ability to sense emotion.

"What of Ferin and Yiloch?" Ian asked.

The lanky youth would no longer meet her eyes, and she swallowed against a tightening in her throat that made it hard to continue.

"I stole the keystones for the prisons and destroyed one inside the other to bring them together. I intended to take them both out with me, but Myac followed me." She held up one hand to forestall interruptions promised by the widening of eyes and parting of lips. "Yes, Myac is in Demin. If he hadn't been so well disguised, I would have known something was amiss long before any of this happened. I would have brought Ferin and Yiloch out of the prison with me, but I knew Myac would try to harm them, so I grabbed Myac and destroyed the other keystone to set them free. Unfortunately—"

Ian jumped in, his eyes lighting up with understanding. "You had no way to control where they ended up."

"So you're saying that they are no longer imprisoned, but we don't know where they are," Adran summarized, a knife-edge to his tone.

"Exactly," Ian answered for her. "The Serroc prisons exist outside the laws of normal reality. Without some kind of keystone, they aren't bound to any one location in this reality."

A wave of dizziness unbalanced Indigo, and she sank heavily back down on the bed. Hax pulled up a chair and also sat, the fury that twisted her features fading to a mask of weariness. The idea seemed to catch on. As Ian and Adran both pulled up chairs, Cadmar returned to his place on the edge of the bed. Looking around at them, she noted the hopelessness in their faces, and her own heart sank. She had theorized that the prison might send Yiloch back where they had taken him from, like the last one had, but the new prisons didn't have the gateway that created an anchor between it and the prisoner's point of origin. Failing that unlikely possibility, she had hoped one of them would at least have some idea how to find him.

Cadmar shifted, clearing his throat. "I have news from the southern Lyran border." When all eyes were on him, he continued. "The Murak were behind the raids Yiloch sent me to investigate, but they ceased without my intervention. They say they are now preparing for an invading army coming from across the Rhuakine toward the eastern border of Kudan."

Ian's eyes lit up. "That's it!"

"What?" Adran asked, the flicker of hope in his pale eyes sparked the same in Indigo.

"Suac Chozai foresaw all of this. Perhaps he could tell us where Yiloch and Ferin ended up."

She stared at him, puzzled. The term suac sounded distantly familiar, like the name of a remote relative. Hax snorted derisively, but Adran looked thoughtful. He stood and started pacing the room, keeping to the far side away from Indigo. She rubbed her temples and tried not to watch him. Exhaustion still pulled at her, but she couldn't afford to give into it yet.

"It's possible. He foresaw the army from across the

Rhuakine... and Indigo's betrayal," Adran added with an accusing glare in her direction, and she shifted back as if it might help her escape the daggers in his eyes. "But would he even help us after Yiloch turned him away?"

"There's also a possibility that Yiloch isn't that far away. He might return before you even reached the suac," Cadmar suggested. "Or he could have ended up in the ocean."

Ignoring that second part, Indigo asked, "Who's the suac?"

Ian turned to her. He looked more cheerful and enthusiastic despite the potential difficulties Adran and Cadmar suggested. Reacting to his optimism, she felt the glimmer of hope take hold and start to grow, warming her.

"Suac Chozai is a Kudaness high priest. He came to Yiloch seeking his aid and warned him he would be betrayed three times: by ally, by family, and by love. Yiloch turned him away, which I can't blame him for," Ian added in hasty defense of his leader. "The man was rude and arrogant, and he had no proof of his claims. No matter what else he was, though, it appears he was also right. If he foresaw these things, it seems to follow that he might know where Yiloch ended up."

"Ian." Indigo waited until he met her eyes. "You're a creator. How much do you know about the Serroc prisons? Is there any limit to where Yiloch and Ferin might have gone?"

With a pained expression, he shook his head. "I know some of the theory behind them, but they're still very new constructs, so most of that knowledge is hypothetical based on what little we understand about them. To the best of my knowledge, nobody has destroyed a keystone while someone was in the connected prison before."

"They could be dead for all we know," Hax snapped.

A cutting look from Adran silenced her. He was clearly no more ready to humor that possibility than Indigo was. If the situation were different, she might have given him a grateful look. As it was, such a gesture would just turn his attention and anger back to her, so she avoided his eyes.

"When I destroyed the keystone for Ferin's prison, it brought him into Yiloch's prison with me and, since destroying the other stone while Myac and I were still inside didn't kill us, I don't think it would have hurt them either." Her burned palm throbbed with the memory of that terrifying moment. "I think this Suac Chozai may be our best option. Our only option," she amended, trying to keep the hopelessness that came with that statement from her voice.

Ian nodded, resolute. "You need some rest before we head out."

Adran threw up his hand. "Hold on. We haven't discussed who is to go on this insane venture."

"Well, obviously you can't go," Hax stated. "Someone needs to supervise Lord Terral in Yiloch's absence. We can't just hand him the reins and let him run free. I don't believe you trust him any more than I do, and there is still that betrayal by family the suac warned of. You are the most qualified for keeping him out of trouble."

Adran shifted from one foot to the other, clenching

his jaw as he struggled with several responses he must have felt were inappropriate. It was obvious he wanted to argue the point. Indigo could understand his conflict, given how much he loved Yiloch, but Hax was right, especially if Lord Terral was the acting authority in Yiloch's absence. The man had always made her uneasy.

"I can't go," Hax added when all the arguments finally died unspoken on Adran's lips. "I'm commander of his army. My responsibility is to keep that army in working order. It's hard to let Ian go, but we do have many other creators and adepts here. None as powerful, but that power might be more useful to Yiloch right now, wherever he is." Her frosty gaze fell on Indigo then. "Indigo should also go. She owes Emperor Yiloch at least that much."

"I'm not letting the two of them do this alone. We can't send a Lyran creator and a Caithin woman into Kudan by themselves. They need someone who knows the Kudaness. Someone like Cadmar," Adran nodded to the dark warrior, and Hax's expression soured.

Cadmar stood and walked over to Hax, taking her hand with a deeply intimate tenderness. "Come walk with me," he entreated.

Hax nodded and let Cadmar lead her from the room. The others watched them go, staying silent until Cadmar closed the door behind them. Ian walked over and placed a hand on Indigo's shoulder, still looking at the closed door.

"Cadmar will take care of her. We have no healers to help you, so you'll have to rest and take care of yourself, I'm afraid."

She nodded.

Ian started toward the door. "I'll get things organized so we can leave as soon as you're ready."

"Thank you," she murmured. "Adran," she started as the other man headed toward the door.

He stopped, refusing to look at her when he spoke. "Find Yiloch. Bring him back here safely. Then maybe I will forgive what you have done."

"Yes."

When they were gone, she lay back on the bed. With the extent of her exhaustion, merciful sleep came quickly.

* * *

"I think you were unfairly harsh with her," Ian commented when they were several doorways down the hall from the room where Indigo was resting.

Adran glared at the creator. "Do you?" he asked, letting his sharp tone convey how little he cared.

"Yes. If she's been dealing with Myac, she can't have had an easy time. He's the only other adept I've come across with a connection as strong as hers is. He almost killed her once, as you may recall."

Adran sighed. Perhaps Ian had a point. Myac was cruel and clever, not to mention alarmingly powerful. He had little doubt that the creator with his strange black hair and eyes was behind the assassination of the king and his family. If he was in Demin, he was there for a reason, and this chaos was making everyone involved in the overthrowing of Emperor Rylan suffer. The problem that remained was figuring out how to prove Myac's guilt and thereby prove Yiloch's innocence, assuming they found him. It was a considerable problem, and not one he looked forward to tackling. Indigo might have information that could help them. If only they could get Yiloch and Ferin back quickly. It had taken substantial effort to keep everyone working together during Yiloch's former absence. It would take a lot more now that they were missing an emperor rather than just an exiled prince.

"Maybe you're right," Adran admitted.

"She loves him," Ian stated with certainty. "She made a mistake, and she regrets it. I don't think you could do anything to punish her as much as she will punish herself with the guilt she feels."

Adran had seen the anguish in her deep blue eyes. He even felt a touch guilty for the satisfaction it brought him.

"When did you get so insightful?" He rested a hand on his cousin's shoulder and squeezed. Ian grinned, the awkward expression reminding Adran how young the skilled creator still was. "Be careful out there."

"Don't worry, Cousin, I'll have Indigo and Cadmar to protect me."

"They had better do so," Adran replied, stifling any further derogatory comments toward Indigo. Despite what she had done, he knew Ian was right about one thing. She loved Yiloch, and it was Yiloch's love for her that drove some of his anger. Nothing noble. Just pure jealousy. If anyone could bring him back safely, it was Indigo, and he didn't doubt that she wanted to. To get Yiloch back, he could live with a little jealousy.

CHAPTER TWENTY-TWO

The sun crept over the horizon, spreading its scalding light upon the canyon-scarred lands of the Rhuakine. The extreme depths of the canyons remained buried in shadow, defying the bright light. Undaunted, it continued to reach westward, toward the eastern edge of Kudan. In some regions, this crisp morning light was the harbinger of day. For the Kudaness, the day started long before the light came. When the first light kissed the northernmost village of the Denilik, it found the dark-skinned inhabitants already busy with routine chores tending to scant crops and livestock, mending clothes, preparing meals, gathering water from a river that reduced to little more than a trickle in the heart of the dry season—anything to make life in the desert possible. They worked with single-minded intensity to finish their tasks before the full heat of the day settled in.

The day that dawned was clear and bright, but thunder rolled in the early hours, bearing down on the village. The rumble gave some warning, but it wasn't enough. Denilik warriors sprinted through the village, retrieving weapons and racing for the eastern border. The rumble preceded its source by several minutes, growing in volume and shaking the ground. It also shook the confidence of those waiting.

Then the horizon darkened with the mass of charging horseflesh. The horses were dark, compact, and muscular, like the men who rode them. The eyes of the men were dark and determined as they leaned low over their horses' necks, short-bladed spears held ready at their sides.

Denilik warriors faced the approaching horde. They had no choice but to defend that which they had spent their whole lives building. Elders and children retreated to their huts. They had nowhere else to go on such short notice. With the villages of the Kudaness tribes widely separated as they were, there was no running to find help or sanctuary. The dark-skinned Kudaness moved into fighting stances, ready to cripple the mounts or take down their riders, whatever opportunity provided. Most carried the wide, curved blades favored by the Kudaness warriors, but the front line carried long spears that could more effectively bring down a horse. Weapons they hadn't needed to use against outsiders in generations.

The horsemen showed no sign of slowing as they rushed the waiting line. Other than the pounding of hooves, they came on in silence. The Denilik warriors let out a battle cry to bolster their courage, and the dark riders leaned forward, pushing into their stirrups to brace for the attack. As the front line of riders reached them, the Kudaness attacked with spear and sword, only to have their weapons knocked aside by some unseen force. The mounted warriors swung their bladed spears, and cries of pain rose into the air as the weapons bit deep into flesh.

The riders continued forward, cutting down any man, woman, or child who got in their path. When all the defenders lay dead in the sun and the compact horses crowded the village, the riders dismounted and entered the huts. They killed the elderly and children with callous efficiency, adding to the blood that already ran thick on their blades. Within minutes of their arrival, the screaming stopped, and silence fell. The riders searched every hut, gathering food and supplies, and regrouped in the center of the village. Here they took time to clean the swept blades of their spears and wipe blood from their faces.

When the last of the army gathered around the village, there were no Denilik left alive to slick their blades with blood. In the center of the village, a single mounted warrior watched while several others divided and packed pillaged supplies. His small eyes, almost black, observed the activity with satisfaction, not from greed so much as vindicated ambition. Like the men who surrounded him, he was stocky and strong with olive skin and nearly black hair. The armor he wore was a lightweight hide with thin plates of red hardwood woven in layers over the chest, back, and thighs.

This man, like the others in all but the air of authority that surrounded him, leapt up on his mount with the ease of a cat. His dark eyes swept the area once more, noting that his army was prepared to move on. The day was young and the sun's heat not yet too intense. They would continue, leaving the silent dead in their wake. With a single command, he gathered the storm and continued north.

* * *

Ferin could extend his ascard ability to find a village, but the walk across endless, sunbaked sand flats after a chilly night took them well into midday before the terrain began changing and they saw the group of huts upon the horizon. Here, at least, there were signs of life. Sand, now mixed with rounded pebbles and occasional plant life, most of it small, spindly shrubs sporting fierce thorns, became increasingly prevalent. His sharp eye also caught movement now and again—ants and other insects, a rare scorpion or lizard. The heat of the day could still be deadly, but the presence of other life made it somewhat less intimidating.

The village was Denilik, so they were still in that tribe's territory, and the villagers received them with more curiosity than suspicion, though they sent most of their women and the younger children into the small huts, away from the potential corruption of the Lyran strangers. Several of the warriors gathered around them, standing guard while an elder spoke for the tribe. Yiloch's announcement that they were heading to Lyra was met with much laughter and so many overlapping remarks that Yiloch didn't bother trying to catch them all.

"Is there a village nearby with horses?" he asked when their initial merriment and flurry of comments had ebbed.

The elder shushed the chatter of the others and raised one wrinkled, leathery hand to point north.

"Some villages further north keep horses," he said. "They will not let you take them, but you can look upon them." He added the last with a grin, amused by his own cleverness.

Yiloch responded with a tight smile. "We shall see. Ilikah watch over you all," he added with a slight nod, trying to remain respectful despite an urge to knock the elder's smile from his lips with a well-deserved punch. These people weren't going to help, so there was little point in lingering.

"And you, travelers," the man returned politely enough.

The villagers watched them for a time as they resumed their journey, women and children venturing out to gawk before they all returned to their daily tasks. Yiloch glanced at Ferin, grateful to have a man of his skills along as the sun blazed down upon them without making much impression.

"Can you sense the next village yet?"

Ferin shook his head. "Not yet, but I'll keep trying."

"How is your energy holding up?"

Ferin smiled, weariness leveling the curve of his lips into more of a pained line. "I'll manage, my lord."

When the last village was no longer visible behind them, Yiloch stopped them and drew out the water skin and some food from the bundle Korik had given them.

"We should keep moving," Ferin said, though he accepted the water skin and then the food with a nod of appreciation.

Yiloch chuckled. "We will, but you can't maintain this level of exertion without sustenance."

Ferin said nothing, focusing instead on chewing his scant ration. When Yiloch felt the other man had enough to keep him going for a while, he started repacking the bundle.

"Do you want me to carry that for a time?" Ferin reached for the bundle.

Yiloch smirked, shaking his head, and threw it over his shoulder. Without a word, he started walking. After a few strides, Ferin appeared at his side, eyes distant, attention focused on protecting them from the burning sun and searching for the next village. While he found the offer to carry the sack amusing, it also worried him that his companion's fatigue was bad enough for him not to realize how ludicrous the idea was. At the next village, he would try to get the use of shelter so Ferin could rest without having to maintain their protection from the blazing sunlight.

As the sun began its slow descent toward the western horizon, Yiloch spotted what appeared to be another village on the distant horizon. Just as he was about to ask Ferin if he sensed anything, he spotted a wide swath of ground leading into the village churned like a storm-tossed sea, as though trampled by thousands of hooves.

He altered his course toward the disturbed terrain. "Ferin."

The other man stumbled to a stop and turned toward him with an expression of mild surprise, as if he hadn't noticed he was walking alone. Yiloch squatted down to examine the sand.

The other man joined him. "What is it?"

There was exhaustion in the slow drag of Ferin's words, and Yiloch looked up, squinting against the sun to search the other man's face. The slack-jawed, expressionless features confirmed the extent of the strain the adept was fighting to maintain his workings. He should have been paying closer attention. Letting Ferin drain himself of ascard energy would leave them vulnerable to many dangers, not the least of which was the risk of overexposure.

Yiloch pointed in the direction they were traveling. "There's a village ahead. Don't you sense it?"

Ferin looked over his shoulder at the distant buildings. He closed his eyes, wavering a little, and Yiloch stood, placing a hand on his shoulder to steady him. After a minute or more, Ferin opened his eyes and shook his head.

"There's no one there."

Foreboding put Yiloch's nerves on edge as they covered the rest of the distance to the waiting village. The swath of churned sand and rock swept in from the east, from the direction of the Rhuakine. Perhaps they were about to catch up with Suac Chozai's prophesied invaders. If so, he needed some way to move faster, because they were heading north toward Lyra, as the Suac had warned. He increased his pace, needing to see what the army had left behind while dreading what he would find.

Scavengers were already busy working on bodies at the edge of the village. Yiloch guessed as many as fifty warriors lay in the sand, their weapons beside them, blood soaking into the moisture-starved earth. Ferin followed him across the line-up of bodies, many trampled where they had fallen by the charging horses. He looked nauseous. As an adept, he seldom got this close to the carnage of war. Yiloch led the way to the center of the village. There were very few bodies among the buildings, which meant the invaders had either taken the elderly and children, or killed them in their homes. The latter seemed more probable. They wouldn't want more mouths to feed when crossing the desert.

"Rest here a moment," he told Ferin.

When the adept nodded, sinking down to sit on an unsullied bit of ground, Yiloch wandered to a hut on the furthest edge of the village. The hut had been ransacked, all the occupants' belongings cast about. Three bodies, those of a woman and two young boys, lay on the floor. The invaders had beheaded one boy, leaving his head lying several feet away next to one of the piles of blankets they used for beds. Yiloch dragged the bodies and bloodied carpets into a hut further down the line, then used some clothing to soak up the rest of the blood on the floor before laying out blankets. With that grim task completed, he returned to Ferin, who sat cross-legged on the ground, half asleep. He helped him to his feet and led him back to the hut.

"Get some rest."

"What are you going to do?"

"I'll be back soon," Yiloch replied. "First, I'm going to search for supplies."

"Stay out of the sun," Ferin muttered, lying back on the blankets.

Yiloch kicked around a few things on the floor until

he found one of the lightweight wraps the Kudaness wore to shield their faces from the midday sun. He put it, glancing at Ferin to see if he approved, only to find him already sound asleep. With a shrug, he walked back out into the sunlight. Without Ferin's protection, the heat was intense, but the wrap would keep his skin from burning.

He did a systematic search of the huts. A corral on the edge of the village might have held a few horses or skek, but it was empty now, part of the fence knocked to the ground. He found bodies in all but a few of the huts and little of use. The attackers had been efficient, cleaning out everything of use that they could carry. The bundle Korik had given them would keep them going for a while longer, but soon they would need to replenish. If they were following in the wake of this army, that could prove difficult. However, the invaders had left something useful behind.

He wandered among the bodies of Kudaness warriors until he found a sword he liked. Strapping the weapon on, he stood for a long time and considered the dead men, learning what he could. Despite the heat, the smell was tolerable, which meant they hadn't been dead long. That implied that the army wasn't more than an hour or two ahead of them. The other thing he noticed was that there were no foreign warriors among the dead. They were all Kudaness warriors with the symbol of the Denilik tribe tattooed on their faces. A closer examination revealed that each one had taken only a single hit from a bladed weapon. Some may have died from the trampling hooves rather than the blow that knocked them down, but they were no less dead. It suggested a very brutal and well-organized attack strategy.

The Kudaness were notorious for their proficiency at facing men on horseback, and all the signs suggested a mounted charge. Their long spears were designed to bring down charging horses. Why were there no dead or injured horses here? He was willing to accept that the invaders might have taken wounded or dead soldiers with them, but they wouldn't drag along dead or badly injured horses. Perhaps the animals were well-armored, but in this desert a well-armored horse would soon collapse from heat exhaustion. The other option was ascard protection, which implied either several very strong adepts or an abundance of weaker ones. Neither of those possibilities pleased him.

He drew the sword he had picked up and moved through a few quick attack forms, startling the birds gathered around the nearest bodies. They took to the air in mass, landing again a few feet away to assess the threat. They weren't willing to be driven from the feast that easily. With a heavy exhale that did nothing to ease the growing tension in him, he sheathed the weapon and returned to the hut where Ferin slept. Night was falling. Traveling at night would save Ferin some strain, but he wouldn't wake the other man yet. The adept needed as much rest as Yiloch could give him. Instead, he lay down to steal a bit of sleep for himself. There was no one left alive to threaten them and the predators and scavengers had plenty to gorge themselves on, so it was safe to sleep for a short time.

CHAPTER TWENTY-THREE

For the next few days, Myac, once again hidden behind the identity of Edan, underwent numerous painful healings to repair as much of the damage as the healers could fix. The hasty healing he did to repair his heart they left untouched, but the rest of the surrounding tissue damage cleaned up nicely. With each agonizing healing, his determination to find Indigo increased, but the Ascard Watchmen and adepts they sent searching continued to return with no news of her. Their failure only fueled his anger.

Today, he and Serivar had an audience with the newly established Prince Caplin. There were many things to discuss, and Caplin was one of a very limited number of people who might have insight into why Indigo would have freed Emperor Yiloch. Whether he would choose to disclose that information remained to be seen, however, and torturing it out of him was, unfortunately, not an option.

Myac rapped on Serivar's office door so hard it set his knuckles to throbbing, but he was angry enough after another painful healing not to care. At least this had been the last one.

"Enter," Serivar invited, though Myac was already opening the door.

A pinch-faced older man wearing the uniform of the Ascard Watchmen sat in one of the chairs across from Serivar. Dark hair dusted with gray and deep lines etched around his eyes and mouth gave testament to his age. He offered Myac a quick smile and nod of greeting that Myac ignored with tight-lipped disregard. The older man was also a member of the King's Order, which apparently made him feel as though they shared some degree of instant camaraderie. Myac disagreed.

"Any news?" Myac asked, shutting the door. He had no desire to sit next to the other man, so he remained standing at the nearest corner of the desk.

"Still nothing," Serivar replied, his voice heavy with resignation.

"She hasn't gone to her uncle's manor?"

The older man shook his head. "There was no sign of her there. Lord Theron has been away on an errand for the king. He doesn't even know she's missing yet. One of his sons was staying at the manor. He thought she was still in the city."

Myac gritted his teeth. "She's just a woman. How hard can it be to find out where she is," he snapped, his temper getting the better of him.

"I understand your annoyance, but she is avoiding all the locations our knowledge of her suggests she would have sought refuge." The older man threw up his hands in exasperation, his own frustration showing through now.

Myac narrowed his eyes at the man, fighting back an urge to teach him some respect. "Then look else-where. You helped force three Lyran adepts to confess to a crime they didn't commit. I would think you could manage this comparably simple task." He drew on enough ascard to crush the man in his own skin just for the pleasure of knowing he could do so.

"Have you any idea where I should look next?"

Myac closed his eyes, struggling with an intense desire to see fear in the man's eyes. For a split second, he almost missed Emperor Rylan. The late emperor would not have tolerated such incompetence, and he would have turned to Myac to mete out appropriate punishment. A task Myac had always taken pleasure in.

"Has anyone tried the Kilty docks?" Serivar asked in the ensuing silence.

"I don't believe so," the adept replied.

"There's a novel idea." Myac's voice dripped with sarcasm. "Who would ever think to leave on a boat?" The other man flinched under his acid glare, bringing him a tiny flicker of satisfaction.

"If she's left the continent, we have little hope of finding her. Given that she has no criminal history, and she's not apt to be equipped to deal with her current situation, it makes more sense that she would seek refuge somewhere familiar."

"Go to Kilty," Myac ordered. "Investigate everyone. Search the minds of every dockworker and seaman for a recent image of her. If you find anyone with information, bring them back here so someone competent can question them. Now go."

The Watchman started to stand then hesitated, looking to Serivar for confirmation. The headmaster met his gaze with frosty silence. Scowling, he stood and gave a cursory bow to each of them before stomping out. Myac raised his lip in a silent snarl after him and dropped into the other empty chair. He winced and let out a small gasp as pain shot through his chest. Serivar watched him with a look that might have been concern. At one time, that might have pleased Myac, but he had lost a great deal of respect for the headmaster since then.

"Should I call on Master Siddael?"

"No. I'm fine," Myac hissed. "Can I kill that man when this is over?"

Serivar shifted in his chair and began rearranging items on his desk. "I would rather you didn't. He has been quite useful."

"Not recently," Myac remarked, enjoying Serivar's discomfort in the absence of the other man's suffering. Serivar, having seen the aftermath of Indigo's actions, was keenly aware now of the type of volatile power he was dealing with in her. He also seemed to have developed a deeper respect for, and fear of, the power that Myac possessed.

"I can handle the meeting with Prince Caplin if you..." Serivar trailed off before his venomous glare.

"I'm not about to leave a delicate situation like this in your fumbling fingers."

A burst of anger rose in Serivar's eyes, but he quickly subdued it. He knew he didn't have the power to fight Myac, and they still needed each other for the time being. When that time passed, Myac thought, a change of leadership at the academy might be in order.

"Well, then, we should probably be on our way to the palace." Serivar stood and hurried to the door as if the close confines of his office had become too stifling.

Myac took a deep breath, appreciating that it no longer pained him so much to do so, and rose from the chair, somewhat disappointed that he didn't have more time to rest there and watch Serivar squirm under his icy stare. Then again, if Caplin had information that would help them, it would be worth the inconvenience of a trip to the palace, even wearied as he was from the recent healing.

* * *

Caplin met them in a second-story sitting room in the west wing of the palace with deep, comfortable couches and a selection of wine and cheeses laid on the central table. The new prince's restless fidgeting undermined the casual setting. Myac, who had expected to be in a similar position by now, recognized as prince of Lyra with his father, Lord Terral, seated as the new emperor, was somewhat mollified by the new appearance of age in Caplin's face and the strain in his eyes.

"Prince Caplin," Serivar was saying, "you must know more than you are telling us. Nothing you have said gives any insight into why Indigo would betray her country in this manner. She has thrown away everything she ever worked for. I cannot imagine that was a decision she came to casually."

Caplin gave him a sharp look, anger rippling off him. That anger was defensive, used to shield himself from deeper emotions. Curious where this might lead, Myac took a long sip of the wine and pondered the various reasons the new prince might have such a defensive response. Serivar and Indigo both mentioned that she and Caplin were longtime friends. Could it be that he considered them more than friends? Or perhaps he simply wanted to protect the beautiful adept and was unsure how best to do that.

Pity the men who cross her path. A burst of irritation flared in acknowledgement of his own attraction to her.

"Why would Lady Indigo free Adept Captain Ferin and Emperor Yiloch?" Myac prompted for the fourth or fifth time since their arrival when the prince's silence lengthened.

There. Finally, something more came through. A deep sorrow and longing radiated from the prince, edged with frustration and something more telling. Although he was engaged to another woman, a student at the academy if Myac recalled correctly, Caplin was in love with Indigo. The last emotion that shot to the surface was jealousy. The emotion puzzled Myac at first, and then an insidious dread began spreading through him. He knew what Caplin was going to say next, and it stoked the fire of his anger to a raging inferno.

"Because she loves him," Caplin stated mournfully, finally sitting and staring forlornly at his hands in his lap. "She loves him," he repeated, as if trying to accept a truth he found hard to bear.

"She loves Lord Ferin or Emperor Yiloch?" Serivar asked, puzzled. "Never mind. It doesn't matter which one. How could she possibly have spent enough time with either of them to fall in love? I thought you were watching over the healers in Lyra."

An excellent question. How could she have fallen in

love with Yiloch in the time the Caithin army was in Lyra? There was no doubt in Myac's mind which of the two men Caplin referred to, but it still made no sense. While he was leading an army, when would there have been a chance for the arrogant Lyran prince to capture the heart of the headstrong young adept? And yet, so many other things made sense if it were true. Her instant affinity for the Lyran adepts sent to study at the academy. Her reluctance about letting him try to woo her long before she knew who he really was. The sorrow and longing always lurking beneath the surface. The risks she had taken to help Yiloch and the way she and Ferin behaved toward one another. She loved a man she could never be with. At least she suffered in that way, but it wasn't enough, not by far.

Caplin glared at Serivar. "I was watching over her. Every time I checked on her, she was with Siddael as directed. The minute I turned my back, she would vanish, and I would find her standing with Emperor Yiloch watching the sunrise or lying half-dead at his feet. Does it matter how it happened?" Caplin said, growing subdued as he lowered his eyes again. "She knew we would put him to death. She came to me that night before she set them free."

Myac leaned forward. "Information that would have been valuable before this." He let frustration come through in his voice. "What did she say?"

Caplin glanced at him, but his guilt drove him to avert his eyes again. "She said she knew Yiloch wasn't guilty."

Myac leaned back then. "She has gone to Lyra." He was certain of it now.

Caplin rubbed at his temples as though his head pained him. "What will you do?"

"What you should have done," Myac hissed. "I'm going to go after her."

"Edan," Serivar snapped. "Remember your station."

Myac glared at Serivar, aware that Caplin was glaring at him in turn. If not for this fool of a prince, he would already be a prince himself or well on the road to it. He took a deep breath, reining in his temper, and faced Caplin, bowing his head slightly. "My apologies, Your Highness."

Caplin dismissed the apology with an abrupt gesture. "You will try to imprison Emperor Yiloch if you find him. No harm is to come to Indigo." He met Serivar's eyes with a look of warning until the man nodded, then turned the look on Myac.

"It will be as you command." Myac infused his tone with a sincerity he didn't feel. Harming her was the least he planned to do. In that moment, he wanted nothing more than to spend a long time harming her, repeatedly, but Caplin didn't need to know that.

Caplin held his gaze this time with fierce intensity. "Yiloch loves her too," he said, perhaps simply to see how Myac would react to the statement. Myac caught himself, clinging to a neutral expression despite the fresh swelling of anger and disbelief. "He told me that the day we left Lyra."

"Perhaps I can use that information to my advantage," Myac replied. If it were true, they would both suffer, as he had never made anyone suffer before.

Caplin gave a curt nod. "You may both leave."

* * *

"You're planning to go after her yourself?" Serivar asked once they were in the carriage on the way back to the academy.

"Yes."

"Perhaps we should discuss this more. Wait until Eric returns," Serivar suggested.

Myac sneered. "Do you really think that incompetent adept will find anything?"

Serivar's heavy sigh only irritated him more. There was no way Indigo could know where Yiloch and Ferin had gone when she destroyed the prison. Fleeing to Lyra would be a brash and desperate move. But would she really go there, not knowing for certain if her beloved emperor wasn't there? Maybe she had figured out a way of determining where they ended up. In theory, it wasn't possible to predict such an outcome, but how many times had a genuine opportunity to test it come up? The Serroc prisons were complex enough that even those who created them didn't fully understand how they worked. Could Indigo have discovered a way to manipulate a prison?

Myac shook his head, ignoring the curious look Serivar gave him. Indigo was clever, but he knew how desperate she had been when she went to free them. When she destroyed the stone, holding him here with her, she appeared distressed by the turn of events. He couldn't imagine her faking such emotions so convincingly. Although with her impeccable skill at masking, there was no way for him to be certain.

What does she see in that cruel, arrogant monster?

Myac clenched his fists, raw anger tearing through him. Yiloch was vain, selfish, and possessed a heartlessness that had helped plant the seeds of an arguably greater cruelty in him.

He forced a deep breath, releasing his fists.

The emperor was also handsome, as a man of such pure Lyran stock couldn't help but be, and powerful. Perhaps Indigo was shallower than he thought, desiring little more than superficial qualities in her chosen mate. Given that she had an ascard connection strong enough to rival his own, he might have projected his intelligence upon her out of a desire to have an equal. The idea of someone who could understand his power and share his ambitions was seductive. Add her beauty to the equation, and the fantasy of her might have blinded him to an unfortunate reality.

"We will wait and see what Eric finds," Myac muttered.

Serivar's brows jumped up. "Really? A wise choice, I am sure," he added hastily before Myac's glare.

Patience.

He needed to be patient, no matter how it made him seethe to think of her getting farther from his reach. All would be as it should be, so long as he wasn't as reckless as she had been. Yiloch would die. No other punishment suited his crimes. Indigo would suffer for making him want her and for the dire injury she had inflicted upon him. With patience, all would be right in the end.

CHAPTER TWENTY-FOUR

They kept their horses moving at a brisk pace during the day, heading southeast toward the Kudan border and the Murak tribal lands that lay beyond. Cadmar, though he much preferred to travel on foot in the style of the Kudaness, rode along without complaint. Ian, however, grumbled about his aches from long hours in the saddle in the evenings, though his manner remained lighthearted enough that Indigo didn't begrudge the effort of healing him. She healed Cadmar as well, though the dark warrior never asked her to, and she never offered aloud. Neither of them spoke of it, but she understood his gratitude when he brought her water and offered to care for her mount.

The unlikely trio of a young Lyran man, a Caithin woman, and a warrior who could pass as pureblooded Kudaness, was bound to draw unwanted attention. To avoid complications along the way, Ian maintained an illusion to make them appear as a trio of Lyran soldiers. They were unlikely to be harassed using such a guise and, as long as they camped or took meals in their rooms at inns so Ian could rest, the illusion wouldn't fail them. Once they were in Kudan, where they needed to draw attention, they could abandon the disguise.

Indigo removed the mourning braids at Cadmar's recommendation. Braids held a different significance in Kudan, and they didn't want to start off by offending anyone. Somehow, abandoning the braids lifted some of the weight of the loss they represented. For now, it made sense to put some of that sorrow aside and focus on their more immediate problems.

Before leaving the palace in Yiroth, Adran had approached them with a few requests. Avoiding Indigo's eyes, he handed Yiloch's sword to Cadmar.

"Take this and take two extra horses for Yiloch and Ferin. Yiloch will want his stallion."

"What if he returns before we do?" Ian had asked when Cadmar accepted the weapon, handling it with a notable degree of reverence.

"Then there are plenty of swords and horses for him to use here," Adran snapped, his quick temper exposing the extent of his worry. "He may have need of his best wherever he is now."

She had dodged his gaze when he turned to her, knowing her own misery might get the better of her if she looked into those tortured eyes. Adran said nothing more, and perhaps he hadn't intended to, or perhaps her turning away discouraged him. She figured at the time that hurt feelings were a thing they could both work on healing once Yiloch was safe. Now, as Yiroth fell further behind and the uncertainty before them became almost overwhelming, she wondered if he might have had something important to say. She could only hope he wouldn't have let her actions dissuade him if that were the case.

So many doubts tormented her while they worked their way south, the gravity of their venture hindering conversation and leaving her to flail about in the mire of her own thoughts.

What if they couldn't find this Suac Chozai? Or they did find him, but he couldn't help them? What if Yiloch and Ferin were dead? It was more than possible, given the innumerable places they might have ended up. And what kind of reception would she face as a Caithin woman in Kudan? The tribes weren't fond of the Caithin people, and for good reasons. Prejudice was its own epidemic in Caithin, especially the further inland one traveled. Visiting there was often unpleasant for anyone of obvious foreign descent.

She stood in the stirrups to give her rear and the horse's back a break as the animal trotted along, so absorbed in her own thoughts that she jumped hard enough to make the horse stumble when Cadmar touched her arm. Glancing over, she caught his quick, amused grin, then followed with her eyes when he pointed off to the right of the road. The forest had given way to open grassland, and a family of foxes was loping along on the far side of a creek that paralleled the road a few yards out. She smiled, appreciating the simple pleasure Cadmar had granted her of watching the beautiful creatures on their own journey.

Ian slowed his mount to a walk, and the other horses followed suit, unwilling to separate unless their riders demanded it from them.

"Any inns coming up, Cadmar?"

Cadmar glanced around them, his trained eyes picking out landmarks neither of them was familiar with. "We will come upon a village in another hour if we keep up our pace. There's lodging there. It's the last decent lodging we'll get."

Ian nodded and urged his horse back to a trot, pulling Ferin's gelding along. Yiloch's stallion, Tantrum, followed behind Cadmar while Indigo used her healing abilities to keep him calm. They found out right away that the big, dappled gray didn't appreciate following when he nearly unseated Ian trying to charge to the front. Now he came along congenially enough under Indigo's influence, though Cadmar kept his lead, hoping he would be strong enough to manage the animal should her working fail for any reason.

The inn was on the far edge of the small town. They kept up a good pace until they reached it to discourage anyone who might have an inclination to speak to them. As soon as they had secured lodging, Indigo and Cadmar retreated to the room, and Ian, who most resembled the illusion they were traveling under, handled arranging accommodations for the five horses and purchasing food.

When the young creator arrived in the room with their supper on a platter, Cadmar was laying out a bedroll on the floor, insisting that she and Ian take the two small cots. After sitting on one cot and realizing it wasn't much softer than the floor, Indigo left off trying to argue. Ian sat on the remaining cot and grimaced, not bothering to disagree. They ate in the pervasive silence that had hung over them since leaving Yiroth. There was tension in the group that she knew was at least partially because of the trust she had broken. For Cadmar, there seemed less uncertainty toward her than respect for Ian's state of mind. It was the young creator's pensive mood that had kept her silent as well, but there were things she needed to know before they reached Kudan.

As Ian started situating himself on the uncomfortable cot in preparation for sleep, she set aside what remained of a passable supper.

"Ian." He startled and glanced over at her, almost as though surprised to find he wasn't alone. "What exactly did the suac say to Yiloch?"

Ian arranged himself cross-legged on the cot, mirroring her position, though she couldn't tell if the mimicry was intentional. He picked at the worn hem of his pants while Cadmar adjusted his position, leaning against the wall to watch them.

"He said Yiloch would be thrice betrayed, by ally, by family, and by love." Ian freed a few threads from the hem of his pants as he spoke, and she wondered if he would get through the conversation with them intact.

"What else?"

"He said a great army would come and the Lyran empire would fall before it, essentially," he added, the last with a slight shrug she translated to mean this was a much-abbreviated version of the suac's prophecy.

"I suppose I must accept my role as one of his betrayers," she murmured. If either of them had feelings about her place in it all, they held their silence, for which she was grateful. "The ally betrayal would be the Caithin alliance. Technically, I think Myac is behind that, though I don't believe he was working alone. But family? What family does he have left?"

Ian leaned against the wall. "His father, mother, and brother are all dead. His cousin, Lord Terral, has been loyal, though Adran doesn't seem to trust him entirely. I think he may have a few nieces and maybe a living aunt or uncle. Adran would know his family better."

Indigo glanced at Cadmar, who merely shrugged. The big warrior apparently didn't see a need to know such things.

"Lord Terral is emperor regent?"

Ian nodded.

"Let's hope it isn't him, then. At least Adran and Hax are there to watch over him. I'm sure they won't let him get into trouble if they can help it. What about the invading army?" She gave Cadmar a querying look, hoping he might know something.

Cadmar shook his head. His pale green eyes were the brightest point in the poorly lit corner. She found herself trapped by them as his deep, soothing voice filled the room. "I know little. Rumors and prophecy mostly. There was some talk before I left the border the last time of a Silik hunter who spotted a massive cloud over the Rhuakine that he believed to be dust from many horses moving at speed. It also could have been a common dust storm."

Following Ian's example, she tore her gaze away from Cadmar and slid back along the cot to lean against the wall. "None of it bodes well," she murmured, willing herself not to pick at her fingernails.

"Do you love him?"

She met Ian's eyes.

So much had happened in the short time since she left Yiroth after helping Yiloch take the throne. She remembered well that last night spent in his arms, and even more so their last kiss the following morning. He had offered her everything he could as the Emperor of Lyra. It wasn't enough to keep her by his side, not with so many things left unresolved and so many uncertainties regarding what role she could play in his life. Still, she had risked her life for him repeatedly. Would she hesitate to do so again? Thinking back on what she had done to free him from the prison, braving Myac and making herself a traitor to her own kingdom, she supposed not.

"Yes, Ian. I can't imagine loving anyone more."

Ian smiled, and the delight in his eyes warmed her.

Cadmar chuckled and stretched out on his bedroll.

"It'll all be all right then," Ian declared.

She returned his smile, though she didn't share his confidence. "Goodnight." She blew out the candle by her cot before climbing under the rough woolen blanket.

* * *

The evening chat eased some of the tension between them. Her admission that she loved his emperor seemed to buoy Ian, and his mood, despite the daunting task ahead of them, was almost jovial throughout the next day. Cadmar found this amusing, and Indigo appreciated the improved humor of the group, though her own worries and guilt continued to trouble her.

The terrain, which had changed from the lush, towering forests outside Yiroth to open grasslands, transformed yet again to a sparser forest colored in the soft palette of grays, greens, and pale browns common to more arid regions. She took it all in, noticing that the deer were smaller as they moved south and the croaking of frogs in the evening gave way to the chirping of crickets. Traveling at speed made conversation difficult, so they spoke little. In that forced silence, the beauty of the landscape alone couldn't ease her apprehension.

They followed the rough roadway at a good pace until the sparse forest ahead of them changed again. There was a distinct line beyond which the trees were a uniform ghostly silver, their outer bark and most limbs burned away. In places, the black of char stood out against the silver of the dead wood. A hint of struggling plant life showing in places on the bare ground.

Indigo pulled up her mount before crossing the line. The animal stopped without a fight, sensitive to her reservations. Ian and Cadmar slowed after entering the dead forest, noticing her absence. They stopped to wait, and she reluctantly urged her mount on. When she was beside the others, she could see a clearing further ahead, full of the fire-blackened remains of buildings. Beyond that, there was another line of dead, silver trees before the forest returned to normal.

"What is this place?"

Cadmar's gaze swept the scene. His lips pressed together in a tight line.

"This is Segys," Ian offered. "It is one of the two cities Emperor Rylan sent Yiloch to destroy. The ones that earned him the nickname of the Blood Prince."

Indigo shuddered at the thought of that senseless slaughter. The man she loved had done this.

Ian swept out a hand out to indicate the burned area. "The fire got out of control on this side, burning part of the forest before the adepts could contain it. AhnSegys, on the south side of the river, was eventually rebuilt. Segys was left like this, preserved by Rylan's adepts as a warning to any who might dare to incite his wrath."

Indigo felt a change in ascard around them and looked askance at Ian.

He shrugged. "I altered our disguise. Imperial soldiers aren't much loved around here."

"I can imagine."

They passed through the dead village at speed, crossing the river into AhnSegys. The villagers, despite their transformed disguise, watched them with open suspicion as they passed through. No one smiled or attempted to speak to them, and Indigo, feeling a guilt she knew wasn't hers to feel, was relieved to leave the place behind.

As dusk fell upon them once more, they found a spot away from the main road to set up camp, and she attempted to indulge her curiosity about her companions while they sat around the fire rather than spend more time fretting over their situation.

"How did you come to be in Yiloch's company, Ian?"

Ian gazed for several minutes into the darkness beyond Cadmar, who sat in silence across from him. She was about to repeat the question when he looked at her.

"I'd been in Yiroth less than a month, hoping to earn a place in the palace, when Yiloch's father exiled him. I probably would have stayed if Adran and Eris hadn't insisted otherwise. At the time, I didn't understand their devotion to him. He terrified me." He lowered his gaze, picking at a patch of grass. "I only knew Yiloch through rumors that abounded after the destruction of Segys and AhnSegys. It shames me to admit I was relieved when he vanished—when his father imprisoned him," he clarified. "I didn't want to be part of his rebellion. Then he returned, thanks to you, and he took me with him to arrange the alliance with Caithin. My role in that was similar to what I'm doing now. I was to disguise the entourage so we wouldn't be recognized."

Another long silence stretched out, and Indigo waited, sensing that interruption might discourage him from continuing.

When his picking had dramatically reduced the patch of grass, he continued. "Along the way, we ran into a rogue imperial patrol, and they picked a fight with us. I tried to show off, using my ability to create shields for our soldiers, only I overextended and blacked out. The illusion vanished, and one of them recognized Yiloch. He killed the soldier when the man tried to flee, but he was furious. I thought he was going to kill me for a moment. A few minutes later, when his temper cooled, he asked me if I understood what I had done wrong. I did, and I respected him for coming back to talk to me about it. That's when I started wanting to help him. A little peculiar, isn't it?" An awkward smile flitted across his features.

She smiled fondly in return. "Not at all. He helped you grow, if perhaps a little indelicately. What about you, Cadmar?" She shifted her position to focus on him.

Cadmar met her gaze easily. "Like you, Lady Indigo, I have never sworn loyalty to Yiloch."

She hadn't expected that. "But you have acted in his service. You stayed behind in Demin to guide Caithin's soldiers and healers to the rendezvous in Lyra at Yiloch's bidding. At least, that's how I understood it."

Cadmar grinned. He disappeared into the darkness with his dark skin, but his teeth flashed brightly in the firelight. "Whether Yiloch asks or orders, the ultimate choice to comply or not remains with me. Hax came to my village and trained in swordsmanship under me for a time. I fell in love with her. That was before the prince's exile from Yiroth. When he turned against his father, and she chose to go with him, I followed her. He knows I love her and has never taken advantage of that knowledge. I respect him for that, and I believe he could be an influential leader, so when I am asked to help, I often do. He has offered me official status, but he never argues when I decline. For the respect he has shown me, I can do no less than I do for him."

She nodded. "He may not have your sworn loyalty, but he has you all the same, just as he has me."

Cadmar eyed her for a minute, and she waited for him to contradict her. Eventually, he nodded and said, "Perhaps he does at that." Then he stretched out and closed his eyes.

CHAPTER TWENTY-FIVE

It took several days for Yiloch and Ferin to reach the first Silik villages beyond the Denilik tribal lands. The Silik were a far more aggressive tribe than their southern neighbors, which explained why they owned much of the land on the banks of the Endwater, the major river supplying the tributaries that kept Kudan alive. The Kudaness called the river Silgandveswyr, which translated roughly as Silgand's tether. According to their mythology, Silgand, the Kudaness water god, dwelt in the oceans and maintained the river as a connection to his people.

Because of their notoriously combative nature, Yiloch had dreaded passing through the Silik tribal lands, but the army that continued its destructive trek north ahead of them had also decimated those villages, leaving no one alive. Careful searching uncovered a few useful supplies well hidden in some of the huts and the river refreshed them. The third Silik village they came to was silent like the rest, but there were no bodies. Though the churned sand and ransacked huts attested to the passing of the army, there was no sign of the Silik people who usually resided there.

After sending Ferin to rest in an abandoned hut and

donning the wrap to shield himself from the sun, Yiloch began his methodical search for supplies. His efforts earned them a second, half-full waterskin, which would be invaluable as they continued north away from the river, and a few food items to help keep their strength up. They were already rationing their supplies. Traveling through the arid lands of Kudan was hard enough without prior planning or knowledge of edible plants in the region. With the villages emptied of people with whom they might have traded, and the food and water scavenged by the army, it was becoming impossible.

Yiloch dropped the few supplies in the hut where Ferin rested and left again. He had more to do. Heading out to one edge of the village, he began a wide trek around the perimeter. It was easy to find where the horsemen had entered and where they left, still heading north. That wasn't what he was looking for.

The muscles in his legs were adjusting to the added effort of walking in the soft mix of sand and rock. He had gained a deeper appreciation for the muscular legs of the Kudaness warriors. Facing the heat without Ferin's barrier, however, made the trek around the village far more arduous. Still, the adept needed rest, or he wouldn't have the energy to continue.

Yiloch stopped. On the western side, beyond the area trampled by horses, he found what he was looking for. A sizeable number of people had passed that way on foot. The villagers had abandoned their homes. Perhaps they received a warning from someone who escaped the slaughter further south. That was unlikely, considering the army would have overtaken anyone traveling on foot, even a Kudaness warrior. The other possibility was that a suac here had foreseen the coming army and warned the villagers. Each tribe had many lesser priests of the Ithik Ani, but only one high priest, or suac. That meant only one village per tribe had a suac in residence. If the Silik tribe's suac lived further north, it made sense that a warning might not have reached the southern-most villages in time.

Knowing that the villagers had deserted wasn't a comfort. They would probably return, and the when of their return could prove critical for them. They needed supplies for their journey. In different circumstances, he would have preferred to trade for those supplies. If the Silik returned, they might not take kindly to finding Yiloch and Ferin in their ransacked village helping them-selves to whatever they needed. Still, they had to rest. There was no denying that. They would risk staying for a while so Ferin could recover from his exertions. The cumulative strain was wearing him down more than their brief stops could restore.

The foreign army's horses need to rest too, he told himself on his walk back to the hut, trying to find some solace in the thought.

The horses were moving faster, though, and that meant that the army drew closer to his empire every day while he fell further behind. Frustration welled up in him, but he forced it away and stretched out on some blankets in the hut. He could fret over such things tomorrow if he wished. It would do no more good then, but at least it wouldn't interfere with his sleep.

* * *

They started out at dawn the next morning. Yiloch hoped to leave earlier, but Ferin was faltering. In the early hours, it was cool enough that they could wear Kudaness wraps to shield from the rays of the sun and travel for a time without an ascard barrier. They had done so for much of the trip, managing until almost noon before turning to Ferin's power for protection from the heat. Yet, even with that effort, Yiloch could see that the adept was fading. It wasn't the strength of his connection that earned Ferin his rank. It was his extensive knowledge of many different ascard skills in combination with his leadership ability. Unfortunately, few of those skills were strong enough to be of much help in this situation.

They weren't yet out of sight of the village when he spotted a group of Silik warriors heading their way. The other party spotted them at the same moment, which meant it was much too late for Yiloch and Ferin to avoid them, not that they had many options for hiding in the open desert.

"Halt!"

The command was pointless. They had already stopped to await the dark-skinned warriors. Trying to outrun Kudaness warriors in the sand would be nothing but a waste of energy and a death sentence besides. Ferin let out of soft groan, his lips twisting into a grimace where he stood at Yiloch's side.

"Why are you here, pale ones?" One Silik warrior, apparently the ranking individual in the group, faced

Yiloch as they approached, having determined him to be the leader of the two intruders.

The rest of the warriors, fifteen in all, encircled them, and one poked at the Kudaness wrap Ferin wore with the tip of the ornate spear he carried. Yiloch turned to scowl at another warrior who tapped the curved Kudaness blade he carried with the tip of his spear before he turned back to the one who had spoken. Given the size of the group, they were probably scouting to see if it was safe to return. Having to abandon the village to begin with would put them in a foul mood. Finding two Lyran men passing through carrying Kudaness supplies and weapons would only add fuel to that fire. He would have to handle the situation with care.

"We planned to barter with your people, but the village was empty and we needed to rest for the night. We used one of your huts for shelter," Yiloch explained in the Silik dialect, keeping a respectful tone. It sounded reasonable enough, so long as one ignored the peculiarity of two Lyran men wandering the desert and clearly ill-equipped for the journey.

The warrior's gaze focused beyond them, and he nodded. Before Yiloch could react, a spear burst through Ferin's chest from behind. The spray of blood stood out in brilliant contrast to the pastel colors of the desert. Yiloch drew the sword and spun in a swift, graceful movement intended to ward off further attack. There was little chance he could defeat so many trained warriors at once, but he was willing to die trying. No one else moved.

Ferin dropped to his knees, and the warrior who

had run him through placed a foot against his back and pulled his weapon free. He then met Yiloch's eyes, his dark gaze cold and emotionless as he stepped back to his place in the circle. Yiloch glanced down at his companion, seeing Ferin's eyes gloss over seconds before he toppled forward on the bloody ground.

The world turned red around the edges of his vision when he looked back up at Ferin's killer. He wanted to demand justification, but didn't trust himself to speak. More than that, he wanted blood for blood. The warrior deserved to die. As far as he was concerned, they all deserved to die now. He could barely think past the fury pounding through his veins.

"Now you have paid for your bed and whatever else you have taken," the ranking warrior declared, his hostile tone daring Yiloch to act in vengeance.

Yiloch took a step toward him. Ornate spears and curved swords lifted around the circle in warning, and he paused. If he attacked in his weary state, he would die. He would never see Lyra saved from the threat of the army from across the Rhuakine. He had to protect his empire. A deep ache of loss spread through him.

"Where are you bound?"

"Lyra," he hissed, reaching deep within himself to find the restraint he needed to survive this encounter.

The dark warrior laughed, though the amusement never touched his eyes. "How did you get here?"

"Ilikah put me here," Yiloch stated, not interested in trying to explain the actual situation to men who considered the use of ascard a form of blasphemy.

"If Ilikah watches you, then you won't need these

things," the warrior said, reaching for the bundle that held their supplies with the point of his spear.

Yiloch knocked the spear away with the sword, part of him still itching to start a fight despite the bleak odds. "You took your price," he snarled.

"Fair enough, pale one, take your baggage and go." He swept his spear out behind him to indicate the unwelcoming expanse of desert that lay beyond the village.

Yiloch hefted the bundle, not sheathing the sword, and walked between two warriors. He hadn't gotten far when the leader called after him.

"You forgot something, pale one." Yiloch turned to see the man nudging Ferin's body with his foot. "You brought this. Take it with you."

The other warriors laughed. Yiloch drew on ascard and swapped himself into the space next to the dark, tattooed warrior. It was a waste of energy, but his sudden disappearance and reappearance in their midst cut off their laughter, and all their weapons rose to the ready. Yiloch met the man's eyes, standing almost nose to nose with him.

"What I brought was a companion. That is a body. You made it. It's your problem now."

Before he turned away, he remembered one thing and bent down, turning Ferin gently onto his back. He searched the adept's pockets until he found the chain with Indigo's ring on it and moved it to his own pocket. The warriors watched with interest. They were less eager to confront him now that they knew he was an adept. Closing Ferin's eyes with two careful fingers, he whispered in Caithin so they wouldn't understand.

"I'm sorry, my friend. You deserved better."

Blood pounded in his veins when he turned his back on the group bristling with weapons and walked away, leaving a cherished part of his world behind. He focused on each footstep and listened for the sound of pursuit. None came. They would expect the desert to finish him off for them. Soon he fell to focusing only on his footsteps.

It was never easy to lose a companion, though it happened all too often in times of war. Now that he had taken the throne, losing Commander Dalce and Captain Eris among many others in the process, he had hoped to avoid such losses for a time. Ferin's death was neither noble nor did it serve any purpose. Reaching into his pocket, he closed his fist around Indigo's ring until the blue stone dug into his palm. When he saw her again, and he would see her again, he would make sure she understood the pain she had caused him and those he cared about.

* * *

In the hottest part of the day, he sat sheltered under the Kudaness wrap. The intensity of the heat without Ferin's workings made forward progress slow and laborious. Heat permeated everything, dulling his senses as it closed in all around him, smothering him. He would wait until the sun began setting and the temperature dropped again.

Without his footsteps to focus on, his thoughts

drifted to Ferin and to the army that rushed toward his home. He could do nothing about either. Every day the army got farther ahead of him. If he made it through the Silik lands in one piece, he still had the Murak to deal with. They were on peaceful terms with Lyra, other than the occasional petty harassment of the border towns, but Yiloch's less than congenial encounter with Suac Chozai and the fact that he was coming from within Kudan on the heels of an invading army wouldn't make him welcome. At best, they would greet him with suspicion. Worst case, well... worst case, he would join Ferin.

Did Adran know what had happened to him? He hated that the other man had to manage this chaos without him again. Still, if anyone could hold things together, Adran could. He had proven that much when he kept Yiloch's plans from collapsing while his father had him imprisoned. What would he be doing now? Was he preparing for the possibility that Suac Chozai's prophecy might come to pass? Yiloch could only hope he was. There was the possibility that Lyra had declared war on Caithin after the abduction of their emperor. If that were the case, his empire faced its doom. There was no way Lyra, still recovering from his takeover, could confront Caithin and this new army at the same time.

Yiloch rubbed his temples, trying to fight the growing headache his thoughts brought him. More than anything, he needed to rest now, while he couldn't travel. It would avail him nothing to sit worrying about things he couldn't control.

He allowed himself to doze for a time, catching some sleep now so that he could continue traveling through the night. As he drifted off, he thought how nice it would be to find the next Silik village full of bodies like the first two had been. His lips pressed together in a bitter line.

Let them suffer for Ferin's death a thousandfold.

CHAPTER TWENTY-SIX

They continued traveling south, and Indigo grew more nervous with each passing day. The road took them along a winding route through a run of steep, but low-slung mountains. The rugged terrain made it hard to keep up their pace. They made the journey up and back down the other side in a few days of relative silence. The arduous trek wore down the horses and their riders, so they set up camp a little early when they reached the bottom of the pass on the second day.

Stopping was a relief. As much as she wanted to find Yiloch, she wasn't sure what kind of greeting to expect from the Kudaness and, more importantly, what kind of greeting to expect from him if they did find him. She wanted to believe he would forgive her once she explained, but if she tried to imagine events from his side, she couldn't imagine him feeling anything less than loathing for her. In her hunger for knowledge, she had ignored her instincts and allowed Serivar and Myac to use her. In short, she had been a fool. Could he forgive her for that? Could she?

Pulling away from her miserable pondering, she sat by the fire and watched Cadmar. He rested back against a log with his eyes closed. Without seeing those out-of-place pale green eyes, one would never know he wasn't full-blooded Kudaness. Did he believe in the Kudaness gods, or did he share the Lyran belief that there were no gods and life was born from divergences in ascard that existed in all things?

Ascard energy, the ultimate power that made so much possible. The common denominator that made them alike and yet so very different. The Lyran belief struck her as incomplete. What brought about those divergences in ascard if not the Divine? Lyra boasted no common religion other than perhaps worship of ascard itself, but even that was undercut by their casual use of it. The tribes of Kudan made ascard sacred, belonging to their pantheon of gods and therefore considered its manipulation sacrilege. Their conflicting beliefs alone made it a wonder that two races didn't kill each other.

"Do you wish to share any of those thoughts?"

Cadmar's deep voice startled her. Lost in her own contemplations, she hadn't noticed him watching her. "I was just wondering about your beliefs. If you follow the Kudaness religion or the Lyran... lack of one." Her brow furrowed, and she touched her fingers to her lips, realizing how inappropriate it was to bring up such a thing so casually. "I apologize. That really is none of my concern."

Cadmar chuckled. "We are not at a society gathering, my lady. All your thoughts are welcome here. To assuage your curiosity, I will tell you that I am the worst of all sinners. I follow whatever belief will keep me out of trouble at any given moment."

Indigo gaped at him, and Ian looked up now, his

interest sparked. "You have no religion at all? No belief system you follow. What about the Lyran belief that everything is born of ascard?"

Cadmar shrugged, the laughter in his eyes suggesting that he found her skepticism amusing. "I am no ascard user, my lady. Any knowledge I have of that is as much hearsay as the various gods are. I believe I exist. That is all I believe, but I can assume any religion you like convincingly enough and will do so if the situation requires it."

She marveled with reluctant admiration at the ease with which he disregarded and used religion, or the lack of it, to his advantage.

A slow smile spread across Ian's face. "Seems like a handy skill."

Seeing the complete fascination in Ian's gaze, staring at Cadmar as though he were a prophet of some kind, brought laughter bubbling up. "What a fine trio we are. We are even more diverse than we appear, and that was already considerable."

"What do you believe, my lady?" Cadmar inquired, turning the tables.

She opened her mouth, intending to speak in support of her one god, the Divine, but the words wouldn't come. Looking into those pale eyes, the only testament to his split heritage, all her recent experiences swept in on her, and the words that came to her tongue out of habit lacked the conviction to make it past her lips. The familiar ache of loss filled her, and the sting of tears came to her eyes. She lowered her gaze to the fire and spoke in a low voice. "I'm not sure I know anymore."

Silence followed. She twisted the ring on her finger. What did she believe? If the Divine existed, why did He let such terrible things happen? Was this all punishment for loving someone who was a nonbeliever?

The smoke from the fire drifted over to her, stinging her eyes and nose. She stood and backed away, scowling at the fire.

Cadmar grinned. "You may sit here, Lady Indigo," he offered, moving to the ground and gesturing to the stump he'd been sitting on.

Accepting the seat, she resumed gazing into the fire. "You can just call me Indigo," she said. "I haven't proven to be much of a lady."

Cadmar touched her hand, and she turned to meet his eyes. "That I do not believe. If I believe in anything, it is your love for Emperor Yiloch and the strength that lies within you. You will succeed, my lady."

Locked in the intensity of his gaze, she could almost accept the conviction in his words. The Divine knew she wanted to believe them.

A soft snore broke the moment, and they turned to see Ian slumped over awkwardly by the fire.

Cadmar chuckled.

Indigo stood. "We can't leave him like that. He'll be a mess of knots by morning."

Cadmar started to get up, and she gestured for him to stay. "I've got it."

Creating a soft barrier of ascard around him, she lowered the creator to the ground and put a blanket over him. He moaned in his sleep, and she regarded him for a moment, startled by a powerful desire to protect him.

With careful fingers, she brushed a strand of hair away from his lips. He smiled and curled up on his side. She turned back to the fire to find Cadmar watching her with a satisfied grin.

"What?" Had she missed some joke?

"Very much a lady."

She blushed, unable to hide the pleasure his words brought her. Sitting back down, she gazed into the fire until her eyelids began drooping, then she too stretched out to sleep.

* * *

"Will we reach Kudan today?" Indigo asked as they rode out the next morning.

"If we keep our pace up." Cadmar nudged his mount up to a trot.

"There are a few larger Lyran cities on the Kudan border, aren't there?"

Cadmar glanced at her and settled in the saddle, easing his mount back to a walk. He regarded her with unnerving intensity. Did he realize her question was as much to delay their progress as to gather more information?

"Further west, there are. Where we are crossing, there is only a small village. They tried once to expand like the cities closer to the coast. The Murak complained, saying they could already see too much of the settlement from their northernmost village. When the villagers ignored the tribe's complaints, they began sending in raiding parties at night, stealing valuable construction tools and materials and frightening anyone foolish enough to be out after dark. The raids weren't violent, but they were costly. Over time, those looking to grow the village gave up and moved west."

"The Murak don't sound like the friendliest people."

Cadmar chuckled. "They are my people. My father was Murak. My mother was half Lyran and half Murak in flesh, all Murak in spirit."

"Will they..." She trailed off, not sure how to phrase the question.

"They will not embrace you, Lady Indigo, but they will not harm you, not while you are in my care. Expect some hostility, perhaps, in their words, but not in their actions."

She nodded. His answers weren't comforting. Still, it could be worse, and she would have to be content with that. If she looked at it from a different perspective, it was a remarkable learning opportunity. It wasn't unheard of for the occasional daring Caithin traveler to venture deeper into Lyra, but not Kudan. The desert was as unwelcoming as the people who lived there. Very few Caithins would risk becoming stranded there among tribes of people who wouldn't hesitate to let them die. She was traveling into Kudan with a man who was at least partly one of them. It was an unprecedented opportunity to expand her knowledge of the Kudaness people through lived experience if she could get past her fear.

Cadmar gave her a questioning look, and she nodded. He urged his mount faster again. The other horses followed suit, Tantrum tossing his head even with her influence on him. She held her mount back some, falling behind the others where she could think without their eyes upon her. A tendril of power revealed that Ian was nearly as nervous as she was. Cadmar remained a pillar of unfaltering calm. She envied him that.

They were only a few hours north of Kudan, walking to give the horses a break, when they heard a rumble like approaching thunder. A storm was coming, but not in the sky above them. The horses began prancing about, and Indigo spread the calming influence she was using on Tantrum to the other four. They left the road, moving well out into the sagebrush at Cadmar's hasty orders.

"What is it?" The big warrior's heightened alert prompted her to speak in a hushed voice, barely audible over the growing rumble. She resisted the urge to investigate with ascard to avoid wasting power she might need soon.

"I hope I am wrong," Cadmar said in a low voice, and a chill coursed through her. "Ian, can you create a barrier to hide us?"

Ian nodded, his face drawn with worry. His eyes lost their focus as he turned to the task. As an extra precaution, Indigo sought Ian's barrier and worked a masking around it so that they would be not only invisible physically, but to ascard sense as well. He glanced at her and nodded his appreciation. While they waited, she had to increase her influence on the horses as the noise got louder and the ground began shaking.

The source of the disturbance came into view over a gradual rise on the horizon. A swath of horsemen riding at a gallop, fifteen or more abreast, some far enough off the side of the road that Cadmar moved them farther into the sagebrush. Behind the first rank of riders came another row, and another, until Indigo gave up trying to count. When the front rank was close enough that she could start distinguishing facial features, there were still more riders coming over the distant rise.

Calming herself with the same skill she was using on the horses, she examined the fast-moving army. They rode horses shorter and thicker than any she had seen before, but the animals were strong and fast despite their stature. They were mostly bays, with an occasional dun or dusty gray mixed in. The men who rode them were also stocky and thickly muscled. Their skin was darker than the Lyrans and lighter than Kudaness, almost a Caithin tone, but more olive gray than light bronze. Their hair appeared to be almost universally black and worn loose around wide, pronounced features and deep-set dark eyes. There was nothing at all familiar about them, not in her personal experience nor in anything she had read. The weapons they carried strapped to their backs looked like short spears, only topped with a thick, swept blade that looked to be nearly a foot in length.

"There is the leader." Cadmar spoke in a low voice, as though worried they might hear him over the distance and the din of their passage.

She glanced over the horde. They all looked much the same to her, but as she was about to question Cadmar further, she spotted him. He rode near the center of the army, nearly parallel to them now. It was not so much the man himself, for his fierce expression matched that worn by the surrounding men. It was the careful consideration of the riders near him. They didn't crowd or jostle for position near him as they did throughout the rest of the fluctuating mass. Upon closer observation, the men surrounding him also wore darker armor, suggesting that they might be a special guard of some kind.

Curious, she reached out with ascard, intending to feel through the army for any adepts and wondering absently how many workings she could maintain before putting the integrity of her own masking at risk. She recoiled with a small gasp of surprise.

Cadmar and Ian both looked at her, faces drawn with concern.

"There is a shield over the entire army," she explained. "A very strong one."

Ian grimaced. "I didn't sense any notable connections, so I assumed there weren't any. Apparently, they were just hidden well."

"There must be quite a few strong adepts to create a shield of that magnitude." She scowled at the passing army. If she dared drop any of her current workings, she might be able to breach the shield and learn more, but the finesse required to do so undetected would require a significant expenditure of energy.

"Can I help?" Ian asked, apparently guessing the direction of her thoughts.

"Can you spare some of your ability without jeopardizing our concealment?"

He nodded.

"I'll let you feed into me then, so you can control how much I use."

When she felt his strength boosting her through their link, she drew upon her own connection, resolving to use his as a backup only. Closing her eyes to increase her focus, she snaked a tendril of ascard out to the shield, masking it as she went. With the utmost care, she bored her way into the barrier, feeling a sudden release of pressure when she broke through. In seconds, she discovered not a few, but hundreds of adept-level ascard users among the hundreds of men, including the man she believed to be their leader. Extraordinarily, the power of all the adepts except the leader was channeling into one adept who combined it seamlessly to create the barrier.

"Indigo."

Her eyes snapped open. Ian pointed, and she looked out at the army to see the leader staring in their direction. Startled, she drew back the tendril of ascard. The man smiled then, a cold, unkind expression, and faced forward. She shuddered. Ian rested a hand on her shoulder, perhaps for comfort, though he looked at least as distraught.

When the army was well past, and the dust beginning to settle, Ian dropped the concealment around them and took a deep, shaky breath.

"So, the army is real," Cadmar muttered.

Indigo thought his tone far too calm under the circumstances.

"That doesn't bode well for what lies ahead." Ian was still staring after the mass of warriors growing smaller in the distance.

Weary, Indigo retracted her control over all the

horses except Tantrum. With one last glance at the army, she urged her horse to walk. The other horses followed with little encouragement.

The combining of power among the adepts troubled her, but it was already too late to investigate it further, and there was little point in worrying her companions with something she couldn't confirm.

"It doesn't bode well for Lyra either," she said, struggling to keep her voice steady. "All we can do now is hope the suac survived their passage. If he knew they were coming, there's a decent chance of it."

The other two said nothing more, and she urged her horse up to a swift trot. They couldn't afford to waste time.

CHAPTER TWENTY-SEVEN

While Myac much preferred to inflict suffering without prejudice, it irritated him some to find himself facing yet another Lyran. He had hoped to take his frustration out, ideally, on some soft, spineless Caithin captain, though he would have settled for a Kudaness or a captain of mixed blood. Of late, he had spent far too much time using his abilities against his own people. That would be acceptable if he were still in Lyra, but here it was becoming ridiculous.

The Lyran captain, Murchadh, glared molten fury at Myac from where he sat in a rough wooden chair, hands and feet bound. Only two candles in the large training room provided a feeble, flickering light, and those they had placed upon the table between them so the man wouldn't see much of the surrounding room. They had not yet decided whether they would let him go when they finished with him or kill him as a precaution. As such, Myac maintained his Caithin disguise. How much worse would the man's anger be if he knew one of his captors was Lyran?

"Why are you a ship captain?" Myac asked, scowling at the man while Serivar stared at him, his pinched brows making it clear he didn't see any relevance to the question.

Murchadh looked just as puzzled by it. "Because my father was," he finally answered.

Reasonable enough. "Why do you sail the Gilded Strait?"

Confusion warred with the anger on the captain's face. He opened his mouth to respond, but Serivar cut him off.

"How is this relevant?"

Myac searched his mind for some way to express his frustration that the other adept would understand and that wouldn't reveal too much about him to their prisoner. He shouldn't be questioning a Lyran ship captain, not in Caithin. What pureblooded Lyran captain in his right mind would work the Gilded Strait by choice? So many other lucrative routes wouldn't require dealing with the people who enslaved his kind. It made no sense at all that he should be interrogating a Lyran man in this situation.

He finally threw up his hands, admitting defeat. It didn't matter. While it was vexing, Serivar was right, the answer wasn't important.

"Never mind," he snapped. "You recently helped a fugitive cross to Yiroth. A young woman by the name of Indigo Milan."

Murchadh's expression calmed as though knowing their purpose erased his concern. He tossed his head so that his long braid flipped over his shoulder. "Perhaps. I take the odd passenger. I don't pay much attention to who they are so long as they pay."

Myac smirked. He had caught a brief spike of unease in the captain at the mention of Indigo despite his bold display. "You would remember her. A young Caithin woman. Quite lovely. She would have approached you with a sense of urgency. When did you drop her in Lyra?"

The man set his jaw and said nothing.

Myac grinned. If the captain continued to resist, he would have reason enough to use his power against him.

Serivar stood, leaning on his fists on the table and staring intently at Murchadh. "Why protect her, Captain Murchadh?" he argued sensibly. "She is Caithin. What is she to you?"

The subtle wave of remorse and affection that came from the man almost broke Myac's careful control. How did she do that? She couldn't have been in the man's company for more than a couple of days at most. How was it possible for her to have instilled such fondness in him in such a short time?

The captain was watching him warily, perhaps concerned by the way he ground his teeth and curled his hands into fists. He looked away when Myac glared at him and said, "I dropped her in Yiroth four days after the death of your king," he admitted, voice thick with resignation. Regret poured from him.

Myac and Serivar exchanged puzzled looks.

"That is not possible," Myac countered. "She was here that night. It takes more than a day to cross the Gilded Strait. Do you think us fools?"

Murchadh smiled then, a slightly crooked, smug smile. "Under normal circumstances, that is true."

Myac drew on ascard and closed off the air around the captain. The look of defiance turned to one of gratifying terror as he struggled to breathe through the invisible barrier that would suffocate him if Myac chose to let it. After a short time, Serivar cleared his throat, and Myac released the barrier. The man sagged forward gasping, and Myac walked over to him. He placed a hand on the chair back and leaned down close to the captain's ear.

"I would love to kill you," he whispered. "You would do well to keep that in mind."

Turning away, he went to sit on a corner of the table and waited for Murchadh to catch his breath. After a minute, Myac returned to push him upright in the seat, since the captain now lacked the strength to do so on his own. He did have enough strength to pull his shoulder away from Myac's hand once he was up again, glaring bitter hatred at him. Myac smiled in response, more than ready to draw on ascard again.

"Lady Indigo paid for her passage by speeding my ship across the Gilded Strait in under a day," Murchadh said, his voice strained. "No captain would turn that away or question someone who could provide such a service."

Myac scowled. After everything she had done that night, it stunned him to hear she still had the strength to manage such a feat. She must have arrived in Yiroth drained to the point of passing out. That would have slowed her down, but she still had a substantial time advantage over him.

"And if I made you the same offer?"

"I would have you thrown off my ship," the captain snarled.

Myac grinned and leaned closer to him, taking the captain's chin in his hand to force him to meet his eyes. "I would love it if you tried."

A shudder racked the captain, the shame of his potent fear clear in his eyes. Pure-blooded Lyrans were so proud. Myac supposed he suffered from that same arrogance, but at least he could back it up with his power *and* his lineage.

Straightening, he turned to Serivar. "I'll take him to his ship tonight and cross to Yiroth. I will need secondary keys to the remaining Serroc prisons." Not that he intended to bring either Indigo or Yiloch back alive, but he needed to keep up appearances.

Serivar frowned. The headmaster still disapproved of Myac chasing Indigo any more than he approved of him trying to court her. He had relented to the idea with some persuasion, admitting that following her might be their best method for finding and recapturing Yiloch. Things in Demin were proceeding as planned and would continue to do so if they could tie up the loose ends. Myac looked forward to doing exactly that.

Drawing on ascard again, he incinerated the ropes that bound Murchadh's wrists and ankles. The captain hissed in pain, his skin blistering from the sudden heat. Myac smiled in satisfaction, ignoring the chastising look Serivar gave him.

* * *

The sound of growling woke Yiloch. The evening was still warm, though nowhere near as stifling as the heat of day. His hand went to the sword he wore, the unfamiliar hilt one of many things that brought the misery of his situation into stark relief. An echoing growl rose in his own throat as he looked around. There were several wild dogs nearby, tearing at something that looked disturbingly familiar. It only took a second to recognize that the something was his pack of supplies. Exhaustion from many days spent walking through the desert without Ferin's skills to counter the oppressive heat was telling on him. He had slept hard enough for the dogs to drag his pack away without waking him. They could have easily gone after him instead. All the food and water he had was in that pack.

Drawing the sword, he rose and went after the dogs. They darted away, keeping a cautious distance, but still lingering much closer than he liked. They were wary of him, not afraid. He used a touch of ascard to speed an attack, bringing the curved blade around to cut deep into one dog's mottled flank. The animal let out a piercing yelp and darted away. The wound gaped open, blood flowing freely. That one would die a slow and painful death unless another predator put it out of its misery. The other dogs backed away, giving him more space.

A burning hunger to make something suffer—for his frustration, for the loss of Ferin, for the relentless dread of what the army he followed might do to his people—pulled at him, compelling him to go after more of the dogs. The exhaustion from the first small exertion, however, was enough to counter that desire. He simply couldn't afford to waste his strength right now. Reining in the bloodlust, he turned to the remains of his pack. The dogs had decimated it with remarkable efficiency. They had torn both waterskins, letting precious water bleed out into the dry soil. He picked up each one in turn, hoping to preserve some of the liquid. It was too late. All his food was gone as well.

He hurled one of the useless waterskins at the nearest dog. The animal darted out of the way and came back almost instantly to investigate the item, watching him as it licked at the traces of moisture. The wounded dog lay a short distance away, panting hard. It had given off licking the still-bleeding wound. Some of the other dogs were milling around it now, sniffing at the injury.

Glancing up at the sky, he determined which direction he needed to continue. He didn't have the ascard skill necessary to search out Kudaness villages. Without Ferin, he would have to walk north and hope he got lucky enough to come across a village or, at the very least, a water source. He glared at the dogs. It was more than possible that they had killed him by destroying his supplies.

Moving on required a substantial force of will. His arms and legs felt tied down by the same weight that dragged at his chest and made his head feel heavy. It was a feeling he knew, one he had hoped never to feel again after escaping his father's prison. Despair.

Turning his back on the dogs, he began trudging north. As far as he knew, he wasn't even in Murak lands yet, though he had no way to tell without coming upon a village. The landscape was much the same throughout the region. Rock and coarse sand spotted with thorny bushes and peculiar cacti alternated with infrequent open stretches of only sand. The terrain here was hilly, but the hills were gradual slopes he might not have paid much attention to at another time. In this setting, with all his supplies gone, each rise stole precious energy and increased the core heat of his body, wearing him down faster.

The dogs followed. They knew vulnerability when they saw it. Being a small pack, only six animals, they weren't as aggressive as they might otherwise be. They would follow and wait for him to falter. When they came too close, he yelled and brandished his blade. The dogs darted away, though never more than a few feet before coming back to resume their patient pursuit. Eventually, the wounded dog lay down. The rest continued on. The animal would never get up again. It occurred to him to wonder if the wounded beast didn't have the right idea. Why not settle down and accept fate when that fate became unavoidable?

He stopped at the top of a rise and stared out at the same landscape continuing on to the horizon in splashes of pastel color, barely discernible in the fading light. Once, he had called the desert beautiful. It was hard not to wonder what he had seen in it then. Whatever it was, circumstances had burned that beauty away. The landscape was harsh and unforgiving. There was no promise of escape on the horizon, no hope of rescue.

No, he wasn't willing to accept that he would die here. He refused to give up until the last breath left his body. He touched the ring in his pocket, hoping the hunger for revenge would help drive him. Instead, he felt pain and a deep aching hollowness within. Grinding his teeth against that hurt, he took one step at a time, making his way down the hill. He continued in the same manner for hours, sometimes counting the steps, sometimes not. At the top of each rise, he scanned the horizon for any sign of a village, trekking always north.

The terrain changed once more, stretching out flat before him as far as he could see. During the night, he stopped to take a brief break. Sheer exhaustion caused him to doze off, and he woke to find the dogs closing in. A hoarse yell sent them backing away while he stumbled to his feet. Knowing the dogs would attack if he slept, he resumed walking. They harried him onward, patient but hungry. Even with the Kudaness wrap, the heat of morning was intense and suffocating, promising a sweltering day. Hunger consumed him, and thirst made him falter. The thirst would kill him faster, though not as fast as the dogs would.

When he stumbled, there was no hesitation. One of the dogs leapt, slamming into his back with more power than he would have expected from the thin animal. Unable to stop his momentum, he fell, catching himself on hands and knees in a thorny bush. Tiny, sharp spikes dug into his palms. They were the least of his worries. Twisting, he punched the nearest dog, boosting the strength of the impact with ascard. Bone cracked, though he wasn't sure if it was in the dog's jaw or in his own hand. The animal's piercing yelp suggested the former.

Teeth sank into his forearm when he reached for the sword, and this time he was the one to cry out, a hoarse animal sound. The other three dogs moved closer, ready to attack. Yiloch seized the sword, feeling wounded muscles protesting the effort as the animal maintained its hold. He grabbed the dog's jaw, wrenching it up with ascard-enhanced strength that made the lower teeth rip through his flesh as he forced it away. With his arm free, he swept the blade around, catching another dog in the shoulder as it dug its teeth into his thigh. The animal screamed and blood flew.

With another ascard boost, he surged to his feet and went after the dogs. Even when they realized the odds had turned and started fleeing, he held onto the power until he had killed them all in a whirlwind of blood and piercing yelps. When it was over, he sagged forward, landing heavily on one knee. Heat, thirst, and exhaustion weighed him down. Blood ran from the wounds in his arm and leg, wetting his clothing. He stared at it, realizing with distant concern that he should do something to stop it.

His thoughts came sluggishly. The carnage would draw more predators. He had to move. For a time, he knelt there, mustering the will to continue, then he stood and began walking. After a few stumbling yards, the landscape lurched around him, and he collapsed, panting in the sand.

CHAPTER TWENTY-EIGHT

They came within sight of the last Lyran village they would pass before they crossed into Kudan about midday. Indigo reached ahead with her ability. The complete absence of living human ascard signatures made her stomach curdle long before they came upon the first body. There was still a faint trace of inner aspect in the dead, she realized after a more thorough investigation, but it felt different. There was a coldness to it that repelled her. Perhaps it was supposed to do so as a kind of warning, to say, "Stay away, there is death here." She wanted to heed that warning and move on. Cadmar insisted they see what the army had left behind.

Nothing was the answer.

The next body they found was well outside the village, a young woman lying face down in the dirt. It looked as though she had been fleeing for her life when someone ran her through from behind. They continued into the village at a reluctant pace, the horses even less eager than their riders to get closer to the stench of death. Many more men, women, and children lay on the outskirts, cut down while running away. They stopped at the outer edge of the village proper. More dead littered the roads, blood creating red mud in the dusty streets. Chairs, cook pots, and myriad other household items were strewn outside the doors of the houses, attesting to a thorough scavenging.

Bitter anger infused her, and she drew on more ascard, stopping only when Ian laid a hand on her arm. Glancing at him, she saw the same rage reflected in his eyes and realized there was nothing they could do about it now. She released the power.

"Can you tell if there is anyone left alive?" Cadmar asked.

She stretched her ability through the rest of the village, finding quite a few rats, a small population of cats, the odd dog or two, and many insects, but no living people. The chilling presence of the many dead sent a shiver through her. Tears crept silently down her cheeks by the time she drew back. It was a moment before she could speak.

"There's no one. Not one human life." She brushed the tears away. "Why kill everyone?"

With a small jerk of his head, Cadmar indicated that they should leave. He guided his mount to skirt around the perimeter of the village proper. Indigo and Ian fell in beside him.

"It is not an uncommon strategy," Cadmar said several minutes later, when Indigo thought the question forgotten. "If you leave enemies alive behind you, they can rally and come after you. Then you might find your-self surrounded by the people you seek to conquer."

She scowled. She didn't really care what the justifi-cation was. It was wrong to slaughter any people in such a way.

"Who are these invaders?"

Cadmar shook his head, and Ian, when she looked at him, turned away, his face drawn and full of misery.

"Do you think they did this to the Murak as well?" She asked after a moment.

"I doubt Suac Chozai would have let them," Ian replied. "He knew they were coming."

"But did he know when?"

Ian gave her a sharp look, unwilling to humor that line of thought. Facing forward, he urged his horse to a trot. Cadmar sped up, staying beside him. Indigo sighed and held her gelding back a few strides behind them.

Cadmar turned off the road a short time later, riding up to the top of a rise. He waited for Indigo and Ian to bring their horses up beside him. Before he gestured to the view beyond, she was already gaping at the scenery in awe. The land dropped off abruptly beyond the rise and, to the southeast, a vast rift opened in the landscape, stretching out so far and wide that it looked as though there was a great crack in the world. Directly south, the arid region stretched out for miles, made up of unwelcoming desert spotted with spindly bushes.

"The Kudan border is there."

She looked up to see Cadmar gesturing to some point in the landscape behind them that marked the border of Kudan. She nodded, feeling a sudden rising unease at knowing she was now in Kudaness territory. Could a Caithin in Kudan ever be welcome? Perhaps their dislike for the Caithin people was exaggerated. Regardless, she felt fortunate to be traveling with the company she had.

Trying to ease her nerves, she searched ahead with ascard, reaching out for the link that connected her to Yiloch. She found nothing. Wherever he was, he was too far away from them for her to feel him.

Or dead.

She pushed the thought away and turned to searching for any human life in the desert beyond. By late afternoon, after several more sweltering hours in the saddle, her search bore fruit. She encountered a few ascard signatures at first, then many more, none of them with a connection of any notable strength. Before long, the village came into view on the horizon, and her nerves began dancing.

"Will they be hostile?"

Cadmar grinned at her, not taking the situation seriously enough in her estimation. "They are hostile toward everyone. I am sure you will be no exception."

She let out a shaky exhale and only loosened her tense grip on the reins when the gelding started snorting and tossing his head in irritation. Cadmar chuckled, though she couldn't quite see the humor.

"He's there," Ian remarked. "I found his signature."

"I thought he would be," Cadmar responded. "This village is on the border. That makes it important to all the tribes. Suac Chozai spends most of his time here."

"They've spotted us." Her hands tightened on the reins, causing the gelding to toss his head again. "Sorry," she apologized to the animal and eased her grip.

Six dark-skinned warriors jogged out toward them from the village, moving more easily in the soft terrain than the horses did. Cadmar stopped his mount and gestured for Indigo and Ian to do the same. The approaching figures were tall and lean, as Kudaness commonly were, and each carried either an ornate spear or a curved sword. When they were close enough, she could see the tattoos on their faces, though she knew little about the significance of the symbols. All she knew was that the black designs on their dark skin somehow made them even more intimidating.

When they got within a few yards, they slowed to a walk and chatted amongst themselves, pointing at the three riders more than once. They stopped a few feet from the horses, their weapons held ready. One man advanced a few strides past the others and scrutinized each of the riders in turn. He scowled at Indigo, then settled his gaze on Cadmar and addressed him in Kudaness. The two spoke for several minutes and, wary of using ascard too much here, she watched their faces to try discerning the mood of the exchange. It became heated for several minutes, both men emphasizing their words with sharp gestures, and Ian shifted in his saddle. Then the Kudaness warrior turned and gestured for them to follow. The other five warriors moved out around them.

"What was all that?" She inquired in a whisper, moving her mount close to Cadmar's.

"They do not want us here. They have only just returned to clean up the damage from the passage of the gray army, and they are very upset," Cadmar replied, watching the backs of the lead warriors as he spoke.

"Gray army?" She recalled the uniform olive-gray skin tone of the foreign warriors and decided it was an apt description. "At least they came out of it better than that Lyran village. They could have sent someone to warn them if they knew the army was coming." Anger toward the Murak swelled in her, and she clung to it because it helped drown out her fear.

Cadmar gave her an unreadable glance and said nothing.

They followed the lead warrior into the village, moving between modest huts and other structures. The villagers were busy cleaning up the disarray the army had left behind. Belongings were being gathered, sorted, and piled outside the small dwellings, and several partially destroyed huts were being repaired. They paused in their work to offer suspicious and hate-filled glares to the trio. She did her best to ignore them, keeping her eyes forward and clinging to her anger to ward off fear. The Kudaness rarely traveled in Caithin, so seeing this many of the dark-skinned people in one place and knowing how little love they had for her people made her feel much like a mouse in a roomful of cats.

They don't use ascard. You could overpower any of them with your ability.

The thought helped some, though she was acutely aware of the spears they carried. An unexpected throw could end her life just as abruptly as it could anyone else's.

The warrior led them to a hut that was taller and longer than the others. Here they dismounted and left the horses with two of the warriors. She had to force herself to relinquish the reins to her mount. The animal was her best means of escape, and Kudaness rarely kept riding animals. She had some doubts that they knew how to properly care for them, though she wasn't about to be left outside. The remaining four warriors escorted them into the sparingly furnished hut. A few low tables and a small cabinet of ornate design stood toward the front. For sitting and sleeping, they had pillows and blankets of far more luxurious material and design than she expected of a tribal people living in the desert. She had always assumed they made the elaborate Kudan blankets in the markets that way to impress people out of their coin. That they also applied such extraordinary craftsmanship to items for everyday use came as a surprise.

The lead warrior announced Cadmar to a man standing in the center of the hut, and then the four warriors stepped to the side. From their expressions, she suspected they would kill any of the three visitors without hesitation if they behaved in a threatening manner.

This new man's muscles rippled under tattoos that wove in complex patterns over his arms, chest, and legs as he stepped up to Cadmar and gripped his arm in a congenial greeting that perplexed her, given their reception so far. The man appeared to know Cadmar. They exchanged a few words, the stranger looking at Indigo and Ian when Cadmar gave their names. His long hair, braided into myriad small braids weighted with beads, swayed with every turn of his head, giving exaggerated fluidity to his movements.

Eventually, the two men approached Indigo and Ian, and she noticed the odd, copper color of the strange man's eyes.

"Indigo. Ian. This is Suac Chozai Galal of Murak un Ani," Cadmar introduced.

Before either of them could offer a greeting, the suac spoke, demonstrating considerable mastery of the Lyran trade dialect.

"You and the creator I expected," he said, indicating Cadmar with a gesture and narrowing his eyes at Ian. "I did not expect *this one*." The last two words he spat out like a rancid berry, though his tone when referring to Ian hadn't been any more friendly. "It is as if you are not here even now, though you stand before me." He eyed her with open distrust, and his eerie copper eyes drilled into her. "Your presence hides from me."

Her initial defensive anger faded some when she realized he was sensing the ascard signature within each of them, even though she sensed no active ascard connection in him. How then, could he sense ascard at all? Maybe she misunderstood him, but it was the only logical explanation for his comment.

"I assure you, I am very much here." She wanted to ask him how he could possibly sense ascard without connecting to it in any obvious way, but she knew enough about the Kudaness to recognize that such a question would almost certainly upset him. Since his full attention was on her and she wanted nothing more than for it to be elsewhere, she skipped to the point. "We come to seek your aid."

The suac scowled, and she reminded herself again of the power she could wield as she held his dark eyes.

"You seek the Blood Prince," he hissed, stepping closer to her. His lip lifted in a silent snarl, revealing teeth filed to a slight point.

Ian took a step back.

Indigo held her ground, hoping Cadmar would step in and offer his support, but the dark warrior was silent, his pale eyes observing their interaction with curiosity. Would he tell her if she did something wrong?

"Yes." She forced the word out past the knot in her throat. "If you knew this would happen, it stands to reason that you might know where Emperor Yiloch is now."

"Where you put him?" The suac smirked at her surprise. "You are the one who stranded him in the desert, yes? You are the love who betrayed him." The dark man looked quite pleased when she flinched at his accusations. "You are the one he hates," he added this in a whisper meant for her alone.

Those last words were a knife blade through her chest. She could only stare at him for a time, fighting the agonizing ache that threatened to tear her apart. His satisfied grin hurt and enraged her. Anger burst through the pain, and she took a step closer to him, looking up into his eyes with courage born of fury.

"Whatever you may know," she hissed, her chest tight with restrained fury, "you know nothing of love. I love him and I will make right this wrong with or without your help."

Cadmar cracked a smile and nodded approvingly.

The suac took three steps back from her, a milky whiteness filming over his odd eyes. Indigo retreated several quick steps, alarmed. When he spoke again, his voice took on a rhythmic, dreamlike cadence.

"The Blood Prince will walk a path of death. Many

trials stand before him and many losses. If the half-breed and the creator come for him, he may survive. If not, he will be forever lost." His eyes returned to normal again, if the strange copper color could be called normal, and he looked at her. "You are not here."

She ignored his last words. "Where is he?"

"I see him in southern Murak. He lives, but he has lost a cherished companion and is near to becoming lost himself."

Ferin?

Silence stretched among the three of them as they absorbed the meaning of Chozai's statement. She felt sorrow and anger from both Cadmar and Ian. It was enough to feel their pain, so she walled off her own.

"Can you give us anything more specific?" She asked, a little startled by the grudging respect in his regard now. Apparently, her bold approach had been the correct choice.

He gazed at her for a long moment, searching her face for something, perhaps looking beyond anything the naked eye could see. "Travel due south from here and your paths will cross. Ilikah will test your spirit if you persist, Silent One."

He was warning her against continuing. She could see that in his eyes, feel it in the blend of emotions coming from him. Her heart gave her no choice. With everything Yiloch had gone through, he deserved an explanation from her, regardless of whether he chose to forgive her. She had to help him. She owed him that much, but the unexpected sympathy that came from the suac now unnerved her, and she averted her gaze.

"It will be evening soon," Cadmar commented. "We should get some rest."

Indigo scowled at him, and Suac Chozai mirrored her expression. He didn't want them there, and she wanted to get moving now that they knew Yiloch was close. Both worked to the same end. Cadmar looked from her to the suac and back, his jaw tightening as if he were considering the value of disagreeing, and she searched her mind for a counter to any argument he might put forth.

Eventually, he shrugged his muscle-bound shoulders. "Very well, we go on."

The suac nodded and turned to one of the warriors still waiting to the side. "Let them water their horses."

Cadmar gripped his arm again. "Ilikah watch over you."

"You need him more than I," the suac replied, his eyes drifting once more to Indigo.

She hesitated, not sure how to say farewell appropriately, but Suac Chozai turned away from them then, so she followed his example and left the tent without a word, following the other two to water their horses and continue on.

CHAPTER TWENTY-NINE

Upon arriving in Yiroth, Myac went straight to the palace to request an audience with Emperor Yiloch, knowing already that the loathsome man wouldn't be there to see him. He followed an usher into a sitting room near the main entrance hall and waited. The room, decorated with a tasteful selection of ornate wood chairs and a large, pale blue couch accented with embroidery in silver and white, hadn't changed since Emperor Rylan's death. It was somehow disconcerting to see that Yiloch had changed nothing in this room or any of the others the usher led him past along the way. The palace looked just as it had when he had been Emperor Rylan's personal adept. It struck him as almost indecent how the things that dramatically changed a person's life could leave no impression on the world around them.

He reclined in a chair, gazing into a fire that blazed hot in the marble-lined fireplace. At least with his disguise, he didn't need to worry about anyone recognizing him for who he truly was. Unless Indigo was in the palace, no one there had the power to break down his illusions. If she had been there, he got the feeling she wasn't anymore. Until the throne was securely in his father's hands, he couldn't risk going undisguised in his old home. Yiloch wanted him dead, and too many of his most loyal followers in the palace might recognize him on sight. Once Terral wore the emperor's crown, they could deal with those individuals.

The door opened, and he rose, clamping down on a defensive reaction when Captain Adran entered. He hadn't seen the captain since the night Emperor Rylan died. Adran shot him in the side with a crossbow bolt, saving Indigo from his counterassault. He struggled to hide the hatred that flared to life with the memory of that pain and the even more unpleasant loss connected to it. Adran regarded him with an air of mistrust, but, given that Caithin had taken Yiloch prisoner without warning, the reaction came as no surprise.

"Lord Edan," Adran greeted with a civil tone that didn't reflect in his curt nod or narrowed eyes. "I'm Captain Adran. I am afraid Emperor Yiloch is unavailable at this time. How might I assist you?"

Unavailable? How long did they expect to get by with that kind of ambiguity?

Myac forced a smile. "I appreciate you taking time to seem me, Captain. I thought Emperor Yiloch might have returned from his absence by now and was hoping to speak with him."

Adran's eyes narrowed even more, and the cutting resentment that came from him was stunning in its force. The captain remained outwardly courteous and cautious, not willing to assume Myac knew everything that had occurred. The absence of any effort to confirm or deny Yiloch's return convinced Myac that he also knew they no longer had the emperor in their custody. That meant one of two things. Either he had spoken with Indigo, or he had spoken with Emperor Yiloch himself. Either would be a positive development.

"Lord Terral is handling affairs on the emperor's behalf and will be joining us momentarily. Please have a seat." His voice wavered ever so slightly under the strain of the chaos of emotions he was suppressing.

Myac offered a gracious smile, enjoying the way the expression aggravated the man even further, and sank back into his seat, relieved he didn't have to come up with a legitimate reason to ask for his father.

"Are things settling in the aftermath of the assassinations?" Adran asked with a convincing show of casual curiosity.

Myac managed a sorrowful expression, matching deception with deception. "We have felt the loss of King Jerrin and his family deeply throughout Caithin, but his brother, King Gavin, has already assumed the throne. The quick transition seems to have comforted the populace."

The door opened, and Terral entered. Myac stood and allowed his father to see through the illusion for a few seconds, hoping he wouldn't react too strongly to the disclosure. To his relief and moderate surprise, Terral showed almost no outward response. Just a few blinks and a hint of fresh tension in his jaw.

"Lord Edan," he acknowledged with a nod to Myac. "Captain Adran. I believe I can handle this from here. You are welcome to go."

Though it was a gentle dismissal, it was a dismissal,

and Adran recognized it as such. A frown tugged down the corners of his mouth, and he hesitated, meeting Terral's eyes in silent defiance.

"I'm sure Lord Edan is no threat, and there are two guards outside the door if I need them. You may as well attend to other affairs."

Adran gave Myac a look of warning before exiting the room and shut the door with a bit of extra force behind him. The instant he was gone, Myac erected ascard barriers around the room to prevent eavesdropping, then turned his attention to his father. Terral was a fine example of untainted Lyran blood. Not quite as perfect as Yiloch and Emperor Rylan, but his long, pale gold hair and matching gold eyes gave him a surreal beauty. His nose was a touch too narrow and his brow a little too bold, but those flaws were slight enough to go unnoticed by all but the most discerning observers. Myac appreciated that purity almost as much as he resented it.

"I thought you had everything under control," Terral commented in a mocking tone, pacing over to gaze into the fire and putting his back to Myac.

Myac bristled. Who did the man think he was talking to? Terral knew he could crush him in his own skin with little effort.

"Once again, I find my plans being thwarted by that woman," he spat, letting frustration with Indigo distract him from his petty irritation with his father.

"The Caithin healer? Lady Indigo?" Terral rested a hand on the mantel.

"Yes. Has she been here?"

"She was here. She headed south with Creator Ian and Commander Hax's big pet, that Kudaness warrior Cadmar."

Myac took a deep breath, fighting not to lose his temper. That was always especially hard with his father. So many things might have worked out differently—better—if not for the selfish decisions Terral made in the past. If he had allowed Myac's mother to stay in the manor, she might still be alive, but he had been married to another woman then and was unwilling to bring his mistress into their home. His wife died less than a year after Prince Yiloch killed Myac's mother, leaving Terral without wife or mistress in his home. He deserved that loneliness.

"You let Indigo leave?"

Terral turned, brow furrowing with frustration. "I am not trusted. We aren't dealing with fools. Captain Adran didn't inform me of her arrival until after she was gone. Apparently, she stayed the night in the palace. I am only a figurehead here unless they declare Yiloch officially dead. Captain Adran and the others are severely limiting my control."

Myac shrugged. "Adran will need to meet with an accident before long, regardless. The man complicates things."

"It must be a convincing accident. His word holds substantial influence over Commander Hax, and I would like to keep her in her position. She's very good at what she does."

Myac nodded agreement. "She is. We have to be careful. We don't want to lose all Yiloch's most diligent supporters. He always had a talent for drawing in skilled people."

"I'd also like to keep his fiancé," Terral remarked, a whimsical smile curving his lips.

"He's engaged?"

Terral nodded. "The Lady Auryl Vyram. She and her parents are in the palace in anticipation of the coming wedding. That's delayed, unfortunately," he added with a smirk.

Lady Auryl. She was an excellent choice. She had all the right breeding and was beautiful besides. It would be disappointing to see her on his father's arm and could complicate his goals as well. He needed to ensure that Terral never sired a true heir, but he could deal with such trivialities later. For now, they had more urgent issues to attend to.

"Do you know where Indigo was going?"

"They went to find Suac Chozai Galal of Murak un Ani."

That was an unexpected answer. "A Kudaness high priest?"

"Yes. The man came seeking an alliance with Lyra a few months back, but Emperor Yiloch turned him away. He tried to warn Yiloch that he was going to be betrayed. If Yiloch had listened to his prophecy, this entire plan might have failed, not that it has succeeded yet." He scowled into the fire. "They thought the priest might know where he ended up when Indigo destroyed the prison, which was a peculiar turn of events. Why did she free him?"

"She's apparently in love with him," Myac replied

through gritted teeth. That revelation still vexed him, more so because he couldn't turn off his desire for her despite that knowledge and the things she had done. Yiloch was born to privilege. Everything he ever wanted became his, including this remarkable woman. No matter what happened, he would face her again, and this time no one else would get in the way. She would regret crossing him.

Terral rubbed his chin. "That comes as a surprise. They did seem rather comfortable together for having just met when the Caithin healers joined Yiloch's army, but they kept any romantic involvement between them well hidden during the campaign."

Myac observed his father, noting how distracted the man seemed. Worried, perhaps. He had never been the aggressive type. If not for Myac pressuring him, he would never have considered making a move to secure the throne. Terral found ample satisfaction in his life of luxury as a landholder, languorously passing his days in the beautiful valley where he had his manor. Now he wiped a finger along the mantel, then lifted it and gazed at it for a few seconds, perhaps searching for traces of dust that would indicate a failing in the cleaning staff. He had always been particular about cleanliness.

"We have another problem," he added after a long silence in which the crackling of the fire was the only sound. "There is an army heading towards Lyra."

Myac's heart stuttered. "An army. Whose army?"

"Well, if Suac Chozai is to be believed, they come from across the Rhuakine. Yiloch sent Cadmar to investigate raids at the border, and he came back with more rumors of the army the suac prophesized. I've sent additional scouts south to see what they can learn. I assume we can expect no aid from Caithin this time," he added with a resigned sigh.

"The rumors may be only that, rumors," Myac said, trying to convince himself in defiance of the heavy sense of dread settling over him.

"Perhaps, but the suac was right about many things he told Yiloch. He knew Yiloch would be betrayed by Caithin and by Lady Indigo." After a pause, his brows crept up a fraction, and he added, "And by us. It's hard to doubt the army when everything else he prophesized has come to pass."

Myac stood and started pacing the floor between the door and the fireplace. This new turn of events didn't fit into his plans at all. Indeed, the timing couldn't be less fortunate. He completed a few passes, then stopped and stared into the flickering flames.

"It goes without saying that Caithin won't send troops given recent events. If Yiloch had been convicted and executed for his crime and you properly raised to the Lyran throne, there might be a chance, but with Yiloch missing and no one officially positioned in his place, I doubt they would even humor the suggestion of an alliance against this supposed army." Myac chewed at a fingernail, a bad habit he hadn't indulged in years.

"You shouldn't do that. It's unbecoming," Terral remarked.

Myac stopped to give his father a quick glare. He spat a chip of fingernail at Terral's feet and resumed his pacing. Terral settled on the couch and watched him.

What to do?

He could go after Indigo. If she had found Yiloch, then he would be in position to destroy them both. However, if Lyra fell to the invading army, assuming there really was an army, then Yiloch's death would serve little purpose.

What to do?

"How is it that this Indigo presents such a significant threat, and yet you failed to eliminate her when you were walking the same halls at the Healers Academy?"

Myac spun to face Terral, seizing ascard in a fit of anger and using it to pin the man to the couch. Gradually, he increased the pressure against his father's chest, forcing the air from his lungs.

"Perhaps you forget who you're speaking to," Myac hissed, leaning over him.

"She captivated you, my son, didn't she?" Terral wheezed, maintaining surprising composure despite his struggle for air.

"Maybe you can handle leadership after all, Lord Terral." Myac released him and stepped back, impressed by this unusual show of audacity. "You are more familiar with the art of war. You will stay and contend with this rumored army. I will go after Indigo, deal with her, and hopefully find Emperor Yiloch in the process. If the army comes, I suggest you put Captain Adran on the front lines. Many die in battle. I'm sure you can arrange for him to be one of those casualties."

"I can handle a fight."

"Yes. That I realize. You could always destroy things with some efficiency," Myac replied with unrestrained resentment.

"Do we really need to revisit your mother's death right now?"

"No." Myac stared into the fire, barely feeling its warmth. Lyra was his home, but wrapped in this hated Caithin disguise, he felt very much apart from it. "If Indigo or Yiloch arrive here, welcome them. I will return soon and deal with it. For now, I need a swift and reliable horse."

* * *

Adran tried to listen in, placing his ear to the door, but he heard nothing, so either they weren't talking, or Lord Edan was an ascard user and had put sound barriers up. He was betting on the latter. There was something about the other man that made him uneasy. It was all too possible that this man could be Myac in his new disguise Indigo had mentioned. But if that were the case, why would Lord Terral hold a secret audience with Myac? Perhaps he was just being paranoid, but the suac had warned that Yiloch would be betrayed by family. Terral was still the closest family he had left.

Not for the first time, he cursed his inability to use ascard. Ian was gone, and the time it would take for him to track down another ascard user with the required skills would undoubtedly be more time than they needed to conclude their business.

I should have insisted on staying. It was too late now to remedy that poor decision.

"Captain Adran?"

Adran stepped away from the door. "Lady Auryl."

She put a hand over her mouth to stifle a laugh at catching him in such an undignified position. When she had composed herself, she brought her delicate hands down to smooth her skirts and smiled graciously at him. "Affairs of the empire proceeding without you, my lord?"

Adran made himself smile for her. He intended to shield her from the reality of the situation as much as possible, though her father was becoming difficult. Vyram was a shrewd man, and he was growing impatient with their evasions and redirections.

"They often seem to," he replied. "Where are you bound?"

She shrugged, sorrow reaching her eyes for a second before she chased it away with a warm smile. "I was just walking. Care to join me?"

Over the many weeks she had been there, Adran experienced a growing sympathy for Auryl. She was a lovely creature and kind, if sometimes shallow in her pursuit of fashion and gossip, but that was a product of her mother's training. Her willingness to learn to love Yiloch was admirable, and knowing she would likely never hold the leading place in his heart only made him feel sorrier for her. Although with Indigo's betrayal, Auryl at least had a chance at securing that position for herself, assuming Yiloch returned. With him missing, she seemed lost in the palace. She hadn't been there long enough to make it her home, and Adran longed to comfort her, but he felt lost himself without Yiloch there.

"I would love to join you," he replied, offering her his arm.

Auryl took it, and they strolled away from the door.

Adran longed to linger, but there was little likelihood the sound barrier would drop so long as anything of significance was being said.

"How are things with you and young Captain Leryc?"

Adran felt his face flush. Leryc hadn't spent a night in his own quarters since the evening he eagerly agreed to help Adran out after the beating Hax had given him in the sparring ring. That relationship was the one thing keeping him sane amid the current chaos. "Very well, thank you."

He adjusted their course toward the throne room. It was empty, so he led her up to the dais, gesturing for her to sit on the throne that would have been hers soon had Yiloch not vanished. Auryl hesitated, giving him an uneasy look, but he nodded encouragement, and she sat. Adran sank down on the steps and gazed up through the created crystal ceiling. Yiloch, like his father before him, loved to sit and watch the sky through that faceted ceiling. It was one of many things the two men had in common.

CHAPTER THIRTY

Ksa-jnai, First Legend of Khajikan, sat silently on his mount at the top of the hill. His seventeen bloodken, the leaders who bowed to his blade and whose souls now belonged to him by the Rights of the Conqueror, sat upon their mounts in respectful silence behind him. There were no men in the world Ksa-jnai could trust more. If these men betrayed him, their souls would be forfeit, cursed to spend the Afterworld in wretched suffering. They would never betray him.

Ksa-jnai became First Legend of Khajikan when he united all the clans of Khajikan under his rule. Within two years of his last conquest, he realized that while his people were strong, their land was weak. Khajikan did not have the resources needed to support the recent growth and advancement of his people. On the advice of his bloodnau, Ini-jnai, the First Maker, Ksa-jnai sent the sons of his seventeen bloodken to seek new lands. One of those sons, Na-ksu, returned with tales of a rich land to the west and north of the Scars. When Ini-jnai read the young man and confirmed his words, Ksa-jnai permitted the boy to kill his father and honored him as Na-jnai, the First Warrior. Then preparations began.

Na-jnai sat on his mount to the left of Ksa-jnai now,

and Ini-jnai waited to the left of the First Warrior. Before them stretched a land that promised greater riches the further north they traveled. A low range, thick with trees, lay ahead, but it appeared passable, unlike the mountains north of Khajikan that had forced them to cross the Scars into the desert lands they were now leaving behind.

That rushed trek through the desert had weakened them all, even with the First Maker's protection. Now he needed to proceed at a more calculated pace to build up the strength of his army again and keep it strong. Ini-jnai's reading of Na-jnai told of a powerful people, but those people were imbalanced by turmoil within. Ksa-jnai never failed in his conquests, and with each one his army grew stronger. This new enemy could not stop him now. Even the Afterworld would bow down to him now.

They had makers here, though. He knew that for certain, as he had felt the touch of one a few days past. The foreign maker shouldn't have been able to breach their barriers. That was Ini-jnai's failing and anger with his bloodnau still bubbled beneath the surface. The First Maker had every maker in the army bound to him and could use their powers as his own. There was no excuse for weakness. An effort to find the source of the touch had only given him a vague direction, so he turned a predatory smile way, hoping to alarm the maker, or makers, behind that contact. The sudden retraction of the foreign power implied cowardice, so he hadn't tried to search them out. Ini-jnai received a warning not to fail again.

Even his bloodnau's mistake wasn't enough to

dampen the swelling of pride as he surveyed the terrain. This land would serve as the new home for his people. His bloodnau assured him they were only just beginning to discover the vibrant wealth of the region. Na-jnai had guided them true and deserved his gratitude.

"Na-jnai, in tribute to your service, I bleed before you," Ksa-jnai declared.

Na-jnai turned to him, his deep cobalt eyes filled with the vigor of youth. "Ksa-jnai, First Legend, I accept your blood and am honored to receive it."

Ksa-jnai sidled his mount closer to Na-jnai's. The First Warrior drew his weapon and held it as Ksa-jnai struck a fingertip fast across the blade. The young man tipped his head back and opened his mouth. Holding the bleeding finger above the young man's mouth, Ksa-jnai let three drops of his blood fall onto that hungry, pink tongue, then retracted the hand. Ini-jnai mended the wound with power, not allowing even one drop more of his precious blood to be wasted. Such a gift was a rare treasure, one Ksa-jnai had offered only four times since his rise to power. Na-jnai swallowed. His smile was euphoric. He would be stronger now before both the threats of this world and the demons of the Afterworld.

* * *

Yiloch stood in the sun's fire. Layers of flesh seared and turned black, then sloughed off so the next layer down could begin the process anew. Each step was agony. His legs grew lighter as more flesh fell away, but the muscles no longer wanted to obey him. Skin, then muscle, scraped away from his feet as he dragged them through gritty sand on the power of will alone. The individual bones of his toes showed through now, stark white against the red and black flesh peeling back around them. That was as far as he could see, for his eyes had begun overheating in their sockets.

Stumbling over his own mutilated feet, he fell to his knees in the rocky sand, awash with agony as it ground into exposed muscle. The bones of his fingers were beginning to fall away, the blackened flesh that held them together disintegrating as he watched until. Then his eyes were becoming fluid, melting in the sockets. Something started scraping the remaining flesh away from his forehead. Yiloch reached up with what remained of one hand and tried to push the offending thing away.

"Stop that." A woman's voice, speaking Kudaness in a dialect he knew but couldn't place through the fog that held his thoughts captive, broke through the nightmarish images. Someone pushed his hand down, and he had no strength to resist. "The pale one is very feverish."

Yiloch tried to open his eyes, but his body wouldn't respond to his demands. He lay trapped in darkness.

"Give him this." A man's voice now. "Here."

Strong hands took hold of his head, lifting it a little and forcing his jaws open. Every point of contact hurt, making him groan. Terror flitted through him as he lay there, helpless. A foul-tasting fluid ran into his mouth, and he choked. The resulting coughing sent waves of pain through every part of him.

"Careful. You don't want to drown him." It was the man's voice again, coming from above Yiloch this time.

"Don't I?" the woman snapped back, but a smaller trickle of the fluid came into his mouth this time, and he swallowed convulsively.

The two started talking again, but Yiloch couldn't follow the conversation. The darkness that had over-taken his world began spinning, and his body grew heavier. Consciousness escaped his grasp.

* * *

"Still feverish, but some better."

The female voice tugged him awake again. She was speaking in the Murak dialect, he realized, finding it odd that he hadn't noticed that before. He opened his eyes, pleased that they obeyed him this time. They were dry and sore. He was lying on the floor of a Kudaness hut, his head propped up on pillows. A Kudaness woman tended him. No one else was in the hut, so it followed that she must have been talking to herself. In the dim light, he could see that she had her black hair braided and bound in an elaborate knot to show she was someone's mate, and a tattoo on one cheek declared her tribe.

She gave him a severe look. "You are a miserable patient. Always moaning and flailing about, fighting my ministrations. Drink."

She held a waterskin to his lips, and Yiloch pressed them together, unwilling to choke down more of the foul liquid. He refused to allow her to put him to sleep again. Moving the skin away, she gave him a long, irritated stare. After several seconds of silence, she put the skin to her own lips and took a deep drink, then held it to his mouth again.

"Water," she added when he still resisted.

He allowed some of the liquid to pass through his lips. Glorious water. The best he had ever tasted. He drank greedily until she cut him off. When he tried to sit up, she raised an eyebrow at him but didn't intervene. She merely watched with a smug, knowing smirk. It took him only a moment to understand why she didn't try to stop him, and he gave up when the interior of the hut began swimming in his vision. He closed his eyes to the sudden ache in his head and focused on breathing until the pain eased. When he opened his eyes, the woman was sitting cross-legged by the blankets, regarding him with a flicker of amusement in her eyes.

"How did I get here?" Even with some water, his throat felt dry. The voice that rasped out through it was rough and unfamiliar.

"A hunting group followed the din of the wild dogs you killed and found you unconscious. They would have left you there, but Rhiak recognized you from his journey to Yiroth with Suac Chozai. He said you were the Lyran emperor and Lyra might want you back, so they brought you here." Her sour expression told him she would have left him there.

He smirked. That was a bit of improbable luck. Only a few in Kudan would have recognized him. Most of those who would probably would have also considered leaving him there. He owed this Rhiak a considerable debt.

"Ilikah must want you alive," the woman commented, reflecting his thoughts in her own terms.

When he went to speak again, his voice cracked, and

he eyed the water skin with longing. With her lips pressed into a bitter line, she gave him another drink.

"What's your name?"

"Akiah un Rhiak," she replied, marking herself as either the mate or sister of the man who had opted to save him. "You are weak. Can you eat?"

He took inventory of his state and decided he could eat something. The weakness needed to be resolved as fast as possible. He couldn't afford to stay here.

"Yes."

"If you move slow, your head should not pain you so much." She twisted around to pick up a bowl from behind her.

Yiloch did as she advised, rising with care this time. She shoved a few pillows around behind him, pushing them up against a support post and gesturing for him to lean against them. Once settled against the post, he was in a better position to look himself over. The clothes he wore were still the clothes Indigo had stranded him in, now dirty and tattered. Bloodstained tears on one leg and arm hung open to reveal bloody bandages wrapped around the wounds he'd suffered in his fight with the dogs. The heat and pain from those wounds was more intense than anything else, though his headache took a close second. The heat worried him. Bite wounds were quick to infect, and it felt like these were well on their way.

When he was steady, he accepted the bowl from Akiah. It contained a cold soup with a bitter aftertaste. It wasn't much to his liking, but he needed whatever sustenance he could get, so he choked it down.

"Eat slow or your stomach will turn," she added, supervising him with hawk-like intensity as he sipped from the bowl. Despite her apparent dislike for him, she appeared determined to care for him as her patient.

Now that he was sitting, he noticed she was rather slight and not very tall for a Kudaness woman. She had a rounded face, not from fat, but from a wide jaw and shallow cheekbones. She was pretty in a rather childlike way, though the black tattoo of her tribe gave a touch of severity to her features.

"How long have I been here?"

"You clutter my floor for three days." She held up three fingers as she might for a child.

Alarm swept through him, making his head spin again and his stomach twist. He placed a hand on the floor to steady himself, and Akiah reached out as if to add support, then hesitated, torn between racial aversion and an apparently powerful nurturing instinct.

Three days? The army would be well ahead of him by now if they had kept up their pace. He had to get moving, and fast.

"You will only kill yourself if you try to catch them like this."

He narrowed his eyes at her, disturbed by her perceptiveness.

She responded with a tight smile. "The Gray Army passed through Murak lands not long before you came. We were not here when they came because Suac Chozai gave warning, but they ransacked our homes. The suac said they would continue to Lyra. I assume this is what worries you."

"The Gray Army?" he questioned, grimacing as he closed his eyes and bowed his head to focus on settling his stomach and quieting the throbbing in his skull.

"Yes, the men and their mounts all look quite similar. They are not pale like your people, dark like us, or even golden like the Caithin." Yiloch groaned when an image of Indigo with her soft bronze skin jumped to mind, and he opened his eyes. Akiah winced in sympathy, undoubtedly attributing the sound to his current physical condition. "These men are more of a gray shade, so we call them the Gray Army. How did you come to be here?"

The soup was soothing his throat, making it less painful when he answered her. "I was stranded in the Denilik lands by a Caithin adept," he said, hoping it would be enough of an explanation.

Her eyes narrowed with hatred at the mention of an adept. "Alone?"

The pain of Ferin's loss struck him anew, as though it had happened only seconds ago. He ground his teeth and closed his eyes. In his weakened and feverish state, it took all his will to fight off tears. There was a quick touch on his arm, like the wings of a passing insect. He opened his eyes. Her brow furrowed with concern, that strong mothering instinct in her overwhelming everything else in that moment.

"The Silik killed my companion. I might have managed better otherwise."

Closing her eyes, she waved her hand in front of her face once, palm turned in. It was a quick gesture to honor the dead, and it touched him, bringing the sting of tears to his dry eyes again. The salty moisture was strangely welcome, though the uncommon lack of emotional control grated on him.

She was silent for a few minutes after that, waiting while he struggled to control his ailing body and continued to work on the soup. The slight bitterness tasted familiar somehow, but his mind wasn't clear enough for him to place it.

"You know I am right," she said, taking the bowl when it was empty. "You need to rest and heal, or your efforts will only kill you. The army will slow. You might still have a chance to catch them."

"Why do you say that?"

She gave him a look that said he was being obtuse, but he couldn't think well enough past the fog of fever and the pain to figure it out. She sighed. "They did not linger in Kudan. There is little to keep an army of that size flourishing here. They will be weary and in need of replenishment after their hurried passage through the desert. The men and the animals will need considerable rest, water, and food to restore them. They can get that more readily beyond the Lyran border. Once they have rested, they will not drive as hard. They will want to stay strong for when they encounter your warriors."

She was right. The desert couldn't have supported their force for long. They knew that, so they pushed through hard and fast, perhaps counting on their strength to keep them going until they reached more hospitable lands. They must have sent scouts ahead to figure out how long it would take to get out of the desert.

Akiah nodded. "See. This you know. I see it in your

pure-blood eyes." She touched his jaw, turning his face to one side and frowning at his cheek. "I do not see the mark of the warrior on you, but I think it is there, hidden beneath the skin. A true warrior must be wise. He must know how to read his enemies. More importantly, he must know how to read himself."

Yiloch wanted to argue with her. He needed to move on, and yet he knew she was right. It was also pointless arguing, he realized too late. The something familiar that he tasted in the soup was the same foul liquid they had given him earlier. Its effect wasn't as instantaneous in this diluted state, but it was now drawing him back toward sleep.

"What time is it?" He asked, noting that his voice slurred a bit, the effect of the drug relaxing his muscles.

"It is late afternoon."

"One more night," he conceded, as though he had any choice now. The drug muted his thoughts so he couldn't even find it in himself to be angry with her for giving it to him again.

"Rest," she ordered. "When you wake again, we will clean you up. You stink of rot. While you sleep, I will tend your wounds."

She waited until he lay back down on the blankets, adjusting the pillows for him, and then stood, carrying the bowl from the hut. The faster he recovered, the faster he could resume his chase. He closed his eyes, letting the drug drag him into dreamless sleep.

CHAPTER THIRTY-ONE

They rose from camp well before dawn and continued south. The sky overhead was still bright with stars, and the air brisk. By noon, they would have been sweltering without ascard to protect them. After dropping the illusion the previous day, Ian had created a different barrier around them that kept the worst of the heat and harmful light away. It felt like an almost sinful luxury, but Indigo and Ian weren't at all accustomed to the harsh desert climate. Before they left the prior evening, they had bartered with the Murak for wraps that would keep the bright sun off their skin during the early hours so they could save Ian the effort of using ascard all day. There was always a chance he would need his energy for something else.

Indigo's anxiety eased some now that she had made it through an encounter with the Kudaness in their own lands. The welcome, while not warm, could have been much worse, and she had impressed herself by standing her ground with the suac. She was now far more curious than afraid. The strange whitening of his eyes and apparent soothsaying without using ascard in any discernible way was frightening and fascinating.

Even with the urgency of their journey, she had a powerful urge to go back and talk to the unpleasant suac again, though some of that was probably a manifestation of her reluctance to face Yiloch after everything that had happened, especially if Ferin was dead. As the one who stranded them here, she expected he would hold her at least partly responsible for that loss. The more she thought about it, the more she felt like she was putting her life at risk for him now more than she ever had before. Only this time, he was the one most likely to end it.

Opening herself to her ascard connection almost completely, she took comfort in the flood of nearly overwhelming power. It might be a false comfort to a degree, but he would have to catch her by surprise to do her any physical harm, unless he used Ian against her.

She watched Ian for a while, wondering if the young creator would harm her on Yiloch's orders. After poking around his emotions for a bit, she decided that, even if it meant defying Yiloch, Ian would never hurt her. It wouldn't be easy for him, though. His strong devotion to Yiloch pitted against his fondness for her would make such a situation miserable for him. She felt a twinge of guilt for the position the young creator could end up in soon. Perhaps she should turn back and let them find Yiloch without her.

Her horse began falling behind, and she realized she was pulling back on the reins. Ian also slowed and glanced back at her.

"Is something wrong?" His sudden tension told her he expected danger.

He would believe anything she said, she realized. He trusted her. She couldn't let him down.

"No. I was merely looking around." She urged the gelding to a faster walk. They were keeping a controlled pace here because of the soft footing and the heat that would wear down the horses even with ascard intervention.

Cadmar slowed to fall back next to her and pointed to their right. "Did you see our followers?"

She peered in the direction he indicated, seeing nothing but dry, thorny shrubs and odd-looking cacti. Reaching out with ascard, she found the signature of a wild dog. Once she knew where it was, she could pick it out from the surroundings. It was standing still as stone, watching them in return. An ascard sweep found several more of the animals even further out. Beyond them, a lone scavenger bird sailed through the hot air.

"They wait for one of us to fall. Game must be scarce."

She shuddered at the thought, and Cadmar, noticing her response, shrugged his big shoulders. "It is the way of life out here. You spend too much time in cities, my lady."

They urged their mounts on again, and this time she kept pace with the others.

"I find it hard enough to survive in the city of late," she commented.

Cadmar glanced at her. "Sometimes it is harder in the city. The predators there can be far more devious."

"All too true," Ian agreed.

Indigo couldn't argue.

A few hours later, Cadmar announced they were nearing the southern border of the Murak lands. That meant they should come across Yiloch soon if Suac Chozai's vision was accurate. She reached out along the link to him, caught by surprise, despite the suac's words, when she ran up against his presence at the other end. Her pulse sped up, and she struggled to keep her breath from quickening.

"He's not far now. I can feel him through the link." Her mount began dancing about and tossing its head in response to her sudden unease.

"Can we move faster?" Ian asked, his horse also starting to prance, betraying its rider's excitement.

"No." Cadmar's firm denial punched cold reality through their enthusiasm. "We cannot push the horses faster. They are not accustomed to this terrain and will injure themselves."

Indigo nodded. Cadmar was right. Ian heaved a sigh, but he brought his mount back under control, perhaps a little too firmly in his disappointment. They proceeded with Indigo leading now, following her link to Yiloch.

"It's kind of eerie, isn't it," Ian remarked into the silence a short time later.

Indigo glanced at him, puzzled.

"That whole prophet thing with the dramatic voice and white eyes." He wiggled his fingers in front of his eyes. "That man's been right about almost everything he said so far."

She smiled, though she couldn't maintain the pretense of good humor for long. Looking down at her hand, she ran a finger around the pearl in the ring. Did Yiloch hate her as Suac Chozai said? If Ferin died because of where she had stranded them, intentionally or otherwise, he might hate her now as passionately as he had loved her before. Ian's comment only made it seem more likely. From Yiloch's point of view, she had betrayed him and, in some sense, he was right.

"Are you all right, Indigo?"

She ignored Ian. Her attention was on the village that had come into view on the horizon in the stark light of late afternoon. Yiloch was there. She could feel him. He was awake and, now that she was closer, she could tell he was not well. They would need to be closer still for her to discern what was wrong. He wouldn't be aware of her unless she wanted him to be. Perhaps it was better that way. This way he wouldn't have time to consider how angry he was with her before he saw her. She drew back from him, figuring it might also be better for her not to be too aware of his feelings when they finally met again. Once that initial encounter was over, she could deal with whatever illness or injury afflicted him.

A hand rested on her arm.

She glanced over at Cadmar.

"You do the right thing, my lady," he assured.

She tried to smile and found that she couldn't this time. He gave her arm a gentle squeeze and released it.

As soon as they were close enough that the individual huts had taken shape and people became visible moving among them, several figures struck out in their direction from the village. When they converged, the lead warrior disconcerted Indigo by offering a smile and greeting them in Lyran.

"You come for Emperor Yiloch?" He looked them over with open curiosity as he spoke, his gaze lingering on Indigo before moving on to settle on Cadmar.

"Yes," Indigo replied, a little too abruptly.

He turned his full attention back to her, and an even broader smile split his features as though some amusing revelation had just struck. "Come this way. I have him." He turned and waved for them to follow. "Best get him out of my sister's hut before she decides to poison him."

Cadmar dismounted to walk with him. Indigo and Ian stayed on their horses, neither eager to waste energy walking in the soft sand.

"I am Rhiak of Murak un Sita."

"Sita is the warrior class," Cadmar explained before introducing them.

The dark-skinned warrior nodded to each in turn, his expression still curiously full of amusement. "I went to Yiroth with Suac Chozai," Rhiak explained. "Because of that, I recognized your emperor, despite the shape he was in when we found him."

"The shape he was in," Indigo repeated, alarmed by the choice of words. "Is he all right?"

Rhiak glanced up at her with unexpected warmth in his dark eyes. "Yes, Indigo un Yiloch, he will live."

Cadmar barked a laugh, and Indigo looked from him to Rhiak, confused.

Rhiak glanced between them with a look of genuine dismay. "I am sorry. I assumed from her concern and presence here that she belonged to him. Is that wrong?"

Belonged to him? Was that how they did things here? "I..." she stammered. "Well... not exactly. I..."

She trailed off and reined in her horse, her gaze locking on the figure now approaching from the village. A brilliant sunset reflected off his long, silver hair as he walked. His strides were slow and deliberate, suggesting a weakened condition, and she noticed a limp in his gait. The clothes he wore were tattered and bloodstained. A quick scan with ascard told her he was running a low fever. There was an infection developing in a wound on his thigh and another on his arm.

Cadmar glanced back at her and gestured for her to continue along with them. Somewhere deep inside she found the resolve to move forward, but she dismounted first, happy to let the sand slow her progress now. It felt inappropriate somehow, to face him from an elevated position after all that had happened. She felt barely worthy of meeting him on equal footing. She had let Serivar and Edan... Myac... use her against him.

She could see him between Cadmar and Rhiak, noting the way his eyes narrowed when he spotted her. Even without actively sensing his emotions, she could feel the sudden spike of rage through their link, riding on a wave of underlying heartache.

The group stopped in front of him. Without a word, Yiloch pulled something out of his pocket and walked between the Cadmar and Rhiak. His eyes blazed with molten fury as he approached her. Grabbing her free hand, he twisted it palm up, placed the item in it, and clamped her fingers over it. His gaze lingered for a heartbeat on the ring he had given her, then, still not saying anything, he turned away and walked back to Cadmar, patting Tantrum's neck on his way past the stallion.

Was he too angry to speak, or did he simply have nothing he wanted to say to her after all that she had done? Glancing down, she opened her hand, and her heart shattered. In her palm lay her old engagement ring, the one he had taken from her so long ago, still hanging on the chain he had put it on. Visceral pain coursed through her, so powerful it was like a violent blow to the gut, and she fought the need to curl down over that agony. She couldn't indulge her grief here.

She slipped the ring and chain into a pocket of her saddlebag, struggling to maintain an outward calm.

"Ferin is dead," Yiloch stated, staring holes through Cadmar's horse.

Again, she felt the surge of anger from him, and this time she put up a deliberate block on their link so she could avoid the anguish brought by his rage.

"We know," Cadmar replied, surprising Indigo with his curt tone. "Suac Chozai told us. Your sword is on Tantrum."

Yiloch nodded, his expression cold, his face much paler than usual. "Good. We need to get moving. Thank you, Rhiak, I am indebted to you and your sister."

Rhiak nodded, his manner subdued by the obvious tension that crackled in the air.

Cadmar was the only one willing to voice what she suspected they were all thinking. "You do not look ready to travel, Emperor Yiloch."

Yiloch scowled at him, though she saw him waver ever so slightly on his feet. "I'm assuming you noticed the army heading into Lyra?"

Cadmar answered with a stiff nod.

"Then you know why we're going now." His tone said he would suffer no arguments.

"Fine," Cadmar relented, "but we should water the horses and barter for supplies before we head out."

Ian dismounted then and walked up to Yiloch.

"It's good to see you, my lord."

Yiloch gripped his arm in greeting. "You as well." His expression softened a touch, enough to make the resentment with which he looked at her that much more painful.

He took Tantrum then, leaning on the animal for support. As they walked back to the village, Ian and Cadmar told Yiloch everything they could about the army they had seen. He responded with an accounting of the destruction the army had wrought in southern Kudan. None of them made any effort to include her in the conversation, and she preferred it that way. She had little desire to speak while she fought with the torment of her emotions. When the horses were watered and supplies gathered, Yiloch removed the Kudaness sword he wore and handed it to Rhiak. He thanked the warrior and the woman who came out to stand next to him, then strapped on his own sword and mounted Tantrum, the strain in his muscles the only show of how much the effort pained him.

When Ian asked, he told them how Ferin died, abruptly and without reason. That ended most of the conversation for the rest of the day. They stopped in the hottest part of the afternoon to rest, and Indigo took advantage of the time to do a physical scan of Yiloch and heal him from a distance. He gave her a sharp glare, apparently noticing the sudden improvement, but said nothing. Ian shifted in his spot, watching the silent exchange.

They stopped to rest again in the darkest part of the night. Unable to sleep, she waited until the others had fallen asleep and walked a short distance from the camp to stare up into the sky. The stars were so much brighter there than in the city.

She couldn't return to Demin, not after freeing Yiloch and Ferin. If she made it out of Kudan, where could she go? There was little point in staying with her current group. They didn't need her, and it was obvious Yiloch didn't want her with them.

The error of blocking Yiloch from her awareness became suddenly apparent when his arm wrapped around her, pulling her back against him, and his blade touched her throat.

Her breath caught.

"Give me a reason not to kill you," he whispered.

Anger surged to the fore, and she drew on ascard, using it to protect her hand and boost her strength as she grabbed the blade and spun away, twisting it from his grasp. It was a rash move driven by anger and panic, and the outrage in his expression told her it may have been the wrong way to handle the situation. No worse than his approach, perhaps, but still not helpful.

"I didn't know," she defended, her anger evaporating, leaving only the ache of loss in its place. His pale eyes and hair picked up the sparse light of the moon and stars. It wasn't fair to her heart that he should look so handsome at that moment. "I didn't know they planned to imprison you. They used me because you trusted me."

"But you believed them, didn't you? You believed them when they accused me of having King Jerrin and his family assassinated."

She couldn't deny it. Deep down, suspicion had taken root in her and begun to grow. Now she knew better, but it didn't change the fact that she had almost believed him guilty for a time. "I'm sorry. I was wrong."

"No amount of apologizing will make Ferin any less dead or put Lyra in any less danger."

She felt as if bands of steel were tightening around her chest. She could think of nothing more to say to him. Clenching her jaw against threatening tears, she held the hilt of his sword out to him. He grabbed it and yanked it from her grasp, either assuming she would protect her hand with ascard or not caring if he cut her. Sheathing the blade, he turned and stalked away. Indigo sank to her knees in the sand and cried, muffling the sound of her sobs with her own hands.

When she was calm again, she reached into the camp with her power and locked the three men in sleep. After she gathered the supplies she couldn't survive without, she mounted her horse and left, allowing them to slip back into a natural slumber.

CHAPTER THIRTY-TWO

The cloud-obscured sun sank toward the distant horizon. In its fading light, Myac gazed out over the forested land below. Once out of Yiroth, he had banished his disguise, savoring the ability to be himself again for a time. Weary of having to be Edan, but not wanting to draw awkward attention to himself, he used his ability to turn his hair icy blue and his eyes light silver, the color they had been in his youth when his mother still lived, before Yiloch and his father taught him the true meaning of hate. That moon-pale hair waved in the light breeze rising from the valley and sweeping over his vantage point on the hilltop. The dark bay gelding he had taken from the Imperial stables stood patiently. The animal reminded him of the old horse he had grudgingly left behind when he fled the palace the night Emperor Rylan died.

It wasn't a pleasant memory. If not for Indigo, he could have influenced that battle, choosing the victor he wanted. She prevented that, granting Yiloch victory with her actions. If the exiled prince had more inclination toward greed and less toward vengeance, Myac might still have bargained to maintain the position he held with Rylan. Unfortunately, Yiloch snubbed his offers to serve him and prolong his youth with ascard. So much nastiness that they could have avoided if only sense were more persuasive than passion. Now he was stuck out here hunting for a woman who should never have played into the equation in the first place. If he found Yiloch while he was at it, he would consider that a bonus, but Indigo needed to disappear forever. She had shown where her loyalties lay. She was far too dangerous to let live. With her out of the picture, Myac would be unrivaled in his power again.

And yet...

Rain was starting to fall, and the unmistakable scent of an approaching storm filled the air. He urged the horse on. Minutes later, a crack of thunder made them both flinch. The next village wasn't far, but the speed with which the weather was changing made it clear he wouldn't reach it in time. The restless calm gave way to thunder that shook the ground, and flashes of crackling light danced across the sky. Spreading his ability, he searched to either side of the road ahead and came upon a small building. Allowing the now torrential rain to soak him through rather than waste power, he angled the horse in that direction.

With the rain coming down as hard as it was, he didn't see the house until he was almost upon it. Another quick scan told him five people were inside, three of them children. This place would do. He wasn't in much of a mood to deal with awkward questions, but he could eradicate that issue simply enough. Peasants died all the time and, secluded as they were, their bodies would go undiscovered for a while.

He drew on ascard, ready to silence the residents before he saw their faces. A bright flash and a deafening crack stunned him for an instant. The horse reared and twisted, letting out a squeal as it leapt away from the nearby lightning strike. A tree branch crashed to the ground a few feet away. Myac also hit the ground, the force of the impact sending bolts of pain through the scarring in his chest, and his heart faltered for a beat. A cry ripped from his throat, a wrenching sound of agony and panic.

He drew in a tempest of power, ready to force his heart to resume working should it not do so on its own. Seconds later, when his heartbeat stabilized, and the pain was less severe, he became aware of figures gathered around him, mere shadows in the downpour.

"Oh dear. We'd best get him inside. Mord, see if you can catch his horse."

I was about to kill you.

A haze of persistent pain left him dazed, making it hard to speak, which was probably a good thing given the direction of his thoughts. Strong hands gripped under his arms, taking care not to worsen any injuries. Another set of arms wrapped under his legs. Fresh agony pulsed through him from his right arm when they lifted him, and a moan escaped his lips.

"We can put him on our bed." A woman spoke from somewhere to his left.

A grunt of acknowledgment came from the man at his head. Unable to focus, Myac closed his eyes and turned his attention to healing the cracked bone in his forearm. Maybe he wouldn't kill them tonight after all.

* * *

Myac's own moans woke him. The deep ache that resonated through his chest kept Indigo at the forefront of his thoughts, whether he was asleep or awake. A brisk breeze blew in through the door of the small home, chilling him in the cot on which he lay. It was the light of day, though, not the chill, that motivated him to rise. Wary of his condition, he sat up slowly. Everything was stiff and achy, muscles resisting when he got to his feet. His body had taken a beating from the fall. Scarred tissues protested when he stretched his chest with a deep inhale.

"You're awake."

A woman hurried in through the open doorway, setting down a basket of greens and wiping her hands on the pale apron that years of wear had stained to a tan almost as dark as that of the simple dress she wore. The choice of color wasn't flattering with her pale gold hair and paler skin, but perhaps that was intentional. She already had a husband and three children. She didn't need to put effort into attracting a man. Still, despite the drabness, there was a hint of beauty that whispered across her face when she smiled.

He managed a nod while he struggled to remember her name. When they brought him in the previous evening, she and her husband had given him their bed and promised him a warm meal in the morning. The chance for warm food cooked and served by someone else, along with a bed that was at least a little above the cold ground and out of the rain, sounded glorious by the time he had finished healing the arm. The compassionate welcome the family offered was a bonus he appreciated under the circumstances. If they hadn't offered, he might have gone on with his original plan, but it would have taxed him after the healing. He had meant to be back on the road before dawn, but, even with the hardness of the bed, his injured body had clung to sleep longer than intended.

"Lady Kynna," he greeted, pulling her name from a vague memory of the rather hasty introductions the night before in time to save himself the embarrassment of asking for it again.

"Lady." She tittered and gave a dismissive wave of her hand, her cheeks picking up a hint of flush. "Aren't you the flatterer? Didn't wake you, did I?"

"Not at all." *I woke myself with my pathetic moaning.* "I must be on my way."

A disapproving frown detracted from that hint of lost beauty. "You took a nasty fall. I don't know that you're well enough to travel."

"I'm well enough, given the urgency of my journey," he countered.

"Well then, it'll please you to hear we found your horse. He's in our pen. Your saddle and things are next to the door. You must have a bite to eat before you head out. Get some strength back," she insisted.

He surprised himself by chuckling at her maternal doting. Perhaps he could forget all this madness and travel around letting other people's mothers care for him. How long could such a ploy last? It would be far less apt to get him killed, whereas confronting Yiloch and Indigo was a dangerous venture at best. The thought had a simplistic appeal to it, simplistic and entirely impractical. He knew himself too well to believe such a life would satisfy him for long.

For me, there is only vengeance or death.

The thought dampened his mood, but he faked a smile for Kynna when she ushered him to the gouged and stained dining table. Not for the first time, he wondered over his choice of direction. Behind him waited a spineless father who would probably betray him in an instant if things went any further awry. Before him he might find Emperor Yiloch, who wanted him dead, and Indigo, who would be all too happy to help the emperor achieve that goal.

Indigo, the beautiful and very lethal adept who was unquestionably more dangerous than any other threat he had ever faced. That way waited confusion as well. Did he want her dead? Her mere existence made him feel so alive that it was hard to want her gone. It wouldn't matter in the end. Regardless of what he wanted, she believed she needed to destroy him. As an enemy, she was far too powerful to ignore.

"You seem a bit troubled, if you don't mind my saying so."

He glanced up as Kynna returned to the table with bread and some spiced cheese warmed over the fire. The aroma made his stomach growl. She chuckled and sat down on a stool, perhaps meaning to ensure that he ate enough before heading on his way. He noticed her knees sat apart beneath the skirt, more in the manner of women soldiers he'd known than any lady. Odd as it was, that simply quirk put him more at ease in her presence. Resting her elbow on the table and her chin in her hand, she settled to watch him.

Amused by her manner, he took a bite of the bread. It was fresher and softer than he would have expected. It took him back to his childhood when his mother baked such fine food for him.

"Is it a woman?"

The bread and cheese lost some of its appeal. He met her penetrating gaze. He shouldn't be lingering here. The world was changing without him outside the door of this dark little hut.

"Isn't it always?" He answered, intending it to be more flippant than it sounded. When had it ever been a woman for him? It wasn't about a woman now, was it? This was about power and vengeance, and about making Yiloch pay for his crimes and for the fact that *she* loved him. His free hand started balling into a fist, but he caught it and forced himself to relax.

"Unless it's about a man," she responded with a wink and the flippancy he had shot for and missed. "Is she beautiful? I bet she is."

His hand paused, holding another bite inches from his lips. Indigo strode to the forefront of his mind, as vivid as if he had looked upon her only seconds ago, all soft curves and fierce determination, the remembered smell of her skin altering the taste of the food. A wistful smile touched his lips as he continued to eat without answering.

"That's a yes then. A handsome gentleman like you should have no trouble with women."

He swallowed the bite in his mouth. "There are all kinds of trouble, my lady."

"A noble lady, then?"

He eyed her curiously.

"You don't talk with your mouth full, and I'd bet, from your looks, that your blood's near as pure as the emperor's."

A weary exhale slipped from him. The comment would have been far more pleasing without the mention of Yiloch. He did find it gratifying to have her recognize the purity of his blood, though. He had kept his pale features contrasted by the pitch black of his hair and eyes, reminders of the insult and injury he had suffered, for so long that he had forgotten what it felt like to be admired. Her admiring regard was a pleasant caress to his somewhat trampled ego.

"Yes. A noble lady," he conceded, hoping to appease her.

"Going home to her, are you?"

He finished the last few bites and rose, grabbing his equipment from inside the door. A deep, unfamiliar ache spread through his chest. Not from the inadequately healed injury this time, but something else. This was a new feeling, one that didn't originate from a physical wound. It made him uncomfortable.

"My life will never be so simple, Lady Kynna," he replied, hearing the bitterness in his own voice.

The woman sat back, a new sorrow in her expression erasing all traces of former beauty from her face. She looked worn down and near to breaking.

"I'm very sorry, my lord," she offered in earnest.

The sympathy touched him. Rarely was he the recipient of such treatment. He reached out with ascard to reverse some of the age in her face in thanks for her kindness, but he encountered something within her. A blackness rooted there. A dark sickness slowly eating her alive that was well beyond his skill to heal. He drew his ability back, the ache within expanding.

"Thank you," he murmured, his shoulders sagging as he turned away.

She said something else as he walked out, but her words didn't reach him, becoming as lost as she would be soon. What did it matter if you lived a simple, honest life? Death came for you in the end, all the same. He saddled the borrowed horse under a heavy cloud of melancholy and mounted, still stiff with the lingering aches from the fall. That was a pain he could heal, but it seemed like too much trouble somehow.

Sitting in the saddle, the horse awaiting his direction, he glanced back the way he had come. It might be easier to go back and wait for Indigo or Yiloch to return. It might be safer as well. Then again, to risk dying at Indigo's hands somehow seemed preferable to living without bringing some closure to his odd relationship with her.

What is wrong with me? He closed his eyes to the cool morning air, the rich, musty smell of the recent rain filling his nose. *I will be prince and, in time, emperor. I will have my revenge on Yiloch. This is what I want. It's what I have always wanted.*

A sharp pain shot through the scar on his chest. He doubled over, gasping. The horse shifted. He ground his teeth and numbed some of that pain with ascard.

How many more times could he dodge death? Was it worth the suffering?

Catching his breath, he sat up in the saddle and looked back once more. Then he kicked the horse, following the trail that would take him to Indigo and, he hoped, Yiloch.

CHAPTER THIRTY-THREE

Yiloch was already awake and adjusting saddle-bags on Tantrum when Ian woke. He felt the brush of the creator's power sweeping the camp and then reaching out beyond. Less than a minute later, Ian ran over to him, face twisted with worry.

"Where is Indigo? I can't sense her. Not even through our link."

Yiloch shrugged, doing his best to ignore the irritating nagging of his own silent anxiety. He had considered killing her for what she had done, but when the moment came, he couldn't follow through. Driving her away was the next best option. Now he had to face the truth. Running her off had worked, and he hadn't honestly expected it to. Some part of him had even hoped it wouldn't. The whole situation, complicated by his unreliable emotions, only made his blood boil hotter.

"Her whereabouts are her concern. If she wanted any of us to know where she was going, she would have said something."

"What did you do to her?" Ian demanded.

Yiloch turned on him, sword instantly in hand, the point coming to rest at the hollow of Ian's throat. The weight of the familiar weapon felt good in his hands, and his rage demanded that he draw blood with it, anyone's blood. The color ran out of Ian's face, but he stood his ground.

"Given what she's done, I imagine her own guilt got the better of her," Yiloch snarled.

Cadmar stepped in then, pushing Ian back from the point of the weapon. Some distant, calmer part of Yiloch found the young creator's show of courage impressive. Not so long ago, he would have cowered before such a show of anger. Mostly, however, it only aggravated him that the young man's courage manifested now, in defense of Indigo. Lowering the blade, he turned away from them and started sheathing his sword when Ian spoke again.

"They used her."

Yiloch clenched his jaw, trying to hold his temper at bay even as his hand tightened on the hilt.

"Now isn't the time," Cadmar said, attempting to intervene.

"What better time," Ian snapped.

Yiloch turned to see the lanky creator trying to push the wall of muscle that was Cadmar out of the way. In different circumstances, it might have been amusing. When Cadmar didn't budge, Ian settled for darting agilely around the other man to continue his defense of Indigo.

"Where would she have gone from here? Where can she go now?" he growled. "She risked her life, not for the first time I might add, to try to save you. She faced down Myac to protect you and made herself an enemy to her own country."

Yiloch hesitated, wishing he could ignore the doubt nagging at him, strengthened by Ian's words. "Myac?"

"Yes," Cadmar answered, placing a hand on Ian's shoulder and moving the creator back again. Realizing he still had a death grip on the sword, Yiloch sheathed it and moved his hand away. The big warrior gave a nod of approval and continued. "Myac has been hiding out in Demin using an assumed identity—an ascard disguise. He followed her into the prison when she went there to free you. That is why she destroyed the stone the way she did and stranded you here. She was afraid Myac would kill you if she brought you out with her."

Yiloch wanted to disregard his words. So many terrible things had happened because of her actions. Holding onto his anger was far easier than admitting he might have been mistaken. If he was in the wrong, then he also had to acknowledge that he still cared about her, that he worried about where she had gone, and he could no longer use his anger to help him endure the many things he had lost and still stood to lose. Then again, if he were to be honest with himself, he had never stopped loving her. That was why it hurt so much. He could still see the anguish in her eyes when she apologized to him, and he had turned her away.

"She should have trusted me." The words sounded weak and false when he spoke them, their hollow ring echoing in the emptiness that filled him.

"She does," Ian snapped, his temper still high. He started forward again, and Cadmar stopped him with a hand on his chest. Seeing the rage flare in the youth's eyes, it dawned on Yiloch how lucky they both were that he hadn't lashed out with his ascard ability. With a little creative application, Ian's skills could be lethal, and neither of them had the ability necessary to oppose him. "She also knows you well enough to know that you have your own goals and will let nothing stand in your way. Why wouldn't you want Jerrin dead? You even talked about eliminating him after you had the empire settled if it was necessary to end the slave trade."

"She should have at least known that I wouldn't have made such a mess of it," Yiloch snapped. Ian's lip twisted in a silent snarl, and Yiloch felt him drawing on ascard now. He narrowed his eyes at the creator. "Think before you act."

Ian closed his eyes, his hands balling into fists. Yiloch could feel him draw on more ascard, his breath coming fast and shallow. If he gave Ian a chance to lash out at him with his power, it wouldn't end well for him. For an instant, he considered plunging his sword into the young creator's chest to stop him, even if it meant injuring Cadmar. He didn't want to hurt the creator, though, and not only because of what his death would do to Adran. Ian had become a part of his inner circle, so he made himself wait. After almost a minute of silence, he felt the power fade as Ian gradually released it.

Yiloch turned and mounted Tantrum. "Come, we have a long way to go, and we've got an army to catch."

Ian stormed over to his mount, making the animal flinch when he snatched the reins. Cadmar shook his head, long black braids swaying with the movement. Yiloch urged Tantrum forward, pleased at least that he no longer had to trudge through the dreadful sand on foot. It wasn't much, but even a minor improvement in his situation was welcome. The other two joined him after a few seconds, Cadmar riding at his side with a deep scowl etched in his face and Ian lagging, his dark expression enough to make it clear he was still at war with his anger. Yiloch shook his head, struggling with his own tumultuous emotions.

Where have you gone, Indigo? Where did my anger send you?

Ian was right, she had nowhere left to go.

* * *

Indigo found her way back to the northernmost Murak village without trouble by following the path of the sun and, when she was close enough, the ascard signature within Suac Chozai. Cold resolve had replaced the ache within her. There was no way she could rectify her situation now. She had turned herself into an exile from her home country and made an enemy of the man she loved. Now that Yiloch was in reliable hands and had made it quite clear he didn't want her around, it seemed as good a time as any to take another chance.

With considerable expenditure of energy, she kept her mount moving at a fast trot along the return trip by hardening the ground under his hooves as they went. The energy it required on top of all the continuous barriers and masks she maintained was draining, but she needed to get well ahead of the other three. She knew she was trying to outrun her sorrow, but a very real possibility existed that they would try to interfere with her plan.

After hearing what happened to Ferin, she suspected begging for Kudan's aid against the Gray Army would be nothing short of repulsive to Yiloch, and the way he had disregarded the suac's warning might make them reluctant to give it even if he did beg. Having seen the army in the flesh, however, she had little doubt that Yiroth would fall to them if left on its own. At least Lyra wasn't at war with Caithin, though that could have changed since her departure given the situation.

The first problem she encountered on her return to the northernmost Murak village was the fact that not all the Kudaness spoke Lyran. As she spoke only Caithin and reasonably fluent Lyran, this presented a challenge, but only briefly. The warriors who intercepted met her efforts to make them understand she wanted to see the suac with threatening gestures and shouted words until someone who recognized her from the previous visit came to investigate the ruckus. Then two warriors escorted her at spear point to the suac's long hut while another held her mount, scowling at the poor animal in such a way that she felt guilty leaving it behind.

She hurried into the hut to stay out of range of their spears while trying not to look as harried as she felt. Her prior encounter with the Murak high priest suggested he wouldn't have much sympathy for any show of weakness.

The suac sat cross-legged on some rugs, carving at something with a small blade. When he looked up, his dark copper eyes narrowed, and his lip lifted in a snarl, showing off one sharpened incisor. With a deliberate show of annoyance, he slapped the blade and the other object down to one side and got to his feet.

"Again, you arrive here unexpectedly," he snapped, coming at her with a fierce glare and a long, sweeping gait that put in her mind the image of a predator about to leap upon its prey.

She stood firm, encouraged by his use of the Lyran tongue. He was at least willing to communicate with her for the moment. "I want you to unite the Kudaness and convince them to go after the Gray Army."

His advance came to an abrupt stop. He blinked at her a few times, his pinched brows suggesting he wasn't sure he had heard her correctly.

She held his gaze and waited.

After a long moment of silence, he shook his head. "No. The gods have not advised such action. You are an insect who does not recognize the danger of a booted foot. Leave this place before you are stepped on." Waving a hand toward the entrance, he turned and started back to where he had been sitting.

One warrior raised his spear and gestured to the door. Ignoring him, she took a few steps after Suac Chozai. The warrior grabbed her arm in a biting grip, and she resisted the urge to sear his palm with ascard. When she stopped and didn't struggle against him, the firm hold eased a fraction.

"You said once that my presence hides from you. If I am not truly here, then it will do you no harm to hear me out."

Suac Chozai turned once more and walked back to her, stopping less than a foot away to scowl down at her. The dark man was quite a bit taller than her, and his muscular, tattoo-covered torso gave him an advantage in sheer physical intimidation. In power, however, although he had a strong connection to his inner aspect, he didn't seem to have conscious control of it, which put her at a distinct advantage, so she continued to hold her ground, staring back up at him.

"If the Gray Army takes Lyra, do you really believe they will leave Kudan in peace? You pose a threat they will be eager to eradicate." She rushed the words out, feeling impatience from the warriors behind her.

"If they return, the gods will warn us, and we will deal with them," he replied, his tone final.

"Perhaps. You can assume you will see them coming next time, but you didn't see me coming." She saw a flicker of uncertainty in his eyes at her words. It vanished almost immediately, to be replaced by a haughty smile, but she had sown a seed of doubt in his mind. "If the Kudaness attack from behind while Lyra defends at the front, you would crush the Gray Army in between. Doesn't that make more sense than waiting to face them when they return here, rested and ready to fight you? Why let them set the terms of that encounter?"

Suac Chozai turned and walked to a corner. For a moment, she thought she was being dismissed again, but the warrior released her arm and the suac drew a waterskin from a small, ornate cabinet. He carried this back to her.

"You confound me, Unseen Woman," he said. "I know what you are. You are a user of ascard. It is sacrilege to use the power of the gods as you do. Yet there is something different about you. Your words also carry a trace of wisdom. It is possible the gods may have given you the power you wield for some purpose, but there is only one way to be sure."

He took a long drink from the waterskin. When he lowered it, a violent shudder passed through him. Then he wiped his lips with the back of one hand and held the waterskin out to her. This time she took a step back, regarding the offering with suspicion.

"If you expect me to consider your words, I must ask you first to walk among the gods with me."

Her heart fluttered with fear so sudden and strong that it left her lightheaded, but this was a crucial turning point. To refuse would seal her defeat. Steeling herself, she took the waterskin, meeting his copper eyes as she raised it to her lips. He started swaying, those thick muscles relaxing into a motion made disconcertingly graceful by the long, weighted braids swaying behind him. The smell from the waterskin made her stomach churn. She hesitated, noticing the way his copper eyes had lost their focus.

With a deep breath to strengthen her resolve, she lifted the waterskin and tilted her head back, taking a swallow of the fluid into her mouth. For a few seconds she thought she would throw up before she could even get the thick, vile liquid down, then she managed a choking swallow. She tried to hand the waterskin back to him, but another hand came forward and claimed it. The warrior closed the waterskin with reverence and returned it to the cabinet. Then he and the other warrior left the hut, leaving her alone with the swaying prophet.

Before she could contemplate what the suac might

expect of her, a wave of dizziness swept over her and a humming sound started up in her head. No, the suac was humming, a deep, almost guttural sound with a strange, hypnotic rhythm. The rhythm filled her mind, taking control of her body and muting her thoughts. She almost began swaying with him, but terror stopped her. Pain coursed through her body then, radiating out from her stomach. She felt weak. Reaching out, she tried to catch herself on the nearest object, which had been Suac Chozai, only he was no longer there.

After what seemed like an endless fall through blackness, she landed on her knees in the sand. Open desert stretched to the horizon on all sides. It was night, and a hint of red tinted the edges of the bright stars. They swayed in the sky as if hung upon strings. The air was crisp, making her shiver, but the pain was gone. No, not actually gone, just distant.

Was she awake or dreaming? Had they drugged her and dumped her in the desert?

She stumbled to her feet again, finding it hard to balance. When she turned, she let out a cry of surprise as the suac appeared in front of her. He placed a firm hand on each shoulder, catching and holding her gaze.

"Don't fight the movement. Let it take you."

His voice was deep and soothing. When his lithe, muscular body started swaying again, she moved with him, not sure she had the power to do anything else. His copper eyes continued to stare into hers, and she felt helpless to pull away when he placed a large, calloused hand against her face.

Thunder rumbled through the air, the sound of

hundreds of horses running. Then the Gray Army surged around them, not touching them. Terror swelled in her, but she couldn't turn to look directly at them. She could only see them in her periphery, passing by on either side as though she and Suac Chozai were naught but a tree in their path. The copper eyes before her narrowed, brow furrowing with intense concentration. Then she saw his eyes widen as Kudaness warriors moved past them by the hundreds, pursuing the Gray Army.

Even in this disoriented state, she felt a smug smirk curve her lips. The suac released his hold on her, all but shoving her away from him. Her balance already compromised, she reeled backward and fell through darkness again.

When she woke, Indigo threw up on the blanket she had fallen on. Sweat dampened her hair and clothes, and her whole body trembled. Her stomach continued to spasm even after it had nothing left to send up. By then she could focus enough to use ascard to settle things down. Rolling over onto another blanket, she closed her eyes and panted until she became aware of the sound of someone chuckling. Opening her eyes again, she noticed first that the soiled blanket was already gone. The next thing she noticed was Suac Chozai sitting cross-legged on more blankets, laughing at her. As soon as his eyes met hers, his merriment vanished, and he stared at her, looking not quite angry, but not pleased either.

She struggled up to a sitting position and met his eyes.

"I was right." Her voice came out sounding hoarse, as though she had been screaming for a long time, and her throat felt raw.

He answered with an irritable scowl. "It appears so. The gods do not lie."

She arched an eyebrow at him, pleased at being able to resurrect the smugness despite feeling like a herd of horses had trampled her. "Shouldn't you be gathering the warriors?"

"I waited for you to awaken. The other suacs must be consulted. We will go to Farid. This is your spirit journey. You must see it through."

He tilted his head, and a beam of light shining through the crack between the door flaps reflected brightly off the metallic copper of his eyes. Those odd eyes had gained an intimate familiarity, and she shuddered as the shared experience that created that intimacy replayed in her mind. Looking away, she worked through her body with a quick healing, doing what she could to mitigate the weakness brought on by the violent sickness. When she was done, weariness tugged at her.

"Could I have a bite to eat and a little rest before we leave?'

The suac nodded. "I must prepare. Rest, Unseen Woman." He gestured to a pile of pillows and rugs.

"Indigo," she countered.

He responded with an absent nod and stood.

Too tired to care what he insisted on calling her, she moved to the pile and curled up among the pillows.

CHAPTER THIRTY-FOUR

Physically, Yiloch felt good. The healing Indigo had done was more thorough than he had initially realized. She had mended his wounds, taking away the fever and weakness from the infection. He felt stronger than he had in some time, more ready than ever to give chase. The Gray Army wouldn't be moving as fast now that they were in a region where supplies were easier to come by and resistance more likely. If he could get to AhnSegys, he knew the backcountry from there to Yiroth well enough to cut considerable distance from their journey over sticking to the main road, which meandered around, avoiding terrain that was less hospitable to wagons and large groups. They could make up time that way and perhaps still get ahead of the army.

The improvement in his health made it impossible for him to put Indigo out of his mind. For the most part, he managed to act as if he didn't care about her whereabouts, but he couldn't convince himself that he hated her anymore. Knowing she had defied her country for him and that Myac was involved made it hard to feel much more than sympathy for her.

He couldn't deny the truth in Ian's accusations either. King Jerrin had been one of his prospective future targets. He wanted someone on the Caithin throne who would work with him to abolish the slave trade that demeaned his people. Even his love for Indigo wouldn't have given him pause when he was finally ready to move against the Caithin king, but he had been far from that point and would have attempted to negotiate an end to the trade before resorting to more violent solutions. Now, even if he could stop the Gray Army, a substantial threat lurked across the Gilded Strait as Caithin continued to seek justice for the death of their royal family. Trying to face two formidable foes now would be the end of Lyra.

Tantrum kicked out in irritation, reacting to his troubled mood. He gave the stallion a sharp nudge in the ribs as a reprimand and took advantage of the resulting twist to one side to glance back at Ian. Would the creator even tell him if he sensed Indigo now? It was highly unlikely that she would alert him to her presence after what he had done, but she might let Ian be aware of her through the link she shared with him. Facing forward again, he weighed the value of asking and decided that, had she wanted any of them to know where she was going, she would have said something before she left. Ian wouldn't know any more than he did.

They were nearing the last village in the Murak lands. It would be easy to pass it by and certainly faster, but he wanted to have a word with Suac Chozai about the ambiguity of his prophetic statements. It wouldn't be a polite word either. The doubts instilled in him by the suac's prophecy had encouraged him to believe that Indigo betrayed him, not only with her actions but also with her heart, and he had treated her more cruelly because of that. If what Ian and Cadmar said was true, then she had been almost as much of a victim in this as he was.

It hadn't escaped him that there was also a chance, however slight, that Indigo might be there. Even if she had left immediately after their argument, she only had about a six-hour lead. If she had dallied anywhere to rest, then they might still catch up with her.

"Are we stopping here?" Cadmar asked when Yiloch angled towards the village.

"The horses need water if we are going to be picking up the pace soon."

"Of course." Cadmar's tone said he suspected there was more to the visit than that, but he didn't press.

No one came to meet them as they approached. Perhaps they recognized Cadmar and Ian and assumed they were no threat. Many Murak watched them with typical wary intensity when they entered the village proper, but no one challenged them as they dismounted to lead the horses to the water. Yiloch noticed fewer warriors than he would have expected to see, given the recent passage of the Gray Army. When he gave Cadmar a querying look, the big man only shrugged. One warrior eventually approached them at the watering hole, nodding to Yiloch, then each of the other two in greeting. The order of that greeting was the only sign that he knew who Yiloch was.

"I would like to speak with Suac Chozai," Yiloch stated.

The warrior shook his head. "Suac Chozai has gone to aid a spirit journey."

"Did Lady Indigo, the woman who was with us before, pass through here?" Ian asked, jumping in to take advantage of a momentary silence.

The warrior nodded.

Yiloch kept his expression neutral despite the sudden spark of hope that made his pulse quicken. Ian was far less discreet. He stepped toward the warrior, eyes lighting with excitement. The warrior stepped back in response, his hand coming to rest on the hilt of his sword. Ian glanced at the weapon and dismissed it, so Yiloch did the same. If the creator was aware of the potential threat, it wasn't likely the warrior would have the chance to inflict any damage.

"When? Is she still here?"

"She was here. She is now with Suac Chozai."

The spark of hope transformed into a painful tightening in Yiloch's chest. "Where did they go?"

"On a spirit journey." Annoyance in the warrior's tone and expression made it clear he had given them all the information he intended to.

"We need to know where," Ian insisted.

Yiloch already knew what the warrior's answer would be. Spirit journeys were sacred to the Kudaness. Did Indigo have any idea what she was getting into?

"A spirit journey belongs to those who take it. No one else can know its purpose or destination. Suac Chozai and the woman walk with the gods. They do not walk among us, and we cannot follow where they go."

Ian took a deep breath, his fists clenching as he scowled at the warrior. "Are you saying you don't know where they went?"

The warrior nodded. "It is not my place to know."

"They took warriors with them, though," Yiloch guessed, sweeping his arm to point out the diminished population of the village.

"Some," the warrior replied.

Then, wherever they went, they expected it to be dangerous. Yiloch looked past the warrior and the huts to the vast expanse of desert land beyond. A light wind lifted an eddy of sand, twirling it through thorny shrubs and sweeping it around in an elegant dance before laying it to rest in a new spot.

He turned to Ian. "Can you sense her?"

"No, but I can't sense her when she's standing next to me if she doesn't want me to," he replied, an edge of frustration in his voice.

Where are you, Indigo, and do you have any idea what you're doing?

Tantrum was still drinking deep, so Yiloch continued to gaze out at the desert, scratching the big animal's shoulder while he struggled with the urge to go looking for her. Then his thoughts turned to the army he had followed all the way north, and he realized he didn't have time to indulge such desires. Wherever she was, she wasn't alone. The suac and his warriors were capable of protecting her from outside danger. There was no one there to protect her from them, though. He had no choice but to be satisfied with that for now. They had much greater problems to solve ahead of them, and they couldn't abandon his empire to the Gray Army for anyone, not even Indigo.

Tantrum began sniffing some pots sitting next to

the watering hole. The other four horses also appeared finished, so Yiloch thanked the warrior for telling them what he could and mounted. The stallion tossed his head, still going strong despite long days of travel. He rested his hand on the dappled neck, and the animal stilled under his touch.

"What about Indigo?" Ian hesitated alongside his mount, staring out at the desert.

"She has more power in her than any of us, and she's not alone," Yiloch replied, hoping the company she was with wouldn't prove to be worse than no company at all. "We need to return to Yiroth."

Ian stroked his horse's neck, then moved his hand to the cantle, but he still didn't mount. When he spoke again, his tone was bleak. He already knew what their path had to be. "I could stay and look for her."

Yiloch suffered a pang of longing to do exactly what Ian offered. "I need you."

Ian turned, distress shining in his pale blue eyes when he looked up at Yiloch. "We *need* her," he insisted. "If not for the simple pleasure of her company, then certainly for the power she can wield."

Yiloch took a deep breath, seeking patience within himself. The misery he felt over driving her off and now leaving her behind made his temper quick, but he also needed Ian and they had talked enough.

"I don't disagree with you," he said after careful consideration. "But the Gray Army will slaughter our people, and they won't wait for us to find her. If I can't have you *and* Indigo, then I *must* have you. I would go after her myself if I could."

Ian met his eyes, a hint of shaking in his hands where they rested on the saddle. "Would you? Would you really? Do you understand what you did wrong?"

Yiloch held the young man's gaze, remembering a time not so long ago when he had been the one pointing out Ian's mistake with those exact words. He tried to generate anger at the young creator's audacity. No anger came, only a deep, sorrowful longing to take back what he had done. Would he ever see her again if he left her behind this time?

"Yes, I do."

Something in his tone or expression must have convinced Ian. The creator mounted up and nodded to Yiloch. Cadmar, who had watched the exchange with passive interest, mounted as well, checking that the lead to Ferin's unneeded mount was secure once seated. They left the village traveling three abreast now, and the mood of his companions was much less bitter, if still somewhat melancholy. It was disconcerting to see how much influence Indigo had over his men.

For his part, Yiloch could only wonder what she might be doing. Why had she gone with Suac Chozai on this supposed spirit journey? I had a hard time believing the suac's intentions were good considering how his people felt about the Caithin and anyone who used ascard. Did the man have any inkling of how great her power was? The warrior said they were walking with the gods. A true Kudaness walk with the gods involved a potent, mind-altering drink that was actually more of a poison, and it killed nearly half of those who tried to use it. That knowledge didn't bring him any comfort. The

Kudaness already owed him for Ferin's life. If anything happened to Indigo, they would suffer a thousandfold for it.

If the Gray Army doesn't destroy us first.

Tantrum kicked out at Cadmar's horse, acting on Yiloch's irritation, and he corrected the stallion again.

"Do you think she'll be safe with the suac?" Ian asked, giving Tantrum a wary glance as he moved his mount closer.

Yiloch's initial inclination was to say no, but he held his tongue. Ian was seeking reassurance, and there was little point in upsetting him more than he already was. The young creator needed to focus, and he wouldn't be able to while worrying about Indigo. Cadmar spoke before Yiloch could come up with a satisfactory answer that wasn't a complete lie.

"That one is rarely safe," the half-breed said with a soft chuckle. He always found humor in life, and Yiloch envied that. "Yet, I think somehow that her story is far from over."

I hope you're right.

Yiloch urged Tantrum up to a trot. The ground here was less sandy, and the faster they moved, the less time he would have to dwell on the woman he was leaving behind. Before him was an army apparently set on decimating everything in their path. If he could solve that rather substantial problem, he could worry about Indigo again.

CHAPTER THIRTY-FIVE

After leaving the hut, Myac kept up a fast pace heading south toward Kudan, pausing only when the horse's wellbeing required it. It wasn't until late afternoon of yet another long day of travel that he found another reason to dread his decision. The sky was darkening fast, and the area they were entering was all too familiar. He didn't want to be stuck seeking shelter from another storm here. The road took him through the silver trees and charred remains of Segys. From there it crossed the river into AhnSegys, the village that had been his home once. He clenched his teeth when lightning flashed low overhead and thunder rumbled moments later. The sky filled with dark clouds bloated with rain.

"Not here," he growled, glaring up at those clouds.

The horse pranced about. More lightning flashed, illuminating the rebuilt inn near the center of town with stark white light. Stopping the horse, he stared down the empty street. Everyone had gone inside to wait out the storm. A few heavy drops of rain splashed down on him. The horse flinched when thunder rumbled again. In the next flash of white light, he saw the house that stood on the corner of the nearest intersection, built over the ruins of the house he had lived in with his mother. In the seconds after the flash, the dark roads turned red with blood from his memories.

Another drop of rain struck his cheek. More followed. Heaving a deep sigh that caused a twinge of pain in his chest, he kicked the horse on and angled him toward the inn. This was the last place he wanted to shelter from the storm, but it was his only option.

Leaving the horse in the care of a skinny stable boy, he entered the dingy little inn. A weak fire struggled in the hearth, offering little light and even less warmth. The innkeeper hunkered on a stool by the front was a grizzled man with heavy jowls and sleepy brown eyes. The only woman in the room, waiting on two occupied tables, had the misfortune of looking similar enough to be his sister.

Myac sought a table near the fire and ordered a glass of wine from the masculine woman. Thunder cracked loudly enough to shake the inn, and a flash of lightning brightened the world outside those filthy windows for an instant. Myac shivered. His pulse quickened. It was unusual for him to be bothered by a mere storm. Perhaps the unfortunate incident in the last storm, or more likely, the memories of this place put him on edge.

The next roll of thunder lasted a long time, and the flash of lightning had an orange cast to it. He stared at one grimy window. The orange glow outside continued growing brighter instead of fading, and a chill crept out from his gut, prickles of unease racing up his spine. Then he heard the first scream.

The lightning must have started a fire in the village.

He joined the other patrons going to look out the windows. One window shattered, and the closest man to it stumbled backward before hitting the floor, a bladed spear protruding from his throat. Myac scurried back, strengthening his barriers and wrapping shields of protection around himself. The door slammed inward, breaking partway off its hinges before the heavy, striking hooves of a rearing horse. The warrior rode his stocky mount into the inn, grabbing his spear from the dead man's throat and sweeping it around in a wide arch that opened the chest of the serving woman. Shock barely registered in her eyes before she collapsed, blood gushing from her chest and between her lips.

Myac thrust out with ascard, using enough force to send the mounted warrior and his horse, as well as many of the inn's occupants, flying back into the opposite wall. The wall cracked and bowed out a fraction from the impact of the horse's body. The man and his mount slumped to the floor in a bloody heap alongside the doorway as another warrior entered, this one on foot.

Myac struck out at this one as well, taking a quick inventory of his escape routes as he did so. This time the attack ran up against a barrier that not only blocked it, but rebounded it back at him. Before he could react, his own power struck him, and he flew back into the wall behind him, using ascard to cushion the impact at the last second. He still struck with considerable force, and the burst of pain in the wound Indigo had inflicted on him debilitated him for a few critical seconds. His new barriers collapsed as he struggled with intense agony.

The warrior hefted his spear and threw it.

With a quick reaction, Myac deflected the weapon, though not before it touched flesh. The point drew a slit in his shirt and jacket, and a shallow cut opened in the flesh beneath as his deflection knocked it to one side. Rage and pain spurred him to his feet. He thrust out with a wall of flame. The warrior staggered back when the flames engulfed him, the barrier that protected him the first time breaking down before this attack. He made no sound when he fell to his knees, his skin melting with the heat of the fire. Within seconds, he slumped forward, dead.

Now the wall around the doorway was burning, and Myac could only stare, driven back to that moment in his youth. Was his mother outside that door? Was an elegant monster waiting out there to cut him down the way Yiloch had cut down his mother in front of him?

Thunder cracked loudly overhead. Broken from the cocoon of memories by the noise, he forced himself to take a step at a time, moving around the burning corpse toward the doorway. Outside the inn, the screaming had already stopped. Was everyone already dead, or had the attackers left?

Stepping into the doorway, he noticed first that it had already stopped raining. In the light of the fires, he spotted a stocky, muscular man in the roadway. This man stood gazing around with dark eyes at the warriors who darted in and out of the burning buildings. Power rolled off him, not just the power of confidence and authority, but ascard power as well.

He was not the only impressive ascard user in the horde. Another man stood next to him, and the ascard power that flowed off him spread out in different directions, stronger than anything Myac had ever encountered. He realized, standing there dumbstruck by the immensity of the ascard might coursing around him, that the adept wasn't wielding his own ability. The power he controlled bore the signature of hundreds of other adepts.

Shuddering at the implications, Myac reached out, erecting a barrier around the first man, meaning to crush him, but when he tried to close it in, nothing happened. The man turned, his gaze settling on Myac where he stood in the burning doorway of the inn. Without a hint of concern, the man touched the arm of the adept controlling the combined power. That one also turned to face Myac. Smirking, the adept pushed outward with ascard, effortlessly if inelegantly blasting away Myac's barrier around the other man. Myac staggered, and the first man smiled. He never opened his mouth to issue any order, but the three nearest warriors turned, dropping whatever task they were about and headed for Myac.

Fighting panic, Myac lashed out with ascard, manifesting three spears of power that appeared in the chests of the three men, dropping them where they stood. The man in the middle of the street frowned, and another two warriors turned their attention to Myac. He struck out again, but this time his power failed, crashing into barriers of combined power that flared up around the warriors. Myac drew the sword he carried. His skill with the weapon was unimpressive at best, but it was his only weapon if they robbed him of his ascard power.

Fear filled him, greater than any he had felt since that moment his burning house collapsed on him so many years ago.

Back then, he expected to die in the burning debris. Now, like then, he wasn't willing to sit back and let death take him. The first warrior reached him and swung his short, bladed spear. Myac brought his blade up to block the attack. The impact of the weapon reverberated through him, and pain burst through his chest. He staggered back and fell, looking up in time to see the warrior grin. Then the front wall of the inn collapsed on the man. Burning debris rained down around Myac. He scrambled back like a crab, trying to escape the destruction. The remaining structure groaned, and smoke filled the air, thick and suffocating. A deafening crack provided warning as the rest of the building gave out.

I will not die yet.

Burning debris came crashing down on him. Before he could erect a barrier, something struck his head, and blackness swallowed him.

* * *

Ksa-jnai wrapped the foreign maker in power, protecting him from the heat of the fire and the debris of the collapsing building. With an outward thrust, he sent fallen timbers flying back off the unconscious man. Ini-jnai followed him to the still form of the pale creature where he stopped, gazing thoughtfully down at him. They had suffered no losses in this campaign until now. His warriors hadn't been under barriers for this attack. There should have been no need in such a place, but this one maker killed five of his men, and stopping him resulted in the death of a sixth.

Ksa-jnai nodded and knelt next to the strange, pale man. His hair was nearly white, with a hint of blue, like ice, and his features refined, almost feminine, giving no hint of the immense power hidden within. Bright blood flowed from a wound on his scalp, so vivid against that pale skin and hair. Scalp wounds always bled with such drama.

Ksa-jnai smiled the way he might smile on a favorite horse and wiped his fingers through the blood. Putting the bloodied fingers in his mouth, he considered the maker a moment longer, swallowing the metallic taste on his tongue. That blood would give him new strength that would help him fight this man's people and give him an unexpected edge when he faced the Afterworld.

After taking a moment to lick the last of the red from his fingers, he stood.

"Bind him and tend his wounds."

"This one is dangerous. He wields more power on his own than any of our makers. We should kill him."

Ksa-jnai looked over his shoulder, narrowing his eyes at his bloodnau. Ini-jnai dropped his gaze to the ground and sank to one knee in a gesture of reparation. "After he is bound, his power will be your power. I will secure him."

Ksa-jnai felt Ini-jnai's power reach out to the pale man. Binding was one of the rare processes for which the First Maker used his own power. Every maker in the army, except for Ksa-jnai himself, was bound to his bloodnau, which meant the First Maker could use their power whenever and however he pleased, while they could only use it if he allowed them to do so. This pale creature would be a potent addition to that store of power. He wouldn't be happy when he woke, but by then it would be too late.

When he had the last weave of the binding secured to the foreign maker's inner core, Ini-jnai finally looked up.

Ksa-jnai nodded approval, then turned to another warrior. "Once that one has been tended to, tie him and carry him on your horse." He paused, considering the men he had lost to the pale man's power. By the Rights of the Conqueror, all their horses now belonged to the foreign maker. Under the circumstances, however, he wouldn't be permitted to take possession of them all until Ksa-jnai was done with him, if that day ever came. "When he can sit on his own, give him Tig-nat's horse, but keep his hands tied."

"It will be done as you say, First Legend," the warrior replied, bowing his head.

Satisfied, Ksa-jnai left his newest maker in capable hands and walked out to the center of the village where his bloodken were now gathering. Na-jnai rode up to him and inclined his head, expressing his desire to say something.

"Speak."

"There is a clearing beyond the village by the river. Plenty of room for your army to rest if you so desire it, Ksa-jnai, First Legend."

"Good, let them rest. You do well, as always, Na-jnai."

The young man smiled, then his expression changing to one of concern. "There is blood on your hand."

Ksa-jnai glanced down and noticed the red that lingered on one finger. "Not mine, Na-jnai."

Turning, he saw his warrior now lifting the pale maker from the wreckage. He placed the bloodied finger to his lips and worked away the last bit of red with his teeth.

THE END

CHAPTER ONE

Indigo moved her mount out at a swift trot to keep pace with the jogging Kudaness. Their stamina in the sand was an impressive thing, but it meant she had to harden the ground under her horse with every stride to keep up his pace on the unfamiliar terrain without injuring him. That effort required significant energy expenditure, though it wasn't depleting her as fast as it had the night she left Yiloch and the others to seek out Suac Chozai. Once she recovered from the side effects of the drug the suac had given her to walk with his gods, her ascard connection felt crisp and strong, almost more intense than it had been before.

Since the Kudaness looked upon deliberate use of ascard as a form of blasphemy, it had already become a source of friction between her and Suac Chozai. Their initial confrontation over the matter remained fresh in her mind. Chozai had stopped them perhaps an hour outside of the Murak village and led her away from the warriors.

"You must stop your use of ascard. Your use of it is an affront to our gods and therefore an affront to our people. I cannot allow it to continue and expect to retain the respect of my warriors."

She had swept the group with her gaze, noting the dark looks they gave her, then met his copper eyes. "Those gods you speak of have already confirmed my path. I cannot keep up the pace you set on foot, and I will not injure this horse. If you take issue with my methods, I suggest you discuss it with your gods."

Chozai's answering scowl had chilled her blood, but he had turned away and ordered them to continue their journey. Her refusal to be cowed by him had earned her his grudging respect, though none of his affection. They shared the vision that sent them on this journey, and it appeared he was unwilling to argue against the will of his gods.

Before leaving his home village, the suac sent messengers out to many other Murak villages to request that they prepare their warriors and send them to the northernmost village. They stopped at the two Murak villages on their route so Chozai could give them the same message. From there, they continued into the Farid tribal lands, resting during the hottest part of the day and traveling through most of the night.

She felt the pressure of time, knowing the invading Gray Army had a considerable lead over them. If this journey were successful, would the Kudaness gather only to arrive in Yiroth and find it destroyed? They might still defeat the Gray Army in that case, but it mattered little to her if Lyra that happened after Lyra had fallen. Yiloch would try to save his empire at any cost. That was who he was, and she shared his desire to protect that empire, even if she no longer held his love.

They came upon the first Farid village mid-morning on the third day, a collection of huts gaining form on the horizon. When they were close enough to make out villagers among the huts, a flood of armed warriors surged out to intercept them, and she gathered ascard to her as a precaution. Chozai signaled their group to stop. She brought her horse up beside him as the Murak warriors moved in close, weapons ready and eyes filled with grim determination.

"They don't look that pleased to see us," she commented, trying not to let the tremor of fear in her chest pass her lips.

Chozai's sour grimace wasn't reassuring. "Murak and Farid have long been rivals. If we can turn them to your cause, the rest will be easy."

"If they can't?"

Chozai said nothing.

She watched the approaching warriors, calming her mount with ascard so her fear wouldn't panic the animal. When they were close enough, she realized that the man in the lead bore no weapons and, like Suac Chozai, tattoos covered most of his visible flesh. Another Kudaness high priest.

"He is their suac?"

Chozai nodded. "He is why we come to this village first. With your power and the aid of a second suac, we can contact the suacs of the other tribes through a walk with the gods."

She shuddered, recalling the vile taste of the liquid he had given her to initiate the previous walk with the gods and how sick it made her. "You would use my power for this? I thought you considered it blasphemous."

Chozai narrowed his eyes at her, muscles in his jaw twitching. "You are a fractious woman. If you would rather travel to all the tribes on foot, I can oblige you. By then, Lyra will have certainly fallen."

"My apologies." She lowered her gaze, hoping he would accept it as a show of deference and sincerity. "What must I do?"

"You will feed power into me to amplify the call," he replied. There was a catch in his voice and bitterness in his eyes when she met them again that told her what it must cost him to accept such assistance from her.

"As you wish." She bowed her head again, this time in respect and gratitude for his efforts.

"I do not wish it," he growled under his breath.

Since the subject was upsetting him, she let the conversation end there and watched the approaching warriors close the distance until they came to a stop a few yards from the Murak group. The warriors on both sides seemed to grow larger, bristling like angry dogs, ready to attack at any provocation. She wondered if they would make it long enough to discuss their proposal before someone lost control and attacked the other side. The opposing suac barked a sharp order, and the Farid warriors lowered their weapons. Suac Chozai did the same. The two suacs stepped up to one another and began conversing in their native tongue. Indigo caught a few words she had picked up in her short time among them, but she learned far more following the discussion through their body language and by reading their emotions with her power.

For a few delicate minutes, the discussion was calm, then it grew heated, both men exuding hatred born of a long rivalry. Careful to keep her activities thoroughly masked, she pushed a slow stream of calm over them the same way she would with an agitated patient. Both men would turn on her in an instant if they had any idea she was manipulating them, but she counted on their lack of conscious ascard control to keep her actions hidden. The heated exchange calmed, and she smiled to herself. Eventually, the other suac gave a gruff nod, and they turned to her.

She caught her breath. *He has copper eyes too.*

Did every suac have such eyes? What would cause such a thing?

"Suac Therah has agreed to walk with the gods. We shall go to his temple."

Doubt swept through her then. She had no desire to experience the side effects of the drug he had given her again, let alone try to choke it down. She didn't belong here. Nor did she belong in Caithin anymore, not after setting free the man accused of having the Caithin royal family assassinated. Along with her place in Caithin, she had also lost Yiloch's love and the possibility of a place in Lyra.

Still, she refused to see him or his country destroyed. There were people she cared for there. It wasn't only about Yiloch anymore. Ian and Cadmar had become dear to her as well. Adran also, for the love and loyalty he gave to Yiloch and for his practicality that balanced Yiloch's passion. If this was the price she had to pay to get Kudan to help Lyra, then she would do it.

She nodded and Suac Therah answered with a curt nod of his own, giving her a suspicious glower before turning to lead them back to the village. Their destination, Therah's temple, was a long hut similar to the one Chozai lived in. Warriors from both tribes escorted them to the door.

Before they could enter, the door flaps opened from within, and a group of warriors emerged, carrying a body between them. Indigo stepped back, bumping into one of the Murak warriors. The man glared at her, and she inched forward again, trying to keep her distance from the emerging group without touching anyone else. She felt small and conspicuous among the tall, dark-skinned Kudaness men.

The body was that of a young man. A reddish foam bubbled from his mouth and nose. His dark eyes stared at the sky, devoid of that distinctive spark of life. Indigo dared a quick inspection with ascard. He had died only moments ago. There was something in his system, a poison of some kind that was uncomfortably familiar. None of the others appeared bothered by the death, though Suac Therah inclined his head, closing his eyes for a quick moment, and she sensed a hint of regret in him.

When the group was clear of the door, the suacs

entered. Indigo followed, staying respectfully behind Chozai. One warrior from each tribe entered with them. Both of the suacs sat, one on each side of a ring of pillows, staring at one another with a dislike so intense it charged the surrounding air. When no one offered any guidance, she sat on another edge of the ring, halfway between the two men. At least they had the good sense to start seated this time. After falling the last time, she felt this was a much safer option.

The Farid warrior walked to a cabinet almost identical to the one in Suac Chozai's hut and retrieved a water skin. This he carried over and handed to Suac Therah.

Therah offered it to Chozai first. She struggled not to fidget as the Murak lifted the water skin, his eyes never leaving the other man. She hoped their standing rivalry wouldn't come into play here. How easy would it be for the Farid suac to eliminate his rival with a touch of poison? She inspected the substance in the skin with ascard, and panic made her breath catch, tightening her chest when she realized it was the same substance she had detected in the dead man's body. Before she could move to intervene, Chozai took a deep drink from the skin. When Therah accepted the waterskin back, he too drank deeply before passing it to her.

She hesitated, remembering the dead man's face, and gave the liquid a tentative sniff. It was the same thing Suac Chozai had given her before. If she refused to drink it now, would he abandon the journey? It obviously hadn't killed her the last time, though it had made her violently ill. Pushing aside fear, she brought the skin to her lips and made herself drink. She drank less deeply than the two suacs had on the reasoning that the men might have developed a tolerance for the substance.

The Farid warrior snatched the waterskin from her and returned it to the cabinet. She was barely aware of the two warriors leaving the hut. Both suacs were swaying now, their eyes losing focus and glazing over. They began humming and, as her vision started to blur, she let herself sway with them, trying not to fight the drug as she had the last time, hoping the aftereffects might not be so violent as a result. This time, the pain that radiated out from her stomach was less severe and the transition less jarring. The hut vanished, and there was only a brief instant of blackness. Then she was sitting under a star-filled sky in the desert. Chozai and Therah sat across from one another in the same positions they had occupied within the hut. A pale, glowing orb appeared in the center of the circle, illuminating the tattooed faces of the suacs.

Reminding herself of her purpose, Indigo focused, drawing on ascard and feeding her power into Suac Chozai. The other man did nothing to show that he was aware of the offering, but the orb glowed brighter. Chozai's lips moved as if he spoke, but no sound came out.

She waited in the strange environment, keeping the feed of power open so Chozai could take as much as he needed.

Another suac emerged from the darkness beyond

the circle and sat across from her. This man appeared older than the other two and was missing his left arm below the elbow. Neither Chozai nor Therah made any move to acknowledge the newcomer, so she followed their example, focusing on the orb. They sat in silence, all of them gazing into the pale orb at the center. The desert pulsated around the edges of her vision, thrumming in her ears accompanying a growing pressure while stars flickered and danced in the sky above. More Kudaness, adorned with the elaborate designs of their priesthood and the varied facial tattoos that declared their tribes, came into the circle from the darkness and sat. The orb glowed brighter with each new arrival.

She dared to glance around, taking a quick inventory of the men joining them. Suac Chozai's hair was longer and woven with more beads than that of the others. Was that significant, or could it merely be a tribal or personal preference?

Now that she had a better idea of what to expect from a walk with the gods, she felt less out of control. The lingering image of the dead man, killed, as best she could tell from her cursory examination, by the poison they had consumed to get here, kept her nerves on edge, but the experience itself was less terrifying this time. Each suac swayed with the pulsing of the desert, and she did so too, understanding now that it helped ward off the nausea the vile drink caused.

When a twelfth suac joined the circle, they all looked up. Most glanced at her first, their judging looks like a collection of daggers waiting to be thrown.

The notorious prejudices of her people did her no favors here. Then they turned their attention to Suac Chozai. Somehow, they appeared to know that he was the one who had brought them together.

"I have called upon you to initiate a Dursik un Kar," Chozai stated. Two of the others began speaking in Kudaness, but Chozai held up a hand to cut them off. He nodded to Indigo. "The gods have brought the Unseen Woman to us. She does not speak Kudaness. I ask, out of respect for the gods' wishes, that you speak the trade tongue."

There was a flurry of discussion around the circle. When it stopped, all eyes turned to Indigo. She struggled to focus past the dizzying influence of the drug and figure out what they expected of her.

Chozai stepped in to spare her embarrassment. "This is your journey. It falls to you to explain why the Kudaness should proceed with the Dursik un Kar." She looked questioningly at him, and he frowned, perhaps searching for the right words. He finally said, "Gathering of blades."

She nodded and looked around the circle, noticing as she did so that they all had those odd, dark copper eyes. Was it a sign somehow of their being chosen by the gods, or could it be a side effect of using the drug? Her gut twisted at the latter possibility. If it was the drug, how long did it take to develop? She had no interest in copper eyes.

There was growing impatience in the expressions of the suacs. Taking a deep breath, she forced her fears aside.

"Some of you have already encountered the Gray Army that swept up eastern Kudan to Lyra. The Silik," she said, remembering Yiloch's description of the army's destructive path. She received a confirming nod from one suac and did her best not to glare at him. Did he have anything to do with Ferin's death? Glancing away from those cold eyes, she continued, "and possibly the Denilik..." the elder suac with the partial arm gave a quick nod, "...have felt the power of that army. The Gray Army now travels through Lyra toward the capital. They have already shown that they do not respect the lives of your people. Should they defeat Lyra, they will not leave the Kudaness in peace. The tribes of Kudan must join against this foe." Several expressions tightened with disapproval, and she plunged ahead before they could voice their disagreements. "Now is the time to attack. If the Kudaness bring a rear attack against the Gray Army while they are engaged with the Lyran army, the Gray Army will fall." She said the last with an assurance that surprised even her, but it felt right, and she needed them to feel it too.

"And what if they take Lyra before we reach them," one suac argued, glancing at Suac Chozai as he spoke.

"Then the battle will have weakened them, and they will be vulnerable to attack," she countered quickly, knowing they would use any hesitation as an excuse to discount her words.

"Who are they?" another Suac asked.

Before she could come up with an answer to that,

the suac from the Silik tribe spoke up.

"They came from beyond the Rhuakine. Two of our villages were decimated, no one left alive." As he spoke, the short, powerful warriors of the Gray Army on their stout horses appeared around the perimeter of the circle. She had to struggle not to react to their presence, but none of the suacs responded, though several glanced up at the Gray warriors, acknowledging this new component of the group hallucination with thoughtful nods. "I do not know how they defeated our warriors, but none of the Gray warriors left their lives upon the sand."

"I came upon them on my journey to Kudan. They have strong adepts creating protective barriers for their warriors," she explained. It was a little simpler than the truth, but the truth frightened her, and she didn't want to share that. One adept controlled the power of every adept in the army. That made him more powerful than she cared to consider right then. For now, she needed to focus only on convincing the Kudaness to act.

"Then how can we hope to defeat them?" Suac Therah demanded.

She met his eyes, holding up a hand as Chozai had done earlier when several of the others started speaking into the opening. Whatever they thought about her for her race and gender, they still respected the gesture, falling silent.

"I can destroy their barriers," she said, hoping that she wasn't promising more than she could deliver.

The suacs turned on Chozai, slinging outraged insults at him for bringing an ascard user among them, several reverting to their native tongue. She kept her silence, refraining from commenting about the way they used ascard themselves, for she was certain that power was involved in this in some way. If not, how could her power have been of any use in calling the other suacs together?

Once more she waited.

The Gray warriors around them vanished, replaced by scenes of Lyran adepts wielding ascard in various destructive ways and the grim outcomes. Fire, ascard enhanced speed, weapons made of power all wielded by Lyran adepts with savage results. Among those images, she was certain she spotted Yiloch at least once, or perhaps she wanted to see him badly enough to impose his image upon the memories of the suacs playing out around them.

"The gods support her words," Chozai defended. "Look."

Around them, the images changed. Gray warriors fought Kudaness, and not just those from a single tribe, but from many of the tribes, judging from their varied tattoos. Indigo wondered if Suac Chozai somehow controlled the images, though she could find no evidence that he was consciously controlling ascard. Blood-spattered Kudaness warriors shouted out in victory around the perimeter of the circle, raising spears and curved blades in celebration. Then the image of the Gray Army's leader appeared among them. His dark eyes picked her out of the circle, and he smiled. She sucked in a breath, terror coursing through her.

Blackness fell, closing around them, the glowing orb's light no longer reaching beyond those gathered. She was trembling. Whether from fear this time or from the effects of the drug, she couldn't tell.

"I, Suac Chozai Galal of Murak un Ani, pledge the warriors of Murak to the Dursik un Kar," Suac Chozai declared, his powerful voice echoing through the surrounding emptiness.

After he spoke, silence reigned for several minutes, and Indigo, her head spinning now, wondered if she could manage to avoid passing out before the others gave their answers.

The Denilik suac pounded his knee with a fist and swept the circle with a challenging glare. "I, Suac Kipith Denilik of Denilik un Ani, pledge the warriors of Denilik to the Dursik un Kar."

Chozai offered a nod of appreciation to the elder. The silence held even longer this time, then the Farid suac sat up straighter.

"I, Suac Therah Hesik of Farid un Ani, pledge the warriors of Farid to the Dursik un Kar."

This time there was no pause. The rest of the prophets each spoke, pledging the warriors of their respective tribes to the Dursik un Kar. As they spoke, she realized tears were tracking down her cheeks. She made no move to stop them, feeling the gesture would be inappropriate in this setting. They needed to know she felt the weight of their decision in her heart. When the last suac pledged his warriors, Suac Chozai met and held her eyes. He nodded once, and she felt he did so in approval of her emotion. The gratitude represented by her tears was not lost on him, though the deeper sadness, the sense that even this would not earn her a place in life, evaded him.

"The Dursik un Kar will gather on the northern border where the Murak lands meet Lyra."

The other suacs nodded and lowered their gazes to the glowing orb. One by one, they vanished, the orb fading more with each departure, until only the original three remained. Suac Therah nodded to Suac Chozai and vanished. Chozai turned to her and reached his hand out. It looked like a lifeline in that deepening darkness, so she took it and blackness swept in.

When she woke up, she was alone. She threw up again, emptying her stomach, but she recovered faster than she had the first time. Once she had composed herself, she got up from the pillows and stepped outside. Chozai waited there with his warriors and Suac Therah. They both acknowledged her with stern nods and a warrior held the reins of her mount out to her.

"We will soon meet again, Unseen Woman," Suac Therah said. "The gods have a purpose in bringing you to us. Never before has someone from outside the Kudan brought about a Dursik un Kar. But remember, having the attention of the gods is not the same as having their favor."

She nodded, leaning on her horse, too drained to worry about what his words might mean. The suac turned away, exchanging a few words in Kudaness with Chozai. Then she mounted and followed the Murak suac and warriors away from the Farid village.

TO BE CONTINUED...

ACKNOWLEDGEMENTS

As always, I won't mention everyone here, but you are all very important to me. I want to offer thanks to a few specific people.

To Michael for supporting my dreams for years and letting me read you my books.

To my mom Linda for your loving support and for helping me work out and refine my ideas.

To Rick and Ann for reading and giving feedback on my books, and for being the best of friends.

To my uncle Greg for being an avid fan of this series and providing great feedback on this book.

To Kali for spectacular content edits and for being such a pleasure to work with.

To my fellow author Eldritch Black for sharing long rides to the coffee shop full of cathartic rants and commiseration. Also, to the rest of that writing group for making my Thursdays productive and fun for years.

To Aradia for *knowing* I would succeed from the first time we met and for being an inspiration in your dedication to your own art.

To my cover artist, Robert, and my interior designer, Brian, thank you both for your fantastic work and for your patience with through the process.

I must also thank my sixth-grade teacher, Mr. Johnson, for being so encouraging when I told you I was going to be an author and to my eighth-grade algebra teacher, Mr. Siebenlist, for allowing me to ignore lessons because you were so pleased I was writing books in class rather than notes.

AUTHOR BIO

Outside of her career as an author, Nikki is a professional technical and creative writer, spider wrangler, animal lover, and devoted cat mom. Writing fantasy and science fiction stories has been a lifelong passion for her. She loves to draw on her myriad life experiences, doing everything from wild cave exploration and competitive horseback endurance riding to practicing iaido and archery. She invites you to join her on some fantastic adventures.

* * *

Thank you for taking the time to read this novel. Please consider leaving a review if you enjoyed it.

* * *

For more information about Nikki and her work, visit her website at http://www.elysiumpalace.com.

OTHER WORKS BY NIKKI McCORMACK

THE WARDEN'S SON (A Vanris Series)
Child of Vanris
Blood of Vanris
Heart of Vanris
Throne of Vanris

DAUGHTER OF VANRIS (A Vanris Series)
Wave Dancer
Wave-Touched
Wavelord

SILVERBLOOD RAVEN
A Path of Blood and Amber
A Path of Secrets and Dreams
A Path of Storms and Reckonings

CLOCKWORK ENTERPRISES
The Girl and the Clockwork Cat
The Girl and the Clockwork Conspiracy
The Girl and the Clockwork Crossfire

FORBIDDEN THINGS
Dissident
Exile
Apostate

ELYSIUM'S FALL
Dark Hope of the Dragons
Dark Savior of the Dragons

STANDALONE NOVELS and SHORT STORIES
Golden Eyes
The Keeper
Warden's Rise (A Vanris Short Story)
In Silence Waiting (Short Story)
And They All Look Just the Same (Short Story)
Making Monsters (Short Story)

www.ingramcontent.com/pod-product-compliance
Lightning Source LLC
Chambersburg PA
CBHW030647120726
47905CB00001B/98